The Ministry of Hope

But I speak of a shore
Where the sea breaks with fury
On ashen walls

The Shore of our Sad Republic
                    Pablo Neruda

Also by Roy Heath

A Man Come Home (1974)

The Murderer (1978) (US 1992)

From the Heat of the Day (1979) (US 1993)

One Generation (1981)

Genetha (1981)

Later published as a trilogy under the title
The Armstrong Trilogy *in the United States (1994)*

Kwaku (1982) (US 1997)

Orealla (1984)

The Shadow Bride (1988) (US 1996)

Roy Heath

The Ministry of Hope

A NOVEL

MARION BOYARS
London • New York

First published in Great Britain and the United States in 1997
by Marion Boyars Publishers
24 Lacy Road, London SW15 1NL
237 East 39th Street, New York, N.Y. 10016

Distributed in Australia and New Zealand by Peribo Pty Ltd
58 Beaumont Road, Mount Kuring-gai, NSW 2080

British Library Cataloguing in Publication Data
Heath, Roy A.K. (Roy Aubrey Kelvin)
The ministry of hope: a novel
1. Guyanese fiction — 20th century
I. Title
813 [F]

Library of Congress Cataloging-in-Publication Data
Heath, Roy A.K.
   The ministry of hope, a novel / Roy Heath
     1. City and town life—Guyana—Fiction. 2. Antique
dealers—Guyana—Fiction. 3. Poor—Guyana—Fiction.
I. Title
PR9320.9.H4M56   1996
813--dc20   96-8215

ISBN 0-7145-3015-8

Typeset in Penguin and New Brunswick by
Ann Buchan Typesetters, Shepperton, Middlesex.

CHAPTER 1

Life seems to accommodate certain people, while others are forever kicking against the pricks and end up by cursing fate for its unbending attitude. Kwaku belonged to the first group; however low he sank circumstances would conspire to raise him up again. Having endured the pain of seeing his wife go blind, brutalized by his twin sons, toppled from his perch as a healer of repute — at least in his own backyard — he had become, once again, the laughing stock of all and sundry. Even the children of Winkel began throwing stones at him, and the dealers in pig food kept lowering their prices for the vegetable scraps he delivered. Yet, once again, Fate intervened. The disastrous condition of the national economy, which reduced many to being eaters of ungarnished rice, provided the base from which Kwaku's fortunes were resurrected. And it all began with a conversation he overheard in the New Amsterdam rum shop he frequented.

'I hear in town things bad!' a well dressed man had said to his companion. 'But I'm telling you, there's money in hard times.'

The man went on to explain how he had made his fortune as a dealer in old things: old clothes, old books, old shoes and old utensils, the last of which he sold under the description of 'Antiques'. He specialized in old chamber-pots.

'It's the pos the tourists like. Enamel pos, glazed earthenware pos, especially if they're decorated with a floral design. I even got hold of a brass po that one Englishwoman paid a hundred and thirty pounds for — in real pounds. I said it wasn't for sale. That's the best way to make their mouth water, you see. Not for sale! — and genuine brass, too!'

Kwaku felt himself trembling at the simplicity of the scheme, which could have saved his family from going to the dogs in those years of penury. Tourists did not come to New Amsterdam, but nothing stopped him from going to Georgetown. He was not sure what *antiques* meant, but he certainly knew about chamber-pots, having prescribed and carried out scores of enemas on his patients in the good old days.

Kwaku, while turning over the scheme in his mind, thought of the small boy who could read upside down and whose father was a skilled pan-boiler and carried his expertise to the sugar estates in the islands, before computers were installed and made his skills redundant. What a pair he and that boy would have made! There was no point dwelling on his poor education now, at the age of thirty-eight, with a lifetime's experience and seven children behind him. The problem in hand was how to go about acquiring fifty chamber-pots, arranging their transport to Georgetown and finding a place to store them.

Mr Barzey, God rest his soul, had spoken at length about the capital, so that Kwaku felt he was sufficiently well acquainted with the place to survive there once he had a roof over his head. Had he not managed to conquer New Amsterdam as a raw countryman who walked with his legs so far apart people must have thought he was afflicted with hydroseed?

Since his decline Kwaku had conceived numerous plans to raise money for an operation on his blind wife's eyes, but to no avail. Miss Gwendoline, his wife, had long ago lost confidence in his powers of recovery as a breadwinner, and had come to terms with the fact that she was obliged to depend on handouts from her children, all of whom lived away from New Amsterdam.

'I don' believe you no more,' she had told him time and time again. 'One time you use to have power. One time. Now you gone to the dogs.'

So he learned to keep his plans of recovery to himself, or rather confided only in the old shoemaker who was in the habit of bursting into song at certain times of the day. He would confide in him whenever he picked eddo leaves and took them round as a gift, in gratitude for the time he had put him up, a complete stranger in New Amsterdam.

'I got this plan,' he said, the last time he was convinced that his luck was about to change.

And Kwaku exposed his scheme to the shoemaker: he would become a professional matchmaker, advertising his talents on a sign which read: 'Happiness to order. Success or money back'. But no one would seek happiness from a man living in a hovel near the Canje Creek, who could not even go walking with his wife because she was so poorly turned out. The plan had foundered, like most of its antecedents, on the serious shortcoming of his poverty. In order to make money one had to have money.

The po plan was no different in this respect; yet its simplicity and the extraordinary prices on offer for receptacles that deserved to be hidden away under beds had fired Kwaku's imagination.

But with each passing day his enthusiasm waned. Finding no way to raise enough money for his fare to Georgetown, let alone transport his receptacles, he all but abandoned the project.

'Is why you in such a bad mood?' Miss Gwendoline asked him one morning.

And in a fit of candour he told her why.

'Go and see one of the old clients you did heal when you was practising,' she suggested.

'What? Woman, you know you right!'

'Borrow, well, ask to borrow some money to buy the pos. Then, go to town with only two pos and see if you can sell them. If it turn out to be easy you can look for a room to live. Then come back for as much pos as you can carry.'

Kwaku could not believe his ears. Not only did she approve of his plan, she had come up with an original suggestion. In all his life he had met only one woman to match her, and that was Blossom, an old school friend who now ran her own taxi service from Georgetown to New Amsterdam. These women!

Kwaku had always seen his relationship with his few women friends as magical, a kind of unusual growth that surprised those who knew about it. Nearly all the other ladies of his acquaintance despised him for reasons he had never been able to fathom. Most of them would give him one glance and then flee as though he was the bearer of some dreaded pestilence. Whenever he attended a dance as a youngster his approach to the girls standing by the wall would have the effect that Moses had on arriving at the Red Sea: half of them would make for the front door while the other half scurried towards the back, leaving a large empty space where, a moment before, there had been a mass of chattering females. But then the village dogs used to give him a wide berth as well. Indeed, the young ones, those too old to be described as puppies, yet too young to be taken seriously, added insult to injury by howling as they took to their heels, especially at night. Women, dogs and his uncle, they all preferred to do without his company.

What mystified Kwaku above all was the gap between his own view of himself and those that others entertained of him. Apart from his tendency to exaggerate he gave no cause for offence. He would even describe himself as considerate and, without doubt, the possessor of an unusual intelligence. Mind you, he *did* appreciate his uncle's reluctance to have him in his home after he found him a wife. If his haste in building him a house was frenetic — a term used by Mr Barzey, their neighbour, God rest his soul — his uncle's desire for tranquility seemed to be understood by everyone, from the policeman to Mr Barzey's obstreperous daughter. Having brought up Kwaku single-handed since his mother disappeared mysteriously after dolling herself up in her Sunday best and depositing him with her brother 'for the day only', this uncle had done his Christian duty and was entitled to live out the rest of his days without the constant alarms and crises that afflicted his home and any home Kwaku frequented.

Kwaku understood. For, curiously enough, if his insight deserted him where most things were concerned, there were moments when he displayed a rare understanding of his place in the scheme of things. Did he not lay down the qualifications for any wife his uncle might choose for him, impossible to fulfil if the older man was to be believed? And did he not eventually find Miss Gwendoline, who possessed all the qualities he demanded, and more?

Pursuing his wife's advice to borrow money, Kwaku first went to look up Mrs Duncan, one of the first clients who, in those heady days, helped establish his reputation as a healer. She lived in Stanleytown, near the cemetery, and was related to the sexton, a sprightly young man whom he once met, but whose appearance he could not recall. The house, a modest cottage that from all appearances had never been repaired since its erection decades ago, leaned so alarmingly that Kwaku hesitated before venturing up the stairs. At the door he decided to call out rather than rap, for fear that the slightest pressure on the wooden façade might bring the house down.

'Mistress!' he called through the jalousie.

Immediately came the response.

'Is who? You in' got manners?'

The door flew open and Kwaku was faced with the truculent figure of an old woman who bore no resemblance to his erstwhile client.

Assuming a humble expression Kwaku asked if Mrs Duncan was in.

'Mrs Duncan? She dead! Is who you?'

'My name is Kwaku, mistress.'

'Kwaku? I in' know no Kwaku. . . . For a minute I did thought I recognize you. You look a lil' bit like the man that send she to she grave. A healer by the name of Haku or Paku, something like that. This man come out of the blue an' fill she up with garlic. She pay through she nose for the treatment! Poor thing. She was my younger sister and she did want to live till she was a hundred. . . . Come in an' let me treat you to a drink.'

Kwaku, trembling from head to foot, was too agitated to reply.

'Is what wrong to you?' she asked, apparently concerned by his inability to speak.

'Mistress,' he declared finally, 'I. . . .'

'You din' come to dun my poor sister for money she owe you, eh?' asked the old lady, resuming her hostile posture.

'No, mistress. Not me. I did come to look her up, 'cause she helped me out once.'

'Well you got to come in then,' she declared, grabbing him by the arm.

'Oh me Lord!' Kwaku muttered, thinking that once more he had succumbed to his old weakness of saying the wrong thing.

'Sit down in the easy chair. I goin' fix you a drink.'

His instinct for flight yielded to the reflection that his fugue would arouse suspicion. Besides, should the sexton get to hear of his visit he might put two and two together and remember he was indeed the man who had filled the dead lady with garlic. And what with him handling corpses every day, who can tell what he might get up to?

Mrs Duncan's sister left Kwaku alone to reflect on her accusation that he was responsible for her sister's death. Taking comfort from the knowledge that patients of trained medical doctors and their relations rarely turned on them where injury or death at their hands was suspected, Kwaku deemed it only just that he should be accorded similar exemption from blame. But if his defiance was thereby roused, his fear that his identity could be discovered and dismay at the consequences that might follow determined him to put on a show of humility, however much it went against the grain of his rebellious nature.

'Oh life! Why I didn' bring a kerchief?' he thought, wiping cascading sweat from his forehead with the back of his hand.

It occurred to Kwaku that some old people practised a peculiar brand of terror when they took it into their head to stand up for themselves. He shuddered to think what Mrs Duncan's sister would be capable of if she had a good memory.

The dead Mrs Duncan came back vividly to his imagination. A quiet, trusting lady, she never once mentioned a sister. Kwaku recalled how he disliked treating patients with many relations or friends. If, on his arrival at a house, there was a gathering in the bedroom or drawing room he would usually decline the invitation to treat, giving as his reason — once he had examined the patient — that the sick person was too far gone. Among the relations of the most docile patient there lurked, occasionally, a difficult customer who knew all about his or her rights. What might this sexton be like, for instance? He knew him to be sprightly; but what lay behind his sprightliness? One by one Kwaku looked over the furnishings, of which he had little recollection. The room resembled so many others he had visited the length and breadth of New Amsterdam, except for a fluted pedestal — nowadays regarded as a redundant extravagance — which was installed by a window in the corner, and on which a maidenhair fern stood grandly; also a Berbice chair with its extendible arm carefully folded back. Perhaps that was reserved for the sexton. Calling the nephew to mind, Kwaku resolved to leave as soon as decency would permit. It would be the height of folly to ask Mrs Duncan's sister to lend him money in memory of his tenuous and fatal association with her sister.

'Ah!' Kwaku exclaimed, as Mrs Duncan's sister came back with her hospitality tray, in the middle of which was a glass with a red liquid.

He rubbed his hands, pretending to be very much at home. In some countries the guest did well to fondle the host's dog or cat. Kwaku had learned that in his own country you ingratiated yourself by fondling a proferred glass. Before carrying it to his lips he stroked it, kissed it, flattered it and finally enquired whether it was old cut glass, the kind you could no longer buy in the shops.

'Cut glass?' asked Mrs Duncan's sister, 'I couldn' give you glass that cut. What you take me for?'

And once again that fierce expression came over her face.

Kwaku explained what cut glass was, even though he would not recognize it from the humbler variety; and for all he knew the glass might be cut or uncut.

Once more he wiped his brow, anticipating great difficulty in judging what to say in order to humour the lady, whose sister he was supposed to have sent to meet her maker with the smell of garlic on her breath.

Mrs Duncan's sister settled in a chair and at once began questioning him about the kind of work he did, and his marriage. Luckily she did not bother to wait for an answer to any questions she put, so that when she wanted to know if he was in the habit of beating his wife he only opened his mouth, pretending to be embarking on an answer. Mrs Duncan's sister waited for none, impelled by some bug that demanded an everlasting flow of words.

'You're a well bred young man.'

'Not so young any more,' Kwaku confessed.

'How old you is?'

'Thirty-two, mistress,' lied Kwaku, who felt the old capacity for improvisation return with such force he could not resist adding a coda to his false statement.

'Thirty-two next month.'

'You's a youngster. When I had thirty-two I was so frisky . . . yes, very frisky. I never married. Couldn' stand being tied down. But my sister! She couldn' live without a man and was off at sixteen. Eleven children she had. Funny number eleven. You ever hear of somebody with eleven children? It jus' don' happen. But she always do things different to everybody else. You know something. . . . What you say you name was?'

The noise that came out of Kwaku's throat resembled that of a young crapaud learning to croak. Something between 'peep' and 'caugh'. Fearing that by repeating his name Mrs Duncan's sister might suddenly remember that it fitted the man who had sent her beloved sister to Heaven with an overdose of his garlic concoction, he only uttered it reluctantly.

'Kwaku is my name, mistress.'

'How you spell it? You see, since my sister dead the memory going. I can't understand it; I does drink my cod liver oil every day without fail. Anyway, I got to write your name so that when the sexton come I can tell him 'bout your visit.'

'O life!' Kwaku exclaimed.

'What? You can't spell your name? And you look so respectable!'

'No, no,' Kwaku added hastily. 'I just had a thought . . . as . . . like something trampling 'pon my chest. My name spell K-w-a-k-u.'

'And your title?'

'Cholmondeley. . . . Look, I feel a little faint, mistress. Is the sun. It so hot! Is this global warming. You didn' notice? They say. . . . What they say? Mistress you got me so confused, I better be going.'

'Going? You drink my sorrel and two minutes later you say you going?'

Kwaku, desperate at his predicament, wondered if it was not best to get up and leave without ceremony. But he reflected that, living in a small town like New Amsterdam, he would almost certainly meet her again when, with her character, it was not inconceivable that she would raise a hue and cry against him and inform everyone that he had drunk her sorrel drink and would not even repay her the courtesy of conversation. In fact, his experience of old ladies persuaded him that she might even invent some story about him and thereby destroy any chance of resurrecting his status as a decent man.

'I'm not going, mistress. I changed my mind.'

'Good!' she declared.

And the laconic 'Good!' in such contrast to her voluble style unnerved Kwaku more than anything she had said until then.

'What I was talking 'bout before you say you was going?' Mrs Duncan's sister asked. 'Let me see. . . . Oh yes! I was telling you 'bout this healer who snuff out her life.'

'No, mistress. You been talking about something else. My name. You did want to know my name.'

'But you tell me your name. What wrong with you? You tetched or something?'

'I can't take any more of this, mistress.'

'Of what? What you can't take more of?' Kwaku's tormentor asked.

'Mistress, do you know what?'

'What?'

'I got a bad heart.'

She looked Kwaku up and down as if heart trouble was contagious.

'A young man like you got a bad heart! . . . I don' believe you. The way you come up the stairs, with your hand swinging. . . no. You don' got a bad heart. I'd say you got something to hide.'

The smile had disappeared from Mrs Duncan's sister's face and her staring eyes put the fear of God into Kwaku who, now more than ever convinced that flight was the most sensible course, decided to leave as soon as she went aback. He must persuade her somehow to abandon him for a while.

'Can I have a drink of water, mistress?' he asked with a great show of respect.

'So that's what you did want all the time,' she remarked, her expression softening markedly at the thought that at last she knew what his problem was.

'You want another sorrel? Is nicer than plain water.'

'Anything, mistress; sorrel, water, anything wet. Is my throat. Do it quick, please.'

Kwaku hung his head, a posture that had often brought him sympathy in the past whenever he sought a way out of some predicament.

Mrs Duncan patted him on his shoulder solicitously before leaving him on his own. But just as he was about to get up and steal away she put her head round the corner and said:

'The sexton should be coming any time now.'

'You din' . . . you din' tell me he was coming today.'

'Mr Cholmondeley, he does eat here! Where else he going to eat? He's my nephew!'

Mrs Duncan's sister did not know what to make of her guest's desperate look.

'Mr Cholmondeley, some people think 'cause he does deal with corpses every day he's funny. Is that what bothering you? If that's what bothering you, you can set your mind at rest. Raymond was devoted to his mother; he's a normal man with normal feelings. You should've see him mourn when she leave for the great beyond. Grieve? You never see somebody grieve like that. One time I did read about a man who grieve for his father. He grieve so bad he end up taking the cloth, so he could take part in lots of funerals. But Raymond make him look like a picture of happiness. Is after he done grieving that he become a sexton at the burying ground.'

Now, at the revelation that the sexton would be visiting that day some men would have shown the house a clean pair of heels. But not Kwaku! Struck dumb by the news he remained in the half sitting, half standing position in which Mrs Duncan's sister had caught him, apparently unable to revert to his sitting position or stand upright. In short, flight was impossible.

Not that Kwaku was unaccustomed to stress. When, as a young man, the villagers were looking for him after he had damaged the conservancy, he remained holed up in Blossom's cottage, to the chagrin of her husband, who was for disclosing his whereabouts to the police. *There* was a stressful situation! But then the deed had been done and he was, so to speak, staring danger in the face. Now it was the *threat* of danger which now turned his legs into two sticks, the uncertainty, the knowledge that his destiny could be decided either way. The sexton might remember him, then he might not.

'Now I believe you got a bad heart, Mr Cholmondeley. I did hesitate 'cause I not as trusting as my departed sister. Sit down, ne?'

And coming over to the hapless Kwaku, she eased him gently into a sitting position before taking a fan from her cabinet, with which she began to fan him slowly.

'You so faint-hearted!' she said, half reproachfully, half indul-gently. 'I got more balls than you.'

Kwaku nodded agreement with her, while his mind raced on in search of some method of getting away without losing her goodwill. Whatever he did now, he was a marked man, for his long conversation with her had created the bond that facilitates memory.

He watched her go back into the kitchen and recalled how Miss Gwendoline, his wife, used to walk with the same authority and how she lost that authority when her world went dark. His fortunes began to wane as well and he was finally reduced to a condition of such pity that the twins took to thrashing him behind a shed at least once a week. Kwaku reflected that he had gone through a great deal and was now entitled to some luck from above.

'Mr Cholmondeley,' Mrs Duncan's sister said when she returned with the second glass of sorrel drink, 'you don't know me, but I know you.'

She waited to see the effect her words would have on Kwaku.

'You should see yourself now,' she continued. 'Not so cocky, eh? Your hands not swinging like when you climb my stairs. I been watching you before you come through the gate posts. Well, I know you, Mr Healer, and I been watching you for years. Oh yes! And I tell you something: I know your wife, but she don' know me, because whenever I help her cross the road she can't see me, so she go tap-tapping with her stick away in the distance. And if it wasn't for her I would deliver you to the sexton without batting my eyelids. We women got to stick together, Mr Cholmondeley, 'cause is we does do the work and you men does reap the reward. I did tell you nobody does have eleven children 'cause that would be a abomination. And they don' got lazy women neither, 'cause that would be another abomination.'

And she went on talking, caring nothing for the terror in Kwaku's eyes and the way he kept looking at the front door.

'When you find a lazy woman,' she continued, 'is like finding a faithful and honest, yes, *honest* man. People does look on a lazy woman as if the whole nation going to collapse because of her laziness. I was like that once, the despair of my mother's house. I used to sponge on my family and lie around the house all day smoking menthol cigarettes and reading those American love story magazines. What bother my parents was not the laziness in itself, but that I was a lazy *woman*. But my sister was a hard-working, blameless woman. You think I don't remember you, but I remember you good, wearing new clothes and walking like countryman that never put shoes 'pon his foot. Who you think you was fooling? Not me! I did tell my sister; "That man up to no good. Look how he does walk and talk. I bet he can't even spell the word 'medicine', yet he practising as a healer." But she was trusting, poor thing. She heard the word *healer* and thought you know what you was doing. One time I did say to her, "Effie, they got good surgeon and bad surgeon." But she say, "I never hear 'bout that. I can't believe that." Yet she had a appendix scar 'bout a foot long. Whenever I lost my tape measure I used to make her lift up her blouse so that I could measure the cloth from it. And you pull the wool over that trusting woman eyes! . . . As soon as I set eyes on you I remember your face. "He must've fall on hard times," I say to myself. "Look how he dress." And if I didn' rush downstairs and strangle you, is because I'm a Christian *and* 'cause I feel sorry for your blind wife. Anyway, Mr Healer, you got to thank woman solidarity for leaving this house in one piece.'

Kwaku opened his mouth to thank her profusely, but she cut him off with a sharp reprimand.

'Don' come with your sweet talk in this house! I don' got no time for men like you. And if you want to know the truth I don' got no time for men! You better piss off before I set the sexton 'pon you!'

Kwaku was not sure whether to leave at once or indulge her by remaining a few more minutes; at all costs he must not offend her.

'Well, what you waiting for? Christmas?' she asked, in her most truculent tone. 'Haul your tail from my house and look for work!'

Kwaku leapt up from his seat and in his confusion bowed so deep he nearly knocked over the pedestal with its maidenhair fern.

Once outside he looked up the road in the direction of his home and in the distance caught sight of a tall, sprightly man walking towards him. Turning round like an automaton he hurried away in the opposite direction. Although from that distance he could not recognize the stranger's face he was taking no chances, telling himself that it would be a supreme irony if, having escaped the aunt's clutches, he were to fall foul of the nephew.

'Was no point asking *her* to lend me money,' he reflected.

Chapter II

We do not name our dogs. Yet, there is an exception to every rule, as Kwaku's experience will show. His next visit was a great success. Not that he managed to secure the loan he was after. No, he had not yet got so far. But through the woman he visited he was to find a place in Georgetown where he could stay while he tried to launch out as a salesman of old chamber-pots.

Kwaku, in despair at his near disastrous encounter with Mrs Duncan's sister, decided that he would go and look up a friend whom he had once helped, and whose gratitude was, as she said, as eternal as the stars.

Unable to afford a bus or taxi fare, he was obliged to walk all the way to East Canje, the lady's village. He had met her through her son, who had shown him the Kumars' residence, where he had promised to treat a sick child. The large house was owned by a man who, delighted that his call for help had been heeded, ordered a sheep to be killed. But having regaled his guest and bestowed upon him every indulgence, Mr Kumar objected to paying the fee for his son's treatment, claiming that it was exorbitant. Worse still, Kwaku, while leaving Mr Kumar's residence, had to endure the abuse of every member of the family, who stationed themselves at the front windows, and on a sign from their father, began to honour the healer with every known expletive and a few improvised ones as well. Needless to say, Kwaku's pride suffered severely from the collective display of ingratitude. Now he had to pass by this house to get to the cottage of the boy who had shown him the way and whose mother had sworn him eternal gratitude for helping her out with a gift of money, a portion of the contested fee. The same dung heap flourished beside the gate of the first house on the left. A herd of sheep — they bore a striking resemblance to those he saw on the occasion of his first visit — were browsing on the grass beside the drainage canal. In short, time seemed to have stood still in East Canje, the place Kwaku had described in that happier time as the end of the world.

'Mr Kumar numerous children mus' be young men and women by now,' Kwaku reflected. However, neither the size of the family nor that of the children occupied his thoughts for long, but rather the conviction that the Kumars had yet another reason for seeing him as a figure of fun: he had come down in the world! It was one thing to abuse a well-dressed practitioner of herbal rehabilitation whose pockets were fat with dollar notes. It was quite another to see your enemy bereft of all pretence to status! Kwaku looked upon that gratuitous abuse as something to be borne willingly, rather than expressions of ridicule that must surely come his way should he now be recognized by the Kumars.

'You're too brittle,' Mr Barzey (God rest his soul) told him once. 'Your pride's going to do for you.'

Recalling these words, Kwaku raised his head and walked boldly down the middle of the village road, past the dung heap and the browsing sheep, past a herd of cows half submerged in the canal, past the massive tamarind tree reputed to have been planted from seed by an immigrant from India, grateful for surviving the early malarial years; past the habitations of the wealthy and the poor living cheek by jowl on a stretch of land that, for them, represented the essential world.

On arriving in front of Mr Kumar's house Kwaku saw no one and heard no sound, and for all he knew it might have been empty. And in his wrong-headed way he stood before the house where he had first been fêted, then abused, and mused on how things, with him and his family, hardly ever turned out as anticipated, unlike the case of most other people, whose lives were ordered from birth to death in a series of predictable occurrences.

At the end of the street stood a tiny cottage occupied by the lady who saw Kwaku as her benefactor. Since his knocking brought no response he called out to the neighbour's equally small house, but, once more, to no avail. Kwaku, disturbed that until now he had noticed no evidence of habitation in the street, was tempted to conclude that animals had slaughtered all the humans and taken over the village. Anxiously he looked up the road, where the cows and sheep were congregated, only to see them all looking his way. The cows, which had climbed out of the canal, now blocked the street, so that if he took it into his head to flee there would be no place to go except towards the back dam, the traditional grazing pasture of village cattle.

'The healer!' came an unexpected cry behind him.

'Lady! You mustn't do that. You nearly frighten the life out of me. Only yesterday another lady nearly do me in.'

The boy's mother threw her arms round Kwaku, kissed him on both cheeks, then took his hands in hers and covered them in kisses.

'Come in, ne?' she said, still holding him by the hand.

She led him up the back stairs, explaining that the front door was for strangers. Since her son was no longer living there she only used the back.

'He not living here any more?'

'No. Come inside.'

She opened all the windows and light flooded into the small room, revealing the incongruously expensive furniture.

'It all change up, eh?' she said, turning to face Kwaku.

'I didn't come into the house that time,' he reminded her.

'You did. I 'member you standing in this room an' putting your hand in your pocket and saying, "This is for you." I remember that distinct as if it was yesterday.'

'I sure I stay outside,' Kwaku insisted.

'Anyway, in those days I use to sit on the floor an' eat my food from Capstan cigarette tins. I had one plate for the lord and master, the boy father. Look how things change, eh.'

They talked of the old days and Kwaku knew that she had not asked him why he was so badly dressed, out of discretion. Once when he looked up he caught an expression of sympathy in her eye. And it pained him to think that his life now resembled those distressing dreams when he walked naked down the Public Road in the village of his birth.

'What about the boy?' Kwaku enquired.

'Boy? He's a big man in town.'

'New Amsterdam?'

'No, Georgetown. He just like his father. You put them down in a desert an' they goin' survive. They got some people like that. Not me! I born to suffer. But I can't complain. Is the boy that pay for all this. He keepin' his mother in style. I'm a kept woman.'

And she laughed her shrill laugh, belying the picture of a sour-faced woman he recalled so well.

She explained that her son was a Permanent Secretary with the Ministry of Hope. She could not remember its proper name, but she christened it the Ministry of Hope for a reason that was never explained. His success, according to her, was due to the massive emigration to Canada, which left a large number of posts in the Civil Service vacant. Once he had his foot on the 'stairs' he climbed up and up until he became a Permanent Secretary.

'Ten years ago that wasn' a job for country people like us. But they can't stop him now. That boy only got to read a page one time an' he remember everything 'pon it.'

'I know,' Kwaku said. 'I remember how he did tell me he could read a book upside down.'

'He too bright, if you ask me.'

Her son had begun as the creature of a government minister who, struck by his compliance and his ability to follow instructions to the letter, assigned him to what he described as 'confidential duties,' which consisted mainly of spying on people suspected of being disloyal to the ruling party. His success in following suspects without himself arousing suspicion earned him promotion, and he became a trusted informant who came and went as he pleased and could even contact the minister on an unlisted telephone number. But the decisive promotion came when he performed a certain service which earned him a rent-free flat and a small car. The minister's lady friend, another one of his numerous suspects, had been installed in a mansion on D Street with three maids and a companion. None of those whose services the minister had secured to keep an eye on her could discover a flaw in her conduct. Sick to death of their incompetence, he put the young man on her spoor, and within a week received a comprehensive list of those who visited the mansion, conspicuous among whom was a notorious philanderer. When asked by the minister how he managed such a difficult task the young man told him that he kept vigil in a tree opposite the lady's house and only succeeded in staying awake by drinking strong black coffee laced with guarana from a Thermos flask. The gentleman visitor never arrived before two in the morning, and by that time the former watchers of the house must have gone home. Besides, there was no other way to maintain surveillance without being noticed, except from a tree with thick foliage.

After that exploit he got rapid promotion until he reached the point where he came to be recognized as the most brilliant star in the galaxy of young pretenders to ministerial responsibility. When, finally, he was appointed a Permanent Secretary, leaving behind him older and more experienced men with a solid academic education, he boasted that behind ambition lurked a sinister companion who eschewed morality, repeating a famous quip made by the Minister of Hope himself.

His mother had no knowledge of the details of his career, believing that his success had been due to an ability to read well, and discounting his incessant stories about power. And had she learned that he was regarded by his superiors as the embodiment of ruthlessness, she would have declared emphatically that that was the character of another man and not of her son. Yet, her constant complaint about the young man's father centred on his ruthless ways and the influence he had exercised over their only child in the brief periods when he lived at home.

'And he buy you all this!' Kwaku remarked, referring to the furniture and bric-à-brac in her cluttered room.

In the old days Kwaku would not have hesitated to ask her to speak to her son on his behalf, so that he could leave for Georgetown with the knowledge that he had a protector. But since he fell on hard times he became concerned about the way people were vexed by his words, even those that were meant to flatter.

'I can't understand you,' she told him. 'This is the third time we meet up an' every time you different. The first time you give me money an' din' want nothing for it; the second time you take advantage of me; and this time you sit down an' hardly say a word. I feel so bad!'

Kwaku made the gesture a dumb man might have made, by way of apology for not being able to reply.

'Is what wrong with you?' she insisted.

'Lady, you never even tell me your name. I know you good, but I don' know your name. I know the names of a lot of bad people, but you and your son. . . .'

'That's all?' she said, twitching her bird-figure and smiling hugely. 'I call Rose an' my son call Solomon. But some people does call him Me-one, 'cause he's a loner. He don' like company.'

Kwaku had once dubbed her 'Bird Woman' in jest.

'May I call you Rose?' he asked putting on his best style taught him by Mr Barzey — rest his soul — so many years ago.

'May I call you Rose!' she mocked. 'May I *caaal* you Rose? You can *caaaal* me anything. But if you go on talkin' so humble I goin' start to cry.'

'All right,' Kwaku said, emboldened by the respect she still had for him and which he dared not expect from anyone else. 'I want to go to Georgetown to do some business, but I don't know anybody there. You see me here, I'm frightened of big towns. All these people who does emigrate to North America where trains run underground and even fly. I don' know how they can manage to survive there.'

Kwaku kept on speaking out of sheer nervousness, not daring to risk giving her time to say 'No.' He talked of his fear of towns, of his profound distress since leaving his village, where he could speak like a fool without the risk of being accused of slander or walk with his arm round his daughter's waist without attracting the attention of passers-by. He talked so much he began to ramble and let her into secrets of his family life; of the daughter who lived with a man, but was in love with Blossom, his life-long friend. He spoke of his admiration for people of status and his ambition to have his photograph taken with the President. He spoke of old Mr Barzey — rest his soul — who had set him on the road to success with his lessons in photography; of how he missed him because he was the first male to treat him with respect. And the Bird Woman let him speak, believing him to be the shadow of the arrogant man she once knew.

'Miss Rose, inside I'm a big man. I know! But I let myself down on the outside, like if I was a prince in my last life and come back a yowaree that does ferret about the public trash heaps for food. . . . Yesterday I been to visit a lady and things turn out bad!'

He recounted his experience of the previous day, when he visited Mrs Duncan's sister.

'I know her from New Amsterdam,' Miss Rose said. 'Don't bother with her. Everybody know how the first square meal she eat for years was at her sister wake. Everybody know how she inherit the house and the money and everyt'ing. When she was young she use to smoke in public an' embarrass her family, until they cut her off, an' she had to go from house to house begging for food.'

The Bird Woman followed her disclosures with a resounding suck-teeth.

Kwaku, relieved by the news that his accuser was less than perfect, felt that a burden had fallen from his shoulders, and the tone of his talk became brighter.

'You going write your son and ask him to help me?'

'Today. As soon as you gone,' she promised.

Then, seeing that her visitor was in better spirits, the Bird Woman asked Kwaku if he would like to go visiting with her. She wanted to show him off to her friends beyond the back dam.

'But Miss Rose, look how I dress!' he objected, surveying his unflattering attire, which looked as if it had been slept in.

'You din' care 'bout how I dress when you lick me down in the grass an' take advantage of me,' she reminded him, poking him in the ribs at the same time with her bony elbow. . . . 'You coming?'

He nodded agreement and she went down into the bath-hut in her yard to prepare for their sortie. Two hours later she came back to join him, transformed by patient work and the miracle of make-up. An organdy peasant blouse and a matching cotton skirt were crowned by a face whose delicately reddened lips provoked thoughts of seduction in Kwaku, and he was overcome by a surge of retrospective pride at the abrupt way he had seduced her long ago when she resembled a fugitive from a long prison sentence.

She pressed an envelope into his hands. Kwaku opened it and found a clutch of hundred dollar bills and a piece of paper on which was written her son's name and Georgetown address.

'I can't take this, Miss Rose. No, no! I can't take money from a woman.'

She reminded him that the Guyana dollar was worth a fraction of its value of ten years ago.

'In any case, I don' want it back,' she said harshly.

Kwaku put the envelope into his pocket, and when she took his arm, smiling up at him as if he had given *her* money, he knew that it would be churlish to refuse her gift.

Once outside, he asked why she was not locking the back door of her house.

'Me? Lock my back door? Why?'

They walked towards the back dam, crossed the narrow plank over the sideline canal and then rejoined each other on the farther bank, strolling side by side in a manner that betrayed their changed relationship. She was no longer overawed by him, while he, relishing his astonishment at the discovery that she was desirable, kept glancing sideways at her in admiration.

'I din' cook for you,' she said, 'but where we going you can eat as much as you want.'

She turned into a yard, leaping a gutter over which there was no bridge. They could hear voices raised in heated argument; and even before they went up the stairs Kwaku felt he would be at home in this house of strangers, simply because he was a companion of the Bird Woman, who possessed Blossom's sincerity, if not her intelligence.

Once upstairs, Kwaku was introduced to a number of men and

women, all seated against the walls of the drawing room. And no sooner were the introductions over than the main speaker took up where he had left off.

'I'm telling you!' he said, emphasizing each word in reply to a protest that had been made before the couple arrived. 'They stealing from burial grounds in town. Of course it not in the papers. The government does control the papers. Everybody know that! Is not what *in* the papers. Is what *not* in the papers. Gangs of men going to the burial grounds at the dead of night. . . .'

And there was a burst of laughter from his listeners at the word 'dead.'

'Alright, alright!' he said impatiently.

But he had to wait until they were sufficiently quiet before he could continue.

'When they begin about a year ago they used to look for the gold and silver jewelry they bury the corpses with. Then they begin knocking out their gold teeth. And now?'

Taking out an improbably large handkerchief from his trouser pocket, he began wiping his forehead theatrically.

'Alyou give me such a hard time,' he said, 'I sweating like Miss Blanding pig.'

'Anyway,' he began again, while putting away the handkerchief, 'as. . . .'

'Buck man does walk with he hammock,' one of his listeners remarked, pointing at the voluminous handkerchief, 'but you does walk with you bed sheet.'

Another burst of laughter interrupted the account, and the story-teller fixed the man with a stare.

'If looks could kill!' a woman said.

'You want to hear the Georgetown news or not,' the storyteller challenged her, 'or you prefer to rely 'pon your prevaricating news-papers?'

His flight of language was greeted with a round of applause.

'Ow, black man! You does use rich words. Man, we people too talented.'

This outburst from a burly man sitting on a straight-backed chair, which had all but disappeared under him, expressed the general opinion of the speaker, a taxi owner who did three trips to Georgetown in a day. In spite of his apparent exasperation at being interrupted, he actually enjoyed the enforced gaps in his accounts of life in the capital, which he gave at regular Saturday night sessions to the same company of men and women, all of whom lived locally and rarely ever went to town.

'As I was saying, they begin with the jewelry, then move to the gold teeth; and now they breaking off the skulls and selling them to America. Truth o' God! Let lightning lick me down if I telling lie. They exporting skulls!'

Many of his listeners, who knew him to be a notorious liar, did not believe what he said, but in fact he had spoken the truth. The number of open graves was worrying politicians, who believed the depredations to be an alarming sign of things to come.

'Man, Vibart, you lie too bad!' an old lady said. 'I been to a *fineral* in Georgetown two months ago an' I in' see a single open grave.'

'You been cross-eyed ever since you was a little girl. You tell me so yourself.'

A howl of laughter nearly caused the house to collapse, and even Vibart began laughing at the effect his remark had achieved.

Kwaku, usually the comedian in any gathering, felt deeply envious of Vibart, who knew how to reduce his companions to laughter without covering himself with ridicule. This talent must surely have been developed because of his frequent trips to town! He exchanged glances with Rose, who made a gesture which seemed to say, 'You see why I bring you here? To learn something about the place where you want to go and live.'

Soon afterwards food was served by three small girls, who had kept out of sight until then. It took a good quarter of an hour before they came round to Rose and Kwaku, and the latter reflected that he thought he knew all about village life until he witnessed such lavish entertaining.

In the village where he had been brought up by his uncle, where he married Miss Gwendoline and raised his children, most of the inhabitants worked for a wage and could not afford to entertain on a grand scale. Here, many were substantial farmers, proprietors of goats and cattle; and if they hardly ever travelled they were nevertheless protected from the woes of townspeople and other wage earners, who suffered unimaginable privations at the time of the fuel and food shortages, when their women had to stand in cooking oil lines for hours and paid exorbitant prices for scarce goods smuggled in over the Courantyne River.

While they were eating, conversation all but stopped. Kwaku was tempted to go over to Vibart and speak to him of his forthcoming mission to Georgetown. But he imagined that the man who knew the secret of entertaining would rebuff him, and he would be made to look a fool in front of Rose.

Deep down Kwaku had not changed. Had he been wearing an embroidered shirt-jac and leather soled shoes he would have been capable of playing any role he chose; but clad in indifferent garb he felt he was nothing. More than ever he husbanded his determination to carry off his enterprise as dealer in antiques and recover the glory of that period which began when he sprayed urine defiantly on the shoemaker's premises and ended with a triumphant return to his village as a famous healer.

The meal was followed by much tooth-picking and the associated hissing, then by innumerable 'ahs' of appreciation and arguments about whether the art of cooking had suffered since political inde- pendence, then by the relative virtues of men cooks and women cooks; by cooking as a form of physical exercise; by a suggestion that there should be established a Ministry of Cooking; by reflections on what proportion of the criminal classes was represented by cooks; should the knife and fork be abolished by decree; should eating with the hands be made compulsory with or without the sanction of imprisonment; whether good cooks were born or made; was group therapy appropriate for the rehabilitation of those suffering from a neurosis induced by inhaling imported curry powder; the relationship between cooking, fooping and arthritis of the tibia; and finally the well-known story of the wife who woke up one morning, discovered that she had lost her memory and believed that cooking had been banned by the government as a mark of respect for the famous Guyanese who passed away while eating the Portuguese dish of garlic pork. This in turn provoked Guyanese Portuguese so much that they emigrated as one man to Canada and the United States.

The taxi driver stood up and, emitting an almighty belch of appre- ciation, announced that he was leaving. However, a howl of protest, especially from the ladies, obliged him to put off his departure for a short while.

'A short while, I say. I got things to do.'

He knew well enough that a guest could not leave so soon after eating at his host's expense and had timed his announcement to provoke the maximum protest.

'One day somebody goin' cut you tail for you' wrong-headedness,' the man sitting on the invisible chair said.

'I got things to do for my father-in-law.'

'You never do a hard day's work in you' life. All you do is sit in you' taxi an' take people money.'

The host himself came back from the kitchen, having heard the turn things had taken.

'Vibart, if you want to go, go!'

And the taxi driver, who had not the slightest intention of going, realized that his host had called his bluff.

'I staying 'cause they beg me to say. I'm a democrat. A democratic storyteller.'

'Eh eh, Vibart,' came a voice from the corner of the room, 'you calling you'self a liar.'

'No,' came the reply, 'I'm a storyteller, a teller of tales. . . . I'll tell you something else. You see them two love birds in the corner. . . ?'

All eyes turned towards a recently married couple who had been feeding each other during the meal.

'That is Love!' declared Vibart. 'But wasn't always like that. And the Lord said, "all I want is a good meal an' a big, strapping woman." An' since that day Love become important. Man–woman story was not like that for a million years. If I did become associated with a woman I had to please her mother and father before we could come together. God did create this love thing, but he hold it back, 'cause he din' care to let it loose 'pon the world yet. Man–woman use to come together out of convenience, not love. But God did know very well what he doing. "Wait, ne," he say to himself. "I goin' unleash this love thing in my own good time." And at the end of a million years he see how things was going on earth an' suddenly decide it was time. So he knead this love good an' put it in the celestial oven till it brown an' crispy; an' when it done he wrap it up nice in cellophane paper an' tie it with a ribbon that had all the colours of the rainbow before letting it down to earth slow, slow. The nex' morning a woman find it, an' being of generous nature she distribute it one-one to she friends an' neighbours them. An' they eat off a piece an' give it out to their friends an' neighbours, until everybody in the world get a bit. Cheese an' rice!

Look story! Everybody change up, even the old people an' the children. They all become infected with the rage of love so bad the children tell their parents not to interfere in their business. An' from then on weddings get smaller an' smaller. An' Jealousy, who was asleep, rise up, like that, from nowhere. An' we begin to love one another so bad it couldn' last, and eventually some of it turn to hate. . . . Give me a drink, man.'

In spite of his doubtful credentials Vibart's audience had become quiet, hypnotized by his gestures and gravelly voice. He drank the water one of the girls brought him, made as if to continue, then suddenly changed his mind.

'I say I staying only for a short while and I did mean it.'

More than ever satisfied with the way he had got them to hang on his words, he stood up, ignoring the renewed protests.

'I gone,' he said, waving his hand. 'I can hear my father-in-law calling.'

And his departure was accompanied by protests more muted than when he declared he was going the first time.

Rose introduced Kwaku to the host, who had been behind the shed in the yard when they arrived. Then, on Kwaku's request to see the backyard, the three went downstairs to admire the animals tethered under the mango trees, whose young fruit hung from long stalks. The yard stretched for about two hundred feet, as far as the drainage canal, a broad, glittering ribbon under the afternoon sun. Kwaku wanted to ask the host a hundred questions relating to the tranquility of his home, about his wife and children, and how he had managed to create a perfect haven in a country in turmoil. Had he never heard of the national debt? Or about the hospitals besieged by people suffering from malnutrition? The plight of schools with too few teachers and the general malaise? He, Kwaku, longing to settle in town, had taken the first indispensable step to that end when, full of his small triumph, he had come across what he saw as a kind of paradise, where people could raise their voices without anger; and Vibart the trickster who, like him, took pleasure in manipulating people, yet was not treated as an outcast.

Impressed, but confused by what he had witnessed, Kwaku bade his host goodbye and left with the Bird Woman as darkness began to fall.

Back home Kwaku gave his wife a detailed account of his day and noticed that his success in securing the Georgetown address of Rose's son upset her.

'Is you that encourage me, though,' he told her. 'And I don' even know any more if is a good idea.'

'You got to go,' she told him. 'It's only that I was thinking how lonely I goin' be with all the children gone away. The house so empty!'

'Well, I got a surprise for you! I earn a few hundred dollars. for singing at this man house.'

'You don't tell me you did sing!'

Kwaku embellished the lie with circumstantial evidence so plausible no suspicion of his invention crossed her mind.

'I goin' buy you a dog with the money. A dog to keep you company and guard the house when you alone.'

'That's good,' she told him, while retaining the mental image of an empty house.

Neither ever mentioned the word *blind*, for to do so would have been to revive memories of her seeing days when, on Saturday nights, the village house would be full of customers who came to buy her black pudding.

Kwaku bought his wife a puppy and called it 'Armageddon'. We do not christen our dogs, but when we do we bestow upon them names chosen with infinite care. Kwaku, with that unfailing instinct for the absurd, had hit upon a name the poor mongrel would have to endure for the rest of its life, as if it were not enough that it was destined to bear the yoke of human attachment.

He put off his trip to Georgetown in order to train Armageddon in the basic skills of companionship; fetching, sniffing out prowlers, ignoring Miss Gwendoline's plate when piled high with food and barking aggressively at strangers. But by the end of the second week the beast was so confused it hung its head whenever Kwaku gave an order, eyeing him suspiciously as he threw up his hands in exasperation. It had no idea what to make of the foul words which rained down on its head when a command was refused; and if at times it looked at Kwaku as if he were tetched, at other times it judged him to be amiable, with a peculiar facility for talking to no purpose. In the end Armageddon succeeded in training Kwaku to leave him alone. Miss Gwendoline liked her new dog.

CHAPTER III

The night before his departure for Georgetown, Kwaku and his wife reminisced about the times they had to part. She never admitted to any anxiety about his welfare on those occasions and now she professed to be confident about the business enterprise. Often, while practising as a healer, his meagre education let him down, more especially his spelling. He had met illiterates from the deep country-side and remembered how once a man travelling in the same taxi as himself confessed that he could neither read nor write. Kwaku was taken with a sudden, inexplicable urge to abuse him and would no doubt have done so had he not feared the reaction of the other passengers.

'You remember how I use to write you letters from New Amsterdam?' he asked Miss Gwendoline, who remained immobile in her bentwood rocking chair.

'I remember. My brother is a better letter-writer than you, but his longest letter was four lines. I got it somewhere in my trunk.'

In her trunk, which now could accommodate all her worldly possessions and in which she kept earthenware plates to protect them from her blind negligence.

'My grandfather use to write letters in Portuguese,' she continued, 'although he did know how to write English. He was too proud. And in our house, when I was a lil' girl we always use to say "Caca", never the English word "shit". And "obrigado" too.'

'Oh,' said Kwaku in a knowing voice, having no idea what 'obrigado' meant.

If they never mentioned her blindness they never spoke of their children either, unless circumstances obliged them to, subscribing to a tacit conspiracy neither would have been capable of explaining. Yet they looked forward to their infrequent visits, when Kwaku plied the girls with indiscreet questions, forgetting Miss Gwendoline's warning that they were no longer children. But he invariably found a reason to go out when the boys came and thereby contributed to the widening gulf between him and them.

'What I goin' tell the other children?' Miss Gwendoline asked.

'Tell them I looking for work in town. But tell the boys I *got* a job in town.'

'If I tell them that,' Miss Gwendoline said, 'I going have to tell the girls the same story, else the boys goin' hear from the girls and. . . .'

Kwaku shuddered at his humiliation and shame at the first thrashing he had received from the twins when it seemed that only a short time before the incident he was looking down at them from a great height. He shuddered at the hostility of Time, especially the way it contrived to deliver him into the hands of his more disreputable offspring. Miss Gwendoline had no idea that behind all his reasons for going away, their poverty, his desire to be respected and the pull of city life, lay the twins with their leering expression and vacant eyes. And if he cared to look deeper into himself he would have discovered a matching hostility on his part, that they had dared to grow up.

'Is who give you all that money?' Miss Gwendoline asked. 'Tell me the truth. Is Blossom?'

'Blossom! I in' see Blossom since she come a few months ago. I *tell* you how I earn it.'

'I believe you,' Miss Gwendoline said softly. 'I got to believe you. One thing I glad about: the buses don' run no more.'

She was referring to the way Blossom, Kwaku's life-long friend, lost her job as a bus conductor when the Transport Corporation gave up competing with the taxis and vans that plied the coast. While Blossom was on the buses she and he used to meet occasionally in New Amsterdam.

'The beetles bumping into the lamps,' she remarked. 'I can hear them.'

It was the time of the year when hard-backed beetles collided with the kerosene lamp that lit up the single room in which they lived. When they were ready to bed down, scores of the insects would have expired on the floor, and Kwaku would be obliged to sweep them away before he unrolled their mattress between the door and the back window. Every time the thought crossed his mind that Miss Gwendoline would not be able to manage on her own he repulsed it, as though it were a malevolent voice whispering in his ear.

He would be taking her with him in spirit, as he would be taking his favourite daughter Philomena in spirit; Philomena, who had grown up to become a woman of great character, widely admired for the way she cared for her deformed child.

'She should've come by now,' Kwaku said.

'You expect Philomena to keep to time?' Miss Gwendoline said, not sparing the sarcasm she could not help investing in any remark she made about her second daughter.

'But she's reliable,' Kwaku countered, for his part refusing to side with his wife when it came to Philomena.

They waited impatiently for Philomena's arrival and grew so agitated a stranger might have come to the conclusion that Kwaku was leaving that very night. A wind which rose and fell fitfully brought the rumour of vehicles from the main road, and with the dying sound of an engine Kwaku would get up and go to the window in expectation of his daughter's coming. He kept asking himself what mood she would be in and whether she and Miss Gwendoline would quarrel before he left the next morning. Would she bring her daughter with her? The most unpredictable of all their children, her parents feared the worst, since she had only been given short notice of Kwaku's trip.

'You better tie down that window,' Miss Gwendoline advised him. 'You know what happen last time the wind was bad.'

Just as Kwaku thought he could no longer endure the waiting, he heard footsteps approaching the house.

'She coming,' Miss Gwendoline said, like someone about to defend herself.

She had heard the footfalls before her husband; and so did the puppy which, tied to a nail driven into the door frame, began wagging its tail vigorously on catching sight of Philomena. The young woman stopped, astonished at the sight of a dog outside her parents' house. Then, making a long detour as though the animal was stricken with disease, she pushed the door and came in.

'Whose dog is that?' she asked unsmilingly.

Kwaku's heart sank.

'Is your mother dog. It call Armageddon.'

'Who gave it to her?'

'Me,' Kwaku answered.

'What for?'

'Cause we did think I'd be alone when your father go away,' Miss Gwendoline put in.

Philomena shrugged her shoulders, unwilling to take up the implied reproach. She was tired from a long walk she had taken to the edge of the Canje Creek, home of the friend with whom she had left her daughter.

'Is where my grandchild?' Kwaku enquired.

'With Sissy.'

Philomena then fell into a stubborn silence, to which her mother used to take exception, knowing that her daughter talked incessantly in Sissy's company.

'You like the dog?' Kwaku asked.

'What?' Philomena asked in turn, shaken, as it seemed, from a long reverie.

'You like Armageddon?'

'No. I don't like dogs. . . . What you goin' feed it on?'

'I got money,' Kwaku said, pulling the envelope with notes from his pocket.

Philomena took the envelope from him and started counting the notes, but before she had even got halfway she looked up and asked her father how he came by so much money.

'I work for it!'

And Kwaku proceeded to tell her about the business venture he expected to make him wealthy.

Replacing the notes in the envelope she asked, 'Where will you get more money to feed the dog?'

'We'll manage,' Miss Gwendoline said, seething inwardly at her daughter's insolence, to which she had never grown accustomed, and which had only declared itself when the whole family came to live in New Amsterdam and Philomena was still in her teens.

Philomena, as usual, was impeccably turned out, with heavy make-up stylishly applied. Her young man, who began courting her 'properly' — as Kwaku put it — after the birth of her child, never got over the contrast between her clothes and the hovel she once shared with her parents. Neither could he understand why she did not seem impressed by his promise to take her away from such squalor. And it was Philomena's apparent indifference that allowed her to establish a hold over him in spite of her lukewarm commitment in their moments of intimacy.

Kwaku attempted to revive the conversation, but Philomena only stared at him when he described the house in East Canje with its many guests and the storyteller who mesmerized his audience.

'You think I make it up, eh?'

But Philomena was preoccupied with her thoughts. Besides, since she had established her own home away from her parents, the hovel seemed like a prison cell where it was impossible to escape her mother's roving, sightless eyes. For that reason alone she had taken her daughter to Sissy.

'This wind!' Miss Gwendoline exclaimed, choosing to merge her resentment with her distaste for the inclement weather.

'Is all the satellites they putting up in the sky,' Kwaku said.

'What satellites?' Miss Gwendoline asked.

Not having access to a radio she had little idea of what was going on in the outside world, except what she learned from her children and the occasional visitor.

'The Russians and Americans sending up satellites and fighting a war up there.'

And while Kwaku felt considerable relief at uttering his lie he felt disappointment as well, aware that it failed to match those falsehoods invented when, at the height of his powers, they acted as a catharsis to his pent-up emotions which bore no name.

'And what they fighting up there for when they can fight down here?' Miss Gwendoline said, puzzled.

But before he could answer Philomena got up.

'Take me with you, Pa,' she said, turning to face her father.

In the silence that followed, the wind could be heard distinctly, its steady, monotonous voice relieved now and then by the puppy's uncertain whining.

Suddenly Miss Gwendoline stood up as her daughter had done; then, without any warning brought her stick down on the floor with such force that the window shuddered in its frame. Kwaku, not in the least surprised at his wife's reaction, gripped his head with his hands.

'I. . . ,' he began, but failed to complete the sentence.

Miss Gwendoline turned her head towards his voice, daring him to accede to his daughter's request.

'I can't. I want to, but I can't,' he said. 'It's a dangerous town. Anybody that been there, ask them, they'll tell you they does rob you in broad daylight.'

The urge to go on, to cocoon himself in a welter of words, gripped him as it always did when he felt cornered or embarrassed. At the same time he wished to know what effect the denial had had on Miss

Gwendoline. Apparently satisfied with his refusal, she sat down once again, feeling behind her with one hand in order to locate the chair.

Kwaku was certain that the storm would break out, for Miss Gwendoline had been restraining herself too long.

'If you take me with you,' Philomena went on, 'I *undertake* to get you the chamber-pots.'

'I know where I can get the two I taking to town in the morning,' Kwaku rejoined, desperate to bring the subject to an end.

'I know. But I'm talking about the future. You'll have trouble keeping up the supply.'

'No!' bellowed Miss Gwendoline. 'He not taking you!'

'I'm not shouting,' Philomena said calmly, 'Pa's a grown man. All he's got to do is say "no". '

'No,' came the swift response from Kwaku, who seized the opportunity to redeem himself in his wife's estimation.

'Story done,' Philomena said.

She took out a cigarette from the packet in her purse, lit it, then replaced both cigarettes and matches before blowing out a puff of smoke.

Kwaku could only guess at his daughter's anger and reflected on the shift of the balance of power in the family since her mother went blind. Philomena had always dressed like a lady, and he could imagine her crossing the great town roads or skirting the canals he only knew from pictures. Nothing would have pleased him better than to go into business with her, thus perpetuating the fantasy that she would never leave him, even after she married and tied herself to a stranger for the rest of her life.

Kwaku's worst fears had been realized. He had always hoped the day would come when the two people he cherished most would put their differences behind them. But he was forced to acknowledge that there was something about their relationship that escaped him, suggesting a struggle beyond their personal confrontation. And it dawned upon him that he knew far less about his wife and daughter than he had imagined, as though Time, far from familiarizing him with the recesses of their characters, cast shadows upon them, until they lay beneath a deep, forbidding pall.

'You know,' Kwaku said nervously, 'You know this man I been to see yesterday. . . . You should've see his yard. He got guinea fowl, turkey, powis. . . .'

And he listed all the birds the man did *not* have in an effort to impress.

'And another man, Vibart is his name, start telling us a lot o' nonsense; an' I never see people so attentive. Talk 'bout the power of nonsense! I sit an' listen to the man going on 'bout people stealing from burial grounds in town. You ever hear people steal from burial ground? Look how them bus drivers does put they foot down 'pon the accelerator when they passing a *little* village cemetery at night. You think thief-man would walk about in that enormous Georgetown bone yard by night? With tools and all? An' you know most of them believe him? But that's Guyanese for you: the bigger the lie the easier they swallow it. Everyt'ing 'bout us is big. When we bright we bright bright; but when we stupid! O loss! We so stupid!'

'Like you,' Miss Gwendoline muttered.

Kwaku had not heard what she said, but knew from the intonation of the two words that the remark was derogatory.

At his wit's end, he clasped his hands so hard his knuckles jutted out above the fingers. He racked his brains for something to say, but in his confusion would only drag up words completely unsuitable for the restoration of harmony. But he, the Lord of Confusion, had learned to hold his tongue at times like these.

Should he have bought a dog? After all, Philomena had surprised him by agreeing to stay as long as he was away, in the wake of her emphatic denial of any attachment to the home during a quarrel with her mother a few weeks before. She detested dogs and cats; and now, with Armageddon's incessant whimpering, it was likely that she would give him away. When the children were young and he earned a derisory wage as a shoemaker, Miss Gwendoline would frequently console him by saying that they would grow up one day and life would be easier. They had grown up and left the home, yet they were a constant thorn in their flesh. Would things have been different had Miss Gwendoline not lost her sight and been forced to depend on the only child with whom she did not get on? He thought of the Bird Woman who, when he first met her, was in such desperate straits he believed she would do an injury to her son or his father, who had all but abandoned her. Look at her now! The once scowling woman smiled continually and had good words for everyone. Everything about her had changed, even her appearance, transformed by the power of clothes. It was as if she inhabited a new body, just as she was surrounded by different furniture and objects of distinction. Hope! He had heard talk of a Ministry of Hope and it occurred to him that it would be more appropriate to set up a Ministry of Action, for only the impotent relied on hope, like those women who take part in collective prayers at the height of a drought. No, he rejected talk of hope and such like. If in the past he rose above a condition of misery he would do so once again, as surely as his name was Kwaku Cholmondeley.

Once more he was distracted by the wind, a sudden gust that set the window rattling.

'That dog!' Philomena exclaimed, crushing out her cigarette in the tin she had placed on the floor. The animal, terrified by the wind, had decided on interpreting its misery at a higher pitch.

'Why not let's go down to the rum shop?' Kwaku suggested to Miss Gwendoline.

'Don' waste your money,' she replied almost indulgently.

'Anyway,' he remarked, 'we can't go in this wind. Is the fishermen on the sea I feel sorry for.'

The last thing that exercised his mind was sympathy for the fishermen; but when not lost in his reflections, he felt an infernal embarrassment, which he attempted to assuage in the only way he knew how, with foolish words.

'Do you read your Bible, girl?' Miss Gwendoline suddenly demanded, directing her words where she thought her daughter was seated.

'You know,' Philomena said, speaking very slowly in an effort to mortify her mother, 'where I does work there's a left-handed man who does read the paper, beginning with the last page an' then reading backwards to the first. . . .'

'My God!' Kwaku said, his patience finally running out. 'Just when things was quietening down alyou at it again?'

Angrily he got up and opened the door, intending to go down to the rum shop alone. But it was wrenched out of his hand by the force of the wind, which threw everything into confusion. Philomena leapt up to help her father close and bolt the door, but it resisted with a violence that seemed to come from within the wood rather than from an external source. And while the two used all their strength to subdue the door Miss Gwendoline remained impassive. Only her head shook imperceptibly in the way some blind people's eyes shuddered, as a disturbing reminder of a presence that could not be taken for granted.

Miss Gwendoline's growing hatred of Philomena (this flowering of distaste for her precocious daughter had begun long before she went blind) had become a kind of necessity, without which she would have felt empty. Seeing no one, having no one for company but Kwaku, she drove her thoughts along unusual paths where obstacles seemed connected with the young woman and the aura surrounding her, like the overpowering scent of tobacco smoke or the menacing rustling of her expensive skirts. Convinced that Philomena had taken up smoking deliberately to vex her, 'to tantalize me' she had told Kwaku, she saw the reasons for her hatred confirmed. Yet, she would not admit to herself that she wanted to see Philomena's destruction and confined her search for vengeance to prayers that God would punish her daughter with the aim of bringing her round to a Christian appreciation of loyalty and moderation.

In spite of their success in bolting the frail door, Kwaku remained standing by it, fearing that it might be blown in once more, perhaps with such force that it would be wrenched from its frame and leave them exposed to the elements.

And the whole evening wife, husband and daughter hung around, waiting for the storm to abate, knowing that the tension between them would not be relieved by a visit, or by the easy conversations for which their home was once famous throughout the village they once inhabited in those far-off days when Miss Gwendoline kept open house as vendor of blood rice and souse.

Chapter IV

Kwaku waited with a score or so other men and women for the arrival of Miss Rose's son, the Permanent Secretary at the Ministry of Hope. It was two o'clock in the afternoon and the sun was high in a cloud-free sky. The building, one of those grand old houses in the eighteenth century style, had a concreted yard on which half-barrels with flowering plants were lined up at regular intervals along the paling fence. Kwaku marvelled at the impassive expressions of his companions in patience, believing their need to see the Bird Woman's son to be as urgent as his. He had arrived the day before from New Amsterdam and by the time he learned how to get to the street in which the Permanent Secretary lived he was told by the watchman that the official was at work. But finding the Ministry building closed he went back to the house, where the self-same watchman informed him that the Permanent Secretary did not receive visitors dressed like that. He would probably see him at the Ministry, however, since he was known as a friend of the poor and had endowed a small children's orphanage only the week before with a handsome, if undisclosed sum of money. Kwaku, weighed down with fatigue, sought a refuge for the night. Unwilling to spend what was left of the money Rose had given him, he wandered about the town until, coming upon a man stretched out on the pavement in Camp Street, he lay down beside him and fell into a deep, untroubled sleep. When he woke the following morning his companion had gone and he alone adorned the paved thoroughfare on which pedestrians walked up and down at a furious pace. If life in New Amsterdam was a speeded-up version of village life with compacted buildings on both sides of the roads, the frenzy of Georgetown filled him, first with terror, and then, gradually realizing that its inhabitants were harmless, with an awesome respect for their stamina and sense of purpose.

Perhaps he should have brought Philomena with him after all. She would no doubt know where to find a place where they could wash before he went off once more to the Ministry of Hope. Anxious to catch the Permanent Secretary before he began his official work, Kwaku made for the Ministry, only to find that the gates were not yet open. A good hour went by before a car pulled up in front of the closed gates and a woman stepped out, said something to the chauffeur and came up to Kwaku, who had placed himself in her path.

'You're the new messenger?'

'No, I'm Kwaku Chol. . . .'

'Oh, I see. Well, you're not allowed in before the gates are opened.'

She thereupon opened the gates and Kwaku followed her.

'I told you, you can't come in until the gates are opened!' she declared haughtily.

'But you jus' open them, mistress.'

'They are not opened, I tell you!'

And with that she pushed Kwaku outside and closed the gates behind him.

He watched her go up the stairs with such a confident step that Kwaku enquired of a passer-by if she was the President's wife.

'No, man. She's a typist.'

Later, sharing the bench with those who were waiting to conduct business, Kwaku reflected that in less than twenty-four hours he had seen three remarkable types of Georgetonians, all displaying character traits so distinctive he could not imagine them living anywhere else. Sharing his bench were the excessively patient; he had woken up to witness the passage of individuals seized with a kind of frenzy; and at the Ministry gate he had been accosted by a mad woman who opened gates which remained closed while she opened them. He called to mind his arrival in New Amsterdam, years ago, when he managed to make friends with a woman as soon as he woke up on the stelling. She, too, was tetched, but she did not persuade him he was no better than a worm. If the typist behaved like the Queen of Sheba he shuddered to think what his reception by the Permanent Secretary would be like.

Kwaku took it into his head to strike up a conversation with the man waiting beside him, but changed his mind. He had better play safe, lest the man jump up and throttle him for no reason at all, he reflected.

The sun rose higher and the bench filled up with people, so that newcomers were obliged to line up. Kwaku, standing up to offer his seat to an old woman, was rewarded with a smile of gratitude, but she was unable to take advantage of his generosity, seeing that a young man had seized the opportunity to occupy the seat even before he was in an upright position. And no sooner had the young man seated himself than his face assumed that look of monumental patience which beguiled Kwaku.

'This is all-day story,' he said to himself, for the sun had already passed overhead, and some workers from the Ministry had come downstairs and gone through the street gates, to lunch presumably.

Kwaku, seeing that patience had borne no fruit, addressed a couple as they arrived at the foot of the stairs.

'Excuse me, sir and mistress. You can say when the Permanent Secretary goin' come?'

'The Permanent Secretary?' the man asked, widening the slits of his eyes. 'You want to see the Permanent Secretary?'

'Yes sir, he's my cousin.'

'Your. . . ?' the woman began, her eye slits outdoing her colleague's.

'Yes, mistress. He's Miss Rose son, an' she's my mother half-sister.'

'The Permanent Secretary won't come to work until later,' the young man said. 'He knows you're coming?'

'Yes, Sir.'

'Wait, then. He should be here in an hour or so.'

The young man went off in the woman's company, repeating, 'Cousin — mother's half-sister.'

Kwaku had decided to revive his habit of lying extravagantly. After all, what had he encountered since his arrival in Georgetown but extravagant behaviour? He had come home! He had found his level at last! In his village and in New Amsterdam he passed for being a freak, an unprincipled offender of tradition, an enemy of stability. Yesterday afternoon he stepped out of the taxi into the territory of freaks. He had waited quietly with dozens of others and was rewarded with indifference and a lack of courtesy. There could be no doubt that the town was full of Kwakus, better educated than he, no doubt, but branded with the unmistakable mark of the peculiar breed.

But, examining his action more closely, he realized that he had gone too far. Suppose the young man or his lady friend reported to the Permanent Secretary that, according to Kwaku, he was expecting him. That, on top of that, the lie about being his cousin might prove too much for Miss Rose's son to stomach. Decidedly, he had gone too far! From now on his extravagance must be tempered to suit the circumstance. In short, he must be master of his actions. Since he was among people who made a profession of misbehaving, he must make of misconduct a fine art. He needed to study the subject in detail; and what better time to exercise his wits to this end than now? Somehow, he must introduce himself to the Permanent Secretary before the couple saw him and warned him that his 'cousin' had come.

Kwaku took up a position outside the gate, having planned to say 'Miss Rose' with a view to attracting the Permanent Secretary's attention.

In spite of his bravado he was worried sick that he would not be allowed past the door dressed as he was, in an old get-up of shirt-jac and trousers he had bought at the height of his fame as a healer.

Kwaku did not have long to wait. When a car drew up, and the chauffeur got out first and opened the door with a show of ostentatious deference, he knew that none other than the Permanent Secretary had arrived. But his heart sank when the features he imagined he would recognize instantly turned out to be those of a perfect stranger. Besides, the figure drawn up to its full height was much taller than the boy he had conversed with at some length, even allowing for the difference in years. He had been short. This was a tall, strapping man who could have passed for a professional boxer.

'Miss Rose sent me,' Kwaku hazarded, and saw with satisfaction and some anxiety his quarry stop and fix him with a stare.

'Who sent you?'

'Miss Rose. She say it's urgent.'

The Permanent Secretary measured Kwaku from head to foot and then, with a brusque gesture, invited him to follow.

Kwaku could have danced with joy. His inspiration had paid off! The same inspiration that had opened up to him a brilliant, if short-lived career and later, saw fit to cripple his wife. . . . If only he could control it, suppress its malevolent tendency, so that it came to him in a pure state!

Kwaku followed him through the empty office on the first floor — the employees had all left for lunch by now — then up another internal flight of stairs to the top floor, where a solitary lady in her early thirties sat behind a typewriter reading a newspaper.

'Leave us alone, Mrs Correia,' the Permanent Secretary ordered the typist in a soft, if peremptory, voice.

The official took his place behind a large table on which two piles of papers were neatly placed side by side.

'Sit down Mr. . . .'

'Cholmondeley.'

'So, you know my mother.'

'Yes sir. I'm a good friend.'

'She sent you. What for?'

Kwaku gave him the crumpled paper on which was written his name and address.

'She say you can find me a job and find me a place to live,' Kwaku said hesitantly.

'I see. . . . But I can't find you a job just like that. My mother thinks I'm some kind of a magician.'

'Mister Permanent Secretary, I did know you when you was a small boy. . . .'

And Kwaku reminded him how it was he who later took him to see his mother.

'I remember you vaguely. You gave my mother money from the fee you charged. It was Mr Kumar's house you came from. . . . Ah ha!'

The Permanent Secretary swivelled on his chair, wondering what to do with Kwaku. Had he not given his mother money when she was down and out he would have dismissed him summarily, knowing from experience that it was not practical to assist every acquaintance. In fact, few people managed to get near him.

'You're lucky you got to see me,' he told Kwaku, as yet undecided how to help him. 'Don't you heal people any more?'

'No, Sir. The power gone from me.'

'The power, eh? So it comes and goes.'

'I think it gone for good,' Kwaku said with a doleful expression.

'I tell you what. Until I decide what to do you can help my watchman tonight. He'll show you where you'll sleep.'

He wrote a note and placed it in an envelope which he sealed and addressed with a fountain pen.

'Take it to this address. It's my house. You'll see Bertie at the gate. If he's not there call out. Give him the note and do what he says.'

Kwaku felt that the moment had come to express his gratitude in a way suited to the occasion. Seizing the Permanent Secretary's hand he covered it in kisses before he could protest.

'Mister, I'm grateful. Wait till I sell the chamber-pots — the pos with flowers and all. . . .'

'What chamber-pots?' asked Miss Rose's son.

'I've got two with flowers, *mimosa pudica* — shame bush. . . .'

'Enough!'

'I'm sorry. I got carry away,' Kwaku said in atonement for his outburst. 'You see, sir, I come to Georgetown to sell antique things and I hear that tourists like to buy pos.'

'Then why did my mother speak about a job?'

'It's to tide me over.'

'Ah!' exclaimed the Permanent Secretary, relieved that he was not expected to do more than find Kwaku temporary accommodation.

'Alright, I've got work to do. I'll see you tonight or some time tomorrow. Meanwhile don't go about kissing people's hands. Somebody will take you for a pansy-boy, and you never know what that might lead to.'

At first Miss Rose's son did not know what to make of Kwaku's character. His outburst about the chamber-pots had put him on his guard after the initial sense of duty aroused by the memory of his scruffy visitor's generosity. What perplexed him more than anything else was the disclosure of Kwaku's fall from grace. How could someone be highly regarded one day and be a nobody the next, especially a healer? In politics, yes. He shuddered at the thought of a possible decline in his own fortunes and the consequences that would ensue.

He recalled how his mother had set Kwaku up as an example for him to follow.

'Black people got brains, but we like too much sport. Mr Cholmondeley don't sport,' she had told him.

That was more or less all he remembered about the flamboyant healer, except the manner of his departure from Mr Kumar's house, when he came running down the front stairs under a rain of abuse from the assembled family.

'What am I to make of this chamber-pot story?' the Permanent Secretary asked himself. 'Could there be money in bedroom objects?'

He had amassed a not inconsiderable sum of money since his political appointment. Not a fortune, but enough to allow him a modest income if he were nudged out of office. He owned a part share in an airline, a tract of land one hundred and twenty acres in area bought on the strength of information regarding a proposed housing scheme in its vicinity, and a special account which accommodated bribes he had not sought, but had been foisted on him for real and imagined favours. After all, his countrymen had become so bribe-conscious, they thrust money into an official's back pocket if he even blinked at them. What is more, while acquiring his fortune, he had gained a reputation for scrupulous honesty, an extraordinary achievement in the social climate of the eighties. And, turning this favourable repute to advantage he succeeded in attracting bribes of greater substance than most of his distinguished colleagues in high positions. His nose for a moneymaking scheme had twitched unmistakably at Kwaku's mention of selling antique things. An uneducated man who could succeed in the healing business might also succeed in selling old objects. In which case he himself was in a unique position to guide Kwaku towards an affair which could benefit them both.

'Mrs Correia!' he called out to the typist who had returned to her desk when Kwaku left.

'Mrs Correia, find out for me the cost of old chamber-pots. Especially the flowered variety.'

She stared at him, mystified.

'Chamber-pots? . . . . P —pos?'

'Yes, pos. The old fashioned ones people don't use any more.'

'Where. . . ?'

'There's a shop. I remember a man in Upper Regent Street, somewhere between Oronoque and Albert Streets, who used to sell things to Guyanese back here on holiday. Old goblets and things like that. Look, I don't know, just do your best.'

Picking up her handbag and parasol, poor Mrs Correia left on what she saw as a fruitless errand and at the head of the stairs turned round with a perplexed look in her eye, by way of pleading that her delicate mission was doomed to failure.

Lest it be thought that the Permanent Secretary's day was taken up with trivial matters like enquiring into the buying and selling of articles with unsavoury connections, it must be stated unequivocally that the very opposite was the case. He was, in fact, the Right Hand Man of a Minister without portfolio, known familiarly as the Minister of Hope, a description applied indiscriminately to a number of other ministers. It needs little imagination to discern that the words 'of Hope' in this connection are the equivalent of 'without Hope', demonstrating that peculiar slipperiness of English words. The Minister without portfolio, in short, presided over a Ministry without hope and the Permanent Secretary, his Right Hand Man, was wont to sit on his left hand at important meetings with other heads of Ministries. He would not have dared sit on his right side, even though he was more intelligent, more alert and altogether better equipped to discuss weighty matters than the well-bred Minister without portfolio, who had tried in vain to discover how, without a portfolio, he should define the remit and scope of his duties. The Permanent Secretary, to the Minister's eternal gratitude, cleared up the matter for him in an obscure memo which the President was persuaded to initial at the end of a long day, when he had more important matters on his mind. And as a reward the Permanent Secretary came to be installed in a grand office overlooking one of the town's most elegant streets.

But writing obscure memos was not the only serious occupation in the Right Hand Man's day, as will be borne out when his experiences unfold. For the moment suffice it to say that he was highly regarded; so much so that his reputation for honesty in no way exceeded his reputation for high competence.

So this was the man under whose wing Kwaku intended to nestle while nurturing his own unbounded ambition. His shortcomings notwithstanding — more especially his ungrammatical speech and country walk — he would climb to a height that surpassed his achievements at the pinnacle of his career as healer and adviser of people in misfortune.

Chapter V

Lying on the small bed placed at his disposal by the Permanent Secretary's watchman, Kwaku could not suppress a certain contempt for the self-made Permanent Secretary. How could he forget that the Minister's Right Hand Man was the son of Miss Rose, who used to frequent New Amsterdam rum shops and rub shoulders with down and outs? On the other hand, this physically imposing man exercised his social power with an ease of manner that could not have been cultivated in the reflections of a looking glass. Kwaku recalled his own torment when he stepped out into the street holding a doctor's bag filled with healing concoctions and believed that passers-by must have been nudging one another and exchanging remarks about his country walk, which suited ill the expensively tailored garb. 'He calling heself "doctor"! If he is doctor parrot mus' be nurse!' Subsequent proof of people's respect for him only brought temporary relief, which was invariably overtaken by an even more acute attack of anxiety.

All things considered, he was impressed by the Permanent Secretary's demeanour, a model worthy of emulation.

Kwaku cowered in his watchman's room behind the outside staircase. On being put out of the taxi near the big market he saw little of what was going on around him, all his efforts being directed towards finding Miss Rose's son. His attempts to picture his arrival brought no more than images of a terrible confusion of cars and taxis, of pedestrians acting in mysterious consort, as though manipulated by an unseen puppet master. He did not remember the traffic lights because he had not noticed them, the puppet strings that maintained discipline among the motley users of the road.

He might have gone for a walk to explore the area, but the watchman who showed him to the room was so brusque in manner and had looked at him with such unconcealed disgust he was afraid of going past him. Now that he had achieved his first aim his courage had deserted him.

'Mr Watchman,' he had called out on arriving with the Permanent Secretary's note, 'the Permanent Secretary send me.'

The watchman read it, lifted his eyes heavenwards and turned away without inviting Kwaku to follow him.

'You want me to come, Mr Watchman?'

'I'm not a watchman!' he said harshly, turning on Kwaku, 'I'm a security guard.'

'Yes, Mr Security Guard. You want me to follow you?'

'You can remain standing in the sun if you feel like it.'

Kwaku guessed that he had to follow the man and did so from a safe distance.

On opening the door to the room, the watchman asked what was in the parcel under his arm. Kwaku had made up an answer in case of such an eventuality, even before leaving New Amsterdam, and was surprised that no one had enquired before.

'This is a pile of documents I carrying for the police in New Amsterdam,' Kwaku lied.

The watchman faltered and the keys fell from his hand. Kwaku bent down to pick them up and their eyes met as he straightened up again.

'You're from the police?' the watchman asked with a poor show of nonchalance.

'Yes, but I dress like this so nobody would suspect.'

'If you want anything,' he told Kwaku, 'call out.'

The Permanent Secretary's secretary had found, to her surprise, little difficulty in discovering the price of chamber-pots, or rather that they were in great demand. The house from which old objects were sold was well known in the Upper Regent Street district and had a reputation for its brisk trade in mortars and pestles, once indispensable tools in kitchens up to the late 1930s. At the mention of chamber-pots for sale the dealer affected a lack of interest, but called her back when she reached the gate. She had not worked for the Minister's Right Hand Man for nothing and demanded that he give her some idea of prices, to which he responded by taking her downstairs to his storeroom, which he began unlocking with a variety of keys while he explained that thieving had become a craftsman's work, like the fabrication of fine jewelry. Apart from his three ferocious dogs, an automatic alarm, a night watchman, barbed wire fencing above his paling and a vigilant wife, he possessed a secret device that protected his premises so well he had only been burgled five times in the last year.

After much jangling Mrs Correia was asked to follow the careful householder into his bottom-house, where were stacked objects of every description, prominent among which were bentwood rocking chairs, pedestals, brass jardinières and all the drawing room bric-à-brac people over seventy would have recognized as belonging to furnishings which vanished mysteriously from the houses of well-to-do families during the last World War. In a corner, disposed behind a large crabwood easy chair was an array of enamel and glazed earthenware chamber-pots.

'What kind you got to sell?' he asked.

Not knowing what her superior had in mind she demanded a price list, so that she 'would inform my supplier'.

'No, lady. Bring your pos and I goin' quote my price.'

'Alright. How much you'll give me for one like that?' she asked, picking up a handsomely decorated blue utensil any high-minded lady would have been proud to ease herself upon.

'A thousand dollars.'

'American?'

'Guyanese,' the man answered.

'No.'

'Two.'

'Goodbye.'

'For you three.'

'Alright, I'll think it over.'

Mrs Correia bade the man goodbye, convinced she could squeeze more out of him.

The Minister's Right Hand Man — the Permanent Secretary — rewarded Mrs Correia with a promise that she could have any afternoon of the week off she chose. Armed with the information she had brought him, he knew what to make of Kwaku's unusual interest in chamber-pots, objects with little intrinsic value.

After taking his dinner alone he asked his watchman to send up the one-time healer.

The watchman had to knock twice to rouse Kwaku, who had fallen asleep, overcome by the afternoon torpor. He came in without waiting for an answer.

'The boss want to see you,' he said to Kwaku, who blinked at him, uncertain where he was.

He smoothed his clothes with his hands and hurried upstairs.

The Right Hand Man began by informing Kwaku that he had telephoned Miss Rose, who spoke very highly of him, describing him as 'honest'.

'And I respect my mother's opinion. But one thing worries me, Mr Cholmondeley. If I'm to help you, I've got my reputation to consider — I can't have people saying I'm associating with a vendor of chamber-pots. A po-seller, to be blunt. You'll have to choose. Either you make your own way in Georgetown — and I can tell you, this is not New Amsterdam — as I was saying, either you make your own way in town or I help you make your way, provided you drop the chamber-pot idea. I'm not keen on any doubtful affiliations.'

'Affi. . . .'

'Pot story people. You have to forego your interest in pos.'

'Well yes, sir. I mean it was only an idea. And thanks for the room downstairs.'

'For the time being you'll have to share it with my day watchman when he decides to sleep here any particular night.'

'Sure, sir.'

'That's settled then. . . . By the way, don't go round telling people you're from the police. This isn't New Amsterdam. Keep your stories for country people.'

He went back downstairs rubbing his hands gleefully, convinced that he had outwitted the Right Hand Man. Encouraged by his benefactor's good will and the unexpected windfall, his anxiety about the future vanished, so much so that he decided to 'do the town' with Miss Rose's wad of notes in his pocket. Resisting the urge to slap the watchman on his back, he went past him without the slightest feeling of fear.

As Kwaku was about to leave to 'do the town' the door of the little room opened and the nearest thing to a giant he had ever seen stepped over the threshold.

'Hey! Bertie! Who is this?'

The newcomer mustered Kwaku critically for a few seconds, then burst out laughing.

'Bertie!' he called out to the day watchman once more. 'Is this for real? Who *is* this freak?'

Bertie, in turn, appeared in the doorway, and from his expression approved of his colleague's assessment of Kwaku.

'He does tell lies. He says the parcel in the corner's got police documents.'

'Is that so!' exclaimed the newcomer mockingly and with that lifted the parcel and began undoing it.

'Please mister, don't open it. Is not police documents. . . . If you want to know the truth is a present for my wife.'

But the newcomer, ignoring his plea, ripped the coarse paper open and, to Kwaku's great embarrassment, disclosed the parcel's earthenware contents.

If the first sight of Kwaku had caused irritation in the one watchman and mirth in the other, the appearance of two chamber-pots provoked an identical outburst of such unrestrained laughter that Kwaku could have died of shame. Not only did he abandon at once his plan to do the town, but he decided to go back to New Amsterdam that very night and give Miss Gwendoline news of his success in finding a benefactor.

To his mortification he was obliged to watch as the morose day watchman sat on one of the pots and made suggestive noises, while the night watchman strutted about the room balancing the other pot on his head.

Kwaku could only stand aside as the two men carried on. Later he was to recall how he and his family had been brought low in New Amsterdam, the city of clocks. Malice had played no part in their downfall, nor even indifference. But here the watchmen's mirth at his expense seemed to him the outward expression of a hostility emanating from the bowels of the city itself, from its elegant houses, its paved streets and well maintained canals.

'Never!' he said to himself, thinking of Philomena's request to accompany him.

The watchmen's antics seemed to last for hours. A display not only physical in its reality, it assumed another parallel dimension in Kwaku's imagination, which filled the room with men and women he had never seen before, strangers in speech and dress, all dedicated to mocking him with exaggerated gestures, all wearing or sitting on glistening chamber-pots. He closed his eyes and longed for the company of Miss Gwendoline and Philomena, the sound of cockcrow at morning and the ghosts of Winkel where the old shoemaker eked out a living. 'Excuse me! Excuse me, madams and sirs!' And Kwaku felt that his voice was coming to him from afar, perhaps from that visionary period he knew intimately — whatever his uncle told him to the contrary — when his hand stretched out towards an object of indescribable softness.

None of the real or imagined persons in the room took the slightest notice of his request to be heard, and hanging his head in despair he reflected that it was perhaps best so, since he intended to protest at the way his plan to set up a business was being turned against him; that the chamber-pots which might have provided the means to dignify his lifestyle were being used to humiliate him. His protest, far from making an impression on his tormentors, could only provide them with ammunition to amplify their orgy of ridicule.

Everything used to be so simple, his poverty and even the twins' hostility! And then there was the river by which he slept for a week when his fortunes were at their lowest ebb.

'Excuse me, madams and sirs!' Kwaku shouted above the din. 'I am a stranger in your town! I'm an ignorant man. Madams and sirs!'

But now, even at his most obsequious, Kwaku was seething inwardly, so much so that his commitment to avoiding conflict at all costs was in danger of yielding to his growing anger and frustration.

'Madams and sirs, listen to me!'

'Hey, you're alright?'

Kwaku looked up to see the giant standing above him.

'All I did was slap you on the shoulder,' the giant said, 'and you go down like a coconut.'

For a moment Kwaku had no idea where he was. Then, catching sight of the chamber-pots on his bed, he asked where everybody else had gone.

'Was only me and Bertie, and he's left for home.'

Kwaku did not insist.

'You got bad feelings or something? You look weak to me.'

'I din' eat since this morning,' Kwaku confessed. 'I was goin' home to take something.'

'Where's home?'

'In New Amsterdam.'

'What? That's sixty miles away. You're crazy?'

Kwaku sat down on the bed, as much weakened by hunger as by his vision of a roomful of persecutors. Now it was dark.

'You want me to get you something to eat?' the giant asked.

'Please, sir.'

'Don't call me sir. If you don't want to call me "Suarez" say "Comrade". What you want me to buy? Dhal Pourri?'

'Anything. . . .'

Kwaku took a handful of notes from his pocket and tried to hand it to Suarez who, however, turned his back on him and left without a word.

Thus began Kwaku's acquaintanceship with the giant who had persecuted him in the beginning and might have been the brother of the day watchman who never smiled, treated him like dirt and surely had something to hide. Kwaku considered the way the day watchman had reacted to the joke that he worked for the police, deemed to be among the most corrupt in the world for being so badly paid and who could not even afford to eat two square meals a day, though they had the air of strutting sensa cocks, with their uniforms and holstered pistols. This did not prevent them from hiding from criminals, who regaled one another with stories about their cowardice and had a stock joke for all hours and all manner of slanderous stories, one of which described their station cells, no more than eight feet by ten and used as a dumping ground for would-be criminals, a score at a time, where a man could die from the stench of the bodies which jostled one another in the windowless, murky darkness. And woe unto the innocent man who fell into their clutches! He would count himself lucky not to be divested of his clothes, his shoes, his bicycle, not to mention his money. This was not the town described by Vibart the taxi driver, a determined lover of everything emanating from its decaying corpse, which was stiffening in a debt-ridden shroud made in America and consecrated in Europe.

Kwaku went back to New Amsterdam the next day, after consuming a cooked meal in one of the eating booths of the market by the river.

Village succeeded village, places with names he had never heard of nor noticed on his trip to Georgetown, only because of the preoccupation with his enterprise. Now that his anxieties had been put to rest, his peace of mind allowed him to read eagerly the board names, La Bonne Intention, Victoria. . . . Look what a mind at rest was capable of seeing! Now was the chance to take himself in hand and espouse a sense of responsibility, so that he could thrive in a place that had threatened to swallow him up as it had devoured its whores, lost souls from the countryside most of them, who ran the risk of being buried in unmarked graves. People like the Permanent Secretary, the Vibarts, were they not the exceptions, protected by the blessing of education or some other quality that made them sprout wings?

What was he to make of Miss Rose's son, the Right Hand Man, who resembled in no way the young boy who at the age of eight was marked with the cross of success. He had shed his brashness to take on instead the terrible assurance of those who wield power.

So Kwaku returned home, wearing the halo of a muted triumph. But Miss Gwendoline refused to celebrate, unable to forget the catalogue of disasters that had dogged the family since they abandoned their East Coast village to settle in New Amsterdam.

CHAPTER VI

The Right Hand Man kept his promise to buy a suitable wardrobe for Kwaku, who would reimburse him from his wages as assistant messenger attached to the Ministry of Hope. Furthermore, he used his influence to secure publication of his own 'In Memoriam' poems under Kwaku's name in the *Daily Chronicle*.

Kwaku promptly wrote Miss Gwendoline — he had returned to Georgetown by this time — and enclosed a copy of the first published verse.

> You are gone
> But not forgotten,
> Buried
> But not yet rotten.

In commemoration of the death of Estella Denbow, who departed this life a year ago.

It is not known what the Denbow family made of the poem, but a year later they commissioned another better known versifier to immortalize their departed relation.

Kwaku's letter to Miss Gwendoline ran thus: 'My dear wife, I know I am coming to see you soon, but I could not wait to show you the poem I publish in the *Daily Chronicle*, the most famous newspaper in the English-speaking world.'

He went on to say that the verse caused such a sensation he was obliged to hide from reporters and cameramen, who besieged the house where he was lodging and only went away after the Permanent Secretary fired a few warning shots over their heads from a Kalashnikov rifle he had never had occasion to use until then.

Kwaku kept the best bit of news for the last: the Permanent Secretary promised to find him a flat in which he would live rent free. '. . . And I am going to send for you as soon as I move in.'

The Right Hand Man had completely taken in Kwaku, as he had some years back taken in Mrs Correia, his secretary, who would have laid down her life for him, even after evidence of his ruthlessness could no longer be dismissed as talk inspired by envy.

Four years ago Mrs Correia had been a Primary School teacher in Lodge. Highly regarded by the headmistress and her colleagues as a disciplinarian and teacher, she was forced to give up her profession in the face of the Government's refusal to increase salaries in line with inflation. At the suggestion of a friend who had similarly abandoned teaching to become a huckster, she followed in her footsteps and began travelling to Brazil by plane in order to purchase goods not available in Georgetown for resale in Kingston market. Week in, week out she could be seen with her bulging, blue striped, indestructable bags at Timehri airport in the company of similarly accoutred hucksters waiting their turn to go through Customs.

'Alyou are a hard breed,' a conscientious woman officer once told her, 'and not trustworthy.'

From being a respected teacher she had sunk low enough to receive the gratuitous jibes of a Customs officer, who only a few months back might have been imploring her to give a son or daughter special attention in the classroom. Like other hucksters she often travelled on unconfirmed tickets and was obliged to endure the humiliations of sleeping rough and begging for a seat on an outgoing plane. The sorority had contributed to the notoriety of Guyanese in Brazil and the Caribbean, where they were described as being 'zigzag'. And it was thus that Mrs Correia, an upright woman and fugitive from an upright profession, had joined the swarm of women who made up a significant proportion of passengers leaving and arriving at the airport bearing goods to be sold in the wrought iron-fenced markets of an impoverished capital. Unfortunately the travellers to Brazil became victims of a new rule requiring them to secure a visa in order to enter that country, which was too much for Amy Correia, who persuaded her husband to pay for a secretarial course with a view to applying for a job at the Secretariat of the Caribbean Free Trade Area. Three times she took the examination, unsuccessfully. Following the third failure her husband suggested that she applied to the Ministry of Hope, where standards were less stringent. Assigned as junior shorthand typist to the Right Hand Man's office she soon caught his eye, not difficult in a place where late-coming was endemic. With time her efficiency and conscientiousness made her indispensable to him, and he guarded her as though she were a treasured heirloom, knowing that with the haemorrhage of skilled labour to the islands and Canada, Ministers and heads of departments were on the look-out for anyone unusually able.

Since emerging from the chrysalis of childhood two events in Amy Correia's life counted to be of the utmost importance to her: a birthday present of a tin of water colours and her two years as a huckster. A marked talent for painting brought her to the attention of her class teacher in the fourth year of Primary School; and though this interest was the starting point of her rapid progress, she was never happy about his intervention, seeing her art as a private, secret world she would have preferred to protect from intrusion. Yet, in the end her growing skill, nurtured by the art master, did have the effect of deepening her passion. Her transfer to Secondary School was accompanied by feelings of relief and sadness. At last she could paint as she liked; but at the same time she believed she had not learned enough about oils to attain the freedom of expression she sought. When she was fifteen she conceived the plan of doing drawings and paintings that owed less to what she had been taught and more to what her teacher had described as her untutored imagination, the epithet prompted by her picture of a ship as a fish might have seen it, from below, while the other children had drawn their boats in the conventional way, as a side elevation. This collection of her new work, built up over a period of five years until she became a teacher, she locked away for the last time out of some vague sense of guilt. Having exploited the most creative period of her life, she was content to take out her images occasionally and dwell on them, like a book read countless times, but whose fascination she would have been hard put to explain.

One day, on returning from work, she found her father at a front window, an unusual position for him for he could not bear to be idle. And no sooner had she come through the door than he asked her to sit down in a chair opposite him. On his lap the collection of paintings and drawings lay open where two naked young men faced each other on opposite pages.

Amy's father said nothing, but she could have formulated his tirade for him: she had been given more freedom than any of her friends and *this* was his reward! And it was precisely because of his silence that she could not forgive him. Her teacher, had he still been in contact with her, would not have understood her desire to paint male nudes either; and she herself began to wonder if her sensuality had indeed been warped by the isolation in which she had worked.

Amy destroyed her collection in a fire that consumed the images slowly, died down from time to time and had to be rekindled more than once. And she imagined the nude flesh blackening in the flames, the obeah dancers and the schooners with sails unfurled, the children rushing outside into the rain that brought an end to a long drought, herself as a small child walking along the Mall flanked by her mother and father, a pair of copulating dogs, the interior of a much loved book, images of recollections and life as she imagined it must be. Her parents' prohibitions had taken root, so that at the age of twenty she was still a virgin, an innocent among her friends. Yet the gulf separating herself and her parents was more profound than she dared believe.

The second experience that seemed to leave its mark was her time as a huckster, when she discovered a freedom of which no one ever spoke. She and her fellow women hucksters had operated in the rough and tumble of a man's world and, in doing so, were surprised at the ease with which they managed to survive. One particularly resourceful colleague, still making her trips when eight months pregnant, complained that she confronted her most serious problem when, encumbered with her foetal companion, she sought a position to bed down for the night, and not in the confrontation with irate officials or the hundred and one problems that beset the commercial traveller. Amy, intoxicated by the collective experience of this women's league, came to understand for the first time the nature of this freedom, which resembled the endless migrations of a flock of birds. Their recourse to subterfuge in order to elude the vigilance of Customs officials — which alarmed her in the early days — came to be perceived as her own bid to avoid detection of her secrets by her parents. Their expressions of relief on boarding the plane to take them home was a magnification of her satisfaction at escaping her parents' control. Obliged by force of circumstances to become a huckster, she had found what she had blindly striven for in those images of childhood and fulfilment which her father saw fit to damn with his oppressive silence.

If the fall of the huckster sisterhood that did business in Brazil left a void in her life, the months in which it had flourished had given her a heightened sense of her worth. She envied the Trinidad branch of hucksters, a still thriving enterprise from all accounts; but then she could not cross a great stretch of ocean, like those Hindu immigrants who refused to embark for Guyana when faced with the reality of *kala pani*, the dark water, the sea that fashioned a girdle round the world.

Mrs Correia's husband bore no resemblance to her, either physical or otherwise; and it was a matter of wonder, even to casual observers, that they ever came together long enough to form a union. Years older than Amy, he professed no interest in art, had no discernable ambition and never sought to discover what lay below the surface, either of things or people. Amy believed she had been attracted to his apparently ordinary character, which made no excessive claims on her; but in reality she admired him for his powerful physique, betraying, perhaps, an unconscious need for masculine protection.

'You could blow me away if you wanted,' she once told him.

But the thought never having crossed his mind, he found no humour in the remark.

Clifford Correia, ever since he was a baby, could only be roused with great difficulty. His placidity and large frame guaranteed him protection throughout his school life, not only from bullies, but from teachers as well. This bland past did not prepare Clifford's parents or his acquaintances for the role he played in the political disturbances of 1964, when the nights seemed inordinately long as every district in Georgetown slept under the expectation of devastation by fire. Clifford became a fire-raiser; and, although the police only got wind of his activities after a score or so of conflagrations were attributed to him, the inhabitants of Alberttown had no illusions about his apparent placidity. None of them dared challenge him, out of fear that he might avenge himself on their district; but they prayed silently that he would confine his pyrotechnic zeal to areas outside Alberttown.

Clifford's parents, for a reason known only to themselves, viewed his unsavoury reputation with no alarm; or at least so it seemed to their neighbours. They only sat up when he began boasting openly about his fire-raising exploits. Of course the police arrested, him and he was committed to gaol for eighteen months by a judge who professed to be appalled at his description of large fires as 'thrilling'.

Years later, when Clifford met Amy, he had already reverted to his childhood placidity and was doing odd jobs to keep body and soul together. Amy learned of his conviction a few days before they married, through one of those missives that are essential reading for Guyanese, the anonymous letter. Written in Roman script, it informed Amy that her intended had been to gaol and was a dangerous criminal, and ended with the expression of a personal concern: 'Take it from me, it is not worth it for a young woman to marry a jailbird.'

Needless to say Amy was deeply distressed. Besides, her work at the Ministry of Hope involved dealing with much confidential material and she deemed it unwise to take any risks which might jeopardize her position. But Clifford pointed out that the woman — he was certain that a woman was the author of the letter — was jealous of her. Why else should she describe him as a dangerous criminal? Many young people with no criminal record had started fires in 1964, just as many otherwise blameless men and women took part in the looting prevalent at the time. Did she think he was dangerous? It took little to persuade Amy. Not only had the banns of marriage been published, but preparations for the reception were already well advanced. Besides, where could she find an indulgent man like Clifford now that males were leaving the country in their thousands? Even hardened criminals were intimidated by the Government's threat that convicted malefactors would not be entitled to a passport. She yielded and went on with plans for the wedding, to which she invited her colleagues at the Ministry of Hope, including the Permanent Secretary, who by this time had taken her under his wing and assured her of his interest in securing her advancement.

Soon afterwards, however, someone at the Ministry learned of Mr Correia's past and, seeing an opportunity to curry favour with the Right Hand Man, did his duty and informed him of the serpent outside his door. But to the employee's disappointment the Right Hand Man did nothing. Judging that the serpent in question was indispensable to the smooth working of his office, he waited for an opportunity to take advantage of the information and, in so doing, secure Mrs Correia's loyalty once and for all. But the opportunity never presented itself, for Amy proved her loyalty at every turn. Believing her superior to be, deep down, an honourable man, she complied with all his requests relating to work. He, in turn, confessed that he knew of her husband's conviction and offered to help him in any way he could.

From that day Amy regarded the Right Hand Man as a demi-god, a man of the same calibre as her father before his silence came between them, and what appeared to others as her obsequiousness was no more than an excessive show of respect for him in the presence of others. It was he who suggested that Clifford should work for him as a currency dealer. And when these pillars of the alternative economy who sold their foreign notes openly were required by law to be licensed, the Permanent Secretary paid his licence fee without demur.

In the early days Clifford Correia could be seen near the Stabroek Market, waving a wad of notes to attract the attention of potential customers among the passers-by. But since he acquired a licence to deal he was installed by the Right Hand Man in a windowless cubicle that reeked of cooked food from the eating place next door. The contrast between his working surroundings and his wife's could not be greater. The air conditioning at the Ministry of Hope worked off the mains, but switched over automatically to a generator during a power cut, while Clifford had to endure an oppressive heat, whose effect was hardly mitigated by a tiny electric fan fixed to the partition. However, he luxuriated in the security his job provided, more especially in the lack of supervision, which allowed him to do much as he pleased. The fact of occupying an *office*, tiny and dilapidated as it was, attracted a consideration unthinkable when he worked from the road and wore a permanent grin while crying his wares like the old coconut seller who plied his trade in front of the Ice House. What is more, he became friendly with the shopkeepers on his stretch of pavement and was able to take part in the mutual exchange of favours that established among them a bond, whose existence was known only to the police and other shop owners.

Amy, Clifford and Kwaku, without realizing it, had become one of a network of protégés set up in one way or another by the Right Hand Man, against the day when they would be used.

Chapter VII

There are friendships and friendships. Some friendships are equal, while others resemble a form of benign slavery in which one friend accepts his or her subjugation, complying with every order issued by the other. Kwaku's association with Suarez, the giant watchman on night shift, was of the latter character. After he moved into his new flat and went to fetch Miss Gwendoline from New Amsterdam to live with him, he made excuses whenever Suarez invited himself, anticipating her display of scorn in front of the stranger at the way he had accommodated himself to life in Georgetown.

'What's wrong?' asked Suarez. 'You're ashamed of your wife or something? She's got three feet?'

'No, man. She's blind,' Kwaku confessed.

'I don't see what that's got to do with it.'

In the end Kwaku gave in, on condition that Suarez showed him the greatest respect in front of Miss Gwendoline. And Suarez showed his friend so much respect when he dropped in to be introduced that Miss Gwendoline took him to her heart at once, declaring him to be a Christian through and through, in spite of her mistrustful nature and her jealousy of anyone who paid her husband more than usual attention. Encouraged to call him by his fond name, Giant, she laughed and said she preferred Suarez.

'Suarez,' she said, 'you don' know how I praise God Kwaku meet somebody like you.'

'Miss Gwendoline, I'm not better than the next man.'

And their conversation ran along those cordial lines whenever he came to the flat. Besides, he took a genuine liking to the blind woman and never ceased wondering how she married a nincompoop like Kwaku, whom he wound around his little finger because he seemed to have no pride and allowed himself to be taken in by every Tom, Dick and Harry.

The more his admiration for Miss Gwendoline grew, the worse Suarez treated Kwaku when they were alone or playing cards in company; so much so that people began to talk and wonder what hold the night watchman had over the assistant messenger who, after all, earned not much less than he did. Suarez believed that Kwaku enjoyed the role of buffoon and slave and was incapable of playing any other.

The fact is that Kwaku was biding his time. Having had much practice since childhood in the home of an uncle, whose only attachment for him had sprung from a sense of duty to his sister, in a village where even the dogs treated him with great suspicion and people used him as a scapegoat for their misfortunes, he had become the Prince of dissembling and the Fool who flaunted his flawed literacy, while taking in everything that went on around him. Kwaku was no more Suarez's victim than the Right Hand Man was content with his position as assistant to the Minister of Hope. It had not taken him long to realize that the people who got on were the virtuosos of manipulation. He saw himself as an apprentice in this city of Sodom where strange growths sprang up in the manner of fungus on decaying wood, like those Chinese restaurants which proliferated in the eighties for no apparent reason until, with time, the secret was out. The proprietors and their families could not emigrate from China to Canada direct and were using Guyana as a convenient staging post. Although the voluble taxi driver had recounted fantastical tales about black-clad grave robbers and corrupt policemen, the reality of living in the capital was altogether stranger, and Kwaku listened and waited while feathering his nest. In less than a year he had managed to secure a flat and bring Miss Gwendoline to live with him. Next he would find a way to persuade her to invite Philomena to follow. And with that the first phase of his strategy would be complete.

Curiously enough the model Kwaku had chosen to emulate was not the Right Hand Man, but Mrs Correia, whose story, common knowledge in the office, had impressed him as being his own. The self-effacing appearance that belied her past worked on him like a potent dream. If every life was a mystery, hers represented an enigma, a mystery turned inside out. There was no doubt, whatever her essential truth might be, that like himself she was a great dissembler. If at first he found her behaviour repugnant — too much of a piece with his own — his attitude towards her changed completely when he discovered her past.

One evening Suarez took Kwaku to see a friend who lived in Meadowbrook, one of the new housing developments beyond the boundaries of the old city, on land that used to be cane fields only a few years ago. The grand houses resembled nothing that Kwaku had seen before. But above all he listened with astonishment to the chorus of frogs and crapauds from the nearby canal and surrounding yards, far denser and more insistent than in the parts of town he was familiar with. He and Suarez had got out of their taxi at the Cuffy monument and walked the long road to Meadowbrook, past the old race course and small, silent houses that resembled dwellings from another country, less from their style than the impression they made of decorating a roadway whose destination was the void. When the two men stood before Suarez's friend's house, the sun had gone down nearly two hours before, and the darkness, relieved only by light from the houses, was dominated by the pervasive night sounds. Just as Kwaku began wondering how Suarez would manage to announce his arrival, the friend appeared at a doorway as though reacting to a signal and without further ado led them by a path to the back door, all the while urging them by sign to make as little noise as possible.

Surinam — he earned his name because of his partiality for Surinam cherries — lived on the premises of an official who owned his house. He was a close friend of Clifford Correia, who was expected at any moment.

Kwaku had been warned by Suarez on the way that he should keep his thoughts to himself during the evening, whatever he saw or heard.

'I know how you shoot off your mouth when people least expect it.'

Kwaku promised and waited eagerly to discover the cause of the warning. The flat they entered was conventionally furnished, with a view into the backyard through open French windows. Surinam himself, a taciturn man of medium height, reminded him of Bertie the day watchman, but with a more agreeable expression.

But Kwaku quickly forgot the prohibition regarding uncalled-for remarks, what with the host's lavish rum hospitality and Suarez's monologues. And when things became hectic soon after Clifford Correia's arrival, he had no recollection of what he had promised not to do.

Soon after Correia appeared, Surinam's landlord went out, and the reason for Surinam's enjoinder to silence immediately became clear. Everybody began speaking loudly, as though an intolerable restraint had been lifted.

'So this is why Suarez never come to my house on Friday nights,' Kwaku thought.

In fact, Suarez kept his private life from Kwaku as much because of the latter's country ways as on account of his unpredictable behaviour. He had not taken him to Surinam's flat before because there everyone drank excessively, and Kwaku could not be trusted to hold his liquor. Besides, the watchmen were clannish, and Suarez was not certain whether his friends would take to him. After all, Bertie never bothered to conceal his aversion to the lowly assistant messenger, a dislike compounded by the speed with which he had acquired a flat while he himself still lived in a room.

Just as Kwaku was beginning to feel at ease and thought that it was his turn to contribute to the conversation, Bertie arrived in the company of a lady much younger than himself. Kwaku's heart sank at the sight of the man he called his 'enemy'.

'That's all I need,' he thought, convinced that it was the day watchman's mission in life to persecute him.

Bertie introduced Eunice to each one in turn, ignoring Kwaku pointedly. But the assistant messenger, his resolve strengthened by the rum he had consumed, got up and bowed deeply to the lady.

'Why you don' curtsey an' get it over with?' Bertie said sarcastically.

Before Kwaku could reply, Bertie addressed Suarez, asking him whether he had difficulty getting away.

'The chief's gone to the country, so it was easy.'

'Sit down anywhere,' Surinam offered.

Thereupon Kwaku leapt up from his chair to allow Bertie's lady to sit down.

It was clear to Kwaku that in this company he had to fend for himself; that however much he was insulted by Bertie no one would intervene, just as they had taken no notice of Correia, who had fallen asleep on the bed.

Kwaku noticed that since Eunice's arrival the conversation had become more animated; Suarez especially speaking more loudly than he had been doing, while Bertie's contributions consisted almost entirely of remarks aimed at cutting the others down to size. In the circumstances Kwaku thought it best to hold his tongue, a resolution all but beyond his powers. The coat of restraint he had worn since he settled in Georgetown would make him ill, he had no doubt, unless he found a way of expressing himself freely.

Suarez began showing off in front of Eunice. He spoke of the Right

Hand Man's father, Miss Rose's husband, the pan boiler. Now, with the advent of computers, which were capable of pinpointing the maximum potential of sugar crystals, there was no longer any need for his expertise, except in a few small islands where no one had ever seen a computer and did things the way God intended them to be done. Suarez railed against authority, ostensibly because he was a rebel, but in truth with the sole purpose of impressing Eunice.

'We're all programmed to live for a certain time,' he declared, looking at Bertie's woman friend out of the corner of his eye, 'and although you can shorten your life by bad living there's little you can do to lengthen it.'

'You talkin' rubbish!' Bertie exclaimed. 'Nonsense!'

Everyone was surprised at his vehement reaction except Surinam, who had noticed how the wind was blowing. Eunice, Bertie's latest conquest, was on her first visit and, dazzled by the company of men, had been encouraging Suarez with her eyes. Failing to notice Bertie's growing agitation and flattered by Suarez's guarded attention, she became more and more brazen.

'Who said I'm talking rubbish?' Suarez asked.

'Me!' answered Bertie. 'You always talkin' tripe. If you brains was as big as your mouth you would talk more sense.'

Suarez, confused at the turn the conversation had taken, looked at their host, who could only shake his head, knowing that Suarez was capable of felling Bertie on the spot. Then, unexpectedly, Kwaku came to the rescue. Even though he had not grasped the reason for Bertie's sudden loss of temper, he stood up and, as though in a dream, went over to Eunice, took her hand in his and kissed it.

'Miss Eunice, I admire you more than anyone else in the world except Miss Gwendoline, my wife. Miss Eunice, one more hour an' I could fall in love with you.'

The others looked on in consternation, scarcely believing their eyes that the odd-looking character who had hardly uttered a word until then should make such an eloquent declaration.

'You palagala!' Bertie said contemptuously.

'Leave him alone,' Eunice butted in, 'he ugly, but he's a gentleman.'

'I'm going to fill your glass up,' Surinam said, visibly relieved that Kwaku had saved the situation.

And Surinam disappeared into the adjoining room, to emerge

almost at once with a bottle of ten year old rum. He pushed Kwaku gently onto the bed from where he had risen to make his declaration, opened the bottle, then poured a bit on the floor in honour of the dead before filling Kwaku's glass to the brim.

Bertie glared at Kwaku to cover up his satisfaction that the threatened confrontation had not materialized. Heaven knows he had often enough wondered what he disliked in the village fool everyone thought of as inoffensive. And out of the blue the self-same fool had saved him from humiliation at the hands of a man people regarded as his friend but whom, in reality, he envied for his popularity and the way he bent others to his will.

Surinam, taking advantage of the turn events had taken, offered to entertain the company with a song.

'Yes, yes!' Eunice shouted, clapping her hands.

He retrieved a guitar from under the bed, sat down and, after playing a few chords, began humming softly. Suarez opened the door that led out into the yard, so that the night sounds mingled with the chords of a guitar and an eloquent voice, and Kwaku, for the first time since he arrived in Georgetown, felt at ease, as if he had thrown off an invisible but palpable burden he had carried all these months during which he could communicate to no one his sense of unease.

The very urge to talk gibberish and make a fool of himself had prevented two men from coming to blows, averting a dangerous situation that might have resulted in damage to Surinam's flat and even the end of Suarez's Friday night reunions. Kwaku had no illusions that Bertie would ever forgive him for daring to kiss his lady's hand, even though, deep down, he was grateful to have been saved from a confrontation with the more powerful watchman.

Kwaku surveyed the scene through his drunken eyes; Clifford Correia asleep beside him with that contented expression of the small child at the breast, Surinam bending over his instrument, and Eunice pretending she had no idea of her effect on the men. Bertie and Suarez, seduced by Surinam's music and his liquor, remained motionless in the manner of guests on a first visit. For some reason Kwaku was overcome by an indescribable feeling of well-being, which made him forget that they had not yet eaten and that he had promised Miss Gwendoline to lay off the liquor. Had it not brought them to the brink of despair in New Amsterdam, after they moved out of the mansion on the road to Canje where the lunatic asylum beckoned with its generous grounds and dilapidated buildings the Government could not afford to repair — despite the threat of chaos when finally the crisis broke and its inmates would take to wandering the streets? Was he himself not drawn to chaos? Even when he craved for and finally achieved success, did he not tremble on the brink? So many of his dreams and reflections told him in no uncertain terms that he was uncomfortable with success! He never felt so free as while he wallowed in the mud, as in that distant time when he was all but forced into a marriage with a young corpse dressed in bridal clothes. The exhilaration of refusal and then of fleeing the death house, never matched at the height of his subsequent fame, could not be communicated to anyone, not even to Miss Gwendoline, who could only see in him a husband whose obligation stretched beyond the children growing up, right to the end, into the dim season of old age. There was something peculiarly satisfying about the company of four men and a solitary woman who, having created the threat to order, could soon afterwards succumb to the seduction of a stringed instrument no larger than a small child.

Eunice, seized by an urge to make it up to Bertie, went and sat on his lap and, like a bird secure on its perch, began accompanying Surinam on the guitar. Then, her song over, the guitarist went to the kitchen to warm up the dinner he had prepared hours before they came.

Clifford Correia stirred, propped himself up on his elbow and then spoke to Kwaku as though he were the only other person in the room.

'I hear you does make up poems for the obituary page of the papers.'

Kwaku, taken off guard, confessed that the Right Hand Man was the composer of the poems. Immediately realizing what he had done, he put his hand over his mouth. The stunned silence that followed threw him into a panic and he pleaded with the company not to repeat what he had said.

'Is what wrong?' Eunice asked Bertie, who did not bother to answer her.

'You mean,' Suarez remarked with surprising severity, 'that *he* does write that tripe?'

'He probably lying,' Bertie put in.

'I telling lies,' Kwaku said, seizing on a way out of his predicament.

'He's the biggest liar in Demerara,' Suarez intervened in an effort to protect his friend.

And no one knew what to believe, except Clifford Correia and Suarez, who were aware of Miss Rose's son's unsavoury deals.

Then Kwaku, tormented at the thought of the consequences that might follow from his drunken indiscretion, shouted: 'Alyou would believe anything. I got the next poem here, in my head.' And his last words were accompanied by three taps on his temple, made with his middle finger.

'I got a hundred poems there. A thousand if you want to know.'

'Let me hear one then,' Bertie challenged Kwaku, delighted at the opportunity to humiliate him.

Kwaku stood up and, like a shaman about to work himself into a trance, took a deep breath, closed his eyes, and with clenched fists began to speak.

> You went when Jesus called
> To his immortal breast
> And we were left to grieve.

'I can't think of the last line,' he added.

'Alright, you prove your point,' Clifford Correia put in, evidently impressed by Kwaku's fit of inspiration. 'You probably learnt it by heart from what the chief gave you.'

'If you want,' Kwaku offered, 'I can start another one.'

'Don't bother,' Suarez objected.

Kwaku stepped out into the yard, trembling like a leaf. Sobered up by the experience, he wiped the sweat from his forehead with the back of his hand. Miss Rose's son had taken him in, found him a job and a flat. How could he face him if he discovered that he had let the cat out of the bag?

'If I'm anything,' he thought, 'I'm loyal.'

He had no idea how the words of the poem had rolled off his tongue so readily. Perhaps Mr Barzey, his dead mentor, was right: there lived in him a friend who stood watch constantly, a kind of sentinel who never slept. Mr Barzey — God rest his soul — never tired of telling him that it was just as well, because he, Kwaku, had so little control over himself.

Kwaku resolved to say as little as possible for the rest of the night, especially as Clifford Correia would not fail to report everything he said to his wife, the Right Hand Man's secretary. Even now he was not certain that he believed his explanation about the 'In Memoriam' poems.

'You're coming in?' Surinam called out.

Kwaku went back inside and was given a patterned earthenware plate laden with dhalpourri. Rumour had it that everything consumed in that room came from Surinam's landlord's larder; that every plate, all the cutlery, the glasses, the rum, the beer and cakes were his, and what is more, were used with his knowledge. Surinam's mysterious landlord demanded only that his carousing should begin after he went out and come to an end as soon as the headlights of his car lit up the yard.

Eunice had abandoned her lover's lap for a more comfortable place on the bed between Kwaku and Clifford Correia, who was now sitting up and eating his portion with great commitment.

On the wall whose single window gave on to the driveway, a small frog had appeared and remained immobile, like a sculptured emblem of the new-styled mansion. Kwaku, surprised that no one remarked on the intrusion, held back his own observation.

He wondered whether the abrupt cessation of conversation was due to his behaviour or the collective act of eating. He had always detested silence, regarding it as directed against him personally, in a conspiracy mounted by all those people he had wronged since his childhood.

'You know,' he found himself saying, in a desperate effort to get a conversation going, 'when I was living in Surinam I get into a fight one time.'

Kwaku had never been to Surinam. In fact, he had never left the country. To tell the truth he had no idea of Surinam's position on the map and would have been hard put to say whether it was an island or part of the continent. But he pressed on none the less, secure in the knowledge that no one would have grounds for doubting that he had lived in that country.

'I get into a fight with a one-legged man. He loss his foot in the last war when he attack a machine-gun post all by himself. Yes, an' this man lurch at me an' I do this!'

Kwaku moved his shoulders in evasive action.

'An' he do so!'

'He missed you?' Eunice asked.

'He jus' miss me,' Kwaku replied. 'An' I miss him too. I never see a one-legged man move like that. But when you come to think of it he had all that experience during the war, dodging bullets an' ducking all the time. . . .'

'Do we have to listen to this?' Clifford Correia asked.

'He's not doing any harm,' Suarez put in, irritated by Clifford's superior tone.

Kwaku, encouraged by the unexpected defence, pressed on.

'The one-legged man swing his wooden foot at me an' I duck, because I tell you, if that peg leg did catch me I would be six foot underground now. "Woof!" he do it again. Then a man in the crowd — a crowd did congregate by then — this man in the crowd shout out, "Go on the attack, mister!" '

'How you know he was talking to you?' Eunice asked.

'I din' know, but the peg leg man was doing all the attackin', so I thought was me he mean. An' I do so!'

Kwaku placed his empty plate on the floor and let fly with his leg.

'So!. . . An' that was the end. I ketch him 'pon the good foot an' he loss his balance. That was the end of him. I become a hero in Surinam, where they *appreciate* me. Not like here, where every crab-dog piss 'pon me.'

'Nobody's going to piss on you here,' Bertie said with mock sympathy.

'I piss on you,' Clifford Correia said. 'I think you're a damn liar, and impertinent into the bargain. You come here for the first time and shoot off your mouth whenever. . . .'

'Leave him alone,' Surinam said gently, feeling that as the host he was obliged to put in a word for Kwaku, whom he neither liked nor disliked, but considered to be, at worst, an awkward guest.

'Every Friday night we get together here,' Clifford continued, 'and nobody ever quarrels. The first time he comes he sows confusion. It doesn't make sense hiding his bad ways from him. A country bumpkin fighting one-legged men in Surinam and writing 'In Memoriam' poems for the dead! This man isn't for real. Left to me I'd throw his ass in the Lamaha Canal and let the alligators maul him. Yes, Mr Assistant Messenger, I'm talking to you!'

'May I ask you a question?' Kwaku said deferentially. 'What I ever do you? I did steal from you? I don' even know you, mister.'

'I wouldn't exchange words with someone like you,' declared the fire-raiser, and he lay down once more on the bed to show his contempt for Kwaku.

'I don' know why alyou quarrelling,' Eunice said. 'Nobody in' do nothing. Women don' quarrel for nothing.'

'Shut you mouth!' ordered Bertie. 'Your mother always quarrelling. She herself does say, "I feel like quarrelling today." Women don' quarrel? An' what about you? You're the queen of sulkers. They see you here so quiet as if butter won't melt in your mouth; but when you ready to sulk is days and days!'

Bertie's unusual outburst was an act of vengeance for her earlier indulgent behaviour towards Kwaku, and its effect was to cause Eunice to seek refuge in the kitchen.

'See what I mean?' Bertie said triumphantly. 'An' that's nothing! You should see her mother!'

'That's what comes from mixing women in man affairs. Women and country idiots!' Clifford Correia said with the greatest calm, as though he were expounding a self-evident truth.

'Play your guitar, Surinam,' Suarez urged him, 'something's got into everybody tonight. Must be the talk of elections.'

Surinam first collected the empty plates, took them into the kitchen, before returning to pick up his guitar, which he had placed upright in a corner of the room.

His music, as untroubled as his conversation, brought Eunice back into the room and she sat down on the bed at some distance from Kwaku.

It was a few minutes after ten o'clock, when the crickets and frogs had already fallen silent. Kwaku, absorbed in reflections on the impossibility of keeping himself within the bounds of respectable behaviour, heard no music, no expressions of admiration, only Correia's last words reverberating against his temples. 'I piss on you!' He had done just that to the old shoemaker to whom he had been apprenticed on the eve of his departure from his village. He had covered his master's front shop in urine, while waving his penis from side to side to make certain that he missed nothing. Now Mr Correia would piss on him if he had the chance. No, he could not go on living like that, the butt of every crab-dog's contempt. In spite of his quick progress since he came to town he felt that something was missing, something that could change his life profoundly.

Kwaku did not know that he had been invited by Surinam on the strength of his 'In Memoriam' poems and the stories Suarez had told him about the odd country man who had been an outstanding healer. From hearsay he considered Kwaku to be someone with secret powers. Himself a painter of considerable talent — this was the opinion of experts at the Ministry of Education, who tried in vain to persuade him to sell some of his canvasses — Surinam wanted to show Kwaku his work. As things turned out he changed his mind, not knowing what to make of his guest. Had Kwaku behaved as Suarez had advised, the two would have remained after the get-together broke up and then been taken into the rooms on the other side of the kitchen. There everything was covered in portraits, scenes drawn from the artist's life, dreams and fantasies; painted on the walls, the bed sheet, his ample cloth bag in which he stored his brushes, and even the hessian that decorated the back of the door. Surinam came from a Courantyne village where his father and grandfather had spent much of their time painting commissions, in the main portraits of people who had died. A photographer from a neighbouring village now received the commissions and Surinam was obliged to paint for himself rather than for others. He refused to sell his work to a Government agency, a stand interpreted by the authorities as arrogance, but which stemmed from his conviction that he would lose his creative power if his canvasses were *hung*.

Kwaku and Suarez left with the others when Surinam's landlord's return was announced by the brilliant headlamps of his Mercedes car. Eunice, Bertie and Correia went off up Vlissingen Road on arriving at the junction, while the two friends continued up D'Urban Street.

'Come out with it, ne!' Kwaku said, unable to stand the tension caused by Suarez's silence.

'I don't have anything to say about your outrageous behaviour,' Suarez answered. 'All I know is I've finished with you. People know you by the friends you keep and I won't have a reputation if you continue to hang around me. I'm sorry for your wife, but there's a limit to everything. From now on I don't want to set eyes on you except at work.'

And that was that. Kwaku closed the top button of his shirt against the night air.

'I could never get accustom to all these roads,' he said pointlessly. 'A road to here, a road to there, East, West, North, South. Is too much for me.'

He felt like overwhelming Suarez with words, as he used to ply him with questions at the start of their friendship. Long ago he would have found some way to discharge his anger and confusion. Now he knew he must act, but not in the old way. He must act upon *himself*. First of all he must see himself for what he is. They could not all be wrong, Suarez, Bertie, Correia, and even Surinam, who must surely have judged him as harshly as the others. He would go into a period of reflection, study himself and try to discover what all others saw in him.

'Anyway,' he said aloud. 'I sorry for the trouble I cause you.'

He stopped, thrust out his hand towards Suarez who, taken completely by surprise, allowed his own to be shaken. Then he watched Kwaku strike out along a road that took him to his flat. And Kwaku, making his way home, could only wonder at what had become of Armageddon, the companion dog he had bought his wife.

The abruptness of Kwaku's departure touched Suarez, who had expected his friend to beg forgiveness in that whining voice that never failed to rouse him. He did not understand Kwaku. No one understood him, Suarez mused. The only way to deal with a man like that was to keep him at arm's length. It was for the best, he told himself, while watching the hunched figure become a shadow beyond the lamplight.

Chapter VIII

The peremptory summons to the Ministry of Hope made Kwaku extremely nervous. Moreover, it seemed to him that Mrs Correia was keeping her eyes on him from her vantage point behind his back.

He noticed a picture on the desk of the Right Hand Man with his arm round a young lady, which had not been there when he spoke to him that first afternoon.

'How long I have to wait?' he asked across the gap between the office and Mrs Correia's desk.

She looked up from her work and, in the space of time she took to answer, Kwaku could tell from her expression that Correia had told her everything that had transpired the Friday night before.

'I have no idea how long you'll have to wait, Mr Cholmondeley.'

'But I did get a message to come right away. I come right away,' Kwaku protested.

She just smiled at him as though he were a child who had asked a foolish question and needed to be indulged.

The telephone on the Right Hand Man's desk rang and Mrs Correia hurried over.

'Yes. . . . Yes, comrade. . . . No, comrade. . . . Very well, comrade.'

She replaced the receiver.

'You won't have to wait long now,' she told Kwaku.

When the Right Hand Man arrived, about fifteen minutes later, Kwaku stood up deferentially.

'Sit down, sit down.'

Kwaku sat down on the edge of the chair and waited to hear the worst.

Correia had indeed told his wife of Kwaku's claim that the 'In Memoriam' poems had been written by the Permanent Secretary, who thought the time had come to compromise his protégé. He himself had been tied to the Minister of Hope, whose place he hoped to take if all went well. Far from being angry on learning that the poems had been attributed to him, he felt flattered that the Correia couple knew. One of them was bound to let slip the information sooner or later and so contribute to the enhancement of his reputation. But Kwaku had to be silenced before his lack of discretion caused any damage. Besides, the assistant messenger must be firmly placed on the list of people who were beholden to him and thoroughly compromised, against the day when he wielded real power and needed an army of trusted minions.

'Do you know what loyalty is, Kwaku?' he asked the hapless messenger. 'Of course you know! Loyalty, gratitude. . . . I'm sure you don't have to take lessons from anyone about the qualities . . . these Christian qualities. Even if you were disloyal I'd have to take care of you on account of my mother. She always talks about you and even calls you a great man. And I'll tell you something: just knowing your story is like reading a good book. I keep saying to myself, "What happened to him can happen to me. I can end up a messenger as well, at the beck and call of every- and anybody. " But besides my mother's opinion of you and your story, I've got another reason to respect you: I'm younger than you. Oh, don't forget I'm from the country too and know all about respect for your elders. Not like these ill-bred Georgetonians who talk to their parents as if they were equals. No, Kwaku . . . . Mr Cholmondeley. Do you respect me? Of course you do! But what's the difference between your respect for me and mine for you? Ever thought of that? Eh? Well, why should you? The difference is that you respect me, a younger man, only because of my status. Now, isn't that right? I don't know. Myself, I think you should earn respect, whoever you are. Don't tell anyone I said so; you know what our people are like. Put crab-dog in a position of power and we'd worship him. Now why am I telling you what, if repeated, would leave me dangerously exposed? Because I trust you, Mr Cholmondeley. And of course because of what I said before, about my mother's regard for you. . . . But is she right? I respected my class teacher in Primary School and thought he was the most remarkable man I knew. But when I met him a few years later — I was sixteen — I saw a pathetic man who couldn't even look me in the eye. So, do you deserve my mother's regard? Yes? No? Of course you do. After all she's not the only one in Canje and New Amsterdam who talks about your healing powers . . . *one time* healing powers. The old shoemaker told me how you once put your hands on an old woman's shoulder and she began leaping about like a dervish, although, before you arrived, she could hardly walk for her arthritis. So, the respect you deserve is not in question, Mr Cholmondeley. No. But something's bothering me, apart from your obsession with freedom of speech. What's bothering me is this: are you up to undertaking something big? I have plans for you, but first you have to prove yourself. . . . I'm sending a certain person — someone you know — on an errand, a kind of mission. I want you to keep an eye on him. It's not spying on him, mind you. Nothing like that. . . .'

'Yes, sir. . . .'

'I don't know if you've ever heard of a law called misprision of felony? It was part of English common law until the early sixties. If you knew that someone had committed a serious crime, it was your duty to report him to the police. Now look at that! If your father committed a crime you had a duty to trip along to the police station and say, "My pa did steal some rice and feed our starving family with it and I eat the rice, wash my hands and then say to my brother, 'Let's do our duty and tell the police about pa.' " Yes, Mr Cholmondeley. Now, while that law was in force in England, hardly anybody spoke out against it. Well, it's the same with what I'm asking you to do, except that you're not doing anything to your family. You see how honest I'm being with you? In fact you're not doing anything at all. When you come back you won't have to report to me, unless the person you're keeping an eye on did something . . . bad. I might not even want you to report if he did anything bad.'

'So why you want me to keep a eye on him?' Kwaku asked.

'Look how shrewd you are!' the Right Hand Man said, accompanying his words with a mirthless laugh. 'The answer to your question is this: he must *know* he's being watched. That's all. I know this character like the back of my hand. He's honesty itself, provided he thinks there's the slightest risk of being caught.'

'Who's the person?'

'It's Mr Correia,' he whispered, leaning towards Kwaku, and then glancing over to the desk where Amy Correia was sitting.

Kwaku looked at him unflinchingly. The thought that the Right Hand Man had been toying with him made him angry, and he regretted bitterly taking part in the carousal at Surinam's flat the Friday before.

'Is something I got to do?' Kwaku asked diffidently.

'You don't have to do anything, Mr Cholmondeley. I have no power over you. My mother wouldn't let me.'

'I see.'

'Well, will you?'

'I don' want to, but I will.'

'You want time to think about it?'

'I don' want time.'

'Good.'

The Right Hand Man then explained that Kwaku and Clifford Correia would be going to Lethem, on the Brazilian border. The currency dealer would be delivering a cloth bag to a man he would meet at a drinking place in Lethem. That was all. Kwaku need only remain with Mr Correia at all times.

'I never travel further than Georgetown,' Kwaku said, suddenly remembering that he had no experience of the purchase of tickets and the other complications that attend a long journey.

But the Right Hand Man assured him that he would be fetched at his flat and only had to remember to carry a change of clothing with him.

'Mr Correia will look after everything else.'

Kwaku shook hands with his superior, while chafing at his impotence.

'Goodbye, then,' Miss Rose's son said.

The chamber-pot shop, set up by the Right Hand Man without Kwaku's knowledge, had done a roaring business during August, the height of the tourist season, and he was thinking of expanding into the adjoining premises, which had been destroyed by a fire some months back. He would add to his stock rocking chairs, stuffed alligators and other bric-à-brac, and combine the operation with his currency shop. This would be a good time to silence Kwaku, who was bound to discover, sooner or later, that he had been duped into abandoning his idea of a business dealing in antiques.

If things continued to go well he would threaten to resign his position at the Ministry of Hope. What with his reputation for excellence and his impeccable style, his superiors would almost certainly offer him a better post, perhaps even a ministry, provided he won one of the by-elections that cropped up from time to time.

Like his pan boiler father, the Right Hand Man was incapable of mediocrity in whatever he did. Unlike his father, however, he was fired by a driving ambition and harboured a secret conviction that one day he would become President of the country. At the important meetings he attended, sometimes as representative of the Minister himself when the latter was not available, he was struck by the incompetence of officials, by the lack of preparation of their briefs and above all by the paucity of ideas emanating from the various ministries. A plan he submitted six months ago had earned him the personal congratulations of the Prime Minister, who summoned him to his office and asked for a more detailed report of the facts on which the plan was based. His star was rising, he had no doubt.

The idea that attracted so much attention he had taken from an acquaintance who was in retirement from a post in England. According to him many Guyanese of pensionable age who lived abroad were afflicted with a terrible nostalgia for the country of their birth and would readily return if conditions were suitable for living out their declining years in peace and security. With a little official encouragement, they could communicate the skills they had acquired in a foreign land at special institutes throughout the country. Most of them would work for very little, considering that their pensions would go far. The Right Hand Man's acquaintance knew of quantity surveyors, lawyers, engineers, teachers and others who would leap at the opportunity.

Originally driven by ambition alone, the Right Hand Man soon became contaminated by the ruthlessness and self-seeking of his superiors, some of whom stacked their gains from dubious enterprises in foreign banks. At first bewildered by what he saw — in the same way as Kwaku was dazzled by town life and townspeople in his first year in Georgetown — he observed without comment and stored away in his analytical mind details of their corruption. One minister in particular had made a fine art of courting popularity with the public, so that while compiling a fortune he acquired a powerful reputation as a people's man, and more especially as a lover of children. His public parties for orphans, larger with each passing year, were accompanied by an ostentatious display of generosity which did not fail to impress Miss Rose's son. His ambition was fortified by a need to emulate the almost magical skill displayed by this man of the people. He filed away every ploy, copied every posture that might contribute to an eventual success, so that in the end the person he moulded for himself, far from being the result of some unwitting process, became the finely wrought end product of a deliberate crafting. He developed a ramrod walk, put his head to one side while listening attentively, smiled with his eyes, spoke with admirable clarity and, all in all, cultivated the appearance of an uncommonly pleasant man whose morals were never in doubt.

The Right Hand Man, more than anyone else, understood Kwaku and saw enormous possibilities in the unusual stamp of his character, which men like Bertie and Correia dismissed as the rantings of a fool. But before he could use him, Kwaku must learn restraint and, equally important, he must learn to respect authority.

Kwaku broke the news of his proposed trip to Miss Gwendoline and promised to send a message by telephone through the New Amsterdam police station to Philomena, asking her to come to town and stay with her mother.

'I can stay alone,' she protested.

'You can't,' Kwaku told her. 'Is who goin' open the glass door 'pon the verandah so you can listen to the traffic.'

'I can find the glass door.'

'An' who goin' do the cooking?'

'That's nothing.'

'And the shopping? And fetch water from the neighbour when the pressure get too low? If one of your children did talk like that you would give them a good box.'

Kwaku dismissed her profession of independence impatiently. He intended to send for Philomena, that was all.

They were living well by the standards of their Canje days, when they often woke up in the morning not knowing where their next meal would come from and their association was soured by differing views of Philomena.

Kwaku had stood by as his wife fretted incessantly when Philomena left and set up house with her young man. She was the last of their children to go. He did his best to revive her interest in the world around her, while thinking that the only remedy lay in taking her back to live in their village, where she would be visited by neighbours and acquaintances and the memories of many births still hung on the air they breathed; where ailing women went to the village elder and requested that he throw a white table for them; where parents simply did what their parents had done before them without suffering the torment of guilt when things went wrong.

Kwaku could not understand that much of her silent grieving was for him; that she was, in one way, glad of her blindness, so as not to witness the scorn on people's faces for his miserable condition. The night when he had danced in the rum shop with two one-dollar notes sticking out of his trouser pockets like paper wings was her enduring image of his humiliation.

'And now at last when I start earning good in Georgetown and we got a flat, you should be happy,' he told her once.

But she did not answer and left him to wonder what the real reason was for her low spirits.

'Anyway,' Kwaku said, wondering how she and Philomena would hit it off when alone in the flat, 'I feel we looking on the Promised Land. I feel it. An' when Philomena come to town she can take you to the church down the road on Sunday. You in' got friends here, but you can go to many churches. . . . When I come back I goin' buy you a whole wardrobe of dresses an' I goin' come to church with you, jus' like when we use to go to the rum shop. We was happy then, you remember? We was poor, but happy.'

The night before his departure Kwaku dreamt that he and Clifford Correia were sitting at a dining table. While chewing his food his companion leaned forward towards him, in such a way that his eyes appeared to have grown and his pupils became magnified several times over.

'You know the Right Hand Man asked me to watch you,' Correia said, using the same hostile tone with which he had addressed him during the carousal at the Meadowbrook flat. 'And I'm not going to let you out of my sight.'

Kwaku, recalling his own instructions not to let Correia out of his sight, said not a word. And on waking he saw it as a triumph that he could keep his mouth shut at such a disclosure, even though it was only a dream. Could it be true that Correia had received the same instructions as himself? If that was the case, what was the Right Hand Man's game? Not once had his dreams instructed him in a meaningful way and, more often than not, they threw him into confusion. Kwaku came to the conclusion that being mortally afraid of flying, his anxiety about the trip must be taking its toll.

He refused to allow his thoughts to guide him along the path of suspicion. There was no reason for Correia to watch him. He knew no one in Lethem and must be the last person to get up to mischief, especially as he had so much to lose.

Kwaku looked over at his sleeping wife before getting out of bed to fetch a drink of water. Not yet familiar with the layout of his flat, he had some difficulty finding his way in the dark. He pressed the kitchen switch and in the bright light saw a swarm of cockroaches on the table where he and Miss Gwendoline were in the habit of taking their meals. They stood their ground and only scurried away when he bent low down over the table.

He poured out some iced water from the Frigidaire and before drinking it ran the cup over his face, now dripping with perspiration. For the first time since moving in he took note of the metal gutter running right through the middle of the kitchen, which the owner must have extended without bothering to alter the drainage arrangements. He had lived in the flat for several weeks and had not noticed such an unusual feature, just as he had never set eyes on the next-door dog which barked ferociously every foreday morning. Was it any wonder, he reflected, that his knowledge of himself was so scant, that others continually surprised him with their remarks? But was Miss Gwendoline any different? She failed to grasp how far a kind word would go with Philomena, who only wanted to be met halfway and hankered after a small sign from her. 'You going take me to church?' his wife would ask. 'Me?' Philomena would respond, surprised and touched at proof that her mother recognized her existence. He had seen similar relationships in many homes during his time as a healer but could give them no name.

Kwaku could not face the fact that the thought of going to the savannahs with Clifford Correia had reduced him to a state of near panic. And if his reflections took in subjects that were not remotely connected to the source of his anxiety, it was just as well, for he would have spent a sleepless night attempting to plan in detail what he would say to him during the days they would spend together at the Guest House.

He had no recollection at what point in his reflections he had fallen asleep but when he was awakened by the neighbour's dog, the window panes glowed with a morning light that announced unblemished skies. He crept into bed so discretely that the even breathing of his wife was hardly disturbed.

Chapter IX

Lethem is one of those remote settlements on the border with Brazil which contrasts so sharply with Georgetown and the coastal villages that inhabitants from the seaboard who go there believe themselves to be in a different country. It was the starting point of the old cattle trail that led to the Berbice River. From there the animals were taken by boat to New Amsterdam and then transported by train to Georgetown, where they arrived, emaciated from the long trek over jungle trails and across the Berbice savannahs.

From Lethem can be seen the Kanuku mountains that separate the territory of the Wapisiana Indians to their South from the Northern savannahs, domain of the Macusi, a Carib sub-tribe. Few Georgetonians have any idea concerning the extent or even the situation of these eerie-looking mountains which serve as a rampart between two peoples whose hostility to one another once erupted in wife-stealing raids and, since the introduction of a centralized justice, mutual accusations of any crime for which a plausible story could be concocted. Now few things distinguish them from one another, at least in the eyes of coastal people. Their two languages and their differing myths cannot disguise the fact that they intermarry assiduously. And if they speak of this in whispers, their children despise the ancient dances which identified their uniqueness, preferring to imitate visitors whom they watch through the spoked windows of the Double Wheel discotheque on Saturday nights.

It was into this brushwood landscape with its scattering of cashew and mango trees that Kwaku and Clifford Correia stepped from the aeroplane. Kwaku, gripping his holdall as if his life depended on it, accompanied Correia to the airline office where he confirmed their trip back to town.

The two men then took the dusty laterite road to the Government Guest House. On one side it fell away towards a path Indians used to reach a Macusi village about a mile away. On the other, two smaller roads branched off to serve various sections of Lethem, in which were another Guest House, a surprisingly large hospital, two drinking places and a few substantial buildings where government officials lodged. Kwaku only took all this in later when he felt at ease in the strange landscape.

A passing jeep raised a trail of red dust that engulfed them, and Correia crossed to the other side, mumbling that he had forgotten which way the wind blew. And indeed there were strong southerly winds deep in the continent, with no dependence on the trade winds that came from across the sea.

Correia opened the Guest House door and went in, leaving Kwaku to wonder why he did not knock or call out.

'Mrs Pestano's there?' he asked a middle-aged lady who looked out from the kitchen.

'Yes?' answered another woman in her late forties who appeared behind her.

'A double room was booked for Mr Correia and Mr Cholmondeley.'

'Oh yes!'

They followed her upstairs and were shown into a large room furnished with two beds, with a door leading out onto a verandah that ran the length of the building.

'You had breakfast?'

'Yes,' Correia answered without bothering to consult Kwaku.

'I din' have breakfast yet,' Kwaku declared, seizing the chance to be by himself.

She invited him downstairs as soon as he settled in, so Kwaku lost no time in emptying his holdall onto the bed by the window, Correia having taken possession of the one with a mosquito-net. Then, without a word, he left to have his morning meal.

When Correia came down he found Kwaku sitting at the dining table. Making as if to go past him he changed his mind, turned round and sat down on the chair opposite him.

'She didn't tell you, did she?'

'What?' Kwaku asked.

'Not to drink the water.'

'No.'

'Then don't. I've got tablets upstairs to purify it.'

'But why?' Kwaku demanded, wondering whether Correia just wanted to be difficult.

'It comes straight from the river. Over the border in Bom Fin the water comes from wells and is safe to drink.'

'How you know all that?'

Correia shrugged his shoulders in reply.

After a long silence Correia suddenly blurted out, almost angrily, 'Let's drop the pretence. You came to keep an eye on me, so let's cut out the damn nonsense. When you fall asleep at night I can be off without your knowing. There's no street lighting here. I'd be gone across the Brazilian border and be back before morning light and you wouldn't know a thing. *You* watch me? It's like putting sloth to keep an eye on monkey. I'm only telling you so you won't look like a fool when I give you the slip. We might as well drop the pretence and come to an agreement.'

Kwaku, lost for words, said nothing. Correia was right. But how could he trust him? Who would row him across the river at the dead of night?

'What you tell me make sense, but. . . ,' Kwaku said, after giving the matter much thought.

'So you *did* come to watch me!'

'I din' say that. But suppose I did, I got a job to do and I have to do it.'

'You're wasting your time,' Correia said.

'I goin' stop pretending,' Kwaku declared, 'if you tell me why you don' like me.'

Correia smiled broadly and his small brown eyes receded into the folds above his cheeks.

'It's not me. It's everybody at the Ministry. . . . You come to work as a messenger and you've already got a flat . . . in a matter of months. Do you work obeah or something?'

As Correia talked Kwaku realized that he must have known a great deal about him before they met at Surinam's flat.

'And how you know I come to watch you?' Kwaku asked.

'Look, I have my sources of information.'

'I got my flat and my job because I know the Permanent Secretary mother. Her title is Rose.'

And Kwaku recounted his meeting with the Right Hand Man while he was still a boy and how he got to know Miss Rose through him. While emphasizing her husband's reputation as a pan boiler, he said nothing about her poverty at the time or the number of households her husband supported.

'You should tell people,' Correia advised him, 'so they'll know you don't have any other connection with him. They think all sorts of things.'

'Let them!' Kwaku said defiantly. 'I had troubles in my life and that's the least of them.'

'You made a lot of money as a healer?' Correia asked.

'Enough.'

'O.K.!' exclaimed Correia mysteriously, wiping his face and neck. 'You don't sweat?'

'Yes, but not like you.'

Beads of perspiration appeared and died on Correia's forehead. The wind from the mountains had picked up and, unobstructed by the scattered trees, seemed to be driving the vultures round and round in ever widening circles.

They got up from the table and went upstairs to sit on the porch in wicker chairs that stood in a line along the wall.

Soon afterwards the proprietress followed them with a cage which she hung upon a hook screwed into the tentest ceiling, then came back a few minutes later with a parrot perched on her right wrist and a glass half filled with coffee in her left hand. Having installed the bird in the cage, she poured the coffee into a tin can on the floor of the cage and then began haranguing it.

'You frigging glutton! You not getting the banana till you done the coffee!'

On and on she went, wearing the calmest of expressions, so that a deaf onlooker might have believed that she was showering the bird with endearments.

Soon she was gone and the parrot, who must have taken her at her word, set about drinking the coffee furiously, throwing back its head with every gulp.

Correia took Kwaku down to the river and showed him the spot where the Indian boatman would take him across 'while you're watching me.'

As they stood by the brown water of the Takutu river, Correia put the question he had been waiting to ask since their arrival in Lethem.

'It's true the Permanent Secretary helped you to get your flat in exchange for teaching him your secret powers? I don't believe your story about his mother.'

'What secret powers?' Kwaku asked.

'There's talk.'

'Oh yes,' Kwaku replied, suddenly glimpsing possibilities in the rumour. 'Is true and is not true.'

'How d'you mean?'

'I don' use them no more.'

'So they say I help teach the Right Hand Man my secret powers,' Kwaku silently reflected. 'So be it! If I help him I can help others. So that's how the wind is blowing!'

Kwaku felt the old urge returning, the inspiration that brought chaos while he was still a youth, but spawned creative lies as a grown man, causing extraordinary things to happen.

'I want to tell you something,' Correia said, speaking with great seriousness. 'Let me tell you what's in store for you when you get back to Timehri airport. . . . The police will be waiting for you.'

'Me? What did I do?' Kwaku asked, thoroughly alarmed.

'Nothing. But certain people . . . a certain person wants to put you in your place. . . .'

'Miss Rose son?'

'I'm not calling names. You'll be arrested, but nothing's going to happen to you. Just keep cool when it happens.'

'Why you tellin' me this?' Kwaku asked, recalling his dream in which *he* was supposed to be watched by Correia.

'I scratch your back, you scratch mine,' Correia answered.

'What you want?'

'I want you to tell me the secret of healing people.'

'An' what guarantee I got that nothing will happen to me when they arrest me?'

'Right! If you want you can keep your secrets until things turn out the way I say.'

'I see,' muttered Kwaku, thinking all the while of the possibility that he might be outwitted by Correia. 'I got to think over the business.'

He now spoke with an air of importance to remind Correia that he was not dealing with just anybody.

CHAPTER X

Kwaku woke up in the dark, looked up at the window above his bed, but could see nothing for the pitch black night, not even the metal screen over the window, an arm's length away. As he got up to go to the toilet he recalled that the light switch would not work, since the lights in the Guest House had been turned off at eleven o'clock; so he crawled across the room in an effort to reach the door until he collided with a piece of furniture. He ran his hand across the top and discovered Correia's empty bed.

It was Kwaku's first taste of a quality of darkness never experienced before in village or town, and he lay down on the floor, shaken by his complete helplessness and the discovery of Correia's absence.

Morning revealed Correia's unruffled sheets, but before he could get up and look around for his colleague he heard the proprietress's voice. She began with the ritual abuse of her parrot, then catching sight of Kwaku who had just peeped out of the door on the verandah, spoke to him for the first time.

'You looking for him? He gone!'

'Mr Correia?'

'Yes. Your friend gone!'

She burst out laughing at Kwaku's bewildered expression.

'Where?'

'Across the river. People like that, all they think of is money. And they all end up bad, watch what I telling you. Just like this parrot going end up bad, the frigging glutton! Mister, excess is a bad thing. But that's just what some people can't do without. It don' matter what it is. Could be gambling, eating, money, work. . . . Is like a demon in them. After my husband dead I leave town to get away from excess. He use to protect me from it, from the frenzy that does grip people in town. Out here everybody does say howdye-do to everybody; and the Indians does put us all to shame with their quietness.'

'Lady, I'm confused,' Kwaku confessed.

'What you confuse for? You not his keeper. Sit out on the verandah and look at the mountains. What more you need? One time he come with another man from town, a good looking red man.'

'Surinam?'

'Yes, Mr Surinam was his name. He nearly drive Mr Surinam wild. So I say to him, "Sit on the verandah, watch the mountains and calm your soul." And this Surinam take his pencil and start sketching the mountains. The four days he was here he must've done about. . . . I don' know, a hundred drawings. He wasn't confused when he leave for home.'

'I'm not the serene type, lady. I can't stand quietness.'

'Like this one,' she said, nodding towards the caged bird. 'You going suffer, mister. I'm telling you. Me? I done with frenzy. You see this glutton of a parrot? I only keeping him 'cause he did belong to my husband. My advice to you is: when you get back to town keep away from people like your friend.'

'How you know you can trust me, lady, telling me all this?'

'Me? Trust you? Who say I trust you? At my age what I care if I can trust you or not? You can tell him everything I say!'

As soon as the proprietress went away to fetch food for her parrot Kwaku put on a shirt and sat out on the verandah to look at the mountains as she suggested. The chain seemed to stretch across the whole horizon, when in reality the clouds beyond the Western edge maintained the illusion of an unbroken mass.

The proprietress began to speak even before she appeared again on the porch.

'Long ago they use to come from town to interfere with the Indian women. Nowadays it's money they after. Alyou men so unpredictable. Your fathers only had one thing in mind: to soak their wick! With the younger generation is money. Frenzy! Shut your mouth!'

The last words were meant for the parrot who, at the sight of the rotten banana in her hand, began to squawk and leap from its perch to the ribbed wall of its cage.

'I looking at the mountains, lady,' Kwaku said, 'just as you tell me to. But you know something? I don' feel anything.'

'That's 'cause you got frenzy in your soul,' she said emphatically. 'What you expect when you born an' bred in town?'

'I born an' bred in a village, lady, like yowaree. I still learning to be a townsman.'

'If you been brought up in the country there's hope for you. Keep looking at the mountains!'

She went off with the coffee can, which she had taken from the parrot's cage before peeling the banana and placing it in a shallow trough beneath the bird's perch.

Kwaku remained alone on the verandah. He made every effort to maintain his gaze on the far-away mountains, only to hark back to the proprietress's words about his condition: 'That's 'cause you got frenzy in your soul.' All the years that spanned his childhood, through his rise and decline as a man of substance, he had rejected advice. On the face of it the woman's garrulousness contained little that was different from the thousands of words emptied over him by well-meaning or malicious tongues; yet that one sentence kept intruding on his attempts to empty his mind, as though it contained a hidden meaning. For him the frenzy was in the world around him, not in his soul. The wind that blew in the frail door of his Canje house had not been in his soul; nor was his sons' hostility; nor Mr Kumar's violent objection to paying him his fee after he had relieved his infirm son. Yet the words seemed to strike home: 'you got frenzy in your soul!' What had the proprietress to gain from thrusting a knife into him on the pretext that it would do him good? Besides, had he not himself confirmed her diagnosis by saying that he was not the serene type? Mr Barzey never tired of saying that everyone knew the truth about himself and need turn to no one to discover it.

Kwaku, remembering that his breakfast would probably be on the dining table, went back into the bedroom to put on his shoes. The sun was streaming through the mesh-covered window which he had been unable to see in the extraordinary darkness a few hours before.

The tray with his milk, porridge and toast was downstairs on a table under a white serviette. Not having paid for his board, Kwaku was determined to eat every bit of the unpalatable fare he would have rejected in his own home.

As he ate his rage grew at his feeling of helplessness now that Correia was away. The plane tickets and the money were in *his* possession; *he* knew the area, the entertainment places, the police station, the means of travelling over the Brazilian border. Kwaku regretted not having encouraged the proprietress to tell him more; perhaps he should have praised her parrot or cursed it in the wake of her abuse, in the way townsmen ingratiated themselves with unattractive women by praising their offspring. His remedial thoughts always seemed to come to him after the event, like a traveller arriving at a hostel after it was closed for the night. Did she know exactly what Correia's business was and where he went? Kwaku decided to take the bull by the horns. He would come straight out and ask her.

After the meal he went upstairs, washed himself and brushed his teeth, then went down once more, muttering to himself the words he had chosen to gain the proprietress's sympathy. But before he reached the foot of the stairs he saw Correia seated at the dining table eating his breakfast as calmly as if he had come down a minute ago. Kwaku, unable to contain himself, shouted out:

'Who the hell you think you are? You think you're the President? I want my plane ticket before you go out again!'

The proprietress and the cook both came out of the kitchen to witness the altercation.

Kwaku, seeing the proprietress, turned on his heels and went back upstairs, where he sat on the bed to wait for his colleague; and in due course Correia appeared.

'I want my plane ticket!' Kwaku told him, with no attempt to conceal his rage.

'What you getting worked up for?' Correia asked calmly.

'I don' know what your game is,' said Kwaku, 'but from now on I staying with you.'

Correia lifted up the mattress of his bed and took out from under it Kwaku's plane ticket.

'Take it. You can stay with me all the time if it makes you happy.'

He then took off his shirt and lay down on his side with his back to the enraged Kwaku who, at a loss to know how to tackle his colleague, could only stand in the middle of the room and look down at him. Then, taking a sudden resolution, he put away the ticket in the chest of drawers and went down to see the proprietress.

'You got a few minutes to spare, mistress?'

He found her in the kitchen beside the cook, who was sitting on a stool plucking a chicken whose feathers, strewn on the floor in front of her, brought to mind the sense of disorder in a busy barber-shop.

'What about? You see I busy!'

'Only a few minutes, mistress.'

She signalled him to follow her and, once in her room opposite the kitchen, she closed the door and offered him a chair.

'Mistress, I got a problem,' Kwaku began. 'I'm confused. You did begin to tell me about Mr Correia and I interrupt you, out o' bad manners. My trouble is I don't have breeding. But don' get me wrong, I got a good heart. Ask my wife an' my children.'

'You bring them with you?'

'No, mistress.'

If anyone was born not to come straight to the point it was Kwaku. But although these circumlocutions cost him dear he was determined to do what he deemed necessary to sweeten the proprietress. He kept thinking of the way she treated her parrot and had the peculiar feeling that, given a chance, she would put him into a cage, nourish him on coffee and bananas and treat him to a round of abuse at least once a day.

'What I really want to say, mistress, is, I have great respect for you and the way you can spot wickedness in people.'

'I can spot it a mile away, Mr. . .'

'Chol-mon-de-ley. Pronounce it Chumley.'

'Mr Cholmondeley, I can spot wickedness a mile away in men and women. Nowadays there in' got all that much difference between them. Look how many women does wear trousers. An' in some countries a lot of the men does wear dresses!'

'I believe you, lady. After the first conversation with you I say to myself, "there's a expert in foreign affairs. And she living so far from town!" Well, is something you born with. I know people who does read their newspaper back to front and remain ignorant, like your parrot. . . .'

'Ignorant! My parrot ignorant? I beg your pardon! That bird's got a vocabulary, Mr. . .'

'Chol-mon-de-ley. Pronounced Chumley. . . Anyway, mistress, I'm on a secret mission on behalf of the President himself. . .'

'The President?' the proprietress asked, opening her eyes wide.

'Sh! You sure nobody listening at the door?'

She got up, opened the door and closed it again.

'No. The cook in the kitchen. Is only we two.'

'I telling you 'cause of my respect for your discretion, mistress. But this delicate mission they entrust me with 'cause I look like a country man, an' so they can throw people off the scent. You understand?'

She nodded and drew closer to Kwaku.

'If they did send somebody distinguish-lookin',' Kwaku continued, 'everybody would've say, "Watch that distinguish-looking gentleman. He's not up to any good." So they choose me. You understand?'

The proprietress nodded and drew her chair even closer to Kwaku's, so that he could feel her breath on his face.

'Well, I want you to tell me what you know about Mr Correia, where he does go and so on an' so forth. He was out all last night.'

'I know. He come straight to the kitchen and demand his breakfast. Demand! Do *you* treat a lady like that Mr Cholmondeley?'

'Most certainly not!'

'It's the first time he ever behave like that. . . . Anyway there's no great mystery about him. They got many like him coming in on the Friday plane and going away on Tuesday. They're smugglers, currency dealers, crooks, all o' them. He take you down to the river yet?'

'Yes.'

'You go over?'

'Yes.'

'Was there a wharf on the other side?'

'No.'

'Well, Mr Cholmondeley, you cross by the unofficial ferry, the one people smuggling goods does take, and the currency dealers. Last night Mr Correia been over to Brazil and stay with a man who got property over here and over there. He does deal in diamonds and gold he buy over here from porknockers who don' want to sell to licenced dealers. But Mr Correia got more to hide than currency dealings. He's a bigamist.'

'A what?' asked Kwaku.

'He got two wives.'

'Mr Correia?'

'Mr Correia.'

'Two?'

'Could be three, for all I know.'

'No!'

'I telling you, Mr Cholmondeley.'

An involuntary smile took the place of Kwaku's usually severe expression.

'So so!' he thought. 'An' to think I was frightened of him.'

'You not listening,' the proprietress said.

'Yes, mistress. I listening.'

'You mean people don't know in town?'

'Well *I* din' know.'

'As I say yesterday, you can tell him I tell you. I not afraid of him. I not frightened of anybody, living or dead. When my husband was dying he threaten to come back and *visit* me. "I goin' visit you," he say. This time he was taking his last gasp. "I goin' visit you!" And then he did so! And dead.'

She gave a violent twitch of her head and closed her eyes in a vivid reconstruction of her husband's demise.

'I won't say he was a wicked man, but he wasn't a good man neither. He do so! And dead! And you know, his eyes close themselves. Some women got to close they husband's eyes. But my Ulric eyes go down of their own accord. And since that day the parrot attitude change. He wasn't a glutton before my husband dead; he was a moderate bird in everything he say and do. I'm sure, Mr Cholmondeley, that my husband spirit take over his parrot. I used to treat him so good! "Lora!" I use to say when I feed him in the morning. "Lora, you're a parrot and a half and a piece 'pon top. You so nice! A real gentleman in your green suit and all, prettier than any macaw.". . . You think I can talk to him like that now? . . .'

Kwaku listened to the proprietress patiently, out of gratitude for the invaluable information she had given him.

She told him of her life in town, of the Rupununi, where no one passed another on the road without a 'good morning' or 'good afternoon'; of her passion for dancing when she was courting; about her father's intense jealousy of her mother, a jealousy which extended to her women friends. Her disclosures went back in time, through her youth and back to her early childhood, when she and her sister, a year apart in age, shared a large pram in which they sat opposite each other. Both of them would fight for the seat facing their mother, so that they could feast their eyes on her.

Kwaku waited until he thought he could take his leave without offending her, but the deluge would not come to an end; so that finally he had to interrupt her, alleging urgent business. In fact, he was anxious to get dressed in case Correia took it into his head to leave the Guest House before lunch without being seen.

He found him sprawled on the bed, fast asleep. Bending over him to make certain he was not pretending, he smelt the liquor on his breath, and there and then decided to take a walk by himself, assured that his colleague would not slip away before he got back.

CHAPTER XI

Kwaku gave up the idea of staying with Correia, who managed to get away from him with the greatest ease, even during the day when the road leading to the Guest House was visible as far as the airport building. There were other ways, paths through the trees going down to the river, where aboriginal Indian soldiers of the Defence Force started fires every morning and stood on the blackened ground to the leeward of the drifting smoke.

Once Kwaku attempted to follow Correia through the trees, only to come upon him, his arms folded, in deep conversation with the soldiers' creole lieutenant, who wore a pistol at his waist. Abashed at his mistake Kwaku stood around, pretending to take an interest in the steep descent on which the trees grew. But the currency dealer ignored him so pointedly he went back to the Guest House and never attempted to follow him again.

Kwaku was in no doubt that Correia had set out to punish him for the intemperate language he had used within earshot of the proprietress and the cook the morning after his all-night absence. Left to his own devices he came to rely on the proprietress for conversation; and the obsessional evocations of her late husband which he found so irritating in their early acquaintanceship came to provide the only interest to which he could look forward in an intolerably long day.

One evening a few days before the morning they were to fly back to Georgetown, Correia joined him on the verandah. He appeared preoccupied, even distressed, and Kwaku had the impression that he had got into some sort of trouble.

'What you think of marriage?' he asked at length.

'Depend on the people who married,' Kwaku answered without thinking.

'Marriage without children is a funny thing, though.'

'Is not funny. Is just marriage without children.'

'I wanted to introduce you to somebody,' Correia said, 'a woman, an extraordinary woman . . . but she won't talk to you now. Anyway, I want you to meet her.'

Kwaku jumped at the offer, willing to do anything to get away from the Guest House and the proprietress, and the cloud-veiled mountains where, it seemed, the winds were born.

If, on leaving the Guest House, you take the main road to the airport building, then branch off on to the path on the right, you will arrive eventually at a rickety bridge over a shallow stream. On the other side, following the path, which turns abruptly back in the direction from which you came, it will take you, after some fifteen or twenty minutes walk, to an Indian village set among a grove of cashew trees. Many coastal people who come to Lethem will tell you that they would never again venture so far down that way; yet, pressed to explain their aversion, they can say no more than that, having done so once, they were overcome by an unsettling sensation that forced them to retrace their steps.

The houses among the trees, no more than a dozen or so, resemble something half-way between a coastal village and an old Indian settlement. The buildings, while adorned with windows — as on the coast — are low and thatched with leaves of the Ité palm, which grows on the very edges of streams running through the parched grasslands of the Rupununi savannahs.

That evening, long after the employees of the supermarket opposite the Guest House and the nearby Government office left for home on bicycle or foot, Correia and Kwaku turned off onto the self-same path, crossed the bridge and made their way towards the village.

Correia had hedged his invitation with cautionary remarks which Kwaku, determined to avoid being made a fool of, ignored. The sun had already set, but the two men were guided by a sprinkling of lights burning in the village.

Correia knocked on the window of one of the first houses in the settlement and the young woman who opened it allowed them to enter before closing it quietly.

A small kerosene lamp barely illuminated the large room, which was surprisingly well furnished with low, crabwood easy chairs.

'This is a friend. His name is Mr Cholmondeley,' Correia said, introducing Kwaku who held out his hand.

He was welcomed by the woman with one of the weakest hands he had ever shaken. Besides, she seemed determined to avoid his eyes.

'Sit down,' Correia told him.

He took his place in a chair near the door.

Kwaku's suspicion that the woman was the second wife of whom the proprietress had spoken was confirmed when she went to the door leading into an adjoining room and said something in another language. Three children filed out one after the other and approached Correia, who patted the boy on the head and lifted up each of the two girls in turn.

'Mine, you know,' he said, turning towards Kwaku while still holding the young girl in his arms. 'I'm proud of them. . . . Go back to bed now.'

The three children dutifully went back into the room, leaving Correia and their mother standing with Kwaku.

'Well,' Correia said, rubbing his hands, 'now you've met the family, what you're going to do. . . ? Go back to the Guest House? I'm only joking. You couldn't find your way out of here in any case. Not in the dark. And besides, it'd be dangerous. . . . Well, you said you had to stick with me, didn't you? You're stuck with me, so you'd better make yourself at home.'

Kwaku could not keep his eyes off Correia's wife, who appeared to be still in her teens and, despite her three children, had an extraordinarily youthful figure.

'Excuse us for a bit,' Correia said, 'she's going to cook for us.'

Kwaku was left alone, surrounded by a silence almost as remarkable as the darkness of the previous night.

Correia had moved his family from their home in Bom Fin across the river only the day before, his wife having complained that more than once at night she had seen the dreaded Kenaima standing beside a tree in the yard, his feet turned inwards and his eyes as red as burning coals. Although Correia did not share the aboriginal Indians' belief in this spirit of Nemesis, he knew that she would succumb to her terror if he left her there. He himself had been threatened by an old Arecuna Indian related to the young woman when she was expecting her first child. If he did not marry Sidonie he would never be able to come back to Bom Fin. His marriage under duress constituted a sufficient defence to a charge of bigamy, a lawyer in town told him later; and with that assurance he came on the Permanent Secretary's business without any undue anxiety. Four or five times a year he came and spent as many hours in Bom Fin as possible, noticing how his children had grown, understanding little of the culture into which he had married and tolerating the sight of numerous strangers in the rented house, all clan relations according to Sidonie, who pretended to have no English or Portuguese, and invariably fixed him with a blank stare he found impossible to interpret.

Now that his little family were installed in Lethem he was terrified of possible reprisals from her relations and had conceived a plan which, to be successful, would need Kwaku's help.

Correia came back alone and sat down in another chair without a word. Kwaku could see that he was struggling with some problem that had arisen since he went into the adjoining room with Sidonie.

'You got a nice place here,' Kwaku said.

'What?'

'You got a nice place here.'

'What the proprietress told you?'

The unexpected question left Kwaku without an answer.

'Very well,' Correia said, now certain that the proprietress had informed Kwaku of his activities.

Then, after a long silence, he said, 'I've got enough problems to worry about what she said. That's part of her job, listening to gossip. Hotel keepers, they're born to spread gossip.'

'She din' say anything bad. Only that you were attached.'

'Attached!' he said, accompanying the word with a gesture of disdain, before falling silent again.

'Listen!' Correia exclaimed, suddenly coming to life. 'There's no law among these people.'

'Who?'

'The Indians. They don't care a damn for our law. Something's not right here. Sidonie thinks something's going to happen tonight and says I shouldn't have come. But how could I keep away from my children? Oh God! These bucks! They don't say much, but when they have it in for you, it's like a death sentence. I know they can't bear the thought of my bringing Sidonie across the river, away from them. . . . You wanted to keep an eye on me. Well you are, aren't you, for the good it's going to do you.'

He laughed, then, standing abruptly, invited Kwaku to come over to the window.

'Look out there. There!'

'It's dark. I don' see anything,' Kwaku insisted.

'Wait.'

He fetched Sidonie from her cooking and shoved her over to the window. She looked out and, without hesitating, declared in a whisper, 'They still there. As long as more than one person in the house they not goin' do anything.'

Kwaku could see only the impenetrable blackness, which had engulfed even the large cashew trees.

Sidonie went back into the kitchen without betraying any sign of anxiety.

'I can't take her to town,' Correia said. 'My wife wouldn't stand for it.'

Kwaku called to mind Amy Correia, who he believed was afraid of the Right Hand Man. That was in the beginning. Her toughness, all too apparent to those who knew her at work, and her reputation for efficiency seemed at variance with a domestic life, especially marriage to a Shango-like character like Correia.

'She can hear you,' Kwaku warned, nodding towards the kitchen.

'If you whisper it would be worse,' Correia snapped. 'In any case they know everything. We'll spend the night here, just in case. But if they intend to snuff you out, you can walk with a hundred people — you won't escape.'

Sidonie brought out two calabashes almost filled to the brim with boiled cassava, pepperpot sauce and meat.

The couple watched Kwaku lift out a portion of cassava and place it into his mouth. Kwaku, who had taken to heart Correia's warning of the Indians' hostility, felt ill at ease.

'Eat up, man. It's not Sidonie who's going to bury you,' Correia urged him.

Kwaku shuddered at the word 'bury', forbidden in his country circles. No sound came from outside, as if the house had been hermetically sealed and they were floating in space. Suddenly he felt he could eat no more, his awareness of the darkness surrounding the house and someone hiding in the yard proving too much for him.

Sidonie remained standing, but kept staring at him with the same assiduousness she had brought to avoiding his eyes at the time of his arrival.

'You go in the bedroom with the children,' Correia advised her.

Once they were alone Correia came to the real point of Kwaku's visit.

'I want you to do something for me. When you get back to Georgetown tell the Permanent Secretary I fell sick. The water at the Guest House made me sick. I'll give you an envelope with money for him.'

'You staying here?' Kwaku asked him.

'Yes.'

'What you goin' to live on?'

'I'll manage.'

During his last visit Correia had left a great deal of money with Sidonie, half of which she had spirited away in a hiding place beside her former home. The rest was secreted in bamboo ornaments around the children's necks. For years Correia had lived in the shadow of his criminal past and anticipated that one day he would be called to account, so that his decision to remain in the Rupununi was inspired as much by the need to protect Sidonie and his children as by a resolve to implement an old plan.

'I've done a lot of bad things in my life,' he told Kwaku.

Kwaku recalled the proprietress's talk about frenzy and her criticism of Correia's temperament, which he had dismissed as mere words. Now it was odd listening to him confirming a stranger's view of himself. Could she have been right about his currency dealings as well and the scale of gold and diamond smuggling into Brazil? How much more went on in the country that was hidden from the population at large?

'You believe she saw somebody in the yard?' Kwaku asked for no particular reason.

'Believe? I *saw* him! Tch. . . ! This part of the Rupununi is Macusi country, and the Macusi don't like going out in the dark. She thinks it's her Arecuna relations.'

Correia was glad of Kwaku's company and wished that he had not treated him so badly in the past.

'You got me vexed when you shouted at me in front of the proprietress,' Correia said. 'In front of that parrot-mamma who doesn't even know how to write out a simple receipt. She's supposed to boil the water for the guests and she can't even be bothered to do it. You've got no idea how many people got diarrhoea from drinking her water. The last proprietress, a Mrs D'Aguiar, was respected by everybody. But this carrion crow! My God! How some people get on in this world. . . ! I did some bad things in my life, I can tell you. It's not that I feel guilty about doing them, only that I didn't have any reason to do them.'

Sidonie came out again and announced in her undertone that the children were asleep. She remained standing, apparently attentive to what the men were saying; and to Kwaku's embarrassment she continued staring at him as she had done before. Every time he looked up he was faced with her blank yet penetrating look, as though he were an acquaintance from the past.

Correia continued his disclosure of the proprietress's shortcomings in an effort to hide his anxiety about the strangers lurking outside the house. While he believed Sidonie's opinion that they were safe from any intrusion so long as they remained together, he found the suspense almost unbearable. Since his visits to the region began eight years ago he had done his best to emulate the Indians' undemonstrative behaviour in the presence of sickness and danger, but without success.

'On Sundays,' Correia went on, 'the proprietress puts on a hat and a dress of thick cloth to go to church. In this heat! You must have seen her yourself, with her parasol, walking the short distance to the church like a rancher's wife.'

Speaking more excitedly than ever Correia continued: 'There are people in this world you can trust. Oh yes! Surinam is one of them. You treat him right and you'll make a friend for life. I never did a thing for him, but when the time came he stood by me. If I'd listened to him I wouldn't have come to this.'

As he spoke Kwaku suspected that behind every disclosure of Correia's lurked an equally important fact he preferred to keep to himself. He had no doubt that the money-changer did not trust him entirely.

'But watch the Right Hand Man! When the time comes he would look straight through you and pretend he never saw you in his life. *When the time comes.*'

Correia remained sunk in thought for a while and then, without a word, began pacing up and down the room, stealing glances from time to time at the window.

'You're afraid to die?' he asked Kwaku, stopping to see the effect his question had on him.

'I never think of it,' Kwaku answered. 'And you?'

'I tremble at the thought.'

Then, as unexpected as a thunder clap from a clear sky, there were two soft raps in quick succession on the window pane. Sidonie crouched down on the floor, while the two men remained where they were, petrified.

She placed a finger in front of her mouth, urging them to say nothing, whereupon they both followed her example and lay on the floor, not understanding what advantage was to be gained by doing so. After several minutes of agonizing silence the rapping was repeated. Then Kwaku, following the impulse of a sudden resolution, got up, stepped over to the door and went out into the night. The brief silence that followed was abruptly broken by a scurrying of feet and a few urgent words in Arecuna.

Kwaku appeared in the doorway and could only think of recovering his composure, having no idea why he did what he had done, which did not rhyme with his fear of the dark. Perhaps Sidonie's unrelenting gaze had suggested that she expected him to do something to relieve the tension. Now he only felt relief at his inexplicable demonstration of courage.

'They gone,' he said. 'Was more than two.'

'Was five,' said Sidonie.

'How d'you know?' Correia asked.

'Was five,' she repeated. 'They not goin' come back.'

And the two men looked at each other in astonishment, incapable of grasping what they had gone through.

In the two free days remaining before he was required to return to Georgetown, Kwaku spent much of his time with Correia in the thatched house beyond the bridge. His antipathy turned to admiration for him when he saw how he adapted so readily to Rupununi life and how seriously he took his children's upbringing. He saw them across the river every morning to attend a Brazilian school, because of complaints that the local school in Lethem was badly understaffed.

Correia imparted to Kwaku much of his knowledge concerning the goings-on behind the scenes in the Ministry of Hope, the potential scandals suppressed, the protection of party members' mistresses, some of them humble typists who took full advantage of their high-up associations to come and go as they pleased. The atmosphere created by the dominance of a single political party caused blackmailers and informers to thrive and made cripples of honourable men, who were not above selling a compliant mistress's services to earn promotion in an underpaid administration.

In a supreme act of vengeance on the man who had given him financial security, Correia told Kwaku of the Right Hand Man's chamber-pot business, which was flourishing beyond all expectations.

'I know about the pots,' Kwaku said. 'I find out a long time ago. He give me more than he get from me. Tobesides, I know his mother good. That's why I keep my mouth shut.'

Kwaku made certain of getting back to the Guest House before nightfall, unable to suppress the association of darkness and violence since his act of heroism, as Correia would have it.

The following afternoon Correia came to bid him goodbye and reported that the same five Arecuna men who lurked under the cashew trees came visiting that morning with their wives and children and admitted freely their responsibility. And Kwaku could not understand for the life of him why neither Sidonie nor Correia protested at the outrage.

He could not live in the bush as Correia had decided to do, in the midst of spirits of Nemesis and surrounded by people whose behaviour was so unpredictable.

Correia's children, fluent in English, Portuguese and Arecuna, were allowed a degree of freedom unheard of among 'decent' coastal children and often went to the river to swim naked and congregate on the midstream sandbanks with their Brazilian friends.

'I'll never understand these people,' Kwaku confessed to Correia.

That night there was a deluge, and the proprietress of the Guest House called upon him to help her move furniture from the verandah into the bedrooms. But the rain stopped as suddenly as it had begun, leaving a garlic-sweet scent on the air and a pall of vapour hanging over the laterite earth and the indestructible termite nests, and a covering of cloud as the harbinger of a long, wet season that would bring great fish from the Rio Branco and cause dried up river beds to heave with red water. Then the sand banks would go under, and boats appear bearing markings of ports on the Amazon and other far-away places.

The proprietress expressed alarm that the money-changer intended to settle permanently in the Rupununi and imagined all sorts of disasters befalling Lethem. Unusual portents spoke for themselves, a plague of bats and a deluge in a single evening. Kwaku, in the certainty that he would be far away, swore that all would be well and pointed to the proximity of church and police station as guarantors of her well-being.

'Mistress,' Kwaku said, 'I dream you las' night.'

'What you dream?'

'I don' remember, mistress.'

Kwaku *did* remember what he dreamt, but had no wish to recount his fantasies to a stranger. In fact he did not dream about the proprietress at all, but said what he had because he was at a loss for words.

He dreamt that he was in a large stubble field, the grass of which had been recently burnt. Smoke was rising from blackened clumps dotted about the landscape, and the carrion crows that usually made widening circles in the morning sky were all perched on the Guest House roof, looking down at him. Far from being uneasy he wondered what in his actions could have attracted their attention. Suddenly, in the distance, a galloping horse appeared with a youth on its back, naked except for a dun-coloured bucktah which matched the colour of his skin. Then, on approaching the Guest House, the rider turned his mount sharply, only to disappear up the hospital road ahead of a cloud of dust that took an unusually long time to settle.

'You coming back to the Rupununi?' the proprietress asked him.

'I don' know. . . . I think I'm on the threshold, mistress.'

'What threshold?'

'Of something. I don' have words to explain.'

'You don' have looks either, Mr Cholmondeley. You're not endowed.'

'I *am* endowed, mistress,' Kwaku said emphatically. 'Is that I don' know how to use my gifts.'

'Ah . . . if I was young again,' she said, 'I would marry a man, not with looks, but with gifts and beautiful hands, a man that does smell good.'

And so their conversation went, with neither saying anything of substance. To long-staying clients the proprietress had a great deal to tell, having so much time on her hands and so few guests to cater for. Kwaku was a bird of passage, not worthy of cultivating. But for Kwaku, she was the most loquacious person he had ever met.

Kwaku boarded the box-shaped plane and was soon looking down on the Rupununi river, which divided the land like the legendary water serpent that sucks all the minor rivers dry. Abandoning himself to his reflections he called to mind the proprietress, her parrot husband and Sidonie, whose character he never managed to make out. He clutched the envelope with which Correia had entrusted him and felt uneasy at the thought of moving from one landscape to the other, from one way of life to another. He had learned one thing in his stay; that behind a placid mask could lurk terrors of unimagined ferocity.

CHAPTER XII

At Timehri airport Kwaku was taken aside by a Customs officer and his bag was searched, just as Correia had predicted. He remained calm, even when he was shown a packet containing marijuana which, according to the Customs man, had been found among his things. However, he protested vigorously on being ordered to strip, declaring that the Permanent Secretary could vouch for him.

In the end he had his way and was taken into another, smaller room with a camp bed, where, he was told, he would have to remain all night if no one could contact the Permanent Secretary by telephone.

But the Right Hand Man arrived within the hour. He had been waiting by the telephone for the call, having already informed Mrs Correia that he was going to the airport and would be away for a couple of hours.

Duly released on his instructions, Kwaku accompanied him to his car.

'You mean Correia left you alone at the Customs?'

'No sir. He say he's coming later, with the next plane,' Kwaku lied.

'Why?'

Kwaku gave him the envelope but said nothing in answer to his question.

'Why? I asked.'

'He sick, sir. The water get to him.'

'He's in a bad way?'

'It look so, sir.'

'And I can only contact the damn place by radio!' he complained.

He drove on in silence, and soon the landscape of white sand changed to lush coastal vegetation, wild eddoe and silk-cotton trees marking the boundary between villages.

'What were you doing with marijuana in your things?' the Right Hand Man asked, disappointed that Kwaku had not thanked him for saving his skin.

It was all Kwaku could do to contain his anger. The thought of Sidonie, unmoved while her family were under threat, came back to him and acted like a balm.

'The marijuana was planted, sir.'

The Right Hand Man took his eye off the road momentarily to look at him.

'Anybody can say so.'

'I don' deal in drugs, sir.'

'But why should the Customs people plant drugs on you especially?' he asked, as calmly as any sincere enquiry, so that Kwaku was moved to look at him in turn and marvel at the duplicity of people in high places.

'I can't answer that, sir. I only know that I didn' leave Lethem with drugs.'

'Anyway, it was a stroke of luck I was in the office. These Customs officers are very serious. In fact you're lucky it wasn't a woman. She wouldn't have released you on my say-so alone.'

The Right Hand Man went back to questioning Kwaku about Correia. And Kwaku could not judge whether he was more put out by the money-changer's absence than by his own indifference to what had befallen him at the airport.

'Thanks for saving me at the airport, sir,' Kwaku said out of the blue.

'I can't do that every time though. Remember that.'

'Yes, sir.'

He dropped Kwaku off in front of his North Road flat, then sped away without a word.

Kwaku stood on the bridge and surveyed his upstairs lodging, with its grilled windows and long staircase which wound back to end in a small porch. The glass door of the verandah was closed, as were the windows, giving the impression that the flat was unoccupied.

'Philomena din' come, I'm sure,' he muttered to himself. 'I wonder how she make out.'

Although far from tired, Kwaku mounted the stairs slowly, and arriving at window height called through a shutter.

'Miss Gwendoline?'

Then, just as he was about to call out once more he heard her stumbling about amongst the furniture.

'Is me, blind woman. Is me come back. You not glad?'

She opened the door for him and pretended not to be touched by his embrace.

'I tired from doing nothing,' Kwaku said, sitting down heavily on a chair by a casement window, which he opened wide.

'Let me look at you,' she said, unable to shed a redundant vocabulary. She ran her hands over his face and smiled.

'You in' changed. Is the same ugly man I married.'

She accompanied her remark with an outburst of laughter, which assuaged Kwaku's guilt about leaving her alone for so many days.

'You right to sit down,' she told him. 'We got a visitor.'

'Who? I din' see anybody.'

'Your beloved daughter come and bring a young man. He's a acute puncturist.'

'You mean acupuncturist,' Kwaku corrected her.

'Yes. He does go around boring holes in people. He's a fraud. I can feel it a mile off.'

'Is where he is?'

'They gone out.'

Philomena had arrived with her young man the very afternoon of the day that Kwaku left for the Rupununi. Had Miss Gwendoline been able to see she would probably have asked him his age in her blunt manner. But all she could go by in sizing him up were his unusually soft hand and his voice, which gave her no idea of his age. In fact he was in his thirties, and had managed to flatter the twenty-three year old Philomena with his attentions. He came back to Guyana from Canada, where he had followed a three-month course in acupuncture. That was two years ago, since when he had acquired an extensive clientele, he told her. Miss Gwendoline's question regarding the number of people he had cured elicited such a vague reply that she leapt at the conclusion that he was a fraud, and might even bear some responsibility for the recent outbreak of cholera.

'He and Philomena jus' gone out shopping,' Miss Gwendoline said.

'You didn' even ask how I get on in the Rupununi,' Kwaku said reproachfully.

'Well, how you get on?'

He recounted his adventures in detail, ending with Correia's defection.

'What going happen to him?'

'Either the Arecuna going get him or the Permanent Secretary.'

'Eh, eh! A letter come for you. It on the table.'

Kwaku found the letter on the dining table and on opening it saw Miss Rose's signature at the foot of the page.

Dear Mr Chumley,

I hope this finds you as it leaves me by the grace of God. As you see I am not dead yet so you can come visiting when you are in these parts. I hear you doing good and got your own flat through that worthless son of mine. I write a other letter telling him if he did not fix you up I would not take a red cent from him no more even if he bend down on his knees and beg me to accept it. You know me. I do not mince my words. Well Mr Chumley I more contented than ever although I don't got nobody to quarrel with. A lady nex door got a television set and me and the naybours does go and look at it most nights. Sometimes more than twenty women in her small drawing room watching the set. We do walk with our own chairs because she do not got enough to go round. She glad because we does all take a piece of something to eat so she end up with a lot of food.

Well I must leave you in Jesus name. Keep your wick out of the ladies oil and all will be well.

Yours truly
Miss Rose

'Is from who?' Miss Gwendoline demanded. 'Why you so quiet?'

'Is from a old patient who want me to go up the coast an' cure his great aunt. She got dropsy.'

'You never treat dropsy before.'

Kwaku was embarrassed to receive such a pleasant letter from Miss Rose at a time when he was planning war against her son for stealing his chamber-pot idea and ensnaring him with the Customs. Kwaku despised him, more especially because he had always showed him the greatest deference. He decided that nothing would stop him now from opposing her son. A thousand letters of the kind from Miss Rose would not make him change his mind. If *she* could not mince her words, he was worse.

Kwaku did not tell his wife about the Right Hand Man's appropriation of his commercial plans, simply because he had praised him to the skies up to then, even after Miss Gwendoline voiced her doubts about his unusual obligingness. She was more accustomed to Kwaku's disastrous effect on people, even men and women of proven goodwill, who would threaten to stone and even maim him.

He reflected on the number of secrets he kept from his wife, in spite of the overall harmony in their relations, and on his contrasting weakness for opening his heart to perfect strangers.

'I got a feeling this acute puncturist want to come and live here in this house.'

'He can always ask,' Kwaku told her. 'That don' mean he'll get.'

'An' then Philomena going start to sulk and work me up for nothing and I going wish I was back with the voices I grow up with.'

They talked until they heard conversation at the foot of the stairs, when Kwaku looked out and saw his daughter in the company of a tall man wearing the expensive clothes of a tourist and bending over her like someone who had managed to get what he wanted and felt he could relax because the fruit was there for the plucking. Even before he met him Kwaku agreed with his wife that Philomena's man friend looked like a crook.

Philomena, strangely subdued, introduced him to Kwaku, who had learned a modicum of good manners since coming to town.

'Do take a seat,' he said, showing the visitor to the deep Berbice reclining chair from which you needed help to extricate yourself.

'Do have a cup of tea.'

'We don't have tea, pa,' Philomena corrected him with a touch of desperation in her voice.

'Do tell me where you come from,' Kwaku pursued relentlessly.

'From Guyana. But I lived in Canada for several years.'

'Do tell me more.'

But before he could answer Miss Gwendoline broke in.

'He's a acute puncturist.'

Philomena, on the point of expiring from shame, could only bite her lip while hoping that her parents would stop tormenting Heliga.

'Excuse my wife,' Kwaku said, 'she's not been in town long. I know you're a acupuncturist.'

'That I am,' said the visitor. 'I'm back in Guyana in a professional capacity.'

'Do tell me how many punctures you've made since your return to Guyana,' Kwaku asked, determined to show the young man that his was not a house of ignorant people.

And Kwaku, in his own way, tried to make the visitor feel at home, in spite of his antipathy towards anyone who courted his beloved Philomena.

After a succession of unsuitable liaisons she was ready to do anything to please Heliga — the first professional gentleman of her acquaintance — and now she could only look on helplessly as her parents appeared to spoil her chances with the acupuncturist. Her disapproval did not escape Kwaku who, overcome by a fit of maliciousness, said, 'You feed the baby, daughter?'

Philomena informed him brutally that Heliga knew she had a child.

'And for your information,' she said, 'I left the child in Canje.'

Apart from Kwaku's suspicion of any male friend of Phil-omena's, he only had to set eyes on a well-dressed man with a self-assured manner to become convinced that he had attired himself with the sole purpose of annoying him; that he had gone into the cloth store and bought the material with him, Kwaku, in mind, then taken it to the tailor, thinking of nothing or no one but him. And that once his shirt-jac or suit was made, he would seek him out specially in the street and strut about in his vicinity, only to annoy him and provoke his envy.

'Pa, I'm talking to you,' Philomena said. 'Heliga wants to treat you to a meal.'

'I only jus' come back from the bush,' Kwaku replied, delighted at the invitation, but worried that Miss Gwendoline would not approve of him eating out with a stranger when he had not yet given her the satisfaction of his company.

'Go, ne,' Miss Gwendoline said. 'Go out and have a good time.'

Kwaku, the one-time healer and Heliga, the Acupuncturist went off together, chalk and cheese, the simple and the flamboyant. Kwaku's opinion of Philomena's friend, altered by the unexpected invitation, was as flattering as it had been deprecating only a few minutes before; and if Heliga now asked for his daughter's hand in marriage he would not hesitate to say yes.

He wanted to confess to the young man that kindness never failed to throw him into confusion, to tell him everything that was passing through his mind, however inappropriate to the occasion. He wanted to recount his experiences at Lethem and the story of Correia, who left a devoted wife and a successful career to attach himself to a wild buck woman with relations who see marriage as an association of groups and abhor any expression of individuality. If God divided the land into countries the Arecunas never heard of such a thing, being at home in both Brazil and Guyana. Murder was their business and the subservience of woman. Could he live among people who laid their loved ones in a hammock tied to a tree when they think that Kenaima was stalking them? And that when dawn came they went outside, fully expecting to find their necks broken? He dreaded any further demonstration of kindness or generosity from Heliga, lest he began prancing about and making a fool of himself. Could he not see that he had never grown up and considered adulthood as a burden, and had never understood how his sons and daughters had slid into the new state with the greatest ease?

Heliga took Kwaku to a Robb Street restaurant with labba on the menu, ringed napkins on the table and meals that cost twenty U.S. dollars a person.

'I have serious intentions towards your daughter,' Heliga said, once they had ordered.

Kwaku stared at him, pretending he did not understand.

'I'm serious about Philomena, sir.'

'Don't call me sir, please,' Kwaku objected. 'Nobody ever call me sir.'

Confused by Kwaku's manner — he had no idea that his guest was nearly faint with embarrassment — Heliga decided to put off talk of his intentions until later. Philomena's beauty had not prepared him for Kwaku's unprepossessing, even coarse, appearance. Yet, on closer examination, the resemblance between father and daughter was undeniable. He sought to make his mark with Philomena before she settled in Georgetown and began attracting the attention of young men; and since she was lodging with her parents it seemed to him of the utmost importance that he should get on their right side. As it turned out, however, Miss Gwendoline did not trust him, so he was determined to make a good impression on Kwaku at all costs.

'How you and Philomena meet?' Kwaku asked. 'I have a right to know.'

Heliga recounted their unremarkable meeting in a Water Street store.

'I did see my wife for the first time,' Kwaku said, 'when my uncle bring her home with a view to marriage.'

'My intentions are serious, you know,' Heliga declared, believing that the moment had come to bring the matter up once more.

'You mean you don' mind that she got child?'

'No.'

'And that you hardly know her?'

'Can I remind you, sir, that you didn't know your intended either. You just told me so.'

'I never thought of that!' Kwaku exclaimed so loudly he attracted the attention of nearby diners. 'Well, look at that. . . . And you know, I wasn' keen. But my uncle did give me a ultimatum. Married or else! And I couldn' wish for a better wife than Miss Gwendoline. The children worship the ground she walk on. All except the daughter you got your eyes on. Is a big mystery to me. And look how Providence arrange things, eh? She's the one who does keep coming back all the time as if she lose something.'

'I'm in love with Philomena, sir.'

'I don' know that it's the best way to begin a married life. Love is a word for what does nestle between a woman legs.'

'Sir! Do you think I . . . ?'

'Yes, I do!'

'I can only say you misjudged me.'

'Yes . . . well. How you stand with your mother? The two of you does get on?'

'My mother's dead, sir. But we always used to get on well,' the young man said with feeling.

'I see. Then what objection can I have?'

'What about my father? Don't you want to know how we got on?'

'I don' know. Fathers, sons, who can tell? You ever hear say that a father got a certain instinct . . . to kill a boy child in the cradle?'

Heliga looked at him, scandalized.

'You never hear that?' Kwaku continued. 'I din' make that up, young man. I din' feel like that when the twins born, I mus' say. I suppose it was 'cause my first child was a girl, Philomena's sister. But it make you think, though. It make you think.'

'I get on well with my father, sir.'

'I tell you not to call me sir. So you get on well with your father? Well, look at that. With mother and father. Well, that don' make you God's gift to women, but is a start. Look at that!'

'I thought in the beginning you didn't like me.'

Kwaku did not react to the remark, but reflected that he and the young man had hit it off, and that the moment it happened had escaped him. He could say truly that Heliga was a decent young man, so far as one could judge such things in less than a lifetime.

'I don' dislike you, young man. Is just that life is so complicated. Everything important does happen in the dark, yet we go judging. . . . All I know is I don' want to lose my Philomena.'

'That brings me to another thing, sir.'

'What's that?'

'I was wondering if I could move into your empty bedroom. I'd pay rent. I'd pay you in American dollars if you like.'

Kwaku burst out laughing with a long, high pitched laugh that took Heliga completely by surprise.

'Miss Gwendoline did warn me you wanted to come and live with us and I got so vex! To think you don' know us from Adam, yet you want to take a room in our flat. . . . But now it come to that I can't say no. Shake my hand!'

Kwaku shook Heliga's hand vigorously, more convinced than ever that he was one of the finest people he had ever met.

The restaurant was now half empty, most of the clients having finished their lunch and returned to work. It occurred to Kwaku that a large cigar would crown his euphoria, but thought it unseemly to take advantage of the moment. He had been treated to a sumptuous meal and several glasses of beer, which had had the effect of erasing the Rupununi experience from his memory, at least for the time being.

And that is how Kwaku became associated with a young acupuncturist of unbounded ambition who, in some way, reminded him of his own callow youth. He dreamt of manipulating him, climbing on his back and riding him like a compliant horse, seeing that he was head over heels in love with his daughter and, in his own words, prepared to go through fire for her. He would go through fire all right, Kwaku thought, for Philomena was no ordinary woman. Earth and fire she was; but unlike women of her age she knew her worth and, with it, men's weakness for a well turned backside and the miracle of a painted face.

Miss Gwendoline had been envious of Philomena since her eleventh year and predicted a terrible future for her second daughter; that she would be trampled in the mud and like all selfish girl children end up grubbing in trash cans and opening her legs to all and sundry. But her only misfortune had been to give birth to a deformed child to whom she was devoted.

CHAPTER XIII

Kwaku hung about Heliga's establishment late in the afternoons after work at the Ministry of Hope. The young man had recently changed business premises, having found a much larger place on the ground floor of a building in the line of once elegant shops now boarded up and covered with advertising hoardings. The new establishment was in the centre of a notorious choke-and-rob district where few people apart from the local inhabitants dared walk after dark. But if at night the stretch of street presented a forlorn picture, by day the traffic of people and vehicles made it ideal for commerce of all kinds.

The shop resembled Heliga with its concern for style. A yellow and black sign bore the word 'Acupuncture', below which a window decorated with photographs of Chinese practitioners in highly unusual postures was brightly lit by bulbs of opaque glass.

Every day after work Kwaku spent an hour in his future son-in-law's shop, where he learnt much about dealing with people. If Heliga's reliability and unfailing courtesy struck him as quaint at first, he soon came to understand the beneficial effect such qualities had on his clients. An appointment fixed for Monday at two-thirty meant just that, not three or four. This miraculous timekeeping made such an impression on Kwaku he fancied it to be a gift from above, for how could anyone achieve such a thing otherwise than by superhuman control? Could the clock in the reception room be somehow responsible? Its face was decorated with five circles of varying sizes, each with its own independent needle, and it chimed every half hour with a soft, ingratiating sound. Suspecting that the chronometer possessed some secret power, he took a great interest in its behaviour whenever the moment for the next appointment arrived. But nothing out of the ordinary ever occurred to coincide with the appointed hour.

If Kwaku admired Heliga's timekeeping his good manners were another story. 'Too much please and thank you make eye pass'; such disparaging warnings against excessive courtesy were words that came out of deep experience, Kwaku reminded himself, recalling how in the old days his own clients looked at him askance if he wished them 'Good Morning'. Yet in Heliga's mouth courteous words appeared to be not only apt, but necessary.

Kwaku would have liked to witness the acupuncturist's performance with the needles which, he imagined, resembled the darts those tight trousered picadors used to torture a fighting bull. In his mind's eye he saw Heliga, arms poised above a naked, prostrate client, ready to pounce on the selected portion of her anatomy. For nearly all his clients were women, usually wives of well-off husbands who could afford to indulge new ideas simply because they featured in foreign magazines.

But Kwaku soon discovered that the needles resembled those with which Miss Gwendoline used to do her household sewing when she was still whole. And later his curiosity regarding their placement was satisfied after Heliga disposed in his show window two new photographs of a client smiling vapidly, whose body, bristling with needles, bore a striking resemblance to an amiable porcupine.

But in spite of their good relations Heliga never allowed Kwaku to penetrate into his secret operating room, and the latter was left to concoct scenes from his imagination, stimulated by nothing more concrete than the satisfied expressions of departing clients and the enlarged display photographs.

Nevertheless, pride in his family's prowess — Heliga was now regarded as 'family' by Kwaku, although Miss Gwendoline accepted this development with conspicuous caution — led him to take employees from the Ministry of Hope to view Heliga's establishment. First his night watchman friend Suarez came — after one of his weekly visits to Miss Gwendoline, with whom he had hit it off from the start. Then Bertie the day watchman accompanied him, albeit reluctantly, to meet the extraordinary acupuncturist. And finally Mrs Correia went along, hoping that her cooperation would have the effect of persuading Kwaku to explain the true reason why her husband had remained in the Rupununi.

One Friday night Kwaku sought Suarez's permission to allow Heliga to accompany them on their regular jaunt to Surinam's Meadowbrook apartment, but he refused, claiming that he had his reasons. Suarez had gone back on his decision not to have anything more to do with Kwaku since his visits to look up Miss Gwendoline became regular.

On their way they ran into Bertie and Eunice, who were just coming past the Cuffy monument on Vlissingen Road.

To Kwaku's surprise Bertie was more pleasant than he had ever known him. He invited Kwaku to tell them about his Rupununi trip and spoke of his intention of making a journey into the bush himself one day.

Kwaku attributed the change to his improved appearance, enhanced by a new shirt-jac and expensive trousers. In truth Bertie would not have cared if he were in the presence of the Queen of Sheba. The fact was that he had become engaged to Eunice the week before and was happier. In keeping with his secretive ways he had told no one of the occasion except his relations. Eunice, on the other hand, had done everything to show off the ring short of dangling it from a placard with the words 'I am engaged' written in luminous paint. Now in the half light of dusk she kept stroking her hair, adjusting her sleeve, wiping perspiration from her forehead, uttering ambiguous noises like 'Ugh' and 'Oh' while consulting an invisible watch; in short doing everything to attract attention to the fourth finger of her left hand.

A sharp word from Bertie was enough to make her calm down and, thrusting her arm under his, she walked in step with him as Kwaku elaborated on the Rupununi emptiness, its aboriginal Indians and the fierceness of the morning sun.

'That's 'cause it's nearer the Equator,' Suarez said.

'I hear Correia get sick,' Bertie put in. 'He come back yet?'

'I don' know,' Kwaku answered, anxious that no one should pursue the subject.

The conversation then turned to Rupununi water and the dangers of drinking it untreated. And each one, in turn, had a second or third hand tale to tell about the bush, of which they knew little except from hearsay.

The group arrived at Surinam's landlord's house and might have travelled only a short distance, so little had their minds settled on the long road to Meadowbrook. The ground floor flat was brightly lit and the owner's car absent, a relief to the Friday night habitués, who did not need to restrain their voices.

Night had fallen and the sky, covered with constellations, looked down on a strangely silent district.

Surinam opened up and they soon settled down to the drinking, gossiping and cordial squabbling that characterized their Friday evening meetings.

A while later, when Surinam called Kwaku into the kitchen and asked him to remain after the others left, the latter confessed that he himself had wanted to seek a discussion with a view to clearing up Correia's advice about relying on him. How could Surinam help him? What was he like, actually? His reticence only served to deepen the mystery of getting close to him. The invitation, coming out of the blue, made him so nervous that not only was he unable to concentrate on the conversation, but deliberately kept off the rum in case he could not take full advantage of what he might be told afterwards.

Eunice must have been cautioned by Bertie, for she said very little; but for that she was full of gestures and, in declining any offer of strong drink, pointed her left hand towards Bertie, now her lord and master.

'My fiancé doesn't allow me to drink,' she would say, turning aside the proffered glass.

The conversation centred, first of all, on the latest political sensation. On this occasion they spoke of an electricity generating unit purchased by the Ministry of Hope from the United States of America which, costing several hundred thousand dollars, failed to perform as provided for by the contract. While Suarez and Bertie blamed the Ministry of Hope for the blunder, Surinam claimed that it was the duty of the President's office to oversee all government departments, especially as incompetence was the norm rather than the exception. The argument raged while Eunice kept flashing her ring and Kwaku, out of his depth, sat back in his chair waiting for the company to break up.

'I wonder if you know that more than one hundred Public Corporation vehicles are not accounted for?' Bertie said pompously.

'What you mean "not accounted for"?' Suarez asked.

'Missing, man, missing! And we call this a democracy,' Bertie declared, affecting an exaggerated bitterness.

'It's only one place you'll find a democracy,' the night watchman said, 'in the burial ground!'

The country was going to the dogs, the currency was worthless and a corrupt police was above the law.

Kwaku felt he should contribute to the discussion, but did not wish to put Surinam off; so that throughout the meal which followed the drinking and the drinking that followed the meal he maintained a discreet silence.

Bertie, who was conducting himself as though he had laid down a burden, proved to be the mainstay of the animated conversation, raising subjects others would have preferred to remain untouched.

'And what about the passport business?' he asked, now thoroughly roused. 'The government won't issue a passport to anyone with a criminal record. And since they made the threat they say the crime rate's gone down.'

'Doesn't surprise me,' Suarez said, 'everybody want to emigrate.'

'You believe the crime rate's falling?' Surinam asked.

New versions of theft appeared every few months, the latest being stealing clothes from a washing-line. Thieves were no longer deterred by fierce dogs, which they poisoned mercilessly; and various tales were told to support the general opinion of lawlessness. Eunice offered to recount the bicycle story, a version of which most of them were familiar with, only to be interrupted by Bertie, who claimed he knew the authentic tale.

A man who had had five bicycles stolen in as many months, decided to go everywhere on foot. The six miles to his workplace he walked stoically week in, week out until, overcome with fatigue, he changed his mind and bought yet another cycle. Determined that he would not lose the latest one he chained it to his bed before retiring for the night. Alas! The very next morning on waking he found that it had been stolen while he slept.

'You heard the one about the lady who woke up and heard a thief sawing through her floor boards?' It was Suarez's turn. 'When she called out and threatened him he didn't take a blind notice of her.'

Eunice, peeved at the way she was being ignored, decided to brave Bertie's wrath.

'My grandmother never wear shoes 'xcept when she was going to a wedding or a *fineral*. You ever see people goin' about without shoes now?'

Bertie gave her a withering look and said, 'What's that got to do with what we're talking 'bout? What's shoes got to do with stealing bicycles? Now you see I'm not vexed! . . . Very calmly, answer me.'

Hanging her head, she whispered, 'Nothing.'

'Well,' he continued, 'if you want to contribute anything tonight, go in the kitchen an' do the washing up. You see I'm not vexed.'

Slowly she got up and went off to the kitchen. Bertie, it seemed, had acquired an ascendancy over her through their engagement, the very ring she could not help displaying to anyone who cared to pay heed.

The men launched into their conversation again, moving from subject to subject, speaking about things they understood and things of which they had little understanding. While Surinam rarely intervened, Suarez and Bertie took full advantage of possessing the floor to declare their often conflicting views.

When, finally, Bertie announced his intention of leaving, Surinam challenged him to demonstrate to the gathering that he was capable of walking straight, despite the rum he had consumed. He obliged and, on reaching the other side of the room without deviating from the line, declared, 'There isn't anyone in this country who can drink like me!'

Suarez, in answer to this indirect challenge, gave a mighty suck-teeth, since he was known for a legendary capacity to hold his liquor.

Kwaku asked Suarez to inform Miss Gwendoline that he would be home late. Surinam then saw them off with a teasing remark about love, meant for Bertie, whose left arm was crooked conveniently to accommodate Eunice's right.

Surinam offered Kwaku a cigarette, which he accepted in his confusion, and began to smoke inexpertly.

'I heard from Correia, you know,' he told Kwaku.

'Oh!'

'Correia! Very nearly a great man,' Surinam said, as though talking to himself. 'You didn't talk much tonight. In fact, you hardly talked at all.'

And it occurred to Kwaku that Surinam himself had hardly spoken all night.

'Correia wrote about the way you ventured out into the dark and how the Arecuna men ran away. He used the word "ventured". That was the very word. Tell me something: you did it out of fright or out of bravery?'

'I don' know,' Kwaku explained, thinking that this was not the time to boast.

'I just asked for so. . . . Come, I want to show you something. In fact, you'd better wait here.'

He came back with a post card which he handed to Kwaku. It was the reproduction of a painting.

'Who did this?' Kwaku asked.

'The original? It's the work of Angold Thompson, our finest painter. A man of vision!'

The representation of a man bent double under a mosquito-net surprised Kwaku who, accustomed to traditional landscapes, did not know what to make of it.

'You could have painted that,' said Surinam.

'Me? I don' know anything about painting.'

'I don't mean *actually* painted it. . . . I mean you're an artist. But I'm deeply disappointed in you . . . a man with such spirituality. All you want to do is make a fool of yourself. You either do that or sit all night without saying anything.'

'When I look at people like you an' Bertie. . . .' Kwaku began.

'Oh my God!' Surinam exclaimed.

He was too much of a man to say what he thought of Bertie, but Kwaku understood.

'Let me show you what I wanted you to see the last time,' Surinam said eventually, when he managed to overcome his exasperation.

Kwaku followed him into a room which they reached by passing through the kitchen. The smell of turpentine filled the air as soon as the door opened, and once the light was turned on Kwaku found himself in a large hall, against three walls of which framed canvases were piled one on top of the other. His attention was drawn to the few paintings hung on the walls. One, much higher than the transom of the door, depicted a koker beyond which the river-bank stretched on an expanse of mud laid bare by the ebb-tide.

'Simple, eh?' Surinam remarked. 'What could be simpler than painting what you see? But is it? What do you see when you walk down the street? That's the first problem to be solved as far as the contemporary artist is concerned. Long ago you saw what the culture made you see. But now you're on your own, my friend. The first problem is selection and in many ways it's the hardest problem of all. But solve it and you're faced with another. You choose what fascinates, but can you convert the fascination of the eye into the fascination of paint? Now comes a very serious problem for me: when I discovered how to project this fascination I exhibited, or rather the man who lives upstairs backed a show of my works. But the interest my work aroused made me decide never to exhibit again. . . . Can you understand that? I was disgusted, not with the appreciation, but by the people who appreciated my work, well dressed tourists with their cameras. . . . You know anything about the Haitian painter Bigaud? You know what North American tourists did to his work? You don't? No matter. All I'll say is that they praised it and bought it and took it back to America with them . . . and destroyed him.'

Kwaku did not understand half of what he heard, but remained spellbound in front of the canvas featuring the koker, and at Surinam's words he had the curious conviction that he was standing *inside* a vision of his own past, not only because his childhood had been spent in the shadow of a huge koker which drained the backlands, but because he had inhabited those very colours, it seemed, and the slight figure beside the beached boat at the foot of the canvas could be none other than himself.

'I don't understand what you said,' he blurted out.

'Wise words, my friend,' Surinam said. 'No praise. And above all, no criticism. Criticism destroys. I do nothing else but paint, you see. . . . But there's another story. . . . You know Correia's wife? Now if Correia is nearly a great man, *she's* a great woman; but our women aren't yet ready to defy convention.'

He spoke of the colours that obsessed him as a child; how he used to put his fingers in his ears to shut out his teacher's criticism, unlike Amy Correia, who took her teachers seriously. He spoke of how a master once hit him on the head because he persisted in drawing the handle of a mug in profile, when in fact he was looking at it head on. He talked like a drunk who had the streets to himself, and Kwaku followed every word, mesmerized by his fluency. He felt certain that something, yet unexplained, bound Surinam and Correia, but dared not ask lest he broke the spell woven by the web of words.

'I'd teach you to paint,' said Surinam, 'but I'd be envious if you were successful. The man who taught me to paint was very friendly while I was his pupil. He used to bring people to his studio to see the work of his "promising protégé". That's how he used to introduce me, "my promising protégé"! Nothing pleased him more than to hear people say how promising I was. He fêted me and lavished gifts on me for my "extravagant" talent. He himself organized a one-man exhibition of my work and personally saw that a score of his acquaintances attended the first viewing. Then a few days later, when an article in the newspaper described me as one of the finest Guyanese artists since Denis Williams, his manner changed overnight. He couldn't let me use his studio anymore because there wasn't enough space. He avoided me whenever we attended the same function, and so on. I can't tell you the effect his behaviour had on me. Anyway, I got over it. I had to! Some people paint out of vanity; others, like Amy Correia, have it in their blood. I paint to keep the demons away.

'One day when I'm sure of you I'll show you what is in the adjoining room, my obscenities, paintings for myself. Isn't that where all our problems are? In the adjoining room? Isn't it where our secrets rot? In the adjoining room we are ourselves. What does talk about the adjoining room mean to men? But to women! They live there. Even while we're penetrating their bodies part of them remains in the adjoining room. You see why I'm quiet in company?'

'Why?' asked Kwaku, pleased that Surinam had come down to earth.

'Can you see me talking like this in company? In front of Bertie and Eunice? Suarez, yes. But Eunice and Bertie! In fact in a lot of countries I'd end up in the madhouse, labelled as a so-and-so. . . . Are you lonely?'

'No,' Kwaku said.

'Odd; you're an outsider, yet you're not lonely. I'm consumed by loneliness.'

If Kwaku had believed him he would have betrayed surprise. But the Friday-night meetings and the admiration of his friends were evidence of anything but loneliness. Kwaku knew that Suarez envied Surinam his flat, his connections and above all the fact that he had the means to entertain. Such a man could only pretend to be lonely.

Yet there were indications on his canvases, dark centres of interest, like sombre moments in a brilliant afternoon.

Surinam described his loneliness as if it were a living thing, to be fed and entertained, an animal capable of betraying him, but to which he felt an abiding attachment. He interrupted his account from time to time, to see if Kwaku might be mocking him; then, assured of his interest, he would continue his precipitate verbal journey, like a boat caught in the waters of rain-swollen rapids.

But as he talked Kwaku became more and more uncomfortable. Loneliness, only a word to him, was not worthy of such examination.

Surinam had organized the Friday meetings after he was taken by an attack of solitude one morning when, inexplicably, he could see no future in pursuing his profession as a painter. But while the gatherings went some way to alleviating his feelings of isolation on the particular day, the condition was all the worse for that during the rest of the week. His tendency to withdrawal, already noticeable at school — when he suffered acute distress following the slightest altercation with a class mate — never struck his parents as being out of the ordinary. And after he was introduced to a young lady who 'brought him out' — they liked to say — he seemed to overcome his reticence and taste for back streets and entered into the spirit of socializing to which she was partial. Marriage and recognition of his artistic talents endowed him with a peculiar power, until the fatal morning when the sense of aloneness appeared to arise from within him, for no reason he could ascertain.

'Correia say you could teach me a lot,' Kwaku told him, breaking the silence into which Surinam had retreated.

'So he said I could help you. Me! Well, let me tell you the reason for asking you to stay behind. I would like *you* to help *me*.'

The two men stared at each other, perplexed by a dilemma, at the bottom of which lay the behaviour of a mutual friend who was hundreds of miles away and whom they might never see again. Surinam felt that he could not bare his soul to someone who himself professed to be in need of help. Believing that Kwaku possessed a cure for his loneliness he had buttered him up shamelessly and told him much he would rather have kept to himself. How could he confide in someone soiled with the reputation as a blabbermouth? He had to struggle against the inclination to throw Kwaku out into the night.

'What did Correia say exactly?' Surinam asked.

'I can't remember. I think he say you did know a lot an' you were reliable.'

Kwaku, unable to bear the silence that followed, stood up and declared his intention of leaving; and, standing in the open doorway, he turned up his shirt collar against the chilly night air.

'I gone, then,' he said, struggling to master his nervousness.

'Until!'

And Kwaku imagined his host's eyes following him down the path.

Chapter XIV

The Right Hand Man, since winning a Parliamentary seat in a by-election, cherished the ambition of promotion to high office, and when the Minister of Hope resigned following a murky affair in which he denied involvement, the ministry was offered to him. His reputation for incorruptibility was common knowledge, so that his appointment had the approval of the *people*.

His new office, in the storey above the old one, was twice as large and overlooked a pair of cabbage palms through a Demerara window decorated with elegant fretwork.

Mrs Correia, who went upstairs with her superior, now supervised two other personal secretaries whom she herself had chosen. Anyone seeking an audience with *her* minister now had to get past three women trained in the art of protecting the most valuable member of the government after the President. Having arrived at Mrs Correia's door — she now had her own office — Kwaku was required to present his credentials, which she examined with the scrupulousness of a policeman executing a search warrant.

Kwaku had been sent for by the Right Hand Man and, although he arrived at the appointed time, he was kept waiting in Mrs Correia's office. He recalled his first encounter with her, more than a year ago, when everything about the ministry building overwhelmed him; its style, the people working there and the large number of cars parked in the compound. Familiarity had blunted his impressions and he now sat, preparing himself inwardly for the confrontation with the Minister who, he was certain, had summoned him in connection with some serious business. Mrs Correia had never been friendly in her dealings with him, but his position as a messenger led him to expect no better treatment. Unable to offer her a satisfactory explanation regarding Correia's decision to stay in the Rupununi, despite repeated enquiries, he imagined that her hostility had grown with every meeting.

The Right Hand Man had decided that the time had come to use Kwaku in the way he used all those who were in his debt. He must be put in his place before he entertained inflated ideas about his independence.

'Come right in, Mr Cholmondeley,' he said to Kwaku, as he swept past Mrs Correia and the last defence of his ministerial fortress.

Kwaku remained standing before the polished hardwood desk until he was offered a seat.

'Sorry to have kept you waiting. These damn meetings! Look, I've got a job for you. Promotion, in fact. I want you to take Correia's place. You know he ran the Currency Exchange Centre?'

'Yes.'

'I want you to take it over.'

'I don' have his education, sir,' Kwaku said.

'You'll have an assistant to do all the calculations for you.'

'Sorry, sir. I can't.'

The Right Hand Man made no effort to conceal his irritation but said nothing, in the expectation that Kwaku would offer a more comprehensive excuse. However, the messenger stood his ground, determined not to waste any words.

'You don't understand,' continued the Right Hand Man, 'I'm ordering you to take the job.'

Kwaku, recalling Correia's stories of corruption, would not give way.

'I'm sorry, sir. I have to refuse.'

'I won't bandy words with you,' came the exasperated retort. 'You'll damn well do as I say or lose your flat.'

'I'll write to Miss Rose.'

'Keep my mother out of this!' he exclaimed, banging his fist on the desk. 'You — do — not — understand! You were arrested for illegal possession of drugs and *I* got you out of trouble!'

Those were just the words Kwaku was waiting to hear. Hardly able to contain himself, he stood up without any particular reason for doing so.

'Don' threaten me, sir. I don' like anybody threatening me, especially as I only got one mouth to feed beside myself. I give a priest a letter I write, and in it I tell him all about your illegal currency dealings across the border. If you leave me alone he not goin' open that letter.'

The Right Hand Man considered Kwaku for a while, then went to the door and called Mrs Correia.

'Get your note book.'

She came back, armed with notebook and pencil, pulled up one of two empty chairs and got ready to take dictation.

'Memo to the chief Customs Officer, Timehri Airport. . . . You are at liberty to charge Mr Kwaku Cholmondeley for any offence you reasonably believe him to have committed on such and such a date. . . . Don't send it through the post, Mrs Correia. Ask one of the chauffeurs to deliver it by hand.'

She left the office and a couple of minutes later was heard typing.

'You can go now, Mr Cholmondeley,' the Right Hand Man said quietly.

'You din' believe what I say about the priest. A'right. . . .'

'You ungrateful bitch! After all I've done for you!' exclaimed the Right Hand Man.

The typing came to an end.

'I'm grateful for the way you help me, sir. I want to repay you. But you don' own me.'

The Right Hand Man went outside and spoke to Mrs Correia, who made a gesture indicating that she understood. He then came back into his office but, instead of taking a seat, went and stood in front of a window.

Kwaku, sensing some sort of compromise, kept an eye on Mrs Correia to see if she would carry out his order. She began typing again, looking neither right nor left.

Certain that he had the measure of the Right Hand Man, Kwaku concentrated on the secretary. What had she done about Correia's desertion? Any other woman would have worn her unhappiness like a banner. At times Kwaku imagined that she was not a real woman but a cipher destined to perform certain tasks. Yet whatever he thought of her he believed that in some way she would have a profound influence on his future. He detested her because she ignored him and he experienced a malicious pleasure in recalling how Correia had abandoned her.

'Very well,' said the Right Hand Man, turning round. 'You have a week's notice, and from now on you'll have to pay rent for your flat. You'll be sent a demand at month end. From now on we have nothing to do with each other, and if you cross me in any way I'll break you like a matchstick. Leave my office.'

'Very well, Minister,' Kwaku said, 'Thank you.'

'Thank you, you bastard,' Kwaku said in a low voice as he went by Mrs Correia's table.

On reaching the top of the stairs he hesitated, then went back to the secretary's desk, bent over her and said, 'You know what I think Mrs Correia? I think you an' me . . . you and I got a lot to talk about. I know you would like to piss on me, but is *you* who goin' come to see *me*. Not the other way round.'

She only looked up at him when his back was turned.

There was an excellent reason for Kwaku's sudden access of independence. He had begun working as a healer again.

Several weeks before, soon after arriving back from Lethem, he had read in the Stabroek News an account of a treatment practised in slave days, called the Creole Massage. Still used in the Berbice countryside it consisted of a gentle massage, first of the head and then the feet, which was reported to induce a mild euphoria in certain patients and a remarkable sense of well-being in others. His first opportunity to experiment with it came when he was asked to treat a rival practitioner, whose wife came from New Amsterdam and knew of Kwaku's reputation. Having dressed as well as he could he called on the patient and was welcomed by the wife, who warned Kwaku of her husband's reluctance to be treated by another healer. Day after day he fought the old healer's resistance to his attentions and in the end persuaded himself that he was engaged in the struggle against a kind of death-wish that had no other source than the irrational urge to punish a rival.

The turning point came after Kwaku told his patient that in future no charge would be made for his visits and that he intended to continue with the treatment until he was cured. From then on the man welcomed Kwaku with a cordiality which matched his wife's, and within the space of a few days there was a noticeable movement in the fingers and toes, then gradually a general improvement in the function of all the muscles of the affected side. And seven weeks later the healer was able to take a few steps on his own.

Bertie learned what had come to pass, and the news soon spread throughout the Ministry of Hope. Kwaku's past was dragged up, together with extravagantly exaggerated accounts of his former wealth. And there were even those who claimed to know the mansion in which he once lived and the rum shop where his character was laid to rest with a drunken exhibition in the presence of layabouts and prostitutes.

The first trickle of patients that followed his success were welcomed by Kwaku in his home. But Heliga, sensing the advantage of a joint practice, invited him to set up business in a back room of his surgery.

For Kwaku the experience was a kind of rebirth. Like the silk-cotton trees that lose their leaves and appear to die in the season of drought only to recover their vigour with the April rains, all his confidence returned.

One evening he, Miss Gwendoline and Suarez examined the new situation from every angle. If Suarez took a vicarious delight in Kwaku's success, Miss Gwendoline was more cautious and kept repeating that Kwaku should not forget the long years of deprivation which prompted them to leave New Amsterdam for Georgetown, where even established fortunes were far from secure. Their discussion ended in a suggestion that they should fête his new success as a healer at the Arapaima restaurant, where you sat on converted barrels under flickering neon signs amidst the constant to-ing and fro-ing of customers, families celebrating a surplus of funds, unattached couples, lone men with veiled expressions and habitués betraying a once-a-week look, all hatless, in a fashion their grandparents would neither have understood nor approved.

Miss Gwendoline sat between her husband and Suarez and, almost in tears at such attentiveness, imagined a future strewn with flowers she could not see. Kwaku took care to wipe away the food dribbled onto the napkin worn during her meals and of which she was more ashamed than the contemplation of her affliction by strangers. Suarez was a son, she told herself, for she associated his kindness with blood-bonds and friendships of long standing.

She could not have known how Blossom once told Kwaku that a woman needed more than one man to minister to demands beyond the capacity of any single husband. Had she heard the remark she would have disapproved on account of her Christian upbringing.

How the world had altered since she stepped into the shadows! Before she and the two men left the house she brushed her hair endlessly to make amends for her inability to arrange it before a looking glass. Now everything she lacked she desired immoderately, out of a desperation she would never have understood in that once bright, bright paradise of colours. And if she discovered a new world of sound and touch it was scant compensation for what was lost. Long ago she once remarked that no one spoke in dreams, but now her dreams were filled with clamour, exactly as at present in the restaurant. And laughter! Surely they were mocking her.

'It dark?' she asked, turning to the right, where Kwaku sat.

'It dark,' he answered. 'But the street lamps bright. I think they change the bulbs.'

'You're enjoying the chicken?' Suarez enquired.

'It eat good,' she answered. 'Like chicken long ago.'

Suarez glanced at Kwaku and could sense his anguish.

From across the road came the sound of music from a discotheque, a raucous pounding that invited dancing.

'The place full up, eh?' she asked.

'Yes,' Kwaku answered. 'How you know?'

'I hear the talking; but it get hot too. Alyou want to go outside and walk?'

They wiped their hands on paper napkins and went out into the night air. Then, after standing at the roadside until a break in the traffic appeared, they crossed the road to the middle walk where Miss Gwendoline had to be guided past the bollards at the intersection.

The two men described the houses and Ministry buildings, for she had never come to Georgetown before losing her sight.

'It quiet up this way,' she observed.

'The business district came to an end back there,' Suarez told her.

'Ah,' she said, not able to visualize what he described.

At the top of the road, before arriving at the Pegasus Hotel, Miss Gwendoline complained of the chill, so they turned back and walked all the way home, through the main business district, where stall holders displayed their wares on the pavements during the day. They then turned into the road that branched off into two streets at a point where the cathedral stood alone.

That night, while lying beside Kwaku, Miss Gwendoline reflected on the familiar view of her life as a stagnant pool since she came to town, into which nothing came and out of which nothing flowed, and vowed that she would banish the vision forever. Yet, in the weeks that followed, the sound of Philomena and Heliga making love in the adjoining room filled her with rage and persuaded her of a conspiracy of perfumes and copulating bodies, all the more potent because it derived from what she could not see. And she resolved that as soon as

Kwaku's practice was established on a firm foundation she would ask the couple to find their own accommodation.

Kwaku's auspicious launch as a healer in town was followed by a promising if unspectacular expansion of his practice. Heliga, convinced that their success owed much to the joint venture — his business had improved markedly since Kwaku joined him — spoke of opening a branch somewhere in the countryside, where they could work twice a week. His father, who used to live in Peter's Hall as a young man, frequently spoke of Dentist Kerry's once-a-week surgery when he charged his patients less than his normal fee.

Meanwhile Heliga spent a great deal of money on furnishings in emulation of American entrepreneurs who spared no expense in furthering a commercial enterprise, he claimed.

The waiting-room, painted entirely in powder blue, was dignified with a couch and a refurbished bentwood rocking-chair, while the consulting-room, on the dark side of the building, was lit by two electric bulbs encased in ancient carriage lamps.

If the truth be told, Heliga knew very little about acupuncture but, fortified by an unshakeable optimism and abetted by his clients' fascination with the exotic science, he experimented on his operating table with an aplomb that would have done credit to an expert practitioner.

Heliga, uneasy at Kwaku's unprepossessing appearance and, more especially his lack of taste in clothing, suggested that he wear overalls. And he attributed the subsequent improvement in the number of clients who came to consult the healer to his timely advice.

In Heliga's view only one problem remained to be solved, namely the contrast between their respective clienteles. His mainly well-off ladies suffered from the juxtaposition of persons of much more modest means who made up the bulk of Kwaku's patients. And although he did not think it wise to raise the matter in their weekly review of policy, he nonetheless bore it in mind for future reference, when the inevitable expansion of their premises could come up for discussion.

Never did two men so different in appearance and temperament constitute a joint practice. Heliga, elegant in attire, smooth-tongued, methodical in everything he did and said, recalled an old calypso which described a man about to go and settle in town:

He got the walk
He got the talk. . . .

Kwaku, on the other hand, appeared to belong to a bygone, unidentifiable age, when unconscious urges must have counted for much more. Heliga recalled his own grandfather who wore a felt hat, even in the house, and played ancient card games with his similarly be-hatted friends and reflected that Kwaku would have been happy in their company. If his assessment of Philomena's father was not far from the truth he could not suspect what a heroic effort Kwaku made to keep his tongue in check; how he was all but overwhelmed by a need to abuse any client who could not afford to pay after the treatment was completed. Had Heliga been able to overhear him open his heart to Miss Gwendoline he would have appreciated the gulf that separated them.

'Get if off your chest, man! Get it off your chest,' she would urge him, knowing how fragile his confidence was, especially in town where a person lived in constant danger of offending some urban taboo.

'Yes, girl, is so! These people skin an' grin with you, an' soften you up with "thank you" an' "please" when they don' have a blind cent in their pocket. I tell you, I does get so vexed!'

And he would relate his latest vexing encounter, like the man who sold all his cattle in 1973 in order to expand into sugar cane planting. When the collapse in world sugar prices came he lost nearly everything.

'An' he expect me to treat him free in 1990 for the collapse in the seventies. Look story! *I* never own a piece of land in my life!'

'Get if off your chest, man, get it off your chest,' would come Miss Gwendoline's consoling words.

'An' you should see his smart shoes! It got a tip so long I had was to leave the door open to give it space.'

He would get so worked up that Miss Gwendoline had to abandon her suggestion to shed his troubles.

'Alright, you goin' burst a blood vessel.'

He would then take her advice and calm down, acknowledging that she was his barometer, just as she was his conscience when he made dire threats of revenge against the twins if they should ever appear in town.

Nevertheless, Kwaku was happy. He began buying his wife little gifts made of material that could be admired by touch, cambric handkerchiefs and boxes of smooth mahogany, which she examined without lowering her head. And more than once, on getting up in order to urge her back to bed at the dead of night, he would find her on the verandah above the almond trees, fondling one of his gifts with the same rapt attention of a listener carried away by music from a short wave radio set. He would then sit by her under the saffron light of the nearby street lamp without uttering a single word, knowing her distaste for conversation after everyone in the house had retired.

Kwaku was as happy as a man could be after so many years in the wilderness of material deprivation, when he suffered less on his own account than for the woman he married on that memorable afternoon and for whom he built a house and gave up his sweat-soaked shirt to soften the intolerable birth pains while she was in labour with their first-born child.

A year passed after he was dismissed as a messenger at the Ministry of Hope and began working full-time as a healer, a year during which he and his future son-in-law opened a branch of their practice at Bagotstown near the new bridge across the Demerara river. At the end of which year Philomena announced that she might be pregnant and a hastily arranged marriage was announced, to be held soon after the required banns were published in the Seventh Day Adventist church across the road in Oronoque Street, where she had been accepted as a member after an application made on the advice of her intended, whose family would only take her into the fold if she was a follower of their faith. In the event, the apparent pregnancy, based on the fact that she had missed a period, did not materialize, to the great disappointment of Heliga.

CHAPTER XV

Kwaku cultivated *style*, unashamedly copying Heliga.

'Do come this way!', 'What seems to be the matter?' and 'Can I be of assistance?' were expressions used in defiance of Guyanese norms of bluntness and became stock expressions in his dealings with clients; so that the 'surgery' acquired some notoriety, not only for its unorthodox methods but also for the excessive courtesy of its practitioners.

It did not take him long to recognize the limitations of his new healing method; but, unwilling to go back to the garlic cure of former times, he devised new forms of the creole massage, while waiting for the inspiration that would enable him to extend his treatment. In the end it was an accident that bred the idea that was to characterize his future practice, rather than inspiration.

One afternoon, a woman in her eighties who rejected the suggestion of treatment by acupuncture was referred to him. On being told by Kwaku she would have to submit to his creole massage she objected, insisting that she knew very well what he was up to, and just because her husband had died recently men should not take it into their heads that she was easy pickings. When Kwaku managed to persuade her that his intentions were honourable she spoke at length of her recent bereavement after sixty-two years of unimaginable bliss.

'Unimaginable!' she repeated, blowing her nose in her hand, then wiping it on the right side of her dress.

'That man was a saint,' she continued. 'Whenever he come through the front door I could see a halo over his head, time and time again. In over sixty years of marriage never a cross word. And he go and dead! He was the most respected boat-builder in West Demerara. And he just keel over one day!'

Overcome by the memory she blew into her cupped hand and this time wiped it on the left side of her dress.

'Our marriage was founded on Christian values and love. I wasn't one of these women who give in to a man and then ask him for a pair of shoes or a blouse. And that's why he appreciate me. I know! He did tell me so. You ever see a man with a halo hovering over his head?

Especially nowadays when they all want to spend half their life in a rum shop? He was more than a saint, Mr Healer. I won't be surprised if he sitting up there next to Jesus and his apostles, his twelve apostles. I mean eleven. That Judas did like too much rum, I sure.'

Kwaku was on the point of putting his arm round her shoulder to console her when she blew mightily into both hands and dried them on the two sides of her flower patterned dress. He gave up the idea of consoling her with an embrace, thinking that the shoulders of her dress might be as besmeared as the sides.

'Auntie, your husband is still there,' Kwaku said with feeling.

'How you mean *there*?' she asked.

'He there in spirit,' Kwaku assured her.

'How you mean?'

'Death is of the flesh, Auntie.'

'But when I go home he's not going to be sitting in his Berbice chair. I'm not going to be able to touch him.'

'His spirit's going to be there, Auntie.'

'Healer, I didn't marry a spirit. Is what you telling me?'

Kwaku spoke passionately, deploying all his patience, carried away by his own desire to bring someone round to his way of thinking. And bit by bit she listened more than she talked, until she was made to see the wisdom in Kwaku's words.

'Is true? You think so?'

'I telling you, Auntie. He's in his Berbice chair! You can't see him, but he can see you an' hear you. You mus' talk to him.'

'I'd better not let visitors sit in the chair, then,' she said, her eyes widening. 'They could crush him.'

'No, don' allow nobody to sit in it,' Kwaku encouraged her. 'Clean it an' keep it in good condition, so he know you care for him. You don' know the joy that will come to you, Auntie, when you sit down at night listening to your radio or talkin' with visitors an' knowing you're not alone. Ho! What joy, Auntie! What joy! In the name of the Lord.'

'Oh, Healer!' she exclaimed.

'Join your hands an' praise the Lord!'

'Healer, you're a consolation.'

She locked Kwaku in a powerful embrace, and if he had remembered the state of her dress, which he did not, it would have availed him little in attempting to avoid her demonstration of gratitude.

People talk! And the old woman, as voluble in her gratitude as she had been in her grief, went around telling neighbours and friends of the *unimaginable* spiritual experience mediated by the Healer. Kwaku's future was assured! And he spared no time in supplementing his massage therapy with his spiritual and, in time, gained enough confidence to reintroduce the garlic treatment which had brought him success years ago.

And now that Kwaku had, as it were, three strings to his bow, Miss Gwendoline was finally able to acknowledge the possibility of permanent security.

Chapter XVI

Kwaku's daughter's wedding was a great success. After the ceremony Heliga and Philomena came back to the flat and were enthroned on two armchairs in the middle of the drawing room to listen to speeches and testimonials. Eunice, responsible for the announcements, flashed her ring whenever anyone was introduced. First, the lady who made the wedding cake was called upon to step forward and be seen by the assembled guests. The cakemaker presented herself, but being extremely shy she covered her face with a napkin from the table, where her many-tiered cake rose almost to roof height. Then the tailor came forward uncertainly. He had been responsible for cutting the page-boy's suit and held up the church ceremony for more than an hour because he was recovering from a hangover and could not manipulate his needle confidently enough to produce finishing of high quality. Suspecting that he had not completely recovered, two men helped him back to his place among the guests.

One by one every person who contributed in some way, however small, stepped forward before it was Kwaku's turn to speak. But the sentences he had prepared so carefully were miraculously forgotten, even the opening words which, according to Suarez, held the secret to retaining the others; and he remained facing the scores of expectant guests who, it seemed to him, were smiling at his dilemma. And the crisis, anticipated from the moment he knew he had to make a speech, threw up in his imagination all the crises and dilemmas of his past; the encounter with the fisherman who blinded his wife and left her helpless; the boy singer with the falsetto voice who brought silence to the revellers in the rum shop and caused him to tremble with foreboding; the journey in the East Coast taxi with the inquisitive woman who challenged him to deny that he was the notorious Kwaku who had breached the Conservancy; these and others rose before him as if to mock his insufficiency. And the old fear of the world seized him by the throat and prevented him from performing a function that every Tom, Dick and Harry in every village throughout the country undertook and carried off with varying degrees of success.

Miss Gwendoline tugged at the person standing next to her chair and asked what had gone wrong.

'Is Kwaku,' she whispered, 'he don' know what to say.'

'I'm not a man of words,' he began eventually. 'I wish the couple one hundred years of health and happiness.'

A furious clapping broke out, reflecting as much the guests' relief as their approval of Kwaku's dignified words.

Then there were calls for the cake to be cut.

'Stick the cake! Stick the cake!'

The cry from Suarez was taken up by several guests anxious to witness the groom's behaviour when the time came to kiss the bride. And after the cake was properly divided at the second attempt Heliga boldly kissed Philomena full on the lips, to the delight of the guests, who accompanied the demonstration of affection with catcalls.

Four men shifted the table towards the edge of the room when the cake had been cut up and the pieces shared out. Then the dancing began with the bride and groom. They took the floor with that confidence which never failed to surprise their elders who recalled their own marriages and their embarrassment at being the centre of attention.

When Suarez invited Miss Gwendoline to dance she accepted willingly, belying expectations of her ineptitude. He led her round the floor, past the group of small children standing together, past the table strewn with remains of white icing and across the centre of the floor, where other dancers made room for them. Then the music stopped and there was renewed clapping, accompanied by whispers of admiration as the guests saw Suarez lead her back to her chair.

All of Kwaku's Friday-night cronies were present, with the exception of Surinam who, in his element when entertaining, did not care to attend social gatherings at which he would be just *one of the guests*.

But Bertie was there, drawing satisfaction from Eunice's attractive presence while at the same time disapproving of the way she made a spectacle of herself. She came and joined him from time to time but, taking advantage of the circumstances, which did not permit him to quarrel with her in front of strangers, she was soon off, like a marabunta incapable of settling in one spot.

'I miss Correia,' Kwaku said to Bertie. 'Things not the same when he not around.'

'When he's around he does only lie down and go to sleep,' Bertie answered, leaving Kwaku to guess at the reason for his gruffness.

'Why not dance?' Kwaku suggested.

'Eunice will only kick up her foot high and show off her new drawers.'

'Dance with somebody else then,' Kwaku advised. 'They got a lot more women than men.'

'When the time come. . . . I in' see *you* dancing.'

'I dance already. Now I got to look after the guests,' Kwaku said, sticking out his chest as befitted a host.

Kwaku went off, unaware that Bertie was envious of his growing professional success. He had anticipated some disaster once his friend was dismissed, knowing the Right Hand Man's ruthlessness, and believed Kwaku's days to be numbered. Every morning he expected to hear the inevitable news; an edict closing the clinic or, at least, his eviction from the flat. Bertie drew particular satisfaction from the misfortune of others and belonged to that ilk who scoured the newspapers for disasters, whether personal, national or international. Surrounded by scores of people enjoying themselves, inwardly he criticized their appearance or conduct. It was unseemly for the middle-aged man to dance so intimately with a young woman; the children laughing boisterously should be banished to the back room; he had attended weddings where better cooked food was served!

During the interval between pieces youngsters would surround the disc jockey and make suggestions as to what should be played next. Most of them were neighbours invited at random, and their friends. Kwaku would look around him from time to time and tell himself proudly that everything, the general contentment, the table with the debris of sweetmeats, Miss Gwendoline's tranquil gestures as she sipped her sorrel drink, the conscientiousness of women helpers, all, in some way or other, depended on him, the father of the bride. If Heliga had met the cost of the celebration, he, Kwaku, had taken him in and allowed him to court his beloved daughter, even against his wife's wishes.

Had he not waited long enough for this day and endured predictions of the family's downfall under his guidance?

'Look at him! What can he do? No trade, no profession, no education, not an ounce of character!'

That and similar remarks he had heard from his uncle, his sole surviving relative from the older generation, and equally from those who thought it right to judge him on slight acquaintance. For him this was a new beginning, like the sun that rose in the East after its perilous journey across the dark nocturnal landscape and which one day would appear once more to Miss Gwendoline in all its splendour, he was certain.

'Nice wedding, Mr Cholmondeley,' one of the helpers said in passing by.

'Thank you, mistress.'

From time to time he invited Miss Gwendoline to dance something slow and, as her breasts touched his chest, he would recall her youthful figure in those far-off days when he seemed destined to remain a shoemaker's apprentice for the rest of his life. Many of the young people present were not even born then. Yet here they were, leaping about as if they had inhabited the earth since its beginning and were not destined to die like their dogs, their cats and the body lice that woke them up at night.

At dusk most of the old people drifted away, but the youngsters remained, and soon after nightfall a crowd gathered on the parapet below between the street lamp and the almond trees to listen to the disco music and voices during the intervals.

In spite of the open doors and windows some found the heat unbearable in the close, humid night. A neighbour fetched an electric fan and set it at maximum, but it made little difference to the atmosphere, so that some young people took refuge on the porch and verandah while others followed the example of their elders and went off home. A handful of dancers, sweating profusely, leaned on one another's shoulders or made languid gestures as they danced apart.

Then Bertie and Eunice said goodbye, and a little later Suarez left as well after assuring Miss Gwendoline that he had enjoyed himself. And one by one the drawing room emptied, until only one helper and her husband remained.

'Where the bride and groom?' she asked.

No one had seen them go off for a car ride with a group of their young guests.

'Miss Gwendoline, we goin' too,' the helper told her. 'I goin' come early tomorrow to clear up for you.'

'Philomena can do it,' Miss Gwendoline protested.

'I comin' all the same. You know what they like, newly-weds.'

And she laughed at her remark, certain that Miss Gwendoline knew what she meant.

Kwaku saw them to the foot of the stairs, then came back to join his wife.

'Was a good wedding, eh?' he said.

'Was a good wedding,' she agreed. 'How she look?'

'Philomena? She look alright.'

He avoided superlatives deliberately, knowing Miss Gwendoline's distaste for the way their daughter decked herself out on special occasions.

'You think it goin' last?' she asked.

'I don' see why not. He does work hard an' she settle down in town. They goin' send for the child when they get a place.'

'So they gettin' a place,' she said eagerly.

'So he tell me.'

'Praise the Lord! I don't know, but something not right with them,' she said.

'Since you lose your sight you seeing everything crooked.'

'I did tell you he was going to want to live here and I was right. I feel things more, that's all.'

The optimistic, ebullient wife of the early days was no more. Someone else had stepped out of the shadows to take her place, a stranger but for their years together, a woman with disturbing insights. It was as if husband and wife had changed places, so that she who once grappled with fate, refusing to yield, now gazed with her sightless eyes on the horizon, full of unease. He, on the other hand, had grown bolder and saw clearly for the first time the past errors that had brought him low; his arrogance, and above all the obstacles fashioned by his own hands, as though something within him refused to countenance his own success. If Bertie could not abide the success of others, he, Kwaku, once refused to tolerate his own.

'Was a good wedding, though,' Kwaku said.

'It was good enough,' replied Miss Gwendoline tiredly.

'There are good people in the world,' Kwaku went on, 'Miss Carpenter. . . .'

He listed the helpers, the cakemaker, the dressmaker, and others who had given their services free.

'Good people, yes,' she said, 'good people in Babylon. . . . I going to bed, Kwaku.'

'I goin' look at the moon,' he joked.

He sat up waiting for Philomena and Heliga, but fell asleep before they came back home, when the streets had emptied under a leaden sky.

Chapter XVII

Ever since Kwaku's return from Lethem Amy Correia had wanted to find out from him why her husband had stayed there. She had lost herself in conjectures about secret currency dealings on his own account, involvement in some crime he did not care to speak of and even a possible affair with a woman he might have got to know on his many trips on behalf of the Right Hand Man. She reckoned that Kwaku must have some knowledge of the motive for his stay and, in the days following his return, had come close to deciding to take the bull by the horns and ask him outright if he could help her. But she hesitated, or spoke in circumlocutions, fearing that the Minister and her husband might have come to an undisclosed arrangement and that she would be questioning Kwaku at her own risk.

Since he became a minister Miss Rose's son had dropped his mask of concern for those working under him and his conduct began to resemble that of certain notorious government representatives who seemed to regard their tenure of office as an opportunity to pursue openly their personal interests. In spite of Amy Correia's promotion she was made to do his bidding in ways she had been spared while still a secretary without any special responsibility. She bullied and threatened employees on his behalf, sought by questionable means information that might be useful to him and attended gatherings where gossip was known to be freely exchanged, in order to judge the people's attitude to the government and its ministers. Only when acquaintances and strangers began avoiding her, and at official and other reunions conversation ceased at her approach, did she come to grasp the consequences of her unswerving loyalty. But by this time she had persuaded herself that she was acting in a good cause. If her minister resorted to tactics indefensible in normal circumstances, these were to be excused by the higher motives which once singled him out as a man of the people.

The morning he asked her to pay Kwaku a visit she saw at once the possibility of combining her official errand with the private purpose of finding out about her husband.

'I want you to find out at all costs everything about his practice,' he told her, 'what he does, the methods he uses and so on.'

'What do you mean "at all costs"?' she asked.

'You're to do everything necessary to come by the information.'

She did not pursue the matter, believing that her show of affability alone would be enough to make Kwaku co-operate. Besides, nothing prevented the Right Hand Man from using others to glean the information he sought, thereby robbing her of her chance to look up Kwaku with a water-tight excuse.

Over the last few months she had had little time to examine her position at the ministry. Having overcome her dismay at the discovery of her pariah status amongst the public at large, the request to throw herself at Kwaku if need be obliged her to think seriously of her future. The warmth of a man's body in her bed had been felt as a desperate need for many months after Correia's failure to come home, to the point where she began entertaining fantasies about the hands and neck of the young messenger who had taken Kwaku's place. As if it were not enough to be deprived of her husband's attentions, she was now requested to comply with demands the Minister would not have dared make a year ago. She had become the prisoner of her own fatal inaction.

It was a slack morning for Kwaku who, whenever he came out to the waiting-room, found that the waiting client had come to see Heliga. After the mid-day break however, the first two clients were his: a young man and a middle-aged woman.

The young man, little older than school age, admitted that he had come twice before but turned back at the door.

'I'm frightened of my step-father.'

Kwaku advised him to write down on a sheet of paper everything he thought of his step-father and everything he wanted to do to him.

'Come back tomorrow and we'll talk about it.'

'Why we can't talk now?'

'Because I want you to take your time and think about it.'

'Tomorrow, then. How much I owe you?'

'We'll talk about that tomorrow.'

Watching the young man depart, Kwaku wondered what he would tell him the next day.

'Do come this way,' he said, inviting the woman to follow him.

She complained of cramp in her stomach and came for his famous creole massage, just like her cousin Eliza, who looked ten years younger since he treated her.

'What I treat her for?' Kwaku asked.

'For cramp in her stomach, Mr Cholmondeley.'

'You makin' fun of me, lady?'

'No. Is true. She was in a state before you do what you do to her.'

Kwaku looked her up and down and decided that she had money to throw away. Although he had made a resolution not to fleece anyone knowingly, he found himself breaking his rule on a number of occasions; and faced with this offer to take the woman's money, he felt a particularly strong urge to relieve her of it after a perfunctory demonstration of his art. Yet there was something in her manner which offended his honour; not just his conviction that she was as healthy as he was, but a certain brashness, a depreciation of the profession of healing.

'Lady, I can't treat you,' Kwaku said, after some consideration.

Her face fell.

'But why?'

'I don' know. Is like that with some people. But if you come back another day with another complaint it might be different.'

'And I was looking. . . . Well, I never!'

'I don' have anything against you personally, lady,' Kwaku said, doing his best to be conciliatory.

But she was offended nonetheless and remained standing before a perplexed Kwaku.

'I tell you what,' he added, 'come back next week if you still have cramp.'

'Alright.'

Out of the corner of his eye he noticed another woman waiting and hoped inwardly that she had come to consult him rather than Heliga. He made a show of seeing off Eliza's cousin as he would a familiar patient.

'Until next time!'

Turning round to welcome the waiting client he was brought up with a start.

'Mrs Correia. . . . Who you come to see?'

She got up in her business-like manner and faced him without flinching.

'Good afternoon, Mr Cholmondeley. I've come to see you.'

'What's wrong?'

'Can we talk in private?'

'Yes. Come this way.'

She sat down in an armchair while Kwaku remained standing, uncertain whether he should treat her with the excessive respect he used to show her while still a messenger.

Amy Correia's decision to put her own business before the Minister's was taken on the spur of the moment.

'You're sick?' he asked.

'I'm not sick, Mr Cholmondeley. I just wanted to talk to you.'

'About what?'

'I'll pay you for your time,' she offered.

But he dismissed the suggestion with a deprecating gesture.

The drumming in his ear and his unwillingness to look her in the eye angered Kwaku. After all, he had spoken to her boldly enough as he was leaving the Right Hand Man's office.

'Dammit all, this proud woman come to see me, not me her,' he thought.

'You said I would come,' she told him. 'Weren't you expecting me?'

'I was,' Kwaku lied and drew satisfaction from the fact that she appeared to believe him.

'Why did you tell me I'd come to see you?'

Kwaku sat down on the couch where his patients were wont to stretch out full length to receive their massage.

'I jus' know, Mrs Correia.'

'But I had to, because only you know why my husband stayed in the Rupununi.'

'There's something else.'

'What?' she asked. 'You and I don't know one another. Why else should I come and see you?'

'Anyway, why you come? What's your business? I might have another client waiting to see me.'

'Can you please tell me all you know about my husband. . . ?'

'No, Mrs Correia. I can't.'

'I beg you, Mr Cholmondeley. It's a matter of great importance to me, almost of life and death.'

Kwaku would not answer her.

'You were with him for several days in the Rupununi, where

there isn't a lot to do. The two of you must have talked. . . .'

Kwaku, intimidated by her intelligence, realized that he must be on his guard. How did he know, for instance, that she had not been sent by the Right Hand Man, who was surely planning for the day of reckoning?

'I can tell you something, Mrs Correia. But why should I? You did always treat me like dirt. Now you talk 'bout begging me as if you ever beg anybody in your life. I'm a simple man. . . .'

'That's not what I heard,' she said, interrupting him with words she was sure he would find flattering.

'Mrs Correia, I not goin' tell you anything. Not one single word 'bout your husband. All I goin' say is he got troubles.'

His words must have struck home for, reacting instantly, she said, 'What troubles?'

'We all got troubles, Mrs Correia. What's unusual 'bout that?'

'You pretend to be simple-minded,' she said, 'but I didn't treat you like dirt. It's my manner. If I go about smiling, men think. . . . Well, you know what they think.'

Then, putting out her hand to touch Kwaku's, she said in a soft, ingratiating voice, 'Mr Cholmondeley, do this for me.'

Kwaku clasped her hands, then kissed her fingers gently. When she closed her eyes he saw the gesture as an invitation, let go of her clasped hands, then placed his right hand on her breast. Mrs Correia sprang up, quivering with anger.

'I didn't come here to sell myself, Mr Cholmondeley.'

Kwaku, thoroughly confused, could not, however, bring himself to apologize.

'Alright, you better go,' he said, 'before I do something else foolish.'

She picked up her purse from the floor and made for the door.

'I know about you an' the Minister,' Kwaku said, voicing a suspicion current in the ministry.

'What? Did my husband tell you that?'

'No.'

'Oh my God!' she stammered, unable to conceal her relief.

'He don' know,' Kwaku added, having discovered the chink in her armour. 'All the hours we did talk he din' say a thing about that.'

Mrs Correia sat down once more and, as if sunk in thought, said not a word for several seconds, while Kwaku listened for sounds from the adjoining room, fearing that Heliga might interrupt them at any moment.

'Can I call you Kwaku?' she said, as though she were asking a big favour.

'Yes, Miss Correia.'

'On no account must that rumour reach my husband's ear. If only you knew! Please promise me you'll never repeat it.'

'I never break a promise, Miss Correia. . . . But I in' make one yet.'

'Will you promise?' she pleaded.

'Since I come to town, Miss Correia, I notice something. I look around and see how people can buy and sell everything. I see little buck girls as servants. They parents get a few hundred dollars from somebody in town 'cause they need the money an' prepared to give away they children for it. Everything is bought an' sold. You ask me a favour an' if I was a real townsman I would ask you to pay for it.'

'I knew you were honourable, Kwaku.'

'Me? Honourable? No, Miss Correia, I not honourable. Townspeople honourable, but not a crude countryman like me. Townspeople pay for what they get; I like things free. Besides, give me a chance an' I would lie an' cheat . . . an' break promises.'

'What do you want from me?' she asked.

'Tch! Miss Correia, I got everything I want.'

'So you don't want anything,' she went on. And here a high note crept into her voice, compromising the impression of control she gave.

'I say I got everything I want, Miss Correia.'

'You're toying with me, Mr Cholmondeley.'

'If you don' know what I want you can go home right away,' Kwaku said brutally.

She approached him and Kwaku felt that she was on the point of bursting into tears.

'You can touch me here,' she said, pointing to her left breast.

Kwaku complied. He began stroking her breast and his heart was like a hammer under his skin.

'Alright, just touch it once, Mr Cholmondeley,' she said as he opened her blouse.

Tears began escaping from under her closed eyelids while Kwaku pushed up her brassière to expose the golden mounds of her rounded breasts. She did not resist when he pulled the blouse off gently so that she stood before him, naked to the waist. Bits of conversation came from the adjoining room, and Kwaku reckoned that Heliga was just about to dismiss a client.

He bolted the door and came back to Mrs Correia who stood, hands crossed in front of her, like a penitent school girl before an authoritarian teacher.

She picked up her garments which were scattered about the room, and Kwaku noticed the resemblance to those fatigue-dogged women who go about their yard, clearing it of rubbish at the end of the day. Patches of lipstick covered her face where he had kissed her and her dishevelled hair hung about her temples emphasizing, deliberately it seemed, the hour-long humiliation to which she had been subjected.

When she stood at the door, her fingers gripping her purse, she said to him, 'You did promise not to tell my husband that. . . .'

'Miss Correia, I won't tell.'

'In any case whatever you heard was untrue.'

Disconsolately, she drew the bolt and left the room.

Kwaku was as certain that Amy Correia had come on a mission from the Minister as he was certain of anything. He would send somebody else, he mused. Meanwhile he would wait at the centre of his web and exercise a degree of vigilance with which Miss Gwendoline would never credit him.

'I learning,' he told himself. 'Every day I gettin' better. Oh yes! An' one day I goin' be able to sit in my house an' say, "So an' so going come to pass", and it will come to pass. Just like those old buck men who does foretell events before they happen.'

Convinced that he himself possessed extraordinary powers which needed to be harnessed, he had decided to search for a tutor who was capable of imparting to him what most schoolchildren knew, so that fortified with a more solid foundation, he would bring to the surface all those thoughts that welled up so readily when he was asleep.

But the Right Hand Man did not send another of his minions to visit Kwaku. It was Mrs Correia herself who came back, dressed with impeccable taste and wearing a stylish hairdo, in striking contrast to the severe, unflattering bun of her working days.

'Come in, Miss Correia. Sit down.'

'You should call me Mrs, you know, not Miss,' she said, smiling.

'Is nice to see you,' he said, thinking that to say more would be to betray his delight at her coming.

'I want to apologize for insisting that you keep your promise not to write to Correia. I mean you might think I don't trust you.'

'You don' have to bother, Mrs Correia. I'm as safe as a . . . as safe as can be. I don' know how to use words like you.'

'But you have other qualities.'

'Like what?' Kwaku asked.

'Sincerity, Mr Cholmondeley.'

Kwaku glowed at this unreflected reply. Perhaps he had misjudged her.

'I come to ask you a question,' she said.

'What, Mrs Correia?'

She took out her handkerchief and wiped her eyes.

'I'm a very unhappy woman, Mr Cholmondeley.'

'What? I wish I had your looks.'

'Looks aren't everything, Mr Cholmondeley. If it was only looks. I love my husband deeply. We've known each other since Primary School days and he's everything to me. I know some people can't forget his fire-raising days, but I can proudly say that since we began going out seriously no one can accuse him of any wrongdoing.'

'What's the question?' Kwaku asked.

'Did he . . . did you see what he did with a bag of money he was carrying? Don't be vexed. I asked as a matter of interest.'

Kwaku's suspicion that she had been sent by the Right Hand Man was confirmed. Angry with himself for crediting her visit with a personal motive, he almost barked at her.

'Bag of money?' he repeated. 'I did bring back an envelope for the minister.'

'But there was less than half of what should have been in it,' she lied.

'It was sealed,' protested Kwaku. 'It was sealed with wax. And why youal didn't tell me at the time that any money was missing? You take me for a fool or something?'

'There's no suggestion of misconduct on your part, Mr Cholmondeley. My husband must have given you one envelope when he should have sent two. Did you go over to Brazil with him?'

'No.'

'You had instructions to stay with him.'

'Look, if the Minister want to question me he got to do it himself.'

'Mr Cholmondeley, you get vexed so quickly. You're so passionate! I 'm just carrying out orders, you must see that. You think it's the sort of conversation I want to have with a friend?'

Kwaku got up and, having walked past her chair, looked at her from the back. She resisted the impulse to turn round and waited until he stood before her once more.

'I don' know what to make of you, Mrs Correia. . . .'

'Please don't get vexed,' she pleaded.

He put his hand on her shoulder, and it passed through her mind that she would have lit a cigarette in the days when she was a smoker. Things were as bad as that afternoon the Minister made her stay on at work when the night insects swarmed round the electric bulbs, and afterwards she swore she would save enough to be able to resign her job.

As Kwaku talked to her, inconsequential words aimed at filling the vacuum, she kept thinking that she could not say truthfully that she was filled with disgust. Then, unexpectedly, events took a new turn. Kwaku's foolish, vacuum-filling words led him into an indiscretion.

'Your husband buck woman friend love him bad, you know.'

'What buck woman?' Mrs Correia asked.

'His Arecuna lady.'

A slap full in her face could not have produced the same effect. She went pale.

'I thought,' Kwaku said. 'I didn' realize.'

'Liar! Liar!' she screamed.

'Is everything alright, Mr Cholmondeley?' Heliga's voice came over the low partition.

'Yes, is just a misunderstanding.'

Kwaku sought appropriate words to calm her down but, unable to hide her despair, she had turned her head away from him.

'All I want to know is why you waited so long to tell me. You let me do this . . . under false pretences.'

The discovery that her suspicions had been well founded proved too much. In her heart of hearts she never dreamt that Correia could go near an aboriginal Indian woman, much less give up all he had for one. Despised, the playthings of townsmen, for her they represented the sum of the stories she had heard tell about them; and whether these stories were true or not, the fact that they were believed would diminish her in the eyes of those who, sooner or later, must learn that she had been abandoned.

Now she longed for vengeance against her husband, the Right Hand Man and most of all Kwaku, who undoubtedly relished his triumph at her expense.

Her first act of revenge would be practised on the Right Hand Man, to whom she decided to pass valueless information about Kwaku's practice. And then she would turn her attention to her husband and Kwaku Cholmondeley.

Later, when the pain of her betrayal by the three men had settled into a quiet, persistent resentment, she could not help thinking of the evening when her father sat waiting with her art work on his lap.

She stood up, smoothed her dress and, without more ado, left Kwaku standing in the middle of his consulting room and thinking that women were far more difficult to understand than men at times.

Chapter XVIII

A strong wind blew from the Kanuku mountains, threatening the frail tentest partition separating the bedroom of the Guest House from the corridor along the frontage. Soldiers from the Defence Force were sweeping the yard, while others were engaged in the endless burning of shrubs, which sent smoke northwards in puffs of white.

Amy Correia, the only client putting up there, had arrived an hour ago and was arranging her affairs in the wardrobe, after laying out the contents of her small suitcase. She had lost no time in enquiring from the proprietress where Correia lodged and was rewarded with a prompt answer and the most careful direction as to the situation of the thatched hut.

'When you find him tell him to drop round,' the proprietress said.

Passing the room again, the proprietress asked if she had brought a hat.

'I don't wear one.'

'The sun different here,' the proprietress said, '. . . you can find him drinking Brazilian beer at twelve o'clock in the shop next the airport building. But you can't go at that time without a hat.'

Mrs Correia went to sit on the porch and look out on the landscape, as strange and forbidding to her as it was to most people who came from the coast. She could not say for certain why she had come. To seek an explanation for her husband's conduct? To persuade him that his place was by her side? To confirm Kwaku's story of his association with an Arecuna woman? Or even to threaten the woman with her presence? It was as humiliating to be the *other* woman as it had been to give herself to Kwaku.

But whatever she saw, she was not one to make a scene. Once Correia told her where she stood she would be in a position to plan her future. As an unattached woman she could resign her post, become a huckster once more and rejoin the sisterhood of travellers whose flights were made on unconfirmed tickets. When she reflected on the humiliation she suffered with every compromise she made along the way of her secretarial career she saw, in retrospect, a past in which a kind of darkness had gathered round her, slowly thickening, like the advent of night in her childhood home when her parents were visiting in a nearby village. It was she who had to give out false information on behalf of the Right Hand Man; she had to inform magistrates of verdicts the ministry expected them to pronounce — the Minister himself dealt with the judges. And through her blackmailing activities, all on behalf of the Minister, and ultimately the ruling party, she learned of the web of control that kept the country in its grip. But she had little to show for the unsavoury catalogue of connivances except a small sum in the bank.

Amy Correia hated her husband, even before she learned for certain what part he had in her moral crucifixion. And yet she hoped desperately for a plausible explanation of his defection, for the disclosure of a simple fact which would dispel her suspicions and prove Kwaku to be a liar who had concocted his tale out of malice or envy.

Looking out on the road which went by the Guest House, she noted that nearly every passer-by was an aboriginal Indian and that they all walked with a relaxed, unhurried gait.

A man dismounted from his bicycle below the corridor to ask her if she needed to change Guyanese currency into Brazilian cruzieros, and to her 'No' he shrugged his shoulders, mounted his cycle once more and rode off towards the supermarket. She consulted her watch, found that it was only half past eleven and wondered how anyone managed to survive in an environment where time dragged like a heavily laden cart. She could not wait to meet her husband.

Twelve o'clock will arrive soon, she persuaded herself, especially if she told the beads of her rosary with eyes closed. She fetched them from the dressing table, where she had placed her toilet paraphernalia, the affairs of a simple woman; but when fifteen minutes later she consulted her watch once more, believing it was time to leave, she was astonished at her inability to judge the passage of hours when divorced from events. Here events were abolished and everything occurred in slow motion.

Amy looked out at the mountains and recalled how as a small child she was plagued with hallucinations which were kept secret, out of fear that they might be interpreted as evidence that she inhabited two worlds. Later, on discovering that her first friend of long standing at secondary school lived in two worlds as well, there was much comfort in the knowledge that she was not unique. But in her early teens the visions ceased altogether, except for one occasion when she attended a wake on the edge of town and saw the coffin rise slowly and sail through the window without attracting the slightest attention. Now the vista between the Guest House and Kanuku mountains induced in her the same feeling of oppression she experienced at that wake, where women dressed in black sang hymns with wide open mouths while their men drank rum in another room.

She was not given to much reflection, but now she kept raking over her past, terrified by the void that must surely follow a permanent break with Correia. Her greatest regret had been the discovery that she was an individual, different from others, and she felt certain that it had driven her eventually into the arms of Correia, whose name she now bore. If she had had to endure the guilt of yielding to the Right Hand Man's advances, she now felt a profounder guilt, the betrayal of her own self in entering into an association made alluring only because it bore a name, marriage.

She had always harboured a contempt for women who had to bring up children on their own. Now she desired a child whom she could bring up, with or without a man; a part of herself, blood of her blood, who would not change mothers as men change partners and on whom she would lavish all the pent-up maternal love that fermented within her. How could she not hate Correia for all her wasted years with him? Even if he came back to her the humiliation of rejection could not be cured.

And her reflections travelled the by-ways, avoiding the thorough-fare she dared not enter, the subject that had to be avoided at all costs, her own infidelity. It was too painful, like the scorpion in the un-opened box.

A slight shift in the direction of the wind brought smoke from the burning shrubs towards the building. The proprietress came up the staircase from the storey below with a cloth she must have brought from the kitchen and covered the parrot's cage; and Amy Correia, unwilling to get into conversation, consulted her watch, put it on her wrist and left to meet her husband at the drinking place in the general store. Had she turned round she would have seen the proprietress looking down at her as she hurried along the laterite road.

The proprietress, no sooner had she informed Mrs Correia of her husband's whereabouts and his habit of drinking at midday in the store, regretted her indiscretion. She did not like the young woman, who seemed stuck up, and had sent her cook to warn Correia about the lady who was prepared to brave the hot sun to see him. Correia, his polygamous wife and children used to come visiting every Sunday after going to the church near the supermarket, where the entire congregation was made up of aboriginal Indians, save for a sprinkling of creole policemen, teachers and their wives. The Guest House proprietress had taken to Correia ever since he installed her old pump which had been lying around for years in the kitchen and he, conscious of the value of her friendship now that he was in hiding, cultivated the relationship with uncharacteristic zeal. His aboriginal lady made a living of sorts growing bora beans and selling her warishees to an agent who came to Bom Fin the first Friday of every month. Nevertheless, what they grew and what Sidonie earned were insufficient to maintain them, and when his embezzled money ran out they were destined to live in poverty.

The sumptuous meal put before them on Sundays by the Guest House proprietress, which they often ate in the company of her clients, was not only an invaluable addition to their fare, but provided Correia with the opportunity of maintaining the illusion that he was still in contact with the coast. Forgetting his status as fugitive for a while, he would display his knowledge of Indians and Indian artefacts, explaining for instance the importance of anato, the pungent red dye which, besides being an effective insect repellent, had a powerful symbolic value for them.

Having yielded to the temptation of socializing on that one day, he would disappear with his taciturn lady for six days, except for his hourly sorties at the drinking place. In fact, what he saw as a luxury was no more than certain ranch owners practised, despite the pressure of work and the great distances they had to travel over the savannah. They, too, showed themselves to the outside world once a week, foregathering in the Double Wheel tavern or the general store to consume Brazilian beer in half-litre bottles in the company of Saturday night revellers. But at these times Correia would remain with his lady in their thatched-roof hut, gazing through the window at the shadows cast by the cashew trees.

The proprietress's message came when Correia was preparing to leave and he knew at once that the lady in question was none other than his wife even though, out of pride, he would not solicit a description of her from the cook. His first thought was to skip the drinking hour, but on reflection he thought it would be better to have it out with her in the general store rather than at his home, the address of which she had been given, according to the cook's message.

Hers was the last visit he expected, although he was so concerned about the Right Hand Man's reaction to the embezzlement and the possibility of being interrogated by the police.

Not only was Correia unwilling to discuss his marital problems in an atmosphere of recrimination, but the mere thought of his wife's injured expression angered him, for he did not wish to be reminded of the dereliction of duty which was bound to be thrown in his face. He could easily pretend that the suspicion of her involvement with the Right Hand Man had prompted him to flee to the Rupununi; but nothing had been proven, and he would risk being accused of jealousy, an emotion he despised in men.

Wearing the broad-rimmed hat Sidonie had made for him, he bade her goodbye and set out for the general store, a good twenty minutes after he normally did.

The stream that flowed into the Takutu river was low, and here and there the brown earth along the banks had broken off in large chunks and fallen into it. Correia crossed the bridge, hurrying his step in case his wife had gone to the drinking place and left on seeing he was not there.

He spotted her from the back; the carefully contrived bun above her graceful neck, the neat yellow blouse of expensive cloth, incongruous on the savannah and, above all, her erect posture. She was sitting alone, a mark of unsociable behaviour in Lethem, of which she was no doubt unaware. In any case, people would have been suspicious of a woman entering the drinking section unaccompanied.

'It's you,' she said, looking up at him and pretending to be calm.

'Yes, I heard you'd be coming.'

'Can I have a soft drink?'

He fetched the soft drink, placed it before her and sat down without buying the beer he usually took at this time, partly because he wanted to impress her with his lack of resources.

'So you're staying here then,' she remarked, suppressing a desire to scream and run out of the store, and up and down the road under the yellow, hostile sun.

'You came to quarrel?' he asked.

Hurt by his aggressiveness, she said, 'But we've hardly ever quarrelled. That's why I can't understand. . . .'

'There's nothing to understand. It wasn't because of you I left. I stole the Minister's money. . . . He knew I would steal it and then couldn't come back.'

'He knew?'

'Yes. You don't understand these people, although you work with them. I'm sure he didn't say anything to Kwaku about the money when he came back.'

She did not tell him about how the matter had just been dragged up by the Minister for no apparent reason.

'If he wasn't concerned,' she went on, 'why don't you come back and make up some excuse for the months you stayed away?'

He seemed to be searching for a reply.

'I don't know why,' he said at last.

'I miss you,' she said, turning away from him.

In spite of her gentle tone and the absence of animosity in her words, he was becoming increasingly irritated, plagued by his own nagging guilt.

'Look,' he said, mustering as much control over his words as he could, 'I don't know why I did what I did. I don't understand how people can say, "I acted like this because of this". I don't know. I've never known.'

'We've not seen one another for months,' she put in, 'and anybody would think that you'd at least. . . .'

'Look, if you begin to cry I'll get up and leave. We've had a good marriage. We've been all over the place together and done a lot together. Bertie and Surinam used to make fun of me because I never said a bad word about you. Everything does come to an end. You are in Georgetown and I'm in Lethem, and that's that. It's over!'

The aboriginal women behind the counter were staring at them unashamedly, their blank expressions belying their interest. They knew he was married to the woman beyond the bridge and wondered who the Portuguese lady from town could be.

'Is it true you've got a woman friend here?' Amy asked.

Correia, anticipating the question long before it was asked, flew into a temper.

'Do you think I'm a machine? Do you? I mean, what do you expect? You think I'm the Guest House keeper's parrot, living in a cage and satisfied with a ripe banana and a "Lora, Lora" from time to time? I mean what do — you — expect — My God! . . .'

She waited for the storm to pass. She was not prepared for this, this unreasonable hostility. *She* had been wronged. *She* had to stand up to the Minister's ridicule and hints of collusion. He used to lose his temper from time to time, but there was always in his outbursts an undertone of repentance. Now his manner made her fear the possibility of a permanent rift.

'I've got a suggestion,' he said.

Suddenly he seemed calmer; but, afraid of his irritability, she said nothing.

'You can come and live with me and the lady in question.'

Now she understood why women were accused of becoming more violent with their men of late, why more and more assaults on husbands were lengthening the lists of Magistrates' Court cases. Her frustrations as a teacher had partly been responsible for her leaving the profession and becoming a huckster, and later her experience as a huckster drove her into the Civil Service. But Correia had always been there to stand by her. Now she was expected to walk alone, as if they had never been married.

'So you want me to come and live with you and your buck woman. . . . How are we to sleep? Three to a bed? Do you want me to work in the fields by her side? When you and she make love do I watch or must I go out of the room? And when you leave again, is it me you'd be leaving or her? No, I don't want to come and live with you two.'

Her words had been delivered without any suggestion of the turmoil within her.

'I am not well,' Correia said. 'I have a constant fear of the minister and of Sidonie's relations. They always come at night, at a certain time of the month. When Kwaku was here he chased them away. . . . What's the matter? You've gone as white as a sheet!'

'Nothing. It's probably the sun. I suddenly felt faint.'

Correia looked round and saw the three women staring at them.

'I've got to go now,' he said, standing up.

'Please stay. I've come all this way to see you.'

'You're a young woman,' Correia whispered, in an attempt to placate her. 'It's not the end of the world.'

She was on the point of confessing her infidelity, out of revenge, but she desisted, believing against all the evidence that all was not lost.

'Can't you sit with me until the sun . . . until it gets cooler?'

He sat down.

Correia, irritated that Amy had not reacted sympathetically to his confession of fear, failed to notice his own lack of interest in what she had been saying. But for that, he had found her anguish almost unbearable, and his tactless offer that she should live with him and his lady had been meant seriously. He wanted to confess to her that it had been impossible to handle all that money every day in the Right Hand Man's shop without being corrupted. On his trips to the Rupununi he had often been tempted to abscond and live in Brazil with his outside woman and their children. At first his honesty and marital attachment stood in his way but as the sums of money grew larger and with them his responsibility, he was seized with rage that he was expected to be honest while people in high positions like the Right Hand Man believed they were entitled to soil their hands. Then what began as no more than an idea grew into a resolution. First he wanted to tell Amy of the plan; but when rumours that she had slept with the Right Hand Man came to his ears, he dared not risk confiding in her and decided to carry out the plan alone.

'You've lost weight,' Amy said.

'Life's harder here. You look well, though.'

'Do I?'

Their conversation touched on insignificant matters, as though they had arrived at a tacit understanding to avoid anything painful. He now knew how absurd his offer to live with him and the aboriginal woman had been. A place without furniture, drowned in a perpetual half-light, in a settlement where all the other inhabitants only spoke Macusi or Arecuna in spite of their fluent English . . . this world in which both silence and words could be interpreted as hostility would drive her mad. She harboured powerful ambitions behind a façade of obsequiousness, behind the affected superiority which she saw as her only defence against an affected world. She was of the town, of its alleyways and pitch roads, its cooking oil shortages, municipal edicts, desperate beggars, leather shoes, deformed toes with manicured nails, continuous entertainment dispensed from illuminated boxes; a world of monsters with elongated anuses, elaborate constructions to hide estranged couples, trees no one can name, cattle with a woebegone expression, churches, churches, taverns crammed with men, abandoned bakeries flaunting brick chimney skeletons, uniformed girls, uniformed constables, old people clinging to life with arthritic hands, explosions of ecstacy at weekends, and everyone with secret plans to emigrate.

She looked at her watch.

Her grandfather, a retired fisherman, used to consult the sky several times a day for signs that foretold a heavy haul, even after his retirement in Cayenne. . . . In alternate fits of anguish and anger she felt like attacking Correia and weeping. On this great savannah she was nothing, incapable even of an uncontrolled impulse.

'I'm going to be here for a couple of days,' she said, stealing a glance at the women behind the counter.

'You have a couple of days to decide, then,' Correia said.

'Decide what?'

'I don't know. Nothing, I suppose.'

'Are we going to meet again?' she asked.

'I don't think it's a good thing.'

'Why?'

He drew a deep breath, determined not to lose his patience.

'We've got to separate some time. Everyone separates at some time or other.'

'Very well.'

She got up and extended her hand. But he drew her towards him and kissed her on both cheeks.

Then he watched her depart for the Guest House up the laterite road.

It crossed his mind that when he, Sidonie and the children went on Sunday to take their lunch on the way from church she would have already left for Georgetown, and only then would he be able to consider her visit in the light of memory, and all those years they spent together come to nothing.

She, unlike him, went away refusing to acknowledge the end of their marriage.

But after her departure Correia was tormented by visions connected with her visit. While making love to Sidonie he would see her sitting on the edge of the bed, her skirt raised to display her nakedness. Or, as he was about to step on the bridge on his way to the drinking place, she would call his name in her unmistakably affected voice.

CHAPTER XIX

Things did not turn out as Amy Correia planned. Her imagined hatred for the men to whom she was attached was put to the test by the Minister soon after she came back from Lethem. Uncharacteristically, after he had given her instructions to arrange an official trip for him to St Lucia, he began to speak about his private life. He recalled his promotion, which brought increasing loneliness and a degree of responsibility few people would suspect. Should he visit friends at night he was expected to leave the address and telephone number at which he could be found; and when he came home the sight of the armed guard standing conspicuously in front of his official residence robbed him of the illusion that it was his home. In short, he no longer existed as a private person. And while he spoke she grew uneasy, wondering why he should single her out for his confidences when — as was common knowledge — Miss Rose was in the habit of coming to town once a fortnight to oversee his domestic affairs and never left without engaging in a lengthy conversation with him.

In fact, the Minister had been not a little worried by his secretary's request for a week's leave to go to the Rupununi, and on her return by her cool, almost detached manner. She was irreplaceable and he intended to keep her, even at the cost of doubling her salary. Yet, before it came to that it was as well to let her know she was valued, not only as a worker, but as a confidante.

'As soon as I get back from abroad I've got a suggestion to make,' he told her.

But her lack of enthusiasm for the implied promise of some advancement made him fear for the worst in his absence.

'What's worrying you?' he asked. 'Since your trip to Lethem you're not yourself. Have I offended you?'

She admitted to nothing, declaring that nothing had changed, while cursing him inwardly for creating a rift between herself and her husband.

Then the Right Hand Man, without having given serious thought to the matter, asked Amy Correia to move in with him and take complete control of his social and ministerial activities. Thrown into confusion, she took refuge behind a dignified request for time to think.

She knew from the moment the Minister asked that she would accede to his request to go and live in his house and postponed an answer only as a concession to her pride. She could not yield so readily after having convinced herself that she hated him.

While he was absent she caught herself giving orders in the same tone of voice he used whenever he sought to impose his authority and, in spite of a conscious effort to act according to her nature, the exterior force that appeared to direct her actions continued to have its way. It had been like that in childhood when she spoke with her parents' voice and imagined that she would grow up to look exactly like her mother. It had been like that in her teens when she copied her father's gestures, believing that in them lay his extraordinary authority or the secret of adulthood.

On the threshold of what she considered to be a dramatic change in her fortunes, she longed to acquire a new wardrobe and flaunt herself for the benefit of the ministry employees. But she resisted the temptation, since the absurdity of the change would become apparent to all when, subsequently, she took up quarters in the Right Hand Man's house.

How strange that the single act of infidelity with the Minister had caused her so much anguish at the time, yet now she was prepared to go and live in his house without the slightest trace of distress, even though her marriage was not dissolved. Besides, she no longer entertained any thoughts of vengeance against Correia, whose name alone had been sufficient to provoke images of violence against him and his Arecuna lady since their meeting in the Lethem tavern.

Occasionally, in reviewing what was to be her new life, Amy's satisfaction was marred by the thought of her father judging her somewhere in the background. But these brief intrusions into her reflections of future happiness were always overcome by the conviction that she had achieved her independence at last, that childhood belonged to the distant past when she exercised no authority and no influence upon her way of life. As a child, she had not been able to speak to anyone about her isolation — defined, it seemed, by the painted fence around her yard, where she spent hours watching her pet rabbit make its rounds, knowing, with mixed feelings of fascination and dismay, that it was destined for the pot.

She frequently made trips up Church Street on her way home from work to glance at the Minister's mansion and its well-maintained front yard, with flowering shrubs and a solitary palm that soared above the neighbouring mosque. Had it not been for the guard she would have stood before the mansion gates and examined everything in detail; garden, the house and backyard, part of which could be seen beyond a half-concealed staircase that climbed to the lower storey.

Amy Correia duly moved in with the Minister of Hope and within weeks learned many of the attachments, even secrets, of his private life. She met his mother, Miss Rose, and could not overcome her surprise that her suave, man-of-the-world boss was the son of a woman without pretensions. She saw some of his lady friends who slipped into the house by the covered staircase after midnight and always arrived on foot. She learned of his taste in underclothes, the infinite care he took in choosing his shoes and his great respect for his mother's opinions on everything. And once she was taken aback to hear him — so secretive in everything he did — confide in her a detail of government policy that was yet to be made public.

But most surprising of all was the little extra responsibility that came with her increase in salary and occupation of rooms next to the Minister's. His housekeeper, a pleasant, level-headed middle-aged lady, continued to exercise the same supervision of his domestic affairs as she, Amy, did over his official ones and preferred to leave matters as they stood. She was in no doubt now that her surliness following her break with Correia had worked in her favour.

Had she been a scheming woman she would have little difficulty in turning to account her hold over the Right Hand Man, but as things stood she was content to share his bed while enjoying the freedom to go and come as she pleased.

Amy Correia made the observation that her ambition had died, that the acceptance of the Minister's offer represented an acknowledgement of a terrible failure. At first sight, her father had been responsible for the suggestion. Yet her resistance to it bore little conviction, and she took to brooding over his words and her mother's tacit approval of their import. He had said more than once that parents were never free of their children, however old they were, and whatever the distance that separated them. But it was she who kept going back to the parental home in a vain attempt to seek her father's approval.

'You're still in love with your husband,' he told her during a visit, a remark he meant to be no more than an expression of his superior wisdom, but which fed her conviction that he was determined to prolong the persecution that began in her teens.

But if Amy was no less lonely now than before she moved in with the Minister, there were some compensations in her experience as his companion of uncertain status. From time to time he would entertain a visitor whose conversation surpassed the currency of dreary intercourse she had come to expect from the local functionaries, the foreign ambassadors, the acquaintances and friends who came and went.

One young woman, a former librarian at the University, whose means of support was a favourite subject of comment in certain milieux, never went away without making a deep impression. Her conversation, her independence and refusal to be overawed by the presence of men persuaded Amy that she was the unknown model she had striven to emulate since her teens. On her first visit the Minister, who usually left the organization of supper to his housekeeper, kept enquiring if everything was in order and, on hearing a car arrive in the drive, he hurried downstairs to open the wrought iron gates himself.

Nothing prepared Amy for the extraordinary presence of the be-jewelled apparition whose lack of inhibitions was apparent soon after she came through the door.

'I hope he doesn't bully you,' she said to Amy after they were introduced. 'If you're not afraid of him he'll treat you right.'

She questioned Amy about her work and spoke of her years at the University library, where serious work was hampered by lack of funds and the Guyanese disrespect for women.

'I myself put forward ideas which were scorned. But when later a man put forward the same idea it was a different story. They listened and praised him for his originality.'

The Right Hand Man smiled, knowing full well that the words were meant as much for his ears as for Amy's.

That was the visitor's way and, as Amy learned with time, there were men who admired her for her defiance. But Amy could never understand how a physically unattractive woman managed to claim and keep men's attention as the guest did. Could it be her filigree earrings that dangled provocatively like gilded lanterns under the eaves? Or her talk of East Indian dancing styles, which had died out in India but retained their popularity in Guyana to this day? Or was it her gestures? All the people she admired were defined by their gestures. The stranger's were as florid as her father's were sparing.

Amy looked forward to her rare visits and noted the Minister's humility in her presence. *She* was not one of those midnight women who slid in and out of the shadows and boasted afterwards to intimates of their hasty encounters.

But there were a few others who made an equally lasting impression on Amy. Like the old pianist who insisted that he had given up the instrument years ago, yet never failed to grant the host's request for a last performance. He would then sit at the piano — treated like a redundant piece of furniture, it was covered with water marks from the overflow of hanging maidenhair ferns — install himself on the adjustable stool, crack his fingers with ritual solemnity and, after a series of ascending arpeggios, begin playing with the virtuosity of a performer who, far from giving up the instrument, had become its slave.

Week by week Amy discovered something new in the Minister of Hope, and her own weakness for attributing to him qualities he did not possess. His sophistication, conspicuous to acquaintances and those who worked in the ministry, was a veneer that covered a solid foundation of a different kind laid down, no doubt, in his formative years. Like his mother he had a partiality for bread poultices and rejected any kind of medical intervention, often declaring that the faith-healer came closest to God through the use of salt.

And once, when Miss Rose condescended to hold a conversation in her presence, Amy heard the tale of municipal workers in New Amsterdam who refused to obey an order to fell a kumaka tree. A young colleague, who did not share the superstitions connected with the silk-cotton giant, offered his services to cut into the ancient trunk. But his first blow having drawn blood, the man dropped his axe and refused to carry on, in spite of the foreman's assurances that the fluid was no more than red sap. The foreman was obliged to do the deed himself while his assistants looked on anxiously. That same night he complained to his wife of listlessness and an unbearable pain in his right forearm which, no sooner had he dropped off, began whispering obscenities to him. Night after night he managed to sleep no more than a few minutes at a time and became painfully thin, and the dark patches under his eyes became pronounced as though he had been made up for a part in a play. The foreman wasted away until, a shadow of his once heavy, authoritative frame, he died in one of his brief periods of sleep.

Miss Rose's son, far from saying anything to suggest that he disapproved of the superstition that lay behind the story, went on to declare that he had heard of a similar occurrence on the East Bank Demerara.

Although in public he supported the women's movement for equality of opportunity, in private he allowed his prejudices a free rein, describing sterile women as *mules* and anaemic Portuguese women as *Maninas Rosas*. The contrast between the discreet politician and the unmasked layman in conversation with his mother could not be greater, and the conclusion was forced upon Amy that the carefully contrived separation of his real Self from the public figure could only have been achieved by a person with no pretensions to morality. In spite of Amy's considerable experience she had preserved the naïveté of those women who, striving for independence in a man's world, believed implicitly in the morality of that self-same world. In truth she resembled women like Miss Rose more than she imagined, for, deep down, she found the idea of a woman occupying a post of public authority to be abhorrent.

Amy Correia was to notice much later that her admiration for the Right Hand Man had turned into its opposite; that the process, begun with her visit to Lethem, had entered its final phase in the mansion next to the mosque, the house where she was able to examine her lover-boss under the unflattering microscope of domestic proximity.

When the Minister was abroad she often stood at the wrought iron gates late in the afternoon to look out on the road, straining to hear a few words from the conversations of passers-by. But only the school children spoke loudly. And if she succeeded in catching the drift of some exchange, she would think of those faraway days when she wore a blue uniform and knew the freedom of a shadowy, unconscious world. Childhood was those secret songs, naively believed to be unsavoury:

> Giddy, giddy gout
> Shirt-tail out

One side in
And one side out.

Childhood was a mass of random impressions; dusty roads, plantain leaves lacerated by the wind, wasps ensnared in lace curtains, immobile fish in a backyard pool, possession dances under a pale, uncertain moon. Now that time from which she once longed to emerge into the seductive light of adulthood seemed infinitely precious. And similarly, she forgot the unwitting persecution practised by the father whom she once idolized, and the un-Catholic thoughts for which she flagellated herself as a substitute for confession.

But, unhappy as she was with the Minister, she looked forward to his return from trips, for while he was at home people came and went; official and unofficial visitors, his lady friends, party helpers and others. And there were the grand meals when vingadol was served and aki fruit from Jamaica. And when the librarian came visiting the conversation invariably took an unusual turn, so that she learned about matters considered by her parents to be unladylike or unfit for consideration by the Christian intellect; time was divided into yugas and in the end will be absorbed into Shiva; that they were at present in the Kali yuga, the last and most disastrous period; but those who were concerned for the cosmic condition rather than their personal fate should not worry because Cosmic Time will start all over again.

And she looked forward almost as much to the reluctant pianist's visits, and even the vapid conversation of inept officials, which took on an importance whose absence left a void.

So life went on in the big house where she discovered something about herself and much about the man whom she once admired as the potential saviour of her people. If she hankered after childhood and her huckster days, she never succeeded in grasping the quality of freedom that distinguished both.

And the influence promised by the Minister when she moved in with him proved to be no more than small concessions of power, like the right to decide when his piano should be tuned.

Chapter XX

Correia was arrested on a charge of attempting to burn down the Guest House in Lethem and brought to Georgetown for trial. Many people believed that his apprehension was part of the Government's anti-crime drive and that he had been framed in order to drag up his old fire-raising activities.

The anti-crime drive had begun soon after the old President's death, when the founder of the religious organization The Church of Salvation was clapped in gaol after a trial in which the pent-up feelings of many he had wronged found expression in their testimony against him. A United States citizen on the run from the police in the States, the American authorities were as reluctant to seek his extradition as the old President of Guyana had been keen to let him stay. The Church of Salvation's members, distinguished by their long white robes and overweening arrogance, professed their humility and willingness to co-operate with the authorities immediately after their founder's imprisonment in a long advertisement in the Stabroek News; but the population at large could not forget their association with the dead President and the widespread belief that they were the murderers of Father D, a Roman Catholic priest.

It was in this atmosphere that Correia was put on trial for arson. The Right Hand Man, Minister of Hope, defender of the motto 'Primacy of the Party' — the principle that ensured that no Auditor General's report had been published since 1981, that magistrates and judges cowered under the threats of physical and psychological pressure if they failed to bring in verdicts dictated from above — the Right Hand Man, who normally slept as soundly as Miss Rose his mother, fell into a bout of insomnia when his attempts to halt the proceedings came to nothing. Unable to bear the suspense of waiting to hear whether Correia — in pursuit of his vendetta against him — would disclose anything about his currency dealings in Brazil over the years, he lost weight so quickly and so alarmingly that soon his clothes hung from him like towels from a clothes-horse. His cheeks sank, dark half-moon rings dug deep into the hollows under his eyes, and within a few weeks he presented the picture of a desperate man.

He regretted not doing whatever was necessary to maintain good relations with Kwaku, whom he could otherwise have contacted directly and used as a go-between in dealings with Correia. His dismissal of him and the demand that he pay rent for his flat now seemed rash.

'Send for him an' ask him direct,' Miss Rose suggested, when he told her that Kwaku might have the key to negotiating with Correia.

'The danger is,' he told her, 'that he might visit Correia in gaol and tell him I'm worried. I don't trust that buffoon. There's talk that he's an obeah man.'

He went on to tell her of the phenomenal success of the surgery kept by Kwaku and his acupuncturist son-in-law.

Obeah man! Is that how he managed to heal people? And acupuncturists? She never trusted Georgetown anyhow. All this honking of car horns and the absence of cattle were bad signs. Unbiblical. And why were there so many eating places? This enormous appetite was unnatural. Obeah man!

She decided to look Kwaku up before going back to New Amsterdam, to see how he had crossed her son, who had given him shelter and sustenance when he could have ended up in the streets with dogs for companions or even perished on the damp parapets of an alleyway, companionless. How two fine men could not hit it off was beyond her! But then men were not like women. War was not peace. She had imagined the sort of harmony that should exist between two gifted men, as once existed between her son and his father.

'You look like a tree with blight,' she remarked to her son.

He had always taken care not to tell her too much about his work but now he desired to confide in her fully. In his position he had no true friends, only hangers-on who never disagreed with him and hearkened to his words as if they were pronouncements from heaven. He had begun confiding in Amy Correia about a year ago, tentatively at first; but since her husband refused to leave Lethem, harbouring information about his secret dealings, he could not trust her, even after she came back from the Rupununi giving a creditable imitation of the deserted wife.

No, trusting someone was out of the question. His mother was right, after all. The higher you climbed the more you were exposed to winds that went unnoticed on the ground.

'You look like a tree with blight,' she repeated.

'I should've employed you as my advisor,' he said, trying to put her at ease.

'Whatever you do, eat good and sleep long.'

He kept his insomnia from her. What could she do about it?

'This Correia they're trying knows more about me than I told you.'

'Bad things?' she asked, full of concern.

'Not good.'

'If you kian' do nothing 'bout it. . . .'

'I can't.'

Although he had already decided what to do about it, the futile exchange was useful, giving him the illusion that his mother could help him in his predicament.

He intended getting word to Correia that he was prepared to spend a fortune to secure him an acquittal, provided he kept his mouth shut. The first step to that end would be to avail himself of an attorney with a good record at the Criminal Bar, for whose services he would pay.

Oh, for the time when the old President lived! Then, a single phone call would have sufficed for the case to be dropped, and Correia would have been back in the Rupununi.

'I'll hand in my resignation,' Amy told him one evening.

'What? You'll do nothing of the sort.'

'But I'm in an impossible situation,' she protested.

'What kind of situation do you think I'm in? You resign and you'll give people an excuse to wag their tongues. Besides, we're all in this together.'

That was that! The peremptory tone of voice, the unspoken threat brooked no opposition.

'Very well,' she said, with her show of meekness.

That night he stood at one of the windows of the ministry and looked out on Brickdam with its grand houses, the culvert at the street corner and the asphalt glistening from a recent downpour. He felt deep down that he would survive and, in the end, emerge a stronger, wiser man, more acutely conscious of his isolation, but understanding it to be the price of his ambition. The higher he rose the more apparent it became to him that positions like his were occupied mostly by men who were essentially weak and those who never had time to reflect upon the nature of the mountaintop on which they stood. The old President had died prematurely, having fallen prey to a taste for caviar and Cuban cigars, a prisoner of sycophants who could not prevent his dead body from suppurating and giving off an odour of sulphur dioxide before the plane that had been chartered to transport it to Russia for embalming flew in from abroad. They never learned. He would. Once this trial was over he would plunge into the cold waters of self-examination and not flinch from the lessons to be drawn from his immersion. But his resolve was betrayed by his nightmares, which were full of raging cayman that threatened to devour him.

And if there were those who interpreted his visible suffering as proof that there was more to the arson charge than met the eye, nevertheless they could not fail to admire the disciplined way in which he continued to run his ministry. Arriving unfailingly on time every morning, he bade everyone good day and set to work at once as though nothing untoward had occurred to disturb his peace of mind.

Of course there were others who insisted that he was above the intrigues imputed to him. Something in his private affairs must be the cause of his wasting away. And these fantasists, above all, contributed to the mythology that grew up around the Right Hand Man at this time. One rumour had it that he had fallen from a horse while out riding early one morning, as was the wont of a few leading politicians who regarded riding as a symbol of elevation and the saddle a metaphor for masculine domination. Another rumour claimed that the source of his weight-loss was a jealous woman, who had been secretly poisoning him since he went abroad and did not write her a single letter, or even a postcard. But other stories even more extravagant were put about, to add to the inexhaustible lore concerning emigration, spiralling crime and the desecration of graves in Le Repentir cemetery. Whatever came out in court, the Right Hand Man had been sanctified by the power of rumour and the capacity for elaboration shown by sympathizers and enemies alike.

Whom should Kwaku see in the waiting-room after a day of many clients but Miss Rose, got up in expensive but modest-looking gear she had bought that very afternoon, specially for her visit to the healer of repute.

'Miss Rose!' Kwaku exclaimed and embraced her in the manner

Heliga embraced his more faithful clients. 'I goin' see you after I attend to this dear lady who must be fatigued with waiting.'

She nodded, scarcely believing her ears, for not only did he speak with a different voice but he seemed to have acquired a different vocabulary.

After a good hour Kwaku came out, accompanied by the lady. Miss Rose followed him into his surgery and took a seat in a new wicker chair he had bought to replace the second hand easy chair Heliga had loaned him.

'Miss Rose,' he said, 'what a relief! This high power language is such a strain. . . . But how you know where I practising?'

'Is you who write me. You don' remember. . . ? But you so change up!'

'What about you?' he taunted. 'You look like Senseh Fowl on the way to a dance.'

She enquired about his practice and learned that most of his work now came from listening to people talk.

'They does call it therapy,' he informed her. 'My son-in-law say it's a good name an' you don' got to have certificate to practise it.'

He spoke of odd clients; of clients who came to consult him and ended up telling him what to prescribe them; of wealthy clients who wanted the benefit of all three kinds of treatment; of one woman who spoke frankly of wishing nothing more than a strange man's hand kneading her body 'like bread', although she had no intention of lying with anyone beside her husband. Men did not appreciate his creole massage, and the few who belonged to his clientele preferred his garlic treatment, a last resort because he could not afford to pay an assistant in town to bottle his preparations as Mr Chalfont once did in New Amsterdam.

'But you rolling in money!' Miss Rose protested.

'Not exactly rolling. But people want high wages in town. I can't afford to pay money like that yet.'

Miss Rose was careful to avoid broaching the subject which had prompted her to visit. She would normally not dream of looking him up in town, thinking it more seemly to receive him in New Amsterdam. For, in spite of the hard times she had been through, she still held to the old morality that she should not visit a man at his place. Indeed she was intensely embarrassed and would have preferred Kwaku to talk and talk until she regained her composure. Having installed himself in town, he belonged to town, and to that intimidating tribe of whom she had heard so much from her chauffeur friend whose passenger-van plied the coast.

'I come to see you 'bout something special.'

'What?' Kwaku asked.

'Why you an' my son quarrel?'

'Tch! Miss Rose, Miss Rose. We been friends so long. . . I don' know how to begin.'

'But he was so good to you!'

'That's why I hang my head in shame,' Kwaku said. 'But I pay him back, you know.'

He explained how the Right Hand Man had stolen the idea of his chamber-pot business and built a thriving commerce with tourists.

'Don' tell him I did tell you,' Kwaku said. 'I forget 'bout it already. I jus' did want you to know why I do what I do.'

'What he got to do with this case?' she asked, 'this arson man? He's a *minister*. What he an' this firebug got to do with one another?'

'I don' know, Miss Rose.'

'He get so thin! I had was to look away when I was talking to him. It hurt me so!'

'Miss Rose, I remember when I take my family from the village to live in New Amsterdam, with those houses so close together and the zinc sheets with "Stick no Bills" on them, an' the big, big market. Was like another country. I didn't understand what was goin' on. I was bewildered! You know what? In Georgetown is worse. You an' me are little ants goin' about our business in another world. Everything so big you can't understand no more. I am not bewildered, Miss Rose. I am in a state of perpetual shock! I don' say my prayers no more. If your son get thin is because he understand what's goin' on. An' if I still in shock at least I in' lost weight.'

' 'Strue,' she said. 'You look as if you eating nut butter an' pears with a silver spoon. Your skin so smooth!'

'You should see my son-in-law, the acupuncturist!'

'When my son say you associating with acupuncturists I din' believe him!'

She was now angry. She had forgiven him for his ingratitude towards her son, but on his own admission he was associating with the lowest of the low after all he had done for him.

'Why you vex?' Kwaku asked.

She reminded him of the case that came before the court four years ago, involving an acupuncturist from England who had swindled more than a score of people by offering them shares in an institute for teaching the secrets of acupuncture to students for a substantial fee. Having collected both the share-money and an advance on the fees from several would-be students, the acupuncturist fled to Venezuela. That was the first time the word 'acupuncturist' had appeared in the press, since when it became a synonym for fraudster and joined words like 'adulterer' that were banned from the conversation of well-bred folk.

Kwaku, who knew nothing of the case, proceeded to explain the history of acupuncture, so far as he understood Heliga's version.

'Is Chinese,' Kwaku said finally. 'An' you know they straight as a die.'

Reassured only because the practice came from the Chinese, whose only vice was gambling at mah-jong, she calmed down, delighted that there was no reason to put her friendship with Kwaku in jeopardy.

'He in trouble?' she asked, after giving her anger time to subside.

'Naw! He's a minister. Ministers does make things happen. Things don' happen to them like you an' me. Naw! Take my word for it.'

'He don' want me to stay an' help him, you know,' she complained. 'He say, "go back to New Amsterdam. I'm not a boy no more." He so thin! The only thing that put on weight is his Adam's apple.'

'He right, you know,' Kwaku advised. 'You mus' go back home where all the news is local news. You read the papers? They full of wars an' rape an' this an' that. And the Government doin' it on purpose, you know. They want to bewilder you an' soften you up. M'dear! My head full of rape an' wars; and sometimes when I giving a lady client a creole massage all sorts of wicked thoughts come in my head an' is only 'cause of my professional standing I do what's right.'

'You mus' start praying again,' she suggested.

'I feel embarrassed, Miss Rose. I feel like putting the sheet over my head if I'm to pray. I don' know. Life's easy now. The money's coming in. But I feel so *un*easy! For me, for Miss Gwendoline an' my children. I did promise that when they grow up I'd start living for Miss Gwendoline an' me alone; but when it come to it I worrying jus' as much as before about them.'

The two settled to talking about old times, as though the past contained the answer to their anxieties. She had had many suitors before she moved to a cottage near the cemetery in New Amsterdam, but she could not/forget her husband. She wore her Sunday best every afternoon to watch the funeral processions passing from behind her blind. And sometimes when she felt lonely she would go down to the sexton's lodge at the Stanleytown cemetery and look at a corpse laid out in a coffin placed on the table and wait for the relatives to arrive one by one because they were too poor to attract a procession. All because she was lonely. She was not complaining! That was her lot, please God. If anyone were to ask her whether she preferred her life now to the days when she lived in a state of unrelenting resentment towards her husband she would not know what to say. Suffering or loneliness? Both were diseases. Perhaps she preferred her present condition because her son had made his way in life and was now one of the most powerful men in the country.

'He like you a lot, you know.'

'Who?' Kwaku asked.

'My son. He tell me about the "In Memoriam" poems. If only you know how proud he was when he saw them in the newspaper under the photographs of the dead people. You wouldn' think that a man in that position would care 'bout seeing his poems in the papers, would you? He so upset you don' do it no more.'

After an embarrassed silence she blurted out, 'I goin' come clean! I want you to go and see this Correia and ask if he'll allow my son to help him.'

Kwaku immediately jumped to the conclusion that Correia's imprisonment had been contrived by the Right Hand Man, and that he was now playing the same game of appearing to be a saviour as he had done at the time of his own arrest by the airport customs officers.

'Well, what you say?' she asked, pressing him for a reply.

Kwaku did not know what to say. His impulse was to accept the offer, but at the same time he feared that he might be walking into a trap.

'Alright,' he agreed, deciding that there could be no harm in putting the proposition to Correia.

She got up, thrust her hand out like a lady, and was touched when Kwaku embraced her, for in spite of her son she could not see him as anything but the dispenser of generosity in those far-off days. He accompanied her to the main road, where she took the pavement under the awnings put out by proprietors of drinking places and tailor shops, along the haunts of out-of-work sleepers and cripples and loitering youths, past sellers of second hand books with lurid illustrations, towards the centre of town and the corner flanked by rubber trees.

Returning to the surgery, Kwaku compared Miss Rose's serene figure with the younger, cantankerous woman she used to be, and he wondered how others saw him. There were things one kept to oneself, for no reason except that they were to be left unsaid. Yet he longed to know what he was like, how he was regarded by those with whom he did business. He recalled the words he had heard during a religious service over the radio: 'Man walketh in vain . . . and disquieth himself in vain.' Shadows had always haunted him, demonic shadows. He never understood why 'in vain' referred to 'disquieth himself'. Were the Correias, the Ministers, Bertie, Surinam, Suarez pursued by shadows? And if so, was it in vain? He had sunk to the depths of degradation when he used to go about searching trash cans in New Amsterdam for pig food, vegetable peel and restaurant garbage. Or had he? The more he learned the more he was plagued with doubts. Was it true — what he had told himself time and time again — that if Miss Gwendoline's sight was restored he would be the happiest of men? Seeing her shuffling from the verandah to the bedroom, hearing her engage in futile conversations with herself, certainly made him the unhappiest of men. Suarez, the wisest of his friends, did not think she was unhappy; but Suarez was not always wise. He was not as wise as Mr Barzey, who hanged himself at the height of his wisdom.

Kwaku found himself sitting on the bench where the clients waited and heard the advice given by Heliga to a departing patient in that unctious tone he still admired.

News of Correia's release a fortnight later was followed by a rumour that Kwaku the healer had bought his friend's freedom with a huge sum of money; but the public, judging the incident to provide further evidence of ministerial corruption, paid no great heed to it. Besides, fire-raisers were held in high regard by certain sections of the population who had profited from the looting which followed the conflagrations that scarred the sixties. Some declared openly that order brought them few benefits, while they recalled the advantages of chaos.

The Minister of Hope was overjoyed at Correia's release as a result of his plea at the commital proceedings that, due to lack of evidence, there was no case to answer. He sent a note to Correia in which he congratulated him, adding that he could have his job back whenever he wished. But the former employee refused the offer, to the evident relief of the jubilant Minister.

Chapter XXI

Miss Gwendoline had persuaded Suarez to give English lessons to Kwaku, who felt keenly his inadequacy when in conversation with clients who consulted him for their 'spiritual problems', as he described them. One lady had intimidated him with her large vocabulary of words entirely unsuited to the description of the problem that was giving her concern, and Kwaku, peeved by his inability to match her, behaved discourteously, thus breaking the cardinal rule he had learned from his son-in-law.

The restraint demanded of town life required a constant, heroic struggle that often got the better of him; and a client who had had experience of his obliging, almost fawning gestures, would recoil in alarm at an uncharacteristic outburst.

'I have a problem that's exercising my husband's patience,' the lady had told him.

At this point Kwaku was still on his best professional behaviour.

'I scratch,' she went on. 'And for some impenetrable reason he takes exception to this and chides me. He reminds me that ladies don't scratch, however much they might be itching.'

In spite of Kwaku's reproving look she carried on.

'Only someone who has never been afflicted with itching would venture such a remark. I have a great respect for my husband but I do draw the line at his bullying behaviour. Scratching is a fundamental liberty. . . .'

Failing to appreciate that his client was doing her best to make an impression on him, he was near to breaking point.

'. . . so I reminded him of his faults, his excessive loquaciousness in particular. "You can't stop once you begin," I told him. There are times when I'm capable of the most brutal candour, Mr Cholmondeley. I could have said much more, but. . . .'

'Lady,' Kwaku broke in, 'What you take me for, a blinking dictionary? What do you want?'

He blurted out the word 'want' with such vehemence that she recoiled like an accouri unexpectedly confronted with a snake.

'I say,' she declared, 'steady on!'

She remained standing before him with her head drawn backwards.

Now, as every competent healer knows, every emotion has its corresponding gesture, and Kwaku's client's cocked head could just as well have dispensed with her timid protest.

'If you tell me your problem in simple language, lady,' Kwaku said, 'probably I can help you.'

She took out a handkerchief, dabbed her dry eyes with it and began all over again.

'Sit down, mistress,' Kwaku advised kindly.

She sat down.

She described the itching once more in simple language and, at Kwaku's prompting, spoke of the way her husband monopolized the conversation, which had not really bothered her until he accused her of scratching in public.

'So what is the problem?'

'The itching.'

'Where do it itch?' Kwaku asked, now thinking it was his turn to display a fine appreciation of grammar.

'Here,' she answered, pointing to the middle of her back, 'and lower down . . . on the unmentionable . . . my beatty.'

She whispered the last word.

'Well scratching your backside in public *would* annoy any decent husband,' Kwaku told her, as though he were making a weighty diagnosis.

His blunt description of her predicament made her recoil once more, but Kwaku took no notice this time.

Having no idea how to treat his patient he thought of asking her to come back the following day, by which time he would have decided upon a suitable placebo. None of his favourite remedies seemed appropriate, and the problem being most un-psychological, it would not benefit from his talking cure.

'Lady, when did the itching start?'

'About three months ago, Mr Cholmondeley.'

'You been quarrelling a lot with your husband about the time it did begin?'

'Not more than usual.'

'I see,' said Kwaku, stroking his chin.

In the end, recalling the dispenser's cure for his lottah when he was a boy, he told her to buy some borax at the doctor shop, mix it with water, and apply it to her back twice a day.

She paid her fee and left, edging past Kwaku, not entirely convinced that his tantrum was over. She stopped at the door.

'Something wrong?' Kwaku asked.

'It's not just the itching, you know, Mr Cholmondeley. . . . He says I'm a prude.'

'Who?'

'My husband.'

'You want to come back in an' tell me about it?' Kwaku asked, making a swift mental calculation of the extra fee he would charge.

'No, it's nothing really. . . . I mean it's not serious. . . . He used to live abroad, you see. And he's come back with ideas, you know.'

'I don't know, mistress.'

'Unchristian ideas.'

'Mistress, you'd better come in.'

'No, it's nothing. I'm making a fuss about nothing. . . . I tend to make a fuss about nothing. At least so he says.'

'But it could be serious,' Kwaku corrected her. 'Why not come in?'

She made one step over the threshold and stopped.

'I don't know why I'm telling you this, Mr Cholmondeley. I came for the scratching. This is completely unimportant. A small fly in the ointment, you might say.'

'Lady, please come in.'

'It's very kind of you, Mr Cholmondeley, but it's too painful to talk about.'

'Goodbye, then.'

'Goodbye.'

She went out once more but stopped as Kwaku was about to close the door and said:

'Do you think I'm a prude, Mr Cholmondeley?'

'I think you don' like spending money, lady. You keep me standing here an' take my time free. How you think I does live? On air?'

'Goodbye then,' she said, assuming her suffering expression.

She left for good.

Kwaku knew that what rankled more than anything else, more than the money his client refused to spend, more than her excessive show of suffering, was the feeling of inadequacy with words she aroused in him. And the encounter had the effect of making up his mind to follow

Miss Gwendoline's advice about taking lessons from Suarez, who accepted only for Miss Gwendoline's sake, anticipating that Kwaku would be a difficult student.

But Kwaku was so keen on improving his language skills he proved to be an exemplary pupil, tackling every obstacle with a zest that surprised Philomena, who believed that he hated books and book learning. Kwaku visited every bookshop in town in search of the American textbooks recommended by Suarez. He had gone past most of them at one time or another without looking inside. Now he discovered to his dismay that they carried next to nothing and resembled those derelict construction sites where half-finished buildings offered their innards to the gaze of passers-by. Most of their stock consisted of old books and a few new ones at exorbitant prices. Whole shelves were empty because the proprietor did not have the foreign currency needed to import his wares.

In the end Philomena wrote to a shop in Toronto, enquiring after suitable material for teaching English; and when the first batch of reading matter arrived, graded text books, novels, books on esoteric subjects that presupposed a background knowledge Kwaku lacked and even an American best seller first published in the nineteen-forties called 'How to Win Friends and Influence People', Suarez and Philomena fell on them while he looked on, unable to take advantage of what was, in fact, stuff for the accomplished reader. He had to wait for the second more carefully chosen batch of elementary readers suitable to his level of attainment.

And as he progressed in his quest for knowledge and competence he imported books for their imposing titles or books that took his fancy only because they were published by a University Press; yet others because of the prominence given them in a catalogue, and even a book written by a Nicholas Cholmondeley who, he told his friends, was his father's nephew, son of an uncle who had emigrated to the United States in the early part of the century. And the fact that no one believed him mattered little, for as far as he was concerned the name he shared with the author justified any tale he cared to invent about him.

That is how Kwaku Cholmondeley built up a library and displayed its contents on shelves put up in his rooms at the new East Bank surgery he and his son-in-law had opened, where there was enough space for half a dozen healers to practise. And nothing gave him greater pleasure than a chance remark by a client about his distinguished collection of books.

As for his progress under Suarez's tutelage, it was 'so-so' he told Miss Gwendoline and Philomena modestly, while harbouring excessive pretensions to intellectual distinction, which would allow him to treat his patients with a confidence commensurate with the profits he and Heliga were making.

Indeed Kwaku's progress was more than so-so. Suarez had sent him the results of his first examination, an elementary test set by the Ministry of Education, which he passed with full marks. Kwaku had arranged for the results to be posted to Suarez's address so that, should he fail, Miss Gwendoline would be none the wiser. In fact, he decided not to inform her of his success anyway, since he was more than a little ashamed that he, a man pushing forty, should be putting himself on a par with children in their early teens.

Kwaku saw the following Friday evening meeting with their friends as a kind of celebration, all the more exciting, he thought, as his success would be kept a secret from them as well. At last he was on the way to being able to claim equality with the likes of his son-in-law who, one day, would no longer have a reason to despise him.

Friday evening finally came and the shadows lengthened, and Kwaku sat down at the window to await his friend. When Suarez finally arrived he made no excuse for being late and went straight over to Miss Gwendoline to embrace her.

'Alyou behave yourself tonight,' she said. 'Suarez, if you bring him home drunk I not goin' talk to you no more.'

And saying this she laughed out loud.

'I gone,' Kwaku told her, patting her on the head.

They were happier than ever since the children had become adults, and her family were scattered to every corner of the country.

'I gone, Miss Gwendoline,' Suarez said in turn.

'Walk good. And don' get drunk!'

As they were going down the stairs they heard her radio, which she always used of late as a companion when alone in the house.

The koker was open, and the trench water made eddies beside the grass, trampled underfoot by boys who fished unsuccessfully for tilapia in the afternoons after school. It had rained heavily during the last fortnight, and at times the trench all but encroached on the grass verge; then the koker would open just in time and draw off the water into the river. The scent of rain was in the air, but both men disdained walking with an umbrella, thinking it more manly to take the risk of getting wet during the long journey through Lodge to Meadowbrook.

Suarez, who had taken pity on Kwaku in the first days of his stay in Georgetown, now viewed the latter's flat as his second home. Unmarried, unattached — a fact that made for endless speculation amongst his friends — he dropped in at Kwaku's whenever he was at a loose end. Kwaku believed him to be sweet on Philomena who, however, hardly took any notice of him. Demonstrative in her relations with her husband, she barely acknowledged his existence, or even her father's for that matter, a neglect which pained Kwaku not a little, especially as he began to see through his son-in-law, judging him to be empty under his façade of worldly wisdom.

Suarez nursed an intense dislike of Heliga but, careful to keep his feelings to himself, his impeccable conduct aroused no one's suspicion of his feelings. Like Miss Gwendoline, he had seen through him from the beginning, on the flimsiest evidence it must be said. He could not stand his elaborate courtesy, his refusal to become embroiled in an argument or his cloying courtship of Philomena.

Suarez's accurate assessment of Kwaku's son-in-law was due, not in small measure, to his jealousy. Smitten by Philomena's beauty, at first he was intrigued that someone like Kwaku could father a daughter of such unusual looks. But it was during the ceremony at the church that, filled with an indescribable hostility towards the bridegroom, a man he only knew slightly, his infatuation became clear to him. Perhaps his torment might have been tolerable if Philomena had paid him some attention, even as a friend of the family. But her indifference had the effect of firing his passion, and he could only stand aside helplessly while he magnified every small failing of his rival.

When Kwaku informed Suarez of a client's husband's remark that the son-in-law was no more than a one month acupuncturist, the news had the same effect on him as if he had learned that he had come into an unexpected fortune.

'He said one month?' Suarez had asked eagerly.

'He say one month.'

Now, on the way to Surinam's flat, Kwaku told him that his son-in-law was coming later. Suarez did not know how to take the news. On the one hand he would have the opportunity of throwing scorn upon him for his pansy-like ways. On the other, the evening would be ruined by his presence, for he simply did not fit in with the ribald conversation that was the currency of a Friday night get-together.

'You invited him?' Suarez asked, with a show of indifference.

'Yes. The words jus' slip out.'

'You can't change,' Suarez said. 'You'll never change. You can read a thousand books, you'll never change.'

'The damage done,' Kwaku retorted. 'He coming. My beloved son-in-law coming.'

They had got as far as the point where the houses began to space out and the lights beyond the old racecourse blinked uncertainly, like the reflections of kerosene lamps.

They walked the rest of the way in silence, and the further their steps took them the more dense the chorus of frogs became, calling from the damp grass and canals and, seemingly, from the air above them and the ground beneath their feet; a pervasive orchestra of wailing, croaking, invisible instruments, broadcasting the desire to mate before the dry season came.

Kwaku could not have foreseen these months of contentment. Even Miss Gwendoline's blindness had been all but forgotten. Indeed, she herself, in one of her lighter moments, described it as a blessing, since she was spared the sight of much misery. He had acquired a certain respect among some of his cronies, who admired him for the success he had made of his business and praised him for the way he had shed so many of his country ways.

But above all Kwaku had managed to dispel the shadow of poverty which had frightened him to the point that, only a few years ago, he was prepared to become any townsman's creature, just so that he and Miss Gwendoline could eat a meal or two every day. Lately, he had to make an effort to recall those times, unless Miss Gwendoline took it into her head to speak about them when she sank, for no apparent reason, into one of her gloomy moods.

As they approached the last road that branched off into the heart of Lodge, a van went past and stopped a few yards ahead, then discharged one by one three wheelchairs through its rear door, and in which were seated three heavily made-up teenage girls with deformed legs. Suarez hurried along between the first and second wheelchairs while Kwaku held back, riveted to the spot by an interest he could not explain. Two girls wore grave, unsmiling expressions; but the third, whose head kept nodding from side to side, giggled continually while two strands of spittle descended from the corners of her red-painted mouth.

Suarez, irritated by Kwaku's lack of discretion, hurried on, walking faster than he normally did. And when Kwaku finally ran up to join him he remained stubbornly silent, even as they turned into Surinam's street.

One of the almost nightly electricity black-outs had just begun and Surinam's flat was shrouded in darkness. His benefactor's car was not in the drive, but another unfamiliar one was parked in front of the door.

'Come in, man,' Surinam called out from inside.

The two men went through the open door into the dark room, lit only by a candle standing in a saucer on a table beside the bed.

Surinam introduced a man sitting on the bed as 'Teach', whom neither Kwaku nor Suarez had ever seen before. Suarez shook hands and sat down on the bed beside him before enquiring after Bertie.

'You know he's always late nowadays.'

Bertie no longer brought Eunice to the Friday night gatherings since they married five weeks ago in a quiet ceremony which was attended only by the minister, two witnesses and a parishioner who happened to be praying in the church at the time. The excuse he gave Eunice for coming alone was that it was not seemly for a wife of his to wash up and act as a servant for so many men. They all missed her gaiety and the small tensions that characterized her relationship with Bertie, who would have tethered her to a post like a horse if he could.

The retired teacher, a portly septuagenarian, had been drinking for some time and regaling Surinam with stories from his school days.

'Tell them what you told me,' Surinam said, 'about the three Miss Bournes.'

Nothing pleased the teacher more, and he began with a flourish.

The primary school he attended as a small boy, St Stephens, stood next to a church as all decent schools did. But one thing distinguished St Stephens: the rise in school numbers outstripped its accommodation, so that the classes with the youngest children, Little A.B.C. and Big A.B.C., were held in a part of the church.

The manner of Teach's telling of the story even more than this amusing fact caused both Kwaku and Suarez to chuckle.

'You telling lies!' Surinam exclaimed in jest.

'Truth o' God!' protested Teach.

'Go on, man,' Surinam said, half apologetically.

Teach continued. An even stranger fact was that three of the school's teachers were called Miss Bourne. The children, in order to identify the Bourne teachers among themselves called the one who taught in the school building 'Little Miss Bourne,' while the other two, both of whom taught in the church, were Red Bourne, as she was brown skinned, and Black Bourne, the darkest of the three.

Kwaku was in stitches. When he was introduced to the stranger he resolved inwardly to make an impression on him by being restrained in his deportment and speech. And here he was, one leg in the air, laughing loudly enough to wake the dead.

'Well,' Teach went on, now at his most assured with an appreciative audience of three, 'the story is really about Red Bourne. She was a *beat general*! She used to flog the little ones mercilessly.'

He went on to tell how, with space at a premium in the section of the church where lessons were held, Red Bourne used to make her Little A.B.C. pupils bend over the window ledge to receive their lashes with the cane.

'Passers-by used to watch their faces recording, out of the window, what was tormenting their backsides inside the church.'

Even Suarez nearly lost control of himself, infected by the merriment.

'Nowdays it would be a criminal offence to punish the young ones like that,' Teach reflected sadly.

Since Kwaku had begun attending the gatherings so much had altered! And with each change the company swore that things would never be the same again. The first time Eunice was brought along by Bertie, Correia and Suarez groaned in dismay. A woman! But they grew to be fond of her showing off and her good-natured banter. Now she had gone, spirited away by Bertie's jealousy. And she was missed in the same way that they missed Correia when he went to Lethem, to lose himself in the limitless Rupununi grasslands where he had no friends. Teach, whom they had just met, promised to be a match for anyone of the present or past company; and what was more he loved his liquor, the strongest testimonial in favour of a newcomer.

Bertie arrived soon afterwards, and about fifteen minutes later Heliga, whom Kwaku introduced to the others. Suarez, breaking his code of courtesy, refused to shake hands, and his reaction was not lost on the others, who, however, pretended to notice nothing.

By now Teach was in full flight. Stories of his experiences as a teacher rolled off his tongue as he thrived on the laughter. Then, in the midst of a comic treat which drew the expected howls of delight Kwaku suddenly became serious, recalling the young invalid whose uncontrollable movements had turned him cold. In the dark no one saw the abrupt change of expression.

The candle flame wavered when Surinam opened a window on account of the intolerable closeness in the room, now that six persons were vying for air.

Kwaku wanted to lie full-length on the bed as Correia used to do, but felt that he was, in the end, still a stranger to these Georgetonians.

Unable to get the smiling, dribbling young woman out of his mind, he hid in the darkness of the room, no longer hearing the teacher's words, and hardly aware of the peals of laughter that broke out from time to time. There was a raw, bitter thing on the night air that penetrated them all in the candle-lit darkness, and he remembered words from a book that Suarez had forced him to read over and over:

Pale shadows
Who will not see
The moon go white with dread.

Then, when everyone had become accustomed to the dark, the lights went on.

'Listen!' Surinam told them. 'Shh!'

They all listened, and one by one they heard the emergency electric generators of the neighbouring houses go off, until the night stillness was broken only by the whistling of the army of frogs.

'Every night!' Bertie exclaimed, embroidering his exclamation with a loud eloquent suck-teeth. 'Every night these damned black-outs.'

Stories of official ineptitude replaced Teach's comic reminis-cences, and each one contributed, even Kwaku, whose malaise had passed as suddenly as it had begun. Teach, who had travelled the new road from the Brazilian border, contrasted the section built by Brazil with the other, for which Guyana was responsible. The latter, in a deplorable condition, discouraged travellers from making the trip overland, he claimed.

'You hear that the Minister of Hope going abroad to try and attract foreign capital to the country?' Teach said.

'Again?' Kwaku asked.

That was his first contribution to a conversation concerning politics, a subject of unfathomable mystery to him. But his sustained reading under Suarez's tutelage had given him confidence.

'Yes,' Teach replied. 'Soon they'll be calling him the Travelling Minister. And these people travel first class, you know. First class, mister. We can't pay our debts or feed our people, but our ministers have to travel first class.'

'We must put our best foot forward,' Kwaku's son-in-law declared, breaking a silence most of the company interpreted as being due to arrogance, an opinion confirmed by his supercilious smile.

Suarez, as though he had been waiting for him to make a blunder, leapt upon the remark.

'So it's alright to go bankrupt, provided we put our best foot forward,' he remarked sarcastically.

Heliga, taken aback by the unexpectedly aggressive reaction to what was intended as proof that he was sociable, protested that if the Government could not do things in style they should not do them at all.

The teacher, a peaceable man when he was not on the subject of flogging children and young people, sought to steer the conversation away from the issue of itinerant government ministers, but the company would have none of it. Bertie said it was a disgrace that they attended most of the international conferences abroad anyway while Surinam, conscious of his position as host, urged them to let Kwaku's son-in-law defend himself.

'Look, I'm entitled to an opinion, like you,' Heliga said, determined to stand his ground. 'If you want me to shut up I will.'

'You been doing that all the time,' Bertie said, putting his knife in.

Most of the company had smelt blood and were ready to tear him to pieces. If Kwaku admired him and fawned on him for his sartorial elegance and business sense, he had never forgotten how he had insinuated himself into his family and taken Philomena from him. Suarez simply hated him. And as for Bertie, who made no attempt to hide his emotions, he disliked everything about Heliga and would not have protested if Surinam had shown him the door the moment he walked in.

Kwaku's son-in-law attracted dislike as some people attracted loyalty or affection. The very quality of aloofness that contributed to his professional success irked those with whom he came into contact socially; and he, the butt of contempt and mistrust in countless encounters, remained completely unaware of why he had this effect on others. So much so that with each new experience he betrayed an injured surprise at the injustice of strangers.

'Food!' said Surinam, choosing that moment to announce the consumption of the victuals he had prepared beforehand.

His dinners had grown more elaborate and, since Eunice no longer attended, he had to invite his guests to serve themselves.

They filed into the kitchen next to his studio and began serving themselves on brown stoneware plates. Portions of chicken and labba, fried rice and boiled rice, mango chutney, curried pork and braised beef, and spinach bhaji were spooned up and arranged beside one another. Kwaku did this with some haste, 'lest the fare should go away,' he thought. The spinach bhaji, which he did not care for, he heaped upon the pork; and in the end he returned to his place on the bed carrying an overflowing plate.

No one dared put the question they were all dying to ask: 'Where do you get the money from to pay for all this, Surinam?' And each constructed his own imagined story regarding relations between their host and his mysterious benefactor.

The persecuted son-in-law as well as his tormentors abandoned their argument in favour of the supper, leaving their half-filled beer glasses lying about on the floor.

Had Miss Gwendoline been able to see and had she been present, she would have been surprised to witness her husband keeping company like any other normal Christian, conducting himself with the dignity befitting a Catholic priest hearing confession without so much as a word out of place but choosing his moment to say 'Aye' or to counsel an appropriate number of 'Hail Marys' on the disclosure of a mortal sin. And it could be asserted with confidence that there were those who, apart from the members of his family, enjoyed his company. Surinam, for one, looked forward to his arrival on Friday nights; as did Suarez, who could now claim membership of his family so far as the term included friends who visited regularly and took part in household rituals.

When Surinam indicated during the meal that he wanted him to remain after the others had gone — an invitation that had not been repeated after the last, more than a year ago — Kwaku eagerly nodded assent. One day, surely, he would earn the right to penetrate into the studio adjoining the lesser studio, as Surinam had promised. This, his last unexpressed wish as an outsider, would be the consummation of a deep longing for acceptance which was the source of his delinquency while still a youth and his unpredictability in his adult years. For, of all the people he had come to know since his stay in the capital, Surinam represented an ideal whose face was, in some curious way, turned away from him.

Chapter XXII

Kwaku stood in the middle of the room adjoining the outer studio, the secret room where Surinam achieved transformations which meant as much to him as living. His life *was* his painting, his ability to start with the colours, most of which he made himself, and create through them canvases that recorded his visions. His yellows, the dominant hue in his work, were made by a secret process taught him by an East Indian gentleman in the village of his birth, long before he had any intention of becoming a painter. Beginning with the urine of cattle fed on mango leaves, it went through several stages of refinement until, as the final product, it glowed with a luminosity that appeared to come from within.

'When I feel inspiration creeping up on me I come in here and *create*. You can't grasp the meaning of that word, my friend. It's a kind of theft. You steal from your visions!'

The room was very different from the studio next to the kitchen. Nearly every surface was painted — the bedcover, the walls and a portion of the floor.

'Look here!' exclaimed Surinam. 'It's this I wanted to show you.'

And with a long pole he took off a huge hessian sheet that covered his latest painting on a framed canvas, which glistened with new paint.

'I was born in 1963, the year of those riots middle-aged and old people can't talk about without frothing at the mouth.'

Kwaku was not listening, for he was absorbed in the contemplation of canvases completely different from Surinam's studio work. Here everything was explicit, yet mysterious. The corpse of a child being brought out of what is left of a burnt-out house; a triptych, the last section of which featured a man lying on the road under a bicycle with twisted wheels. In the first he was seen indicating to the traffic behind him in which direction he is about to turn, smiling as he did so.

'They are all real incidents that occurred during the riots, when Indians and creoles were murdering one another. Look at this one: I called it "Good Neighbours". My father told me about an Indian and a creole who were so friendly they and their children were continually in and out of one another's houses.'

In the painting they were hacking at each other with cutlasses, their faces contorted with rage.

'You see that with your own eyes?' Kwaku asked.

'No. I told you. I was born that year. But my father described the incidents to me. My mother is East Indian and she was murdered a week after I was born. My father is a black man.'

Kwaku looked up at the wall once more, pretending that he had not quite understood. Uneasy at Surinam's feverish manner of speaking, he could not get the words out of his mind: 'When I feel inspiration creeping up on me I come in here and create.' Was Surinam tetched? He had never seen paintings like these, let alone colours like these. Whoever bore the name of a country? Surinam! But what of the Surinam who entertained cordially and spoke in a calm voice to boisterous guests and poured oil on troubled waters?

'Everything has its secrets,' Surinam said. 'Painting too. In a portrait the secret lies in the eyes and mouth. Look at them.'

He pointed in turn to the two men with cutlasses, then placed a finger on their eyes, one after the other. And indeed the eyes of the two men had wild, murderous expressions, which made it difficult to credit the story that they had once been friends.

'But what is frightening,' Surinam said, grabbing hold of Kwaku's arm, 'is that it's going to happen again. And you know why? Because humans are thugs by nature, and politicians know all about exploiting thugs and thuggery.'

'I don' agree with you,' Kwaku said, reacting swiftly to Surinam's extreme view. 'I know a lot of Indians in East Canje and they would never attack me. And I never attack anybody in my life.'

Surinam shook his head while staring at Kwaku but said nothing.

'Well, let's not discuss politics or history,' Surinam went on. 'Painting's the thing. When the whole of this generation dies my colours will still shine. Egyptian murals have lasted five thousand years. You are nothing. I am nothing. Art is everything.'

This opinion went against Kwaku's idea of the individual as master or mistress of destiny and the centre of a miniature world. *He* was the hub of his world. 'I am nothing' meant that all his striving counted for little, except that he had saved Miss Gwendoline and himself from destitution. Surinam *was* tetched, and his art, far from deserving admiration, did no more than support the proposition that he should be committed to an asylum.

All at once the reek of new paint sickened him, and the canvases he had been admiring only a few minutes ago seemed garish and vulgar in the extreme. The painted bedspread, figuring a man with an enormous erect penis, was an insult to human dignity, as were the images of death. Small wonder Surinam saw the individual as nothing. Had he been a less generous host Kwaku would have insulted him on the spot and told him to stick his odious views down his gullet. Kwaku regretted that he had not left with Suarez and Heliga. Now he would have to walk home alone with the suspicion that he might be, after all, nothing.

'I read a book once,' Surinam said, putting his arm around Kwaku's shoulder and leading him out of the room, through the outer studio and back into the room where he received his guests. 'I read a novel — long ago, when every book I read excited me — I read this book about an artist who once painted a field with a well in the centre of it. When the work was finished the artist thought there was something strange about the well and informed the police that it needed to be investigated. The police searched it and found a body at the bottom. After that the police employed him as a kind of investigative painter. That's all I remember about the novel, except that it was winter time and everything was covered in snow. . . . I don't know why I'm telling you this. Why am I telling you this. . . ? Do you know they say it snowed more than once on Mount Roraima? In our tropical country that nearly sits on the equator? Strange, isn't it? I would like to paint on Roraima while it's snowing, and the wind's howling round me and . . . the moon. No, you can't paint by moonlight. What a pity! What a pity. . . ! Your son-in-law went abroad and what did it do for him, the pompous fool?'

Kwaku, although he would readily have run down his son-in-law, felt, nevertheless, offended but kept quiet, waiting only for the right moment to make an excuse to leave for home. He no longer doubted that Surinam had only a tenuous hold on his sanity.

'You know Thomas Goodland,' Surinam continued. 'He led an expedition up Roraima and when he came back to town he was only fit for cultivating flowers.'

'Why?' Kwaku asked.

'He himself said that's all he was fit for. After his brilliant feat!

Now there was a man! The experience changed his life. And the day he reached seventy — I mean the very day — he went out and on his way back home asked people where he lived. "But you are Thomas Goodland! Everybody knows where you live," they told him. He'd lost his memory. On that very day . . . ! I haven't got the slightest idea why I'm telling you about Thomas Goodland or anything else. . . . You're no different from the others, Kwaku. Before you began making lots of money you used to do things, make odd things happen. Now I hear you read many books. The poet wants to be educated. No, I've lost all respect for you.'

'Look here!' Kwaku protested.

'Why're you vexed? Do you respect me? Does Bertie respect me? He says I'm a fool because I invited you to sponge on me. And he'll say the same because your son-in-law did too. . . .'

'I don' understand you,' Kwaku said in a loud voice. 'If you were married and responsible for a household, you wouldn' talk like that.'

'But I *am* married and I have two children. But you're right: I haven't any money responsibilities. My wife supports me. . . . I don't know why you're surprised. You know nothing about me. Why did you assume I'm not married? Do you look through the window and say "He's married; she's not married," about passers-by? Yet you assume I'm not married. Oh, I am disappointed in you; in your foppish clothes and the way you lick your son-in-law's boots and in your passion for saving money.'

'Who told you I saving money?' Kwaku demanded to know.

'You're making it, but you don't even ride a cycle or live extravagantly.'

Kwaku was now openly hostile and prepared to utter the forbidden words he had left under his breath while they were in the inner studio. But he held back, imagining that Surinam might be inviting an insult deliberately and was doing everything to rouse him. But while holding back his expression gave him away, and Surinam was moved to say, 'I don't mind if you curse me. But I must tell you; the superior man would welcome the mirror I'm holding up to you, the man who knows he's inferior to a good painting, for instance.'

'If I did think you been trying to insult me,' Kwaku said, 'never mind. I eat at your home, so I not goin' start insulting you now. But I'll never set foot in this flat again.'

'My wife used to buy my paintings while I was in the mental asylum, before we married,' Surinam said in the most normal, unfeeling voice imaginable. 'And I used to insult her and call her every name under the sun. You want to hear some of the things I called her? No? Anyway she fell in love with me. So she said. The doctor told her once when she came to visit me that I wasn't capable of love, but she married me all the same; and I fell in love with her because she was so persistent. I went to see the doctor after I was let out and told him I'd fallen in love. But he believed in his books so firmly he insisted I wasn't capable of love.'

'So you are. . . .' Kwaku stuttered, unable to utter the word on the tip of his tongue.

'Mad?' Surinam said.

Kwaku nodded in confirmation.

'Yes, I'm mad.'

Kwaku reflected for a moment; then, emboldened by the feeling of superiority that overtook him on learning that his suspicions about Surinam were accurate, said:

'You not qualified to lecture me 'bout money when you so comfortably off. I mean you don' have the right.'

'Suppose I was poor and wore rags, would you've taken me more seriously?'

Kwaku did not answer, having no idea what his attitude would have been in that case.

'Once,' Surinam continued, 'I said you interested me because you're an artist. But why should I still be interested in you now that I know you haven't got any talent? Or, better, that you prefer to ignore your talent and earn money. Now I think I know. I'm sure, in fact: it's because you're mad, like me. Like recognizes like. You're as nutty as a fruit cake, my friend. But you have no character.'

'I'm not goin' stay here an' be insulted jus' because I eat your roast pork an' drink your beer. Why you ask me to stay? "Stay, man. I got something to show you." An' what you show me? A lot of smelly paintings anybody could've done.'

Surinam burst out laughing, leaving Kwaku disarmed. He stood by the door, helpless. He had intended to wound Surinam but instead was now the victim of his mirth. Surinam laughed without constraint while brandishing a paint brush with which he had been pointing out to Kwaku features in his canvases.

'Why? Why you brought your son-in-law here tonight?' Surinam asked derisively. 'You wanted to show him off? Eh? Little Trickster showing off Big Trickster? Here? I mean, you're looking at the father of Tricksters. Those animal urges that drive you I rehearse every night when I'm alone. I stand in front of my mirror and shout, "Please, lady, come to my exhibition of paintings, I beg you. I want a little attention. I feel so ashamed if the hall is empty. Oh my God! Just a little appreciation. You can look at the paintings quick, quick, then go out with a smile." But . . . but, and here's the little twist, I've got the opposite reputation. People say I'm indifferent to appreciation. And they're right. The twist within the twist. . . . I *am* indifferent to attention, yet at the same time I thrive on it. But you wouldn't understand.'

'You *are* mad,' Kwaku muttered, now thoroughly disgusted with Surinam's exhibition.

'Go, then! What's stopping you? You stand at my door mouth as though you're screwed to the spot. Go! It's not so easy to go, eh . . . ? Go! Damn you!'

Surinam took up a chair and was about to throw it after Kwaku, who fled into the darkness, now smothered with sounds on every hand. The Lamaha canal, unseen only a short distance away, must have harboured every species of frog that cavorted around the countryside and suburbs of Georgetown.

Kwaku ran the short way to the main road and, after making sure that his demented host was not coming after him, began walking slowly homewards, dazed by the quarrel he had not sought.

Mentally, he re-ran his previous visits to Meadowbrook, seeking clues to Surinam's state of mind, revealed so unmistakably in the last hour. But he found nothing, except his passionate outburst the first time he allowed him into the outer studio.

Anyway, the past was the past. On no account would he go back to Meadowbrook. But having made the resolution his thoughts returned involuntarily to the room that reeked of beer and sweat on those humid Friday evenings when Surinam placed his electric fan on the floor below the wall haunted by the pale frog from the yard. He thought of Eunice and Correia, sorely missed at first, but whose memory grew weaker, like the waning moon, until they were forgotten in the passing months. Perhaps he should have been more circumspect. What would he have lost? His pride? He used to pay little attention to his pride in the early days, so much so that Miss Gwendoline was in the habit of repeating like a litany, 'You don't have pride?' Why had his pride become so important so late in life?

A great sadness filled Kwaku's heart, as though he was afflicted with a bereavement. He went past the houses on the Lodge Public Road, some of which at this late hour — it was past one in the morning — were lit with a night light to deter would-be burglars, while others were shrouded in a darkness that gave their closed windows and staircases a peculiar prominence.

Kwaku was forced to acknowledge that the company of Surinam and the others had taken root in his life and that its denial would leave him stranded. And nothing instructed him more clearly in his blind wife's plight than this awareness of his own deprivation. He walked through the night, bewildered by his loss, by the imperfections in his character and the forbidding obstacles to a knowledge of one's Self.

CHAPTER XXIII

Certain customs and ideas persist long after the revulsion that gave rise to them has weakened or disappeared altogether. So breadfruit, a highly nutritious product of the tree of that name, is not eaten by creoles, who dismiss it as slave food. Similarly, the creoles' contempt for aboriginal Indians is explained away as the cultural memory of runaway slaves being tracked down by the notorious Caribs.

Kwaku, being his own man, was as little concerned with cultural memory as he was about the planets that circled the sun. Besides, the days of penury before he came to Georgetown had reduced him and Miss Gwendoline to eating kinna foods like breadfruit and manatee, in the same way that trouble obliged monkey to eat pepper. Defying cultural memory, he took on an Amerindian janitor who thought nothing of walking long distances which a creole would have considered a serious risk to his health.

Kwaku had become wealthy. But with the growth of his wealth there had developed a commensurate miserliness that had been entirely absent in his first period as a successful healer. His employees, the janitor and an occasional nurse, had threatened to withdraw their labour on three occasions, often complaining that they could not live on starvation wages.

His swift rise to fame and his acquisition of a substantial bank balance — due in some measure to the very tourist trade the Right Hand Man had exploited in the now defunct chamber-pot business — had brought about other changes as well. His son-in-law, whose acupuncture practice had shrunk when the novelty of his *needlework* wore off, moved into a back room on the ground floor of a large house in Houston, which Kwaku bought with his own money. He had managed to outwit Heliga, who sought to contribute to its purchase with a paltry deposit, only so that he could claim joint ownership.

Philomena's protest at her husband's treatment threatened to bring about a rift between the two generations, but Kwaku, mindful of his attachment to his favourite daughter, offered Heliga the two back rooms rent-free. Eventually the couple moved into the top floor of the building while Kwaku practised in the large ground floor area, one small section of which was walled off to make the janitor's room.

Philomena was able for the first time to arrange her own furniture and cook her own food and fetched her small daughter from Berbice to set up house 'properly', she said. And Miss Gwendoline, as much as she had come to depend on Philomena's company — a fact she could not bring herself to admit — was not sorry they went, for Heliga's presence in the flat made her uneasy. Neither time nor his exaggerated efforts to win her over had allayed the deep suspicion she harboured on his account.

Kwaku, at Miss Gwendoline's prompting, got in touch with the New Amsterdam police and asked them to assist him in tracing his eldest daughter, in order that he might persuade her to take Philomena's place, but from all accounts she was no longer living there. So he had to engage an old lady to be a companion for his wife.

Miss Gwendoline was the only one exempt from her husband's stinginess and she felt obliged to remind him that the presents of Moroccan leather and diamond rings and all the other expensive objects were lost on her since her imagination was no longer capable of summoning up images of long-forgotten objects. So his gifts were confined to rectangular pieces of cloth; velvet and organdy and other materials opulent to the touch, which he presented to her in batches on Sundays after their return from church.

Now that Philomena lived elsewhere Kwaku and his wife had long talks in the evenings on the porch while her paid companion looked on, too shy to join in their exchanges. Kwaku spoke of his patients and their problems and told strange tales of deprivations that would not have come about in the country, he insisted. One man, who was afflicted with a severe tick, admitted that his wife had urged him to visit months ago. He complained that he saw everything in reverse and that recently his condition had deteriorated so badly he began to collide with the furniture. Approaching vehicles appeared to get smaller and rush away, only to go past him with the sound of a great wind. Opening his newspaper, the page would more often than not be upside down; and his wife, in an effort to reassure him that all was well, would float away towards the skylight, her mouth contorted in a grotesquely exaggerated grin. Now he remained home, fearing that the traffic would be the death of him. He had consulted drug doctors, homeopathic specialists and two obeah men who practised openly now that the craft had the approval of legislation introduced since independence. Kwaku, apparently, was his last resort.

He deployed his three methods of treatment in the way a market trader would set out a stall; in sections. First he gave the patient a garlic concoction to be taken twice a day. And twice weekly he was required to submit to a creole massage, the greatest attention being paid to the head rather than the feet, since he was a man. Then, when at the end of three months the patient's condition showed no sign of improvement, Kwaku introduced him to the talking therapy, which had become much more sophisticated since his wide reading under Suarez's guidance. The couch on which his clients lay had been imported from Venezuela, where its owner had imported it from Spain before the last world war. And even to the unpractised eye the dark patina acquired with age gave the walnut legs a distinction that enhanced the damask upholstery on which the patients were made to recline.

Kwaku would sit opposite the patient, rejecting the view that eye contact between healer and client should be avoided. In fact, at times intoxicated with his words, he would go much further and establish actual contact without the slightest feelings of disquiet, remembering how Christ the healer himself indulged in an orgy of touching.

However, in the case of the patient with the reverse disorientation, Kwaku sat behind the couch rather than at its foot when, disturbed by his tick and overwhelmed with details regarding his condition, he began to falter and avoid his gaze, in the way the climber of a steep ladder is unable to look downwards for fear of losing his foothold.

'Talk 'bout yourself,' Kwaku urged him.

'How do you mean?'

'Say anything 'bout yourself.'

'I'm five feet nine and a half.'

'Go on,' Kwaku said.

'I'm a presbyterian.'

Kwaku saw that the method might not suit his man, but persisted.

'Tell me about your small days.'

'That was a long time ago.'

'You were happy?'

'I don't know what you mean,' the man answered.

'You laughed a lot?'

'I can't remember. My father used to laugh a lot. . . .'

'Your mother?'

'She was always working. She didn't have time to laugh. . . . Whenever my father went in the bush she used to read her Bible twice a day instead of once.'

'Was she unhappy?'

'I told you she wasn't happy or unhappy. She just worked a lot.'

'You got brothers an' sisters?' Kwaku asked, pursuing his line of questioning with a touch of desperation in his voice, believing that his client was evasive.

'Fourteen . . . one brother and thirteen sisters.'

'Tell me about them.'

'The oldest — my brother — is in the army in America. I'm the youngest. It would take too long to talk about the others. There're good ones and bad ones. Look, I don't like talking about my family to a stranger. And tobesides, you ask too many questions.'

'But I tell you to talk,' Kwaku said. 'Just talk! You start hemming an' hawing so I had to ask you questions. I don' want to pry in your. . . .'

It occurred to Kwaku that he was getting carried away and held back just as he was about to accuse the man of being the most boring patient who ever consulted him.

'I'm a healer,' Kwaku told the man. 'A carpenter does use his saw and hammer and other tools. Words is my tools. If you don' co-operate is like taking away my tools.'

'But I don't *know* you,' the man protested. 'I don't know your family. I don't know any Cholmondeleys. Why should I tell you my secrets, let alone the family secrets?'

'So you got secrets?' Kwaku asked, leaping into the breach.

'If! My *name* is secrets.'

At this point he got up, thrust his hands in his trouser pockets and went to the window.

'You supposed to lie on the couch,' Kwaku reminded him, now convinced that nothing good could come of the man's uncooperative attitude.

He went back and lay down willingly as though he was waiting to be asked.

'So you don't want to talk 'bout your secrets?' Kwaku asked, suggesting from his tone of voice that it was all the same to him whether the man kept his secrets to himself or not.

'Secrets are a burden,' the patient declared portentously. 'They drag you down. . . . I know what you're trying to do, but it won't work with me. . . . My aunt went to a healer once, in Rosignol. He threw a white table for her, and fifteen people did take part. I was small then, but she took me with her. She used to take me everywhere. And I remember how the trees were shaking in the wind that night. The white table was set up in his yard in the moonlight. The ginnip tree with leaves so thick you could shelter from the rain under it, was shaking, shaking in the wind. But you know, not one of the seven candles on the table went out. The flames burned like there wasn't a breath of air. . . . You don't have any candles here; it's just me and you. You don't look at me while you're talking. And . . . what is most disturbing I don't know you.'

Kwaku changed position so that he now sat opposite his patient, as at the start of the consultation.

'You satisfied now?'

'Yes. That's a little better.'

However, he turned away from Kwaku, embarrassed that the situation was rectified at his prompting. He kept wondering how Kwaku could have acquired his powerful reputation, for nothing he had done until then impressed him. Yet the healer had come near to catching a glimpse of what lay behind his mask when he asked about his secrets.

'You goin' talk about your secrets?' Kwaku asked once more. 'Just now when I ask you didn' answer me. You going to talk?'

'You want to know too much, Mr Cholmondeley. And I have too much to hide. Tobesides, I don't know what my talking's got to do with healing.'

A silence settled between the two men, a long, gravid silence compounded of reproaches and thwarted revelations. Faced with a hundred possibilities Kwaku had no idea what approach was most likely to bear fruit. He sensed a desperate urgency on the client's part, which resembled the expression on the face of a gambler who, in the knowledge that there remained to him one last throw of the dice, could only stare at his trembling fingers.

Overhead, the sound of Heliga pacing his room made Kwaku think that he should fit a soundproof ceiling to the floor above.

'You start telling me about your father who did work in the bush,' Kwaku said with one final attempt to get his patient talking about something that stirred him.

'I'll tell you what you want to know if you answer me a question right,' the man said. 'The animals went into the Ark two by two. But do you know how they came out?'

'I don't play games,' Kwaku retorted, peeved at his lack of success.

'You don't know,' the patient continued, 'because they don't tell you. And if they told you they'd probably lie. Do you think we are capable of telling the truth? They say that Noah slept with his daughters while he was drunk, yet the old sources mentioned nothing about drunkenness. Now why is the Bible version doctored? Why? You're a healer, but you don't know that, do you. . . ? I'll tell you why I came here. But I want you to remember this: you didn't get it out of me, Mr Cholmondeley. I *volunteered* the information. I resisted all your attempts to tell you what you wanted to know, remember that. I know you people like to boast of how you healed this patient and that patient by using this and that method. But you take care to say nothing about your failures. . . . You remember I told you how my father was always laughing?'

Kwaku listened with great satisfaction, reckoning that his patience had paid off.

'He's singing like a bird,' he thought. 'Let me hear how the song does go.'

'I used to laugh a lot,' the patient continued, 'just like my father. I was the big teller of jokes at school. I was always skinning and grinning. I couldn't stop. It was like a disease that made me turn everything into a joke, only because I was nervous. One time the teacher of English explained the meaning of the word "patrimony" as property left a child by its father. And I said, "Sir . . . ," and the class started to giggle, because they knew something was coming. "Sir," I said with a straight face, and innocent-like, "if patrimony means money left by your father does matrimony mean money left by your mother?" And the class roared with laughter. That's what I liked, the laughter. It was food and drink to me. Some pupils did want good marks, but I would do anything to make people laugh. Anyway this laughing came to an end a few months ago.'

'What happened?' Kwaku asked eagerly, now completely absorbed in the client's story.

'I was the laugh man. My mother told me once that she caught me laughing in my sleep. . . . Anyway that's a different story. One morning I got up and felt different.'

'How d'you mean?' Kwaku asked.

'I can't describe it. I felt like I was a different person. But I didn't think too much about it. Then at work people started looking at me as if I hadn't washed or something, and one afternoon my best friend came into the office and asked what was wrong. I didn't know what he meant. And when I told him nothing was wrong he said I looked sour. It was like that every day from then on. Something had gone out of me, some kind of spark. That's my secret: I don't laugh anymore, and now I've begun to see everything in reverse, usually in the mornings. In the afternoon things get much better and by two or three o'clock everything falls into place again. Usually!'

'And now?' Kwaku enquired.

'No, it's alright. After all it's past midday.'

'Are you a Christian?'

'I am, but I don't go to church every Sunday.'

Then, without warning, the man got up from the couch, stared at Kwaku reproachfully and said, 'This is futile! I'm not coming here any more. You can keep the money I paid you.'

He had paid for his treatment in advance and Kwaku thought this to be the reason for his anger. But the random question about *church* had struck home, and the client, convinced that Kwaku had been wanting to put it since the session began, attributed to him enormous powers of perception. How could the healer have known? He had received the call to found his own church while walking alone one evening and, determined to resist it, was hoping that the healer would cut the knot that had grown in his chest, nurtured by the conflict between what he knew to be his duty and the need to pursue his carefree life. Ashamed of his refusal to heed the call he saw lies on every hand; in Kwaku's therapy, his friend's utterances and even in the Bible. The world was constructed on lies, of which the present politicians took full advantage, to lead the people into a desert of debt and despair.

Kwaku got up, ready to escort him out in the knowledge that he had done only half the work for his handsome fee.

As they made for the door Kwaku asked the man why he had denied that he laughed a lot while still a boy.

'I didn't deny it. I said I didn't remember. . . . I resent all these prying questions. It's not healthy. Now I can go out into the fresh air and *breathe*.'

'Breathe as much as you like,' Kwaku countered. 'The air's free. I only sorry I couldn't help you.'

The man left without another word, hurrying away towards McDoom.

The East Bank Demerara Public Road and the arteries branching off from it were full of churches, some of which bore the strangest names inspired by an individual experience interpreted as a call, and many people had departed life afflicted with the burden of guilt at their inability to respond to this peremptory order and found a new church to carry out the true mission of Christ. Kwaku, familiar with some such cases from hearsay, would have been hard put to give suitable advice to his client, who returned home dissatisfied.

But a high proportion of Kwaku's consultations were sought by tourists who, having heard of his reputation while on holiday in the islands, came to him complaining of sham illnesses with portable tape recorders and requests for interviews. One anthropologist, well into a thesis on 'Ethnic methods of healing', sought to observe his methods; but Kwaku's fee so alarmed him he called into question his countrymen's view on the hospitality of native peoples and embarked upon another thesis about the erosion of ethnic values in the second half of the twentieth century.

They came, excessively courteous, arms bare, cameras hanging precariously over their shoulders, anxious to discourse and take snapshots for their holiday albums. And unlike their grandparents they loved everyone and everything they set eyes on and would have elevated Kwaku to the rank of saint had he not insisted on being paid. They came nonetheless, insisting that nothing was more picturesque than images of poverty, like standpipes around which women clustered to do their washing and gossiping. Some even brought their children and lectured them loudly on the need for equality throughout the world, inviting Kwaku to support their views, which he did with a degree of passion, depending upon the money he was contracted to be paid.

So Kwaku prospered in Demerara as he had once prospered in Berbice, achieving the ambition he had always aimed for, namely to arrive at a state that placed him beyond the reach of destitution. Having been assisted in his quest for security by his son-in-law, he now found himself in the position of helper and distributor of largesse during the son-in-law's premature decline. Thus was Miss Gwendoline's prophecy about Heliga's future dependence fulfilled.

Chapter XXIV

Kwaku bought himself a large car and paid for his janitor to have driving lessons, so that he could take him and Miss Gwendoline around.

'If only I could see where we going,' she told him.

Numerous tests on her eyes produced the same results: there was no congenital weakness in her eyes, neither were they injured. Hers was a hysterical blindness caused by the fisherman's malicious attentions years ago when Kwaku failed to fulfil a promise. The last optician concluded his consultation with the advice that Kwaku should take his wife to see a healer!

But in truth Miss Gwendoline had become accustomed to her circumscribed world in which the images of Kwaku, Suarez, Philomena and Heliga were embodied in their voices. Every birthday Kwaku would present her with a short wave radio, each one more powerful than the last, so that she could listen to stations throughout the world in any room or on the porch.

Whenever Miss Gwendoline woke up at night she was able to tell the hour from the quality of the stillness and the frequency with which cars and taxis went by; and at certain times of the year, when the humidity drove her to hang dry towels from her bedside table, she would hear cockroaches frolicking on the kitchen table a good twenty feet from where she was lying. But she no longer spoke of such experiences to Kwaku or Suarez, because her world of sound seemed as strange to them as the old lady's next door was to her, when she spoke of the Boer War as if it had taken place a month before.

On being told by Kwaku that he wanted to purchase a house in which her companion could have a room of her own, Miss Gwendoline protested that she had no intention of agreeing to such an idea. Both she and her old companion were village women and would have no truck with 'this own room thing'. Kwaku had been reading too many books and should keep such unwholesome ideas to himself. He had already infected Philomena with them, and their grand-daughter of six was expected to sleep alone.

Kwaku never raised the matter again, and his wife's lady companion continued to sleep on the floor at the foot of the couple's bed, untroubled by the hard boards and the draught that penetrated under the ill-fitting door.

By dint of practising her sense of touch on the pieces of cloth which Kwaku gave her, Miss Gwendoline took a fancy to wearing frocks made of similar material, more especially as her companion could give her advice on their suitability. Her vanity, revived through Emelda's eyes, could be indulged now that money was no object, and she had recovered her zest for living.

On Sundays, whenever the weather was fine, Kwaku, Miss Gwendoline and Emelda would be driven to the Sea Wall, where the chauffeur stopped by the old bandstand, so that they could listen to the concert given by the militia band.

Nothing afforded Kwaku greater pleasure than to witness the interest of passers-by in his brand new car; and had it not been for Miss Gwendoline's moderating influence he would even have demonstrated to them how the windows went up and down at the touch of a button and that by pressing another one he could make his headlights disappear behind screens of polished metal.

But Miss Gwendoline's enjoyment of the music was not marred by such distractions and she listened, her head turned towards the sea, to brass instruments and clarinets and the contrasting sound of the kettledrum with its brief, intrusive roll. Recalling these moments of intense pleasure, she confessed to Suarez on more than one occasion that through the bereavement for her lost eyesight she had achieved a certain tranquility.

It was on one of these excursions that Kwaku, while watching the Sunday crowds during the concert intermission, saw an aboriginal Indian lady go by on the wall. She was carrying an infant on her hip and, apparently fatigued with her burden, rested it on the wall in an upright position it could hardly maintain. Then, as if uncertain whether to stand a while or pick up the infant once more, she looked down at the tiny figure with a questioning expression. Finally she eased herself down on the other side of the wall, took up the baby and continued on her way.

Kwaku excused himself, but before Miss Gwendoline could ask where he was going, he shot off in the direction of the woman who by now had disappeared among the crowd. When he managed to climb over the wall he found his way barred by a secondary sea defence of massive stones. It occurred to him that the woman must have come down to let the child urinate behind the wall. But where could they have disappeared in the short time? He hurried in the direction of Kitty as best he could through the throng until, despairing of finding the woman and infant, he turned back. And then suddenly, rising like an apparition from a sitting position, she appeared before him at the very spot where he had last seen her.

Ill at ease because all aboriginal Indian women seemed to have identical features, he asked tentatively:

'You're Mr Correia lady?'

She nodded affirmatively, betraying neither embarrassment nor surprise.

'This is Mr Correia baby?'

Now she smiled, looked down at the child who was clinging to her legs and then put her hand on its shoulder.

'Mr Correia's in town?'

In answer she picked up the child and struck out towards the bandstand.

'Mrs Correia,' Kwaku said respectfully, walking abreast of her, 'I'm his friend. You don' remember me? You don' remember the night when I go outside and chase the men away?'

But she walked on without answering.

'I got a car an' can drop you home,' Kwaku offered, hurrying his step to keep up with her.

'No, please,' she replied, and then almost broke into a trot in order to shake Kwaku off.

'Alright, I won't bother you,' he said, pretending to lose interest.

But as soon as she went by his car he ran up behind her and gestured to Manny, his chauffeur, to join him.

'Go after that lady,' he whispered, 'and find out where she staying. If you're long I'll drive the wife home.'

Manny had not come back when the bandsmen started putting away their instruments, and the crowd that had gathered round the pavilion began to disperse, and the cars parked beside the wall moved away slowly to the noise of revving engines. Kwaku drove away more than half an hour later at Miss Gwendoline's insistence. She complained that she never liked staying out after dark and in any case she should have brought her shawl if she had known they would be exposed to the night air.

Back home Kwaku waited for Manny in the porch while Miss Gwendoline and Emelda chatted on the other side of the sliding glass screen. Next door the red prayer-flag of their East Indian neighbours hung limp on its bamboo pole. Beyond the canals on the other side of the road the white paling fences stretched in a long, unbroken line, which stopped abruptly at the road separating the block from the Seventh Day Adventist church with its unpretentious façade. Philomena and Heliga still attended there every Saturday, the sect's Sabbath, even though they had to make the trip all the way from the East Bank in a crowded taxi. In spite of Kwaku's extraordinary encounter two hours ago, his mind wandered to his daughter and her husband and even accommodated images of himself as a spectre floating above a city in which he once dreamt of surviving and about which he now entertained ambitions of conquest. His petty strivings, for the time being at least, no longer preoccupied him; and he had all but lost interest in putting the Right Hand Man in his place, or even Surinam, whose jibes he had taken to heart, perhaps because they had exposed him to himself and trivialized the things he longed for.

Now there was the possibility that Correia had come back to town, the one man alive whom he respected without reserve, apart from Suarez, his book teacher and friend, who had begun by making fun of him but in the end demonstrated a unique tolerance towards his wrong-headed ways. They were the friends whose criticism made him ponder, disturbed his nights and even caused him to suspect the stirrings of a deeper conscience within himself that extended beyond the duties he owed his immediate family.

In his impetuous way Kwaku was tempted to rush round to Suarez's house and inform him that Correia was in town but he restrained himself and waited for Manny's return before he acted.

Kwaku fell asleep on the porch as he often did when in the midst of his reflections and only awakened when Emelda tapped him on the shoulder and informed him that Manny was waiting outside the door. At a loss to know what the chauffeur wanted him for at that late hour, Kwaku got up and went out. But as soon as he saw the expression on his face he recalled the errand.

'Why you been so long?'

'She living in a backyard,' Manny answered, 'an' I had was to go deep inside. And a dog start barking fierce, an' I come back out. You know me an' dogs! I not a dog man.'

'Well, what happen?' Kwaku asked.

'I stand at the entrance to the yard, but nobody come out.'

'So you don' know which house in the yard she living in?' Kwaku said, exasperated at his chauffeur's incompetence.

'No, Mr Cholmondeley.'

Manny would have preferred to call Kwaku 'Sir', which was shorter; but Kwaku would have none of it.

'You know you useless, Manny?'

'If you say so, Mr Cholmondeley.'

'You remember the road an' the lot number?'

'Oh yes, Mr Cholmondeley.'

Kwaku set out at once, after explaining to Miss Gwendoline that he had to go and dun a client who owed him money.

The yard in which the second Mrs Correia lived was indeed deep. Strewn with all kinds of debris and the fallen fruit from an unusually large tree whose branches overhung the two adjacent yards, the three houses at the back were divided from one another by fences of their own.

To Kwaku's surprise there was no evidence of a dog, and he came to the conclusion that Manny had not wanted to take the risk of penetrating so deeply into unknown territory.

He went and knocked on the front door of the second house, preferring to tackle the first one last of all.

'Yes?' came an uncertain female voice from inside. 'Is you neighbour?'

'No, is me,' Kwaku answered. 'I come to see Mr Correia.'

'Mr who?'

'Correia.'

'They in' got no Correia in here,' came the reply in a gruff, almost truculent voice.

'I meet his wife on the Sea Wall today. I call Kwaku Cholmondeley.'

There was no further reply, but Kwaku thought he could hear whispering. He stood on the top tread of the low stairway, wondering whether he was expected to go or remain. But a few moments later a bolt being drawn broke the silence with a heavy, metallic sound; then several bolts were released in quick succession, giving the impression that many hands had been put to opening the fortress door.

'Please to wipe you foot,' a creole voice half-covered in plaits ordered.

Kwaku complied with exaggerated movements of his legs, in order to reassure the lady who stood aside to let him enter; and immediately she set about the task of securing the numerous bolts once more. By the feeble light of a small kerosene lamp he could see vague forms sitting on the floor against the wall, but was unable to distinguish their sex. And as he stood waiting to be told what to do a door on the right opened, and a child appeared, only to disappear at once accompanied by a volley of children's laughter from the other side of the partition.

Kwaku was not offered a seat by the woman who let him in and afterwards went to lose herself among the squatting forms in the darkness of the small room. The house, flanked by trees on two sides, was filled with the whispering of leaves and occasionally, when the breeze rose to a wind, a branch would brush against the window panes. He felt that he had been standing alone for a long time, while in fact only two or three minutes had passed since his arrival. Eventually someone lifted the kerosene lamp from its resting place and came towards him.

'You sure is Mr Correia you want?' the voice of an old man enquired.

'Yes,' Kwaku said, almost gasping with relief.

'A'right, come.'

He followed the lamp, afraid that he might stumble against someone or something; but he managed to reach the back stairs without mishap while the lamp descended into the unlit yard and made for the third house, behind the one he had just left. A bright electric bulb lit up the two front windows, which were decorated with blinds.

Kwaku thought of Manny's reluctance to go deep into the unfamiliar yard; yet here he was being escorted, by someone whose face he could not see, towards the back, so that if he was attacked his narrow escape route to the street could easily be cut off. Following the lamp-holder up the stairs of the brightly lit house, he heard him rap three times.

'Mr Correia got a visitor,' the lamp-holder said to the person who answered the door, then turned away promptly, leaving Kwaku alone.

'Who's it?' came a voice from within.

'Me, Kwaku. Kwaku Cholmondeley,' Kwaku answered eagerly.

Correia came to the door himself.

'Come in! The wife said you talked to her. You of all people! But how you found the house?'

Kwaku told him.

'You! You've got a car and chauffeur. Wonders never cease!'

'It's new. The wife didn't tell you? I did offer her a lift.'

'She didn't say anything 'bout that.'

Correia stood back and looked Kwaku up and down as if he were a freak, while his wife held off a short distance away with the infant on her arm. Everything was as bright here in the backyard house as the other was shrouded in darkness, and Kwaku, on being offered a seat, settled in a deep easy chair next to a small table on which a pile of magazines lay.

Correia fetched an earthenware jar from a shelf and handed it to Kwaku, who took out one biscuit and placed the jar beside him on the floor.

The two men talked of their evenings at Surinam's flat, and Kwaku told him that he no longer visited him, as they had quarrelled. And while they talked Correia's Amerindian wife could be heard in a back room.

'So you got another child,' Kwaku remarked, thinking it indiscreet to ask about the other children in Lethem.

'That's why I came back,' Correia said.

Each time the conversation approached the subject of Correia's future in town, he changed the subject and tried to bring up Surinam's Friday evenings or some other matter they had already discussed.

Correia learned from Kwaku how his account about what would happen at the airport on his return from Lethem proved to be accurate, and what transpired subsequently between him and the Right Hand Man.

'So we both have something against him,' Correia said cryptically.

'I suppose so,' Kwaku replied.

Kwaku also disclosed how he had promised Miss Rose to visit him in prison but read of his release the day before he had arranged to do so.

They continued talking during the meal Correia's wife brought out for them after she had put the child to sleep.

'She does ever stop working?' Kwaku asked after Correia's wife disappeared once more.

'She used to get up at four in the morning to prepare the cassava when we were in Lethem. In the five months we've been here she hasn't got accustomed to buying everything from the shop. So she still gets up at four.'

'An' does do what?'

'Ask her! I don't think even she knows.'

Correia went on to say that she was not as quiet as she appeared. When he learned to speak her language he discovered another side of her.

'So you been back five months,' Kwaku said.

'Yes. I saw you once. But I wasn't ready to show myself yet. I'm still not ready.'

Correia did not enquire about Kwaku's business because he was not certain how successful it was, even though he could afford to run a car.

On learning that his first wife, Amy, had moved in with the Minister he was deeply offended, not having forgotten how the latter had used him. Much worse, however, was his bitterness towards Amy, who rejected indignantly the suggestion that she should share his bed with a buck woman, yet was able, soon afterwards, to set up house openly with another man. Had he been asked why he came back to Georgetown he would have lied, unwilling to admit that he entertained vague notions of revenge and that he had been unable to protect his other children from his wife's relations, who had abducted them one by one. His excuse, nonetheless true for being an excuse, would have been that he intended putting pressure on the Minister of Hope to find a way to get himself chosen by the ruling party as a candidate in the national elections that were expected to take place in 1993, the following year. When Kwaku confessed that he had amassed a small fortune he conceived the idea of enlisting his help in dealing with the Right Hand Man. Kwaku owed him a favour after all.

Correia had conveniently put out of his mind that Kwaku's action in chasing away the Arecuna prowlers in Lethem might well have saved his life, preferring to concentrate his recollection on what he, Correia, had done for him.

If Kwaku's driving force was his impetuousness, Correia's was his infinite capacity to scheme and, in spinning an elaborate web, to deceive himself about motives that were no secret to those who, like his Amerindian lady, could observe him in close-up.

Kwaku did not suspect how glad Correia was to see him. Having made up his mind not to get in touch with any of his old friends until the matter with the Minister was settled, he was obliged to live a reclusive life. But now his presence in Georgetown was known he felt relieved. Provided Kwaku kept his secret, life in the backyard would be far more bearable.

'You remember the old man from the house in front who showed you the way and knocked on my door?' Correia asked. ' 'Twas the old man, wasn't it? Well, he owns the house.'

'This one?'

'No, the one in darkness. Twenty-three people're living in it; seven of his children, their husbands and their children. They put on the kerosene lamp on Sunday nights only. Today's Sunday. That's what the ruling party's done to these people. They say the East Indians can't win the elections because they're doing well under the black government. The merchants may be doing well, but the majority of Indians suffer just like us.'

'So you think the Indians will win?' Kwaku asked.

'I think it's a foregone conclusion if the elections are properly supervised. When you repeat a lie over and over you convince yourself, not only other people. They keep saying that East Indians only make up fifty-two per cent of the population, and with some of the Indians voting for them they'll win. Now suppose the Indians are nearer sixty per cent, what then? Eh?'

'You think they're nearly sixty per cent?' Kwaku asked, his interest reflecting his intensive reading under Suarez's tutelage.

'The Indians themselves say they're sixty per cent. Now each side's got an interest in exaggerating the figure. If you take the mean figure you arrive at what's nearer the accurate one, fifty-six per cent, in my view. And that's more than enough to win.'

'I can't understand how a man like you can lose himself away in the bush,' Kwaku said, full of admiration for Correia. Correia barely grunted an acknowledgement of Kwaku's remark; it was unnecessary, he thought, since he had explained how things were while they were both in Lethem. He decided not to ask Kwaku for help until a subsequent meeting; meanwhile he must pretend to be independent of anyone.

Kwaku's interest in the outcome of the elections stemmed not only from the general creole anxiety about an East Indian victory, but more particularly from the situation of his surgery. The East Bank between McDoom and Houston, predominantly an East Indian area, had proved to be an excellent place to practise, being close to the capital but far enough from the hurly-burly that facilitated crime.

'D'you think there's going to be violence . . . I mean the same kind of violence as in the sixties?'

'Things could be worse,' Correia said. 'The police and Defence

Force are mainly black and if the Indians win they'll have to rely on them for public order.'

Kwaku groaned inwardly, calling to mind the graphic details of the period when Death marched across the landscape, and mixed creole and Indian villages became exclusive ramparts of a single race overnight after one section fled. He thought of Philomena, still in her early twenties, and her little family. One moment his future seemed to be in his own hands, another moment he was like a dead leaf in the wind. If he and his family became the victims of events which got out of control that would be a supreme irony, for he often boasted to Miss Gwendoline how he managed to overcome an inadequate education and ignorance of town ways to achieve success.

He was a small boy when British soldiers wearing skirts landed from a warship anchored beyond the lightship, and everything that threatened the country seemed to be reported rather than experienced in the East Coast village where he lived. If things came to pass as Correia predicted he would be in the thick of it. And Miss Gwendoline? He might as well be blind too, for he would stick by her, and so be as vulnerable as she was in her dark world.

In Kwaku's opinion Correia spoke too readily about violent events, and with too much relish. In no doubt about the money-changer's propensity for danger and dangerous enterprises, he saw him as a man of the labyrinth, for whom tranquility represented a kind of death.

It suited Kwaku to shut out from his thoughts his own past when, as a young man, his fellow villagers would have gladly fed him to the crows for his delinquent ways. Money had brought him stability and given him a moral standpoint, and now he had no doubt that public order should be secured at all costs. If Correia was certain with which community his loyalties lay, Kwaku was prepared to support any party, provided that it knew how to keep chaos from his door. He would even back the soldiers who marched with their knees exposed if they could guarantee the inviolability of his money and his person.

Correia accompanied Kwaku to the street, brushing aside his protest that he was not afraid to go unaccompanied. But the passage between the houses and the paling fence, much longer than Kwaku remembered it, was murky, and the large trees, forbidding, immobile sentinels, appeared by their presence to deepen the gloom.

'Tell me one thing,' Kwaku asked before saying goodbye, 'How you managed to get out of prison without a trial?'

'I don't know. Somebody was frightened I would talk about the smuggling controlled by officials. . . . I don't know.'

The two men parted at the entrance, where the street lamps fanned out in both directions like illuminated trees. Kwaku walked briskly, his hands deep in his trouser pockets, and experienced the same exhilaration as when he sat at the wheel of his car soon after he learned to drive. Correia had treated him as an equal and must have wondered at the transformation brought about by his reading, Kwaku reflected. And even if this was an illusion, the fact was Correia had accorded him more respect than he ever had. His usual shrill, hectoring manner had softened into something less patronizing.

Chapter XXV

There had been a sustained falling-off of Heliga's business, and he would sit disconsolately in his consulting room, praying that he would escape the humiliation of passing a whole day without seeing a single client. Then, one Tuesday, he got off by the skin of his teeth. Past the hour of four in the afternoon an old lady dropped in, only 'to see' what he did; and he kept her talking for more than half an hour, in order to be able to report to Philomena that he had been consulted that day. But the following afternoon he skipped his lunch, tormented by a premonition of disaster. By three o'clock he was in such a state that he kept going back and forth to the waiting-room to see whether a client had come and neglected to ring the warning bell.

Heliga, whom Kwaku regarded as a paragon of self-control, whose gestures and figures of speech were to be emulated because he had seen the world, took to wringing his hands in private and beseeching the Almighty to spare him the humiliation of confessing to a wife much younger than himself that he was without resource.

But even worse, behind his wife there lurked the figure of Miss Gwendoline with her unspoken contempt for him. She had called into question his credentials from the beginning, to Philomena's intense annoyance. And now he would have to admit that he could not support her daughter and her grandchild. They would not even be able to afford to make the trip to church on Saturdays.

Heliga compared himself with Kwaku, whose precarious start had not augured well for the future, especially when one took into account his coarse manner and the way he abused clients to whom he took a dislike.

'And to think he's never even been as far as the lightship!' he cursed inwardly.

Kwaku did his best to cheer up his son-in-law, while believing in his heart of hearts that acupuncture did not suit Guyanese and was like those exotic plants which needed a winter break and resisted the most sympathetic attempts to cultivate them in tropical soil.

While Heliga was doing well he liked introducing him to acquaintances and friends as 'my successful son-in-law'. The latter's failure, however, roused feelings that had been carefully concealed by the overlay of admiration; and now, the envy which once masqueraded as fascination itself became transmuted into a kind of avuncular tolerance. Kwaku would listen to his plans about a more modest establishment in a fashionable part of town; then, after nodding with apparent approval, he would declare a lack of interest with remarks like, 'You had a few weeks' training. I mean, a scheme like that would be like throwing water down the drain', or 'Keep thinking . . . you know that's what I here for, to listen!'

Listening to these remarks, Philomena would bite her lip and suppress the urge to call her father to order, as she had been in the habit of doing since the age of eleven or twelve.

The time came when something had to be done, for Heliga could neither pay the rent nor support his wife and her child. It was agreed that a family conference should be called to thrash out the young people's problems, to which Suarez would be invited, though he had no blood connection to the family. As Miss Gwendoline pointed out, his offer to find Heliga a post as watchman at the ministry was the only practical contribution to the search for a solution to his dilemma.

Kwaku, fearing the effect of Suarez's presence on Philomena, would have put off the meeting but could find no plausible excuse. Besides, Miss Gwendoline's restlessness as the date approached persuaded him that the business was best settled as quickly as possible.

The day of the evening when the meeting was arranged, every footstep above Kwaku's consulting-room transmitted a message with an urgent need of interpretation. And when — during a session with a young woman who was seeking advice about marrying someone of a different religion — Kwaku heard a door close with a loud noise, he was certain that Philomena was on her way downstairs to vent her anger on him.

But six o'clock came without any interruption, and he put away his garlic-boxes methodically before sweeping out the surgery and waiting-room with a pointer broom he had made himself from an old coconut branch. Then he secreted his overalls in a chest under the couch on which patients were massaged or made confessions to him before receiving his counsel.

A handsome income was no reason to abandon frugal habits, he once told Heliga, while chiding him inwardly for an implied criticism of his country ways: 'How far your gloves and fine manners got you? And where your elegant clients now? Is it that they didn' survive your rusty needles with ruby heads? A lot of my clients poor an' need credit an' time to pay, but they come in droves. You yourself might want to consult me one day when your body and soul not in tune no more, Heliga, and is not lack of money will keep you away.'

When he was ready to leave Kwaku went upstairs and knocked on the couple's drawing-room door.

'I goin' wait in the car,' he called out.

Downstairs, his chauffeur had parked in front of the door and, now half-reclined, half-sitting at the wheel, his cap pulled down over his eyes, he kept one eye on the door.

'You an' that good-for-nothing in the backyard!' Kwaku exclaimed, 'What I pay alyou for? Sleeping? You must be the onliest employees in this country who does get pay fo' doing nothing.'

Manny sat up respectfully and adjusted his hat.

Kwaku was on edge only because he knew he would have to endure Philomena's silence all the way home. Several minutes passed without any sign of the couple; then when Kwaku least expected it the front door opened and Sosie, his granddaughter, came rushing out towards the car.

'Come an' sit on grandpapi lap,' he said, opening the car door for her.

She fairly leapt up on to the seat and climbed on his lap. Heliga installed himself next to the chauffeur while Philomena took her place beside Kwaku.

'Alright, Manny. Burn up the road!' Kwaku ordered, almost sick with anxiety on account of his daughter's refusal to greet him.

Taxi-vans raced by, carrying their full complement of passengers and occasionally a vehicle would rend the evening air with its horn. The car drove past the last Hindu temple before it approached the outskirts of Georgetown and was obliged to slow down against the denser traffic ahead. Over the Punt Trench hump it crawled, entering Georgetown like a stranger disinclined to take any risks in an alien land.

Miss Gwendoline, dressed for the occasion, was sitting in the drawing-room in anticipation of their arrival, and Sosie embraced her dutifully, never having been able to come to terms with her blindness.

Her grandmother had another explanation for the indifference shown by the child, but did not protest, for God knew how to deal with ingratitude.

Kwaku kissed his wife on the forehead, and Philomena uttered a laconic greeting, in which could be detected two decades of estrangement.

Shaking his mother-in-law's hand, Heliga enquired after her health and sat down on the cane-bottomed settee against the wall.

Then, without being asked, Emelda, Miss Gwendoline's companion, fetched the ivory-handled fan Kwaku had given his wife on the occasion of Mashramani and which she had christened on the verandah while listening to the songs of revellers as they passed by under the almond trees. Since then she always carried it whenever she needed to give herself confidence.

'Suarez in' come yet,' Miss Gwendoline announced to the company. 'He telephone to say we musn' start without him.'

Emelda served coffee and corn pone to the ladies and little Sosie, who remained stock-still on a straight-backed chair next to her grandmother. Kwaku and Heliga installed themselves in a corner of the gallery to drink beer and eke out the time until Suarez's arrival, neither relishing the imminent confrontation. But both were determined to pretend that all was well on that tranquil evening, with the ladies separated from the men, and the child showing a proper regard for the rituals of the adult world.

Emelda hovered about them, ministering to their requests; a glass of water for Sosie, whose mother forbade her to take coffee; another piece of pone for Miss Gwendoline, grown bulky from over-eating and a debilitating inertia.

The front door opened to reveal Suarez smiling on the threshold, pretending to be unsure whether he should come in or not.

'Sorry, I've got the wrong house,' he joked, and Miss Gwendoline laughed.

'You ever arrive early anywhere?' Kwaku asked, using the formula thought up by his wife who, at the beginning of their acquaintance-ship, used to be exasperated at their friend's cavalier attitude to time.

'If youal harass me,' Suarez rejoined jokingly, 'I'm not going to give you the present I brought.'

'Let me see it, Uncle Suarez,' begged Sosie.

'Know your place, child!' Miss Gwendoline said sharply.

Sosie straightened her back on the chair, determined not to forget her place again.

Suarez opened a box he had been hiding behind his back and took out a bouquet of artificial flowers, Miss Gwendoline's favourite ornaments.

'I don' want your flowers,' she once told Suarez, when he brought her a spray of night-blooming jessamine. 'They smell of a funeral parlour.'

And from that day he held to plastic blooms.

Fondling the artificial bouquet, she pressed Suarez's hand in appreciation.

'T'anks. You're a good man. You should get married.'

'You hear that, Kwaku? Your wife says I should get married.'

And every word Suarez spoke was meant for Philomena's ears.

'Emelda, look after Sosie,' Kwaku said, talking from the corner he was sharing with Heliga.

Sosie went aback with Miss Gwendoline's companion, turning round as she was led away, her expression confirming that she disliked the house without children.

'Well,' Kwaku began nervously, 'I better clear the air. We talking 'bout me supporting the two of you.'

The five adults were now sitting in the gallery, so that Emelda and little Sosie would not hear their discussion. The beer bottles from which Kwaku and Heliga were drinking stood half filled in the centre of the low table with a transparent top. Emelda had brought an extra glass for Suarez, from which he sipped nervously at intervals. Philomena, sitting beside her husband, looked even more severe than she usually did in her parents' presence, an expression cultivated from the days when, as a girl, she was acutely embarrassed at her father's buffoonery, unlike her brothers and sisters who accepted him as being different from other men.

Kwaku had caught his daughter's disapproving look and found it difficult to go into detail about the subject-matter of their meeting.

'Your father not a money tree,' Miss Gwendoline said, breaking the silence into which Kwaku had stumbled. 'He can't support you no more. Out of the goodness of his heart he'll allow you to keep the flat over the business for a year without you having to pay rent. But alyou got to find your own money for food and other things.'

The silence that followed this business-like statement was longer and more oppressive than the last. Kwaku, puzzled by Heliga's refusal to say anything, invited him to contribute with a nod. But he remained stubbornly silent.

'What I want to know,' Philomena said at last, 'is what he's doing here?'

'Who is *he*?' demanded Miss Gwendoline.

'Mr Suarez,' Philomena replied, challenging her mother by the prompt answer to a question which suggested that Suarez had some status among them.

'I'll tell you who *he* is,' Miss Gwendoline replied. '*He* does do more for me than you ever did with your airs and your selfishness.'

'Alright, alright,' Kwaku intervened. 'We not goin' to get anywhere quarrelling. Le' me hear what your husban' got to say.'

'I am a professional man,' began Heliga. 'I've never asked anyone for anything since I began working.'

His agitation was so evident that Kwaku feared he might burst into tears.

'I came to this house in good faith,' he continued. 'I married your daughter who has a child. A child with a disability. I married her because I was in love with her. But since I entered this house I was treated like a sponger, even though I paid my way. If you didn't want me here why didn't you say so? You talk about withdrawing support. . . From who? Me? From your daughter? . . . your granddaughter? . . .'

While he spoke Philomena sat with her head bowed. In private that was the way he spoke to her, reminding her at every turn that he was her saviour, especially since they moved into the East Bank flat above the surgery and could talk freely, without fear of being overheard. From the time he set up as an acupuncturist he had anticipated his failure, taking care to conceal his anxieties behind an excessively confident manner and plant the seeds of loyalty in her impressionable mind.

And as he spoke Miss Gwendoline wore a faint smile, content to hear him finally drawn into the open and exposing himself mercilessly.

'If you say go,' he said, winding up his impassioned speech, 'we'll go. Wouldn't we, Philomena?'

His wife nodded, dismayed that all this was being said in the presence of Suarez.

'You expect me to support you for the rest of your life?' Kwaku asked Heliga.

'Mr Cholmondeley, you can order us to go now, if you want,' Heliga answered. 'I'm grateful for what you've done. But give us the word and we'll go.'

'He give you the word already,' Miss Gwendoline said.

Suarez was more reluctant to speak than ever, having witnessed Miss Gwendoline's implacable opposition to the couple and Philomena's public declaration of her dislike for him.

'Miss Gwendoline,' said Heliga, 'I know you didn't like me from the beginning. I don't know what you don't like about me, but I respect you as my wife's mother and as a woman of fortitude . . . .'

'You want to know what I don' like about you? You want to know for truth?'

'Yes, Miss Gwendoline. I'm anxious to know.'

'The day you talk *one* sentence straight I'll change my mind about you. You make too much styles an' got too much double-talk. Is not styles an' double-talk goin' feed Philomena and the child. I don' think she see through you, yet she was the first to judge her father when he was struggling to keep the family together. . . .'

'I see you don't like me,' Heliga rejoined, interrupting her, 'but I still respect you.'

'Oh, you respect me, eh?' said Miss Gwendoline sarcastically. 'If I curse you, you goin' still respect me? Suppose I spit 'pon you, would you respect me?'

'Miss Gwendoline!' Kwaku exclaimed, 'He's a guest!'

He wanted to add 'and our son-in-law', but drew the line at such an assertion when they were trying to get rid of him.

'What you say, Suarez?' Miss Gwendoline asked.

'I don't want to interfere in family affairs.'

And then he added something to his planned answer which came out as if in response to some inner compulsion.

'But I can't bear to think of Philomena suffering.'

'Now I understand!' said Heliga, leaping up from his chair.

Unable to find a way out of the impasse into which he had been driven, he seized the opportunity to protest at an imagined conspiracy.

'Now I understand where the wind's blowing!' he exclaimed,

directing his anger at Kwaku. 'That's what I get for trusting people and treating them like. . . . Oh my God!'

'What you driving at?' Kwaku demanded.

'If I left Philomena I'd never hear the end of it; but some people take loyalty for weakness. Very well, if you want to take Philomena from me . . . but for the love of Jesus do it in front of my face!'

No one saw through the ruse except Miss Gwendoline who, on her own, would have let him stew in his own juice.

Philomena, dazzled by her husband's fancied superiority over the common run of men, was entirely taken in.

'You've got the wrong idea,' Suarez protested, ashamed of the confusion his remark had caused, 'I wouldn't dream of. . . .'

'Let him think what he *want* to think,' Miss Gwendoline shouted. 'And as for you, madam. . . .'

She turned towards the place from which Philomena's voice had come.

'As for you . . . flaunting yourself at another man when you're married!' Miss Gwendoline exclaimed.

Everyone started shouting, so that recriminations, accusations and protestations were mingled like some malicious cocktail. And Heliga, the picture of a bellowing, enraged husband who had just pretended to discover his spouse's infidelity, viewed the scene with satisfaction while shouting at the top of his voice.

Kwaku did his best to pacify the offended Heliga while Philomena, horrified at the possibility of being abandoned by the first man who matched her dream of the ideal husband, burst into tears.

Miss Gwendoline began to fan herself languidly, waiting for the storm to pass before proposing a solution which would give Heliga and Philomena more time, while ensuring that they understood that they would have to give up their flat by a certain date.

Eventually Kwaku was able to speak and gain the attention of the others.

'Look, Heliga. . . . No, no, don't interrupt me. I don' know where you get this scatter-brain idea that we ganging up on you. Long ago my wife use to say that everything I do was in Philomena's interest. I love my daughter an' Miss Gwendoline, whatever Philomena does think, love her too. But we want you to go 'cause you don' have any means. I got a duty to feed a guest and a double duty to support family. But there's a limit to everything. I *cannot* keep you for the rest of your life!'

'The rest of his life?' Miss Gwendoline interrupted. 'We can't support him at all.'

Kwaku's conciliatory note so angered Miss Gwendoline she abandoned her compromise plan.

'We'll take little Sosie until you find a job,' she added.

'No!' Philomena protested. 'Nobody taking Sosie. We'll go if you want us to go.'

Heliga would rather she had not spoken. He had warned her the previous night to let him do all the talking, and the wisdom of that advice had been borne out by what went before. Now she had undone his preparatory work with one untimely outburst.

But Philomena had held out as long as she could, resisting the temptation to let her views be known whenever her mother intervened. The unspoken objections to her autocratic rule since childhood, when every outcry was thwarted by the biblical precept of 'Honour thy father and thy mother. . .', longed to find expression now that she was mother and wife. Here, in the presence of Suarez, who never ceased pestering her with his eyes and tacit attentions, she desired passionately to speak her mind once and for all.

But Heliga silenced her with a severe look.

'Mr Cholmondeley,' he said, 'what is it to be? Where do we stand?'

'You got a year,' Kwaku said. 'You can have the flat for a year, an' I goin' support Philomena an' Sosie in that time. But I can't hand out all that money to keep you in Indian cotton shirts an' soft leather shoes. Enough's enough.'

Heliga's heart sank. His first impulse was to threaten to abandon Philomena and his step-daughter but, aware that he ran the risk of overplaying his hand, he pretended to accept Kwaku's decision.

For Miss Gwendoline's part, she felt that Heliga might conjure up some ploy in the year he had left, and the image of a malignant scorpion scurrying to an underground nest with its tail curled as a warning to its enemies occurred to her.

And thus the meeting came to an end, with Philomena feeling bewildered at her inability to influence events. Despite striving to resist the maternal influence so far as she detected it in her own ways, she saw her role in marriage as that of shaper of events, recalling, unconsciously perhaps, how Miss Gwendoline had kept the family together by making and selling black pudding when Kwaku was out of work. But in this sprawling, amorphous city she was more impotent than the dogs that gave birth in the dank, rubbish-strewn alley-ways.

Yet, Philomena reflected, she had been spared the humiliation of hearing Suarez offer to find Heliga a job as messenger at the Ministry of Hope, as her father had hinted he would do. It must have been some secret, providential intervention that saved her from being the victim of his pity.

Chapter XXVI

Kwaku knew he was educating himself at a price, that every lesson he took from Suarez and every book he opened weakened his connection with an underground spring which provided the inspiration for the miracles of healing he performed when his children were still small. While, before, an idea would *come* to him, he now went in search of facts and knowledge, and the vivid images that inhabited the world of daydreams and half-sleep were replaced by written words. At times he felt that even his arms and legs had been weakened and that one day he would be obliged to rely on some mechanical device to supplement the loss.

The latest volume, bought on his behalf by Suarez, described in detail the practices of an East Indian sect whose calendar month, inspired by the Tantrists, was four days shorter than the lunar month and coincided with tidal movements. Tantric farmers planted certain root vegetables at the time of the waxing moon and others during the waning moon, depending upon the way of growing. These essays almost matched the inner conviction of that distant time when he often talked like a fool and incurred the ridicule of acquaintances; yet the volume was not entirely satisfactory, for the exhilaration of mastering words was invariably tempered by the monumental tedium of scholarly argument.

However, in a town where writing was held in such high regard, Suarez's help had given him a sense of security and protected him from the constant threat to his self-esteem. And if during his first years in town he went out of his way to avoid altercations with educated people, he now stood up for himself, whatever the circum-stances.

As he prospered academically, and in business his confidence grew to the point that he could look upon the world around him with a tranquility that suited ill his old character, and in moments of recollection he would wonder if this redundant character lay in wait for him like a neglected companion, thirsting for vengeance, or whether for want of energy it had fallen into a perpetual sleep. There were indeed times when he was awakened by a feeble voice that appeared to come from a great distance, beckoning him with incomprehensible baby-talk; then he would sit up in bed and look around the darkened room and through the window panes to the façade of the neighbouring house.

Wide awake, he would go over the last years, fancying that he was at one of Surinam's Friday night gatherings, with Bertie holding forth, and Eunice doing her best to conduct herself as he wished, knowing too well the pathological jealousy that overcame him when amongst friends, even though it was he who insisted on taking her with him and dressing her in short skirts because he experienced great pleasure in the way they devoured her with their eyes. Or Surinam, preparing elaborate meals for his guests; a madman with sane gestures and generous ways, driven by an urge to paint while mistrusting public praise, who possessed a portfolio of erotica in acrylic paint. And Correia, the Friday night acquaintance he missed most after he went to Lethem; overjoyed at his return, he hoped to assist him in a bid for political power. 'I owe him everything,' Kwaku was never tired of repeating to himself; for it was Correia, bigamist and fire-raiser, who had opened his eyes and alerted him to the reality of politics as a cesspool. While he did not profess to understand the money-changer, (why should he seek political power when he claimed that politics was a cesspool and that the only way to achieve social justice was to burn everything to the ground and start all over again?) he regarded him as the strongest character he had ever met, the only one except Surinam who possessed the power and intelligence to bend the world to his will. But unlike Surinam life had not taken its revenge by making him mad.

In his practice he had seen everything that could happen to a human between infancy and the decrepitude that comes with extreme age. In these hours when he was deserted by sleep the extremities of suffering recounted to him in his sessions of therapy frequently came back with disturbing force, and a tacit reproach for having taken money from patients who had confided in him. A woman — nearly all his confidantes were women — who had left her ailing grandmother to see her lover, returned home several hours later to find her in great pain. Drawing the blanket back, she found that her body was covered with red ants. Since that night she was consumed with remorse and sought from Kwaku some formula which she might use to make her anguish bearable. However, he was unable to bring her the solace she sought and refused to accept any remuneration. But, having embarked on the road that brought him a fat bank account, there was little room for compromise, and he usually demanded his fee whether his treatment proved successful or not.

Correia it was who sought Kwaku out and asked him point blank to back him with money in his bid to seek election to parliament, a request the latter had anticipated and to which he agreed readily. The only problem that remained to be solved concerned the Right Hand Man's cooperation in supporting his candidacy.

Correia, much too wise to take advantage at this juncture of his former employer's association with Amy, his wife, or indeed to exploit the knowledge of his shady currency deals, wrote him a respectful note suggesting that they should meet to discuss matters of mutual interest. But a good week passed before he received a letter in return, explaining that pressure of work had delayed consideration of his request.

The Minister, far from underestimating the unspoken threat contained in Correia's letter, had deliberately put off replying to him on the assumption that any show of anxiety would weaken his position. Although Correia had worked with him for several years, he only knew the currency dealer as an employee and had still not gotten over his defection with the one thousand US dollars entrusted him. How dangerous was he? Since they both had reason to fear each other it might well be that Correia would be amenable to reason. Should he support such a candidacy, would Correia see his compliance as a weakness, in truth? Moreover, certain people in high places were bound to consider a strong recommendation highly suspicious, especially as the former employee had never worked assiduously for the party in power.

All these questions and many others needed urgent answers if he were to make the best of his situation.

The following Sunday morning he and Amy Correia got to talking after the maid brought them breakfast in bed and left them to their long, obligatory Sunday chat, in which they dealt with the coming week's business, like two working directors rather than lovers enjoying their only guaranteed break.

'You know Correia's back in town,' the Right Hand Man said, apparently embarrassed by the need to break an unspoken rule not to mention him.

'I know. I got an anonymous letter.'

'And why didn't you say anything?'

'I don't know whether he's staying in town or not. What was the point?'

'He's staying,' he informed her.

Amy sat down on the edge of the large bed.

'How do you know?' she asked.

'He wants me to sponsor him as a candidate for the next elections.'

'You're going to?' she said, leaving him to wonder why she failed to enquire whether they had met.

'I haven't got a choice. Although his letter was respectful I know how dangerous he can be. . . . When he stayed in Lethem I was so angry I wanted to break him. Now I wish he hadn't come back. If only I knew what he was like I'd be able to handle him, but you don't talk about him, so I could never get to the bottom of his character. All those rumours about his early life don't help.'

His indirect appeal for her assistance did not appear to have any effect at first. Yet, when he least expected it she said, 'He's married again . . . without divorcing me.'

'How d'you know?'

'The same unsigned letter that said he's in town.'

'What else did it say?'

'Only that he had a child with his buck woman.'

'Why don't you ever talk of these things? Are you afraid of me?'

She did not answer. Then, when he repeated his reproach about her reticence, she replied.

'I'm afraid of being alone.'

Stunned by the revelation, he searched in vain for evidence of her professed vulnerability. In spite of his elevated position he deemed himself fortunate to have 'caught' her, considering that he had little time to frequent what he termed the 'flesh markets'; the society parties, fashionable clubs like the 'Lions', and suburban meeting-places in expensive areas like Prashad Nagar and Bel Air Park, where ambitious young women gathered at hastily organized discos in the hope of a useful encounter. Nearly all the women he knew were procured for him from the pool of time-servers, whose specialty was being laid by high officials.

The Minister had not entirely recovered the weight he had lost at the time of Correia's trial and had suffered ever since from bouts of colic and paranoia, common ailments among his well-placed colleagues who presided over an economy in disarray. His reputation, secure in certain circles, was threatened by his consistent stand against corruption. In his opinion, his own illegal currency dealings did not constitute corruption, so he persisted in the illusion that he was blameless.

Amy's admission of fear at being left alone had touched him, and he was reluctant to press her to reveal more about her husband's character. If indeed he had committed bigamy, this knowledge was of no use to him, since Correia was capable of harming him with equally damaging revelations.

'If only I understood his character,' said the Minister, 'it would be easier to do business with him. All I want is to protect myself.'

She would have preferred him to claim he was seeking strife, so that she could join forces with him and break Correia on the wheel of her festering revenge. The anonymous letter she had received disclosed much more than she revealed to him. It gave details of the child's age, his mother's physique and finally the address of the lodgings she shared with Correia, deep in a backyard. Time and again she was tempted to make the trip to see the house in which the couple had made their nest, but her pride would not permit her to do this.

Now she had to find a way of thwarting her lover's plan to help Correia. Why should he facilitate the association between her husband and a wild bush-woman, who in all likelihood had gone around naked before she met him and must surely, by now, know of his legal wife's existence?

What completed Amy Correia's anguish was that she had not been able to give Correia a child, a lack she felt all the more deeply because he pretended that the matter was unimportant and never failed to add that, in any case, he was no family man.

'You think that by helping him to get into parliament he'll forget what you did to him?' Amy asked, deciding to take a bolder line.

'What you mean?'

'You wanted to know about his character. Out of loyalty I remained silent, but the way I see it he's after your skin.'

And to drive the point home she proceeded to concoct a tale of vengeance Correia had practised on his parents.

'Knowing him,' she ended, 'he won't rest until you're six feet under the ground.'

She had said enough. Sensing that her lover was becoming impatient she saw fit to let him digest what he had heard. In the two years they had been living together she was as far apart from him as when she moved in, mesmerized by the sumptuous meals, his three servants and the mahogany furniture strewn about the house like ikons of good taste. Furthermore she remained the secretary, the paid servant, who, on hearing his car on the gravel, would immediately busy herself with some futile task, interpreting his inability to find time for her during the week as a manifestation of superiority.

Disappointed at the lack of genuine intimacy between them, the Right Hand Man had decided that in some way he failed to understand Correia had come between them. And for that reason he was surprised that she, the most careful woman he knew, should suddenly display such ill will towards her husband.

However, what Amy had said confirmed the Right Hand Man's deepest anxieties with regard to Correia. If his reputation for mischief had gone before him it was certainly founded on a solid base. And after all, who should know him better than his wife?

Their conversation drifted off into the banalities of office affairs and the President's impending visit to the Rupununi in order to meet the Amerindian captains and offer them control of certain lands with a view to securing their votes at election time.

When Amy left him to get dressed for church the Minister went down into the yard and sat on the bench Miss Rose described as the most beautiful retreat on the property. The sundial close by reminded her of a dumb waiter, she said, because it was a similar height and told the wrong time. The Minister, deep in thought, took no notice of the sundial or the sound of church-bells coming from various directions. On occasion he would go to the top of the yard, which was separated from a church by a well-maintained alleyway and, standing motionless as if deep in thought, he would listen to the preacher's sermon through the open windows, and the congregation's solemn responses of 'Praise the Lord' and 'Tell them, Preacher!' Then he would feel left out and be gripped by a longing to go to New Amsterdam and take Miss Rose to church dressed in her finery. New Amsterdam, where the deacons preached with passion in those small wooden churches with grounds encased in lofty palms, under whose fences hibiscus flourished beside the dusty roads.

Today, however, his reflections remained moored to a single raft, and the last thing that entered his head were the tranquil certainties of New Amsterdam. Correia had returned to haunt him with exorbitant demands. Would anyone believe that he once used him like an office boy who, content with the odd coin thrown his way for good behaviour, was expected to owe him loyalty into the bargain?

Since his trip to Venezuela, where he went on a mission connected with that country's claim to two-thirds of Guyana, he had been plagued by dreams of ruin inspired, he felt certain, by scenes of dilapidation along the new Venezuelan highways; gutted shop fronts, tumble-down concrete walls, machinery rusting by the wayside and a general air of abandonment. This vision of an oil-rich country had made a deep impression on him and provided some consolation for Guyana's experience of inveterate malfunction. It was also, apparently, a source of dreams that instructed him on his personal condition, but whose meaning, try as he might, he could not unravel. His life being blameless, what lessons could he draw from pictures of devastation in concrete and iron? Now that he was threatened by Correia's demands, however, it occurred to him that the elegant highway flanked by images of decadence might be a presentiment of vengeance by the likes of Correia and Kwaku, whom he had raised from the gutter at a time when no one took any notice of their plight.

Often he was on the point of confiding in Amy Correia. But how could he broach a subject in which her husband was the villain? Even now that evidence of her hostility to Correia had surfaced, he was not certain that he should read much into it.

The bells from the three churches stopped ringing almost at the same time, and the restoration of Sunday calm left a deep void in the morning. There and then he decided to go to New Amsterdam and look up his mother, who never stopped accusing him of neglect and complained that if she did not make her fortnightly visits to Georgetown she would not see him for years on end.

Chapter XXVII

One afternoon, as Kwaku was ushering out his last patient, he found Surinam waiting for him, a canvas wrapped in brown paper under his arm.

'I can come in?' he asked Kwaku.

'I suppose so but why not come home with me?'

'You know I don't like visiting people's houses. Anyway, it won't take long.'

On seeing Kwaku going back inside, his chauffeur made a gesture of exasperation but did not protest, because of late he had been allowing him to take the car home twice a week.

The two men sat down on the waiting-room bench, whereupon Surinam began untying the parcel he had brought with him.

Kwaku took the painting, placed it on the bench and then got up to examine it from a few feet away. A woman with staring eyes and unkempt hair occupied the centre of the canvas. On her lap sat a small child whose innocent imperturbability contrasted sharply with its mother's wild expression.

'It's for you.'

Kwaku, still harbouring a sense of grievance at the way he was expelled from Surinam's flat, could not hide his embarrassment.

'You don't like it?' Surinam asked.

'Oh yes. It's good. I like the colours.'

Having no idea how he was expected to judge a painting, Kwaku could only pretend to be impressed. He would rather Surinam had kept away, for he had no intention of taking part in his Friday reunions again.

'You're alright?' Kwaku asked, detecting in his visitor a change he could not define.

'Cool, cool.'

'You had anything particular you want to see me 'bout?' Kwaku asked nervously.

'Yes and no. . . . Eunice and Bertie have been asking after you. He started bringing her again. And the teacher too. You remember the teacher? The one with all those stories about flogging children?

He comes every Friday now and sometimes during the week. He's retired, as you know, so he's got the whole day. He says every day's like Saturday and he's never been so happy in his life. Now me! I've got to work all the time at something or other. Funny how people're so different. For me work is life. Or life is work, whichever way you want to look at it. He can loll about the whole day and talk about little children. His conversation is all about children, as if he wants to banish adults from the world. I know you didn't care for him, but if you got to know him better you'd change your mind. Somebody offered him a part-time job supervising staff at a store, and he said he wasn't a spy and the man could stick his job up his batty. The real reason was it would've tied him down. I know. I think teaching drained him and put him off work for good. . . . Eunice misses you, you know. She thinks the world of you, but doesn't dare say anything because Bertie is still a messenger and has got it in for you because you came to town with nothing. We had a long discussion last Friday about people who come from the fringes and do well at the centre. Bertie said all our best writers come from New Amsterdam and the best cricketers are from Port Mourant. He's got something there. Anyway it's all a matter of opinion, isn't it? Or the way you look at things. People from Georgetown are too arrogant to have it that they're inferior to people from the fringes. . . . As I say, Eunice and Bertie miss you. He's started bringing her again to prove he's not afraid of competition. . . .'

Surinam interrupted his monologue of a sudden and bowed his head. Kwaku, astonished at his show of humility, hardly knew what to say. For most of the time he was speaking he had kept his eyes averted, unlike the last occasion they met when his hostile words were matched by the obsessive concentration in his eyes.

'It's the firs' time I ever meet you outside your place,' Kwaku said, groping for a hold on any subject that would keep the conversation going. 'I thought you never leave home.'

'I wanted to see you to borrow money,' Surinam declared, now looking Kwaku straight in the eye.

'What? You?' came the incredulous retort.

'I'll pay you back in a week or so.'

'You don' have to explain,' Kwaku said. 'I mean I owe you so much. . . .'

'You don't owe me anything!' Surinam interrupted sharply.

'How much you want?'

'Five hundred US dollars.'

Kwaku's quickly suppressed expression betrayed his surprise.

'O.K.,' he assented, proud that he was in a position to help a friend in need.

'You're entitled to know why I want to borrow the money,' Surinam said, 'but I'll tell you another time. You don't mind, do you?'

'Me?' Kwaku declared, 'why should I mind? No, man, you don' have to explain. If I was in your shoes I wouldn' even bother to explain.'

'Good. You would've made a good painter.'

Kwaku could not see the connection.

'Talking 'bout painting,' Kwaku said, 'I can't hang your picture in the surgery or the waiting-room. Most of my clients are women and it would disturb them.'

'That's the idea,' Surinam said. 'It's meant to disturb.'

'Anyway, I can't hang it. Not at home either. You know, Miss Gwendoline don' appreciate art.'

'But you said she's blind.'

Kwaku, trapped by his old weakness of saying the first thing that came into his mind, gave a lame excuse about the remarks visitors were bound to make.

'You know,' said Surinam. 'You're the last person I came to ask for the money. I been to my aunt, I begged the man who owns the flat and I asked Bertie. None of them would help. And I said to myself, "Why not go to the only person that I ever wanted to show my adjoining room?" Good! Yes. I knew you'd lend me the money.'

'You did know?' Kwaku said.

'Yes.'

'An' why you din' come before?'

'Because I knew you'd lend me,' Surinam said without hesitating.

Kwaku looked Surinam up and down. His visitor's expression was as humble as when he began talking.

Surinam had spoken the truth. Not doubting for a moment Kwaku's generosity, he nevertheless felt ashamed to ask him for help, thinking that his plea might be interpreted as arising from the expectation of payment for his hospitality. His aunt was blood. Bertie he had known since childhood. And as for his benefactor, who let him have the flat free and helped finance his early exhibitions, he had lost all shame in that regard.

In any case Surinam felt that there was unfinished business between himself and Kwaku and could not come to terms with the likelihood that he would never see him again. His Friday night gatherings, when he lavished attention on his guests, had been at the expense of his savings into which he had to dig more and more deeply as he struggled to maintain the quality of the fare with which he regaled them. Unable to bring the gatherings to an end, unwilling to stop feeding his guests, he spent more and more time painting, only to find that as the number of his canvases grew, their price fell.

'When you can get the money?'

'Tomorrow,' Kwaku replied. 'Come by me at about eleven. Here, not home. And for God's sake don't tell anybody. Miss Gwendoline can't forget the hard times we been through.'

'I'm off then.'

Kwaku's sympathy for Surinam would have persuaded him to take the money from the two thousand dollars he kept sewn in his mattress and hand it over that very night, had it not been for Miss Gwendoline's exceptional hearing, which would not have failed to catch him in the act.

Two weeks later the first client who came into the surgery was dressed with unostentatious elegance, and Kwaku judged at once that she had not come to be helped in any way. As he showed her in he was certain he had seen her recently. Perhaps her photograph had been in the papers. Since he went everywhere by car now he seemed to meet fewer people, so it was more than likely that her picture had appeared in a newspaper. He had tried hard to overcome this feeling of inferiority in the presence of a well turned-out woman, but with no success; and now, after greeting the stranger with the obligatory formula he had learned from his son-in-law, he waited to hear her business. But she waited as well, as if for a sign.

'Please take a seat lady. What's your name?'

'My name is Mrs Tasker.'

'What can I do for you?'

For an answer she opened her purse and took out a large, unsealed buff-coloured envelope with Kwaku's name and address on it.

'I've brought this on behalf of my husband. I believe you call him Surinam.'

Kwaku took out the contents of the envelope.

'Please count it,' she urged him.

'Oh, I sure it's all there. . . . Why he didn' bring it himself?'

'He's been committed,' she said.

'You mean . . . Canje?'

'Yes, that place. . . . I can't thank you enough for lending him the money. He didn't need it, you know. He wouldn't take anything from me over the last year or so, and he got deeper and deeper in debt. The day before yesterday, during a ceremony in court at which I was introducing a new barrister to the bar, he walked into the court and gave me the envelope. I knew . . . suspected he wasn't well since he moved out and went to live in the flat at Meadowbrook. But you can't be sure. He was always a bit eccentric. He was a wonderful painter, you know.'

'I don' understand anything 'bout painting, Mrs Tasker. He did give me one, but I couldn' hang it on my wall.'

'Ah. . . . Since he moved out he only painted at night. Strange, isn't it? He said the flat was just right for him because it was near water.'

'What he did to get committed?' Kwaku asked.

'He came at me with the pestle from the kitchen. But that's not important.'

Her speech had become more agitated, and the words came more rapidly.

'I still think he's perfectly sane . . . well, sane enough,' she said. 'In fact, I'm sure he is.'

'But if. . . .'

'There are some men who beat their wives mercilessly and don't end up at Canje,' she said, interrupting Kwaku.

Kwaku reflected that if anyone came at him with a kitchen pestle he would do his best to have him put away at once. He lived in mortal dread of a distressed patient attacking him, and for that reason constantly thanked Heaven in his prayers that nearly all his clients were women.

'Lady, a pestle? When all is said and done!'

'You don't understand,' she said. 'He wouldn't have hit me.'

'Why you had him put away, then?'

'I panicked and ran out of the house, and the neighbour called the police. It happened twice before, so the police wouldn't allow him to come back. The first time I made a resolution to stand my ground if he ever did it again, because I *know* he wouldn't have hit me. But each time I lost my nerve. It's obvious I'm not strong enough to stand by him.'

Kwaku reflected that this was not the woman who introduced herself a while ago with an intimidating self-assurance.

'I know your husband wasn' well, Mrs Tasker.'

And Kwaku told her how he had abused him and thrown him out of the flat.

'When was this?' she asked.

'A few months back.'

'Try and remember exactly when.'

But he could not.

'You men live in a different world from us,' she said bitterly. 'You're always consumed by some kind of fury. If it isn't women, it's gambling or drinking or . . . painting. What *is* the matter with you?'

Kwaku recalled a similar observation by the Lethem Guest House owner.

She looked at him as if the reproach was meant personally for him, as if he was personally responsible for Surinam's commitment, as if she was challenging him to deny that he, too, was consumed by a fury, like other men.

'I'm sorry, Mrs Tasker. Surinam is a good, generous man. That's why I lend him the money right away.'

Recognizing that Kwaku was pleading in his defence, she said something conciliatory about Surinam speaking well of him.

For some time they did not exchange a word, as though all was said that had to be said. Kwaku knew he could not reflect on his friend's fate until his wife left and he hoped that she would go soon, before he let loose one of his indiscretions. The urge to look at his watch was so strong he turned his arm, only to be interrupted by an unexpected outburst.

'The worst thing a woman can do is to indulge a man to the point of self-effacement. My God! I yielded until I dared not oppose him. At first I wanted to see him happy . . . but, oh God! He's gone where he belongs. . . . Oh, I know how his friends worshipped him. Some of them at least. You're not the first he chased out of the flat. Oh no! If you think that's a unique distinction you're mistaken. He had a close friend years ago, who . . . oh, what's the use! What is my future at the bar now? I was told that my chances of being appointed the third woman judge in the country were high. Now I'll be surprised if I don't have to begin touting for clients, like some who shall be nameless.'

'Lady, why you quarrelling with me?' Kwaku asked, alarmed at her shrill tone.

'Yes, you're right. I'm sorry. . . . I hear you're a successful healer, Mr Cholmondeley. People speak highly of you. So I'm told. . . . But what are you really like?'

'That's not for me to say, Mrs Tasker. I try to be a useful member of society.'

'How empty words are!' she continued, speaking as if she were announcing a serious loss.

Kwaku now consulted his watch openly.

She, in turn, rose from her seat.

'Will you please count the money?' she asked.

'Oh, I know. . . .'

'Please, I insist.'

Kwaku counted the notes and nodded to her.

'One more thing, Mr Cholmondeley. Can I have back the painting he gave you? You said you couldn't hang it.'

'Sure, Mrs Tasker.'

He left her and went up to retrieve the canvas from Heliga, to whom he had lent it. And when he came back down he found her by the gate.

'Goodbye, Mr Cholmondeley. I'm sorry I took up so much of your time.'

Her car went past his on the gravel, and Kwaku could tell from Manny's resigned expression that he would be asking for time off during the week to compensate for having been held back for so long.

'Don' be vexed with that lady, Manny,' Kwaku told him. 'One day she might have to defend you in court for reckless driving. You never know.'

'Not me! Women lawyers jus' like women drivers. I does praise them from far off.'

It was not until he went to bed that night that Kwaku's thoughts dwelt on his friend's committal. He called to mind the sprawling asylum buildings at Canje, past which he used to walk with a hurried step. Once he had gone into the grounds to watch a cricket match and brought back with him memories of a lady patient shaking her fist out of a window, of dilapidated buildings and nurses immaculate in white uniforms. He shuddered at the possibility that he himself might have ended up within the asylum walls when he depended on his children to support him and Miss Gwendoline and lived in dread of the twins appearing on the doorstep of the hovel in which he lived. Perhaps he had been too hard on Heliga who, after all, was 'family'.

Never in a hundred years would he find a Friday night haven like Meadowbrook, near the old canal. Kwaku regretted bitterly that he had not made the first move towards becoming reconciled with Surinam. Was it so important to hold to one's dignity? Especially with a friend? How many embarrassing situations did he not have to endure as host? And at one time or another they all had to put up with Bertie's insults.

In his practice marriages were as various as friendships, yet Surinam's marriage must be one of the strangest he ever heard of. And why did he keep his wife's profession a secret when most men would be proud to claim a barrister as wife? Perhaps he never disclosed his surname for that very reason. No one should have any cause to connect him with her.

The more Kwaku read the clearer it became to him that his consulting-room was at least as instructive as his books; and, more so than his books, his patients were a constant reminder of the fragile hold he had on his destiny.

Kwaku was so unsettled by Surinam's committal that he went to see his wife to ask what he might do to help. But, far from welcoming his visit, she accused 'his friends' of being responsible for his descent into insanity, even though the Friday night reunions only began after Surinam moved into the flat in Meadowbrook.

From that day Kwaku took an interest in Surinam's wife's career and began to cut out news of her which appeared from time to time in the newspapers.

Life went on as though his friend had sunk into the ground with no more evidence of his disappearance than the published news of his wife's activities in the courts. And once, when Kwaku met the teacher in Water Street and was asked what had become of Surinam, he professed to be ignorant of his whereabouts, aware of the odium attached to lunacy. Surinam had disappeared, no more. And Kwaku said nothing of his friend's marriage to the barrister either, not knowing whether she had confided in him and expected his silence in return. In short, Kwaku had become a model of discretion.

Chapter XXVIII

Spotting a stranger in the looking glass, Amy Correia spun round and was on the point of saying that the building was not yet open to the public when she recognized her husband. Thrown into utter confusion at the unexpected visit, she fumbled with the mirror while attempting to find a suitable place for it in a drawer of her desk.

'Hello,' she said feebly.

'I've come to see your boss.'

Recovering from her embarrassment she said that the Minister had not yet arrived at work and was only due in an hour, at the earliest.

'I'll wait,' Correia said, taking a seat.

Knowing how stubborn he could be, she did not attempt to put him off but found it impossible to work now, with him half turned towards her. She pretended to be busy sorting out a few papers and carried them into the Minister's office, from where she took a good look at him through the glass partition.

Above the chair on which he was seated was a legend written in Georgian script, which announced the Minister's loyalty to the administration; an incongruous rubric for a discredited party.

She tried to put some order into her thoughts, for there was much work to be done. But as soon as she managed to concentrate, her intentions foundered in her confusion and resentment. He had not even greeted her and might be any ill-mannered stranger who walked in from the street with a request to see the Minister. Taking his detachment as proof of his contempt for her, she looked back on the Sunday morning when she hinted to the Minister that her husband was untrustworthy and vengeful. And she was more certain than ever that she would spare no attempt to destroy him.

She resented his cotton buktah shorts; she regretted that, unlike many men in their forties, he showed no signs of incipient baldness, and deplored the tolerance with which, as she anticipated, the Minister would receive him.

Employees of the ministry began arriving singly and in twos, mostly young women who sat down before their old typewriters and prepared to thumb through papers or files stacked in neat piles.

One man took his place in front of a computer and at once started tapping the keys energetically, giving the impression that he was carrying on where he had left off the afternoon before. And within a quarter of an hour the clatter of typewriters, interrupted now and then by an intrusive voice, became the dominant element of a purposeful routine.

When Correia looked over towards Amy's desk he saw her staring at him so intently that she had no time to turn away. He got up, stood for a few seconds where he was, then went over to say that he could not wait.

'I told you he'd be long,' she apologized. 'You want to leave a message?'

Correia reflected a moment then said, 'Tell him . . . don't tell him anything. I won't come looking for him any more.'

She watched him depart under the inquisitive glances of those who knew she and he were man and wife.

After the Minister arrived Amy waited for a suitable moment to break the news of her husband's visit, but to her surprise he made light of it.

'Don't worry, he'll come again,' he assured her.

'Why d'you think so?'

'He'll *have* to come, because I won't go to see him.'

And she left it at that, not knowing the source of his new-found resolution. On Sunday she would find out, during the hours when he brooked no interference from the outside world, except for a call from the President himself.

Amy, now that matters seemed to be coming to a head, decided to do nothing that might jeopardize her plan to nudge the Minister towards a decisive act. But after he went out that night, leaving her alone with the housekeeper, she took it into her head to go and prowl around the house in Kingston where Correia and his aboriginal lady were living.

As she was getting ready it began to rain. Through the window she could see the dark clouds stretching beyond the trees in the backyard, and reflected that it could rain all night. She waited for more than a half-hour for the rain to come to an end, but by then it was lashing the shrubs below the window.

Amy rang for a hired car and waited at the foot of the front staircase. She stood by the lattice-work watching the road lit up at intervals by bright strands of light which went out with the passing of each vehicle. The minutes went by, as palpably as the deluge, but the car did not arrive.

'You not going out tonight, Mrs Correia?' the housekeeper asked, looking down from the landing at the top of the stairs.

'Only for a while,' she replied, thinking she detected a note of sarcasm in the question.

The housekeeper withdrew.

Amy, reflecting that perhaps it was unwise, after all, to go out in such foul weather, gave herself a further ten minutes waiting, after which she intended to ring the garage and cancel the car. Then, almost at once, she heard the dying engine and saw the light slow down and stop before the iron gates. Closing the top button of her raincoat, she ran out to take her place on a back seat, on which the chauffeur had laid a folded cloth.

As the car drove slowly through the rain, its windscreen wiper swinging back and forth like an inverted metronome, Amy realized that she had no particular plan in mind, the only certainty being that the chauffeur would have to wait for her while she was in Correia's yard.

'The humiliation of it,' she reflected. 'He dealt with me like a stranger after all we've been through together. I know why he's come back to Georgetown . . . as if I don't know. Politics? He's never had any real interest in politics. All he wants to do is flaunt the child at me. The nights I lay awake thinking of him when he was in Lethem, believing that he'd only stayed because he was worried about the consequences of his theft! And all the while he was holed up with his naked-skin woman! I will see you writhing on the ground in pain and I won't lift a finger to help you, my husband. So you want two women! Well, you have two women!'

Amy was so engrossed in her reflections that they achieved the power of a fantasy. She *saw* an aboriginal Indian woman with jet-black hair who, she was certain, was insatiable, and capable of copulating for hours on end. Then she saw herself looking down from the rafters — the Minister had told her only a few days before of a woman who woke up in the middle of the night and saw a burglar staring at her from the rafters — and she saw the couple in bed, with the woman's hair spread out over Correia's body like a dark, loose-woven sheet.

'This is it, lady,' said the chauffeur, who brought the car to a halt at the entrance to the tenement yard.

She told him she would not be long and stepped out into the rain.

The ground in the alleyway leading to the backyard was soft, and her high heels sank deep into it. She cursed herself for coming, for being weak and yielding to a temptation that could bring her nothing but pain.

As she penetrated into the yard she heard laughter which, mingled with the sound of the rain, might have come from any of the three buildings. Then, beside the last house, another outburst of laughter left her in no doubt of its source.

Amy went round the low-pillared building in which Correia lived, past a barrel where the rain, channelled from the roof by a conduit, made a gentle gurgling sound. And just as she was about to retrace her steps, despairing of ever finding out in which of the three houses Correia lived, she noticed a chink of light at a point where the wall did not meet the floorboards and left a gap wide enough for a newspaper to be inserted. Looking about her to make certain she was not being observed, she saw, in the house next door, the shadow of a man whose back was pressed against a sash window. Bending down cautiously to avoid slipping on the water-logged ground, she put her eyes to the slit; and for the first time she got a glimpse of the aboriginal Indian lady who was sitting on a low stool, busy with a bowl of what she imagined to be rice. She measured her from the feet upwards, found nothing attractive in her features and had no doubt that, standing up, her rival would be revealed as being stout, with a figure as unattractive as her face.

Close by the wall through which she peered she saw a man on an easy chair, while on the far side Correia stood with a glass in his hand, beaming at some remark that had just been made. Her heart began to thump for no reason, but she maintained her bending position none the less, even at the risk of succumbing to the faintness that threatened to overcome her.

'Kwaku, you're talking nonsense, man,' Correia's indistinct voice came to her.

'I telling you!' was Kwaku's answer.

Amy could hardly credit what she heard, for Correia had always professed to dislike the healer, whom he dismissed more than once as a charlatan and a fool. Was Kwaku in league with him?

Amy thought it extraordinary that three of the people she hated most should be in the same room laughing and talking as though she did not exist, while she could only cultivate her rage on the outside, peering through a peep-hole like an inquisitive child.

Drained of her dignity, she stood up once more and for the first time became aware that her feet were soaked. She had often described her years of teaching as a long, degrading experience; now, in a matter of *minutes* the icy fingers of an indescribable anguish had tightened round her throat. No longer caring if she were seen by a neighbour of Correia's, she applied her eyes to the gap once more and tried to catch every word, every gesture arising from an intimacy she did not share. Irrational ideas crossed her mind: suppose it rained so hard and so long that Correia's house, weakened by the water, detached itself from its foundations and drifted away, out into the ocean. She imagined other disasters to match her pain, and in the end began to relish perversely the indulgence of her suffering.

And all the while the rain came down, making a noise resembling the innumerable strokes of a demented drummer.

Blinded by tears of frustration, yet unable to wrench herself away, she stood her ground until the urgent, repeated sound of a horn called her attention to the waiting car.

Afraid that someone might come to the door to investigate, she made her way back to the road, negotiating a path between the puddles and runnels of water.

Taking her place in the car, Amy could not help gazing up the forlorn alleyway that led to her husband's house and, as the vehicle moved off, she looked back through the rear window, recalling how she had once refused to yield to the temptation to do what she had just done. How many times in the past she had deplored the spectacle of a woman conducting herself in an undignified manner!

'Take the back streets,' she told the chauffeur.

She wished to avoid the bright lights, thinking, absurdly, that her despair was visible and that the people huddled under the awnings waiting vainly for a break in the downpour would, with the help of the weak sodium street lamps, glimpse her through the dark pane. The car turned, drove past the high convent walls, past the Astor cinema and into the stretch of road that came to an end where the trench divided it from Vlissingen road.

The guard at the nearby Venezuelan embassy came to the gate and looked up the road briefly before returning to his cubicle. Amy told the chauffeur she would send out the housekeeper with the money she owed, bade him goodnight and disappeared past the armed guard into the shadows of the palm-fronted yard.

Amy informed the Right Hand Man that Correia's aboriginal Indian lady had come to see her while he was out and told an extraordinary story. According to her, Correia had planned, if he were elected, to wreak vengeance on him for the years he worked in the ill-ventilated back shop. He intended to report all his activities as a currency dealer and claim that he was forced by threats to do as he was told. If he was not chosen as a candidate he would burn down the Minister's house. Correia's lady also said that Kwaku supported him and promised to defray any expenses the Party was not prepared to meet.

The Minister listened with that detached manner many people who dealt with him took to be a lack of interest and only nodded when she suggested that he invite Correia to the house and test his reaction when Kwaku's name was mentioned.

This elaborate lie had been conceived during the trip from Correia's home back to the house, while the rain was flooding the gutters and the streets became pitch dark following the nightly electricity failure.

'What did I tell you!' she exclaimed.

'When did she come?' he asked, the first of a series of questions.

She had prepared her answer to any possible challenge and was ready to amplify each with circumstantial detail that lent credence to her story. Her answer was that the visitor had come at such and such a time and wore an ill-fitting frock. She even spoke of the way her hair was plastered down, the effect of walking in the rain. And suddenly it crossed her mind that if he did see Correia he might mention his lady's visit, thus giving her husband the opportunity of denying it. But it was too late to alter her story.

The Right Hand Man had, in fact, taken her earlier warning seriously and decided to invite Correia to dinner, with the intention of offering him a country house should he fail to secure his candidacy.

The memory of the way he had suffered before and during Correia's detention was still vivid. He could not go on living in fear of the currency dealer, especially now that Amy's revelations made it clear that any compromise with him would only have the effect of buying him off for a few years at the most. To cap it all Kwaku had chosen the same time to join forces with his enemy.

First, he must apply Amy's test and draw his own conclusions from Correia's reaction to the mention of Kwaku's name. He was beginning to have doubts about Amy herself for, after more than a year of silence on Correia's account, she had suddenly begun to pile up evidence of his treachery. Yet she could not have invented the aboriginal Indian woman's visit or Correia's association with Kwaku, both of which were capable of being checked.

This the Minister did, only to find through one of the ministry's spies that the two men were as thick as thieves. Amy was right! He made up his mind to act quickly rather than wait for Correia to come to him, as he had predicted would happen.

Chapter XXIX

There was talk that an American commission led by a former President would supervise the forthcoming elections to make certain that excesses of the past were not repeated, when people long dead had voted and ballot boxes from electoral districts loyal to the opposition parties disappeared mysteriously. But objections from the opposition parties that the electoral lists had not been properly drawn up became grounds for a postponement of the elections. News was rife that the ruling party had no intention of relinquishing power and that the American government did not look with favour on the supervising commission; which was not surprising, given that it had been responsible for installing the creole government in the first place.

It was in this atmosphere of intrigue and rumour that Correia went to see the Right Hand Man at his home one night.

The guard had been dismissed, and Correia was welcomed by the Minister himself, who led him to the long back verandah overlooking the extensive yard.

'What're you taking?' the minister asked.

'Nothing. I've just had a big meal and a lot of water. No room.'

'Well, when you want anything to drink you only have to say the word.'

The Minister enquired about life in Lethem and whether he had travelled on the new road to Linden. But Correia, impatient at these circumlocutions, declared his eagerness to get on with their business, as he had promised his *lady* to return home early.

'Very well,' said the Minister and thereupon he changed places so that he could be nearer his visitor.

'I've arranged that we go and see a party activist tonight,' he told Correia. 'He knows the ropes and thinks the matter of your candidacy will only be a formality after he's consulted the right people. He wants to see you, of course, but if you have to go back to your lady early. . . .'

'Hold on,' Correia broke in, 'you were able to arrange it in such a short time?'

'You obviously don't know the ropes. I could have arranged the meeting even earlier. Damien, the party man, will be able to tell you which constituency you could be put up for. . . . Look, you can choose your day. It's up to you. But elections will have to be held by the end of the year, so the longer you wait the less chance you'll have of being put forward. Every Tom, Dick and Harry wants to represent somewhere or other. I've never yet seen such an outbreak of civic consciousness.'

'Tonight. . . . If we must, we must, I suppose,' said Correia.

'And what about your lady?'

'She'll be alright.'

'I hope you told her you'll be coming here.'

'No,' Correia said.

The Minister turned away, lest the relief on his features could be read.

'Where's everybody?' Correia asked.

'They're all out. The housekeeper should be back any time now.'

The two men set out in the private car, watched by Amy Correia, who had been waiting in one of the numerous empty rooms. It was she who had had the responsibility of making certain that guard and housekeeper would be away. The case of the guard proved to be far more difficult, since the Minister was not responsible for his roster, but in the end she suggested that he take off only the couple of hours Correia could conceivably remain at the house.

The plan worked so well there were no witnesses to Correia's arrival or departure.

As she stood at the window Amy dwelt on the flaws of the plan and on the character of the two men closest to her.

'I can never get to the bottom of what he says and does,' she reflected, unsure of the Minister's enthusiasm for silencing Correia.

And in that thought lay something of the humiliation that clung to her resentment against Correia. Had the Right Hand Man proved to be affectionate, had their relationship grown as was the case with Correia in the early days, she might have risen above the jealousy that afflicted her on learning about the latter's association with the Indian woman. But, stranded between a defunct marriage and a union of convenience, she found herself in the grip of quiet desperation.

There was no doubt that she was still in love with Correia. How else could she explain the violence that welled up in her at the mere sight of his lady? Every Sunday she went to church and prayed for her own soul. She prayed for guidance in her struggle to deal with feelings alien to her and the family from which she came, solid God-fearing people to whom no one could point a finger of reproach. But even on the same day some remark, some allusion to marriage, would deal a blow to her Christian resolution, and she would brood on her fate at the hands of men.

She saw the guard arrive on foot and almost immediately after he went out of sight past the lattice-work partition she heard the click of his rifle and imagined him fixing his bayonet and getting ready for his long vigil.

Three years ago when Correia's behaviour began to verge on the eccentric — she had been responsible for 'straightening him out', according to his family — she consulted a card-cutter to find out what she could do to help him. 'Get a child!' was the laconic advice. 'But we've tried.' 'Then adopt one.' Correia had refused, for he regarded adoption as an admission of inadequacy. The Right Hand Man, no less uncompromising, rejected her plea to have a child on the grounds that, as a Minister, he could not afford to father illegitimate children; a curious pretext, considering that it was the rule rather than the exception that well-off officials supported two families. Indeed, there were cases when the *low* family was more highly regarded than the one sanctioned by law.

In Amy's extremity she did not know whether her anger was directed as much against the minister as against Correia. If the woman and child served as a focus for this anger, like a magnifying glass concentrating the heat of the sun, it was easy to pretend that the resulting conflagration was meant to engulf the one most closely connected with them. In fact it was doubtful whether Amy understood the depth of her animosity towards the Right Hand Man. Working with him at the ministry was one thing; it was quite another putting up with his absences abroad, his unrelenting devotion to government business, his reticence about official matters which interested her, and above all with the realization that he regarded her as little more than his secretary. The trap into which Correia had fallen unwittingly had been set as much for the executioner as for the victim, and she hoped fervently that the executioner would not lose his nerve.

She had not noticed the housekeeper come through the gate but, hearing her footsteps on the stairs, she began rocking nonchalantly in her chair to mask her agitation.

'Goodnight,' the housekeeper greeted her.

'Goodnight. You enjoyed yourself?'

They exchanged civilities before the housekeeper left her, aware from Amy's manner that she was not in the mood for conversation.

'Isn't it odd how people can buy loyalty with money?' Amy thought, reflecting on the fact that the housekeeper would not tolerate any criticism of the Minister. 'Or is it easy to buy women? He bought me as well, and I couldn't bear to hear anyone bad-talk him. But he could not buy Correia and Kwaku. At least not for long.'

And she brought to mind the women who would have gone through fire for the dead President, in spite of the authenticated stories of his vindictiveness and the violence he practised against those who stood in his way and the manifest corruption which he encouraged.

With her disaffection had arisen a distaste for anything connected with the Right Hand Man: the housekeeper, his dogs, and those at the ministry who fawned on him.

She kept her position at the window, nodding off from time to time and waking up at any unusual sound.

With a start she realized that the Minister was standing by her.

'You mustn't do that! she complained. 'Why do you creep up on me like that?'

'Wake up!'

'But I am awake,' she objected. 'Did you. . . ?'

'Did I what?' he asked.

'Nothing,' she whispered, while wondering what would be her position in law if he were dragged before the courts.

'Did you take my husband home?'

'Go to bed. . . . Everything's alright.'

She wondered if he could see the fear in her eyes.

'Good night,' she said. 'How late is it?'

Consulting his watch he answered that it was not very late.

'What time is it?'

'Five past twelve.'

She dared not ask him if he knew whether Correia had told his lady where he was going.

Once upstairs she waited for him to follow her to bed, judging that the time he took would give some indication of his state of mind. And while waiting she did not fall asleep, as she had done downstairs. Whatever he had done could not be undone and, in thinking this, she was aware of a terrible weight on her chest. She longed to be able to confide in someone, to explain that the moment the Minister refused to reveal how his mission had turned out she wanted to rush round to the house in the backyard in order to find out whether Correia had returned home.

It was only the following morning that Amy Correia's misgivings about the Minister's journey were replaced by anger at the way her enquiry as to its outcome was dismissed. He was in a vulnerable position, not she. And yet she felt as impotent as ever in her dealings with him, as though it was ordained that things should be so.

Whatever had happened the night before she was determined to find out whether Correia was back with his Indian woman.

When the Minister set out with Correia in his car, he had no clear idea how to get rid of a man who had become his mortal enemy. In his dealings with underlings he had abandoned his policy of total control, Kwaku and Correia having provided ample proof that it had failed. It only needed an erratic, ambitious character like Correia to make nonsense of the most carefully laid plans to manipulate his staff.

At first he planned to give him the fright of his life: perhaps one of the government thugs could flog him within an inch of his life. But, on reflection, he came to the conclusion that a man who was prepared to set fire to buildings would not be neutralized so easily. When Kwaku's turn came that would be the way. Correia must be dealt with once and for all.

Driving along the coastal road — past recently built schools, a shoe factory, advertising hoardings, village burial grounds, raised water tanks — he felt the pull of the countryside and the imagined figure of Death hovering over Stanleytown cemetery, where the sexton slept for most of the day on his bench in the lodge. If his country folk were not afraid of death, whence this hesitation to commit someone else to the other world? Was it only fear of the law?

'How far are we going?' Correia asked.

'We'll soon be there. We can turn back if you like.'

Correia was reassured.

The car veered off the coastal highway into a remote road that soon became impassable.

'The last time I came here,' the Minister said, as nonchalantly as possible, 'we had to get out on the way back and step into a tray with a grey solution, against anthrax, foot and mouth or something.'

They set out on foot.

'You're not locking the car?' Correia asked.

'Here? The people round here wouldn't know how to steal it.'

They continued on their way, side by side, skirting the trench which led to the main canal that drained the backlands. On and on they walked until they approached the Conservancy, whose expanse of water shone in places under the bright moonlight; the same Conservancy Kwaku — while still a young man — had breached, flooding the villagers' crops and rousing them to demands for his imprisonment in the interest of public order.

On their left the canefields made a compact, indistinct mass and beyond, like a line of immobile trucks, stretched the dwellings of estate workers.

'It won't be long now,' the Minister said. 'Our man lives in the most unlikely place.'

The Right Hand Man was slightly ahead of Correia as the road narrowed.

'You'd better go ahead of me,' he suggested, stopping to allow Correia to pass him.

'Very well.'

He stepped aside and remained standing on the edge of the path. And in the moment when the two men were side by side on the dam, at that very moment the purpose of their proximity high above the water came home to Correia with such clarity he remained rooted to the spot, convinced by some quirk of time that what was about to happen had already happened, perhaps many years before. And while he stood, so paralyzed by fear he had no thought of defending himself, he recalled briefly the exhilaration he experienced at his power over the Minister as they drove along the coastal road.

Walking along the dam, the Minister became obsessed with the idea of the side on which he would allow Correia to go past; should it be the right- or left-hand? The success of the undertaking seemed to depend on his choice. Yet when the moment came to invite Correia to step ahead, he lost his head and allowed him to approach on the right, the side he decided should be barred at all costs. In the dark he could only stare at the immobilized figure of his former employee who, he believed, had stopped because he did not care to lead the way. And this last act of apparent defiance drove him into such a rage he conceived Correia as the embodiment of all the opposition he had encountered during his rise to the top.

Suddenly the night was rent by a piercing shriek, and a flock of birds flew up from their roost beneath a nearby clump of trees.

By the time the Minister's car was back in town the tyre treads that had come in contact with the muddy village path had long shed their clods of earth, and when it turned into the driveway and moved slowly between the tall pillars of the mansion, only the most observant onlooker would have noticed anything unusual about its wheels.

Chapter XXX

The house was in darkness, and the absence of any sign of life tempted Amy Correia to knock on the front door but, resisting the urge, she went round to the back just as she had done a few nights before. Although the yard bore few traces of the unseasonable downpour that had ruined her pair of high-heeled shoes she found herself looking for obstacles none the less, as though the last visit had made an indelible impression on her mind.

In the grip of a terrible fear that the Minister had committed the deed to which she had guided him, she realized that she had no stomach for homicide. Impulsively, and quite inexplicably, she climbed the few treads of the back house's stairs and knocked on the door gently instead of following her plan to listen for the sound of a man's voice. She knocked again and again, each time louder than the last, but to no purpose.

While retreating, anxious at the possibility of meeting someone, she thanked God that her features could not be made out in the dark.

The following night she returned, but dared not enter the yard at first. Then, yielding to her insatiable curiosity, she crossed the bridge once more and went as far as the large tree, hoping to be able to make out a light in Correia's house from there. But, unable to see the whole frontage even when pressed against the paling, she advanced all the way to the back.

Correia's cottage, as dark as the previous night, now seemed full of menace and, prodded by some premonition of danger to herself, Amy turned and all but fled to the street, convinced that she must return to the safety of her home as quickly as possible.

The thought came to her that she had never been as happy as when she was a huckster, in that time when she *strove*. Every change of job was the equivalent of a move upwards; the continual, implacable ascent towards an illusion of security. And the triumphant culmination of that ascent had brought her to the mansion; the place of many rooms, the house of silence, behind which travellers' palms spread out their branches with the symmetry of finely crafted fans. How many times she had passed that house as a girl and envied those who lived in it, whose occupation of it could only be guessed at from a vehicle in the carport or a gardener among the flowering shrubs.

At a teachers' seminar she once attended the lecturer elaborated at length on the function of illusion and, at the end, initiated a discussion on the subject. She, too shy to contribute, listened with awe to his repeated point of view: that illusion was itself a part and function of reality and only when it was perceived as such could one hope to avoid its dangerous fascination. But it seemed that her interest was not shared by her fellow teachers.

Her thoughts wandered over matters she had longed to discuss with the Right Hand Man in the days when she regarded him as an intellectual. Men were a great disappointment. Or perhaps she had expected too much of them. Correia, the only man she knew who did not set too great a store by material things, himself fell prey to the magnet of money. And she herself had succumbed to the illusion of a status behind whose seductive face lurked a terrible emptiness. It was as though the corrupting influence had sucked them in with their own connivance. If she hated him in the end, might it not be that she hated being exposed for what she had become, the creature of a man without substance?

She walked through the streets without a thought of the dangers to a woman on her own and, as she went by St George's Cathedral, the sound of its organ escaped into the night like the arresting voice of a counsellor trailing soothing but portentous words. Life flowed on, with its music, its secret forces impelling people along uncharted paths; its conflagrations, betrayals, self-immolations, treatises on religion, priests in black habits, altar boys dispensing wine in silver chalices, vehicles of hope; self, *self*, the desire to be cleansed and clothed like children, the door into the bevelled looking-glass, a sea of words, egrets at roost, the immensity of experience dismembered into comprehensible parts.

'Dear God,' she prayed, 'if my husband is alive I will throw myself at his feet and beg forgiveness. I'll live with him and his lady and ask nothing in return but to revive our friendship!'

The following day Amy Correia went back to the house in the backyard after nightfall and once again she found it in darkness. And every night she did as much, seized by an obsessive need to know if her husband was still alive.

When, ten days after the minister's night journey, it was reported in the papers that the corpse of an unidentified man was fished out of the

Conservancy of such and such a village, Amy asked the Minister point
blank if the body was that of her husband.

'Do you think I am a murderer?' he asked.

Chapter XXXI

'I use to sit down under a table when I was a girl an' listen to the grown-ups talk. The things I use to hear!' Miss Gwendoline said, regaling the company with stories.

Philomena and her husband were there with her daughter. After a period of estrangement they had become reconciled to Miss Gwendoline through Kwaku's good offices, when he claimed to have converted her to the virtue of forgiveness. And she, comfortable in her middle age and buoyed up by Kwaku's devotion and Suarez's friendship, became known in that stretch of road for her boisterous laughter.

Miss Gwendoline spoke to them of the time when the East Coast train could be waved to a stop by a would-be passenger and of her grandfather's dog, which became friendly with an engine-driver and used to go two stops with him — stories passed on from generation to generation.

'He use to put him out; an' you know that dog would run back along the train lines an' find his way home. I telling you!'

Miss Gwendoline and Philomena were no closer than before. But as Heliga shed his pompous ways — at least when he came visiting — and in his state of dependency concealed his delusions of superiority over Kwaku, she learned to tolerate him in his fall from grace. He and Philomena even got into the habit of spending their weekends at the house in town and would have come more often if Miss Gwendoline had been less strict with her granddaughter.

'My grandmother was so strict!' Miss Gwendoline went on. 'When she was dying I had to take my turn keeping watch. I was only five then. Eh, eh! One night she grab my hand and say, "Gwen, I know you frightened of me, but you needn' be. I didn' hurt you while I alive an' I not going harm you when I dead." Truth o' God! That's what she say to me. She use to frighten the life out o' me with long, long silences. . . . She did know a lot o' things, more than my mother an' father, I tell you. But she din' talk much. Just as I blind, she was kinda dumb.'

She was now completely at home in her unlit world, a fact Kwaku attributed to Philomena and Heliga being cut down to size. Philomena, on the other hand, was of the conviction that her mother benefited from the companionship of two men, her father and Suarez. And it was as much for that reason she detested Suarez as for his cloying attentions.

During the storytelling session Kwaku arrived home and, without greeting anyone, whispered in Miss Gwendoline's ear something that changed her expression so dramatically Philomena asked what was wrong.

'It's nothing,' Kwaku answered. 'Well, is something, but you can't do anything 'bout it.'

'Somebody dead?' Philomena asked again.

'Yes. A friend.'

He signalled to Heliga to come with him on to the porch where he told him of Correia's death and the police interest in the activities of all his friends.

'I only met him once,' said Heliga.

'The police not interested in that. You got to be prepared. They might want to see you or they might not.'

'So what you're going to do?'

'I staying home to wait for them,' Kwaku answered. 'The chauffeur downstairs. He goin' take youal home. If they don' find you here they mightn' question you.'

Heliga and his family bade Miss Gwendoline good night and hurried away.

Kwaku was particularly worried. He had reported Correia missing at the Alberttown station on behalf of his polygamic wife, whom he found huddled in a corner of the unlit cottage when he went to see Correia. It was the third day of his disappearance.

But it was the discovery of the body in the Conservancy of the village where he grew up that made him think that suspicion would almost certainly fall on him. The fact that he had breached it once only added to his woes. There were people in the village who still harboured feelings of resentment, even enmity towards him.

'You in' do anything,' Miss Gwendoline told him when they were alone. 'Stop worrying. Nothing goin' happen to you if you think nothing goin' happen.'

As it turned out she was right. Correia's lady spoke so well of Kwaku the police subjected him to no more than a routine interrogation. Once the marks near the Conservancy were found to be different from those made by the tyres of his own car they lost interest in him as a suspect.

Correia had told Kwaku the day before his fateful visit that he was going to see the Right Hand Man, a piece of information he would have passed on to the police had he been arrested. But his knowledge of the murky world of party and government business, gleaned mainly from Correia, guaranteed his silence. Even if he had known that the tyre marks at the scene of the crime matched those of the Minister's car, he would have remained silent. Since nothing he said could bring his friend back to life the best he could do was to support his wife and child, in the same way as he had come to terms with Philomena's family's dependence on him.

On every occasion that Amy Correia had gone to the house in the back-yard her husband's lady was at home. The first, when she knocked several times on the door, the woman put her hand over the mouth of the child who was sitting on her lap. But she had no idea who Amy was and, in any case, would not have recognized her had they met.

The secret of Correia's visit to the Right Hand Man was proving to be too much of a burden for Kwaku, who decided to share it with Suarez.

His friend saw him through the window and called out even before he turned into the yard. He lived with an old aunt and, reluctant to abandon her, had not formed an enduring relationship with a young woman. While he professed to be a loner and unwilling to attach himself permanently, the fact was, his wages as a watchman at the Ministry of Hope being barely sufficient to support himself and his aunt, that a number of associations with women friends had foundered on his lack of means.

The two friends went downstairs to be able to talk in private, and installed themselves on two crates taken from a pile of discarded objects Suarez obtained from the Ministry of Hope and resold to supplement his income.

Kwaku disclosed for the first time his close association with the dead man since he returned from Lethem, and his knowledge of the intended visit to the mansion.

'You're a hell of a man!' Suarez said reproachfully. 'I bet you didn't tell Miss Gwendoline either.'

'She did know I use to go an' see him, but not 'bout his ambition to get elected.'

'So why you've come to cry on my shoulder?' Suarez asked, irritated by Kwaku's secretiveness. 'When you came to Georgetown first you used to say all the wrong things and people could read you like a book. Now you spend half your time doing things behind people's back.'

'Tell me something,' Kwaku rejoined heatedly. 'How come you so educated an' got such a low job? Every an' anybody is manager of this an' manager of that since people queuing up to leave the country. You in' got no ambition?'

'No,' Suarez replied coolly. 'I don't have any ambition, and that's why I haven't ended up in the morgue, like Correia. You believe you're safe? You think because you keep your mouth shut that the Right Hand Man's going to leave things at that? How do you think he got where he did?'

'So you suspect him too. . . . Jeeeesus! To kill a man in cold blood!'

'How d'you know he killed him?' Suarez asked.

'I suppose he take Correia all that way up the East Coast to go for a swim.'

Suarez ignored the sarcasm and remarked that he could see no reason why the Minister should have wished to kill Correia.

'You yourself say he get where he did. . . .'

'Yes,' Suarez interrupted him, 'but there must be a reason for killing him. He had to be a threat of some kind to him.'

'Your trouble is you think too much,' Kwaku said.

Suarez preferred to hold his tongue, for with every word his irritation grew. Besides, he sensed that Kwaku's unease was probably deeper than he made out.

A prickly silence settled between them, while Suarez's aunt moved from room to room as though she was herself uneasy at the conversation below.

At last Suarez spoke, declaring that somebody should stand up and denounce the corruption in the country.

'A local bank that lends money to party people and doesn't bother to demand repayment; Government vehicles unaccounted for; the Government auditor producing no report for years; Treasury accounts years behind. And these people who practise corruption and lies and thuggery preach morality to simple folk. It makes you sick.'

Suarez, with uncharacteristic bitterness, listed the published misdeeds of the administration, while Kwaku, more concerned about Correia's fate and the Right Hand Man's part in his death, listened without interrupting. He gained the distinct impression that Suarez cared less about Correia's death than he did.

'I think his lady know more than she will admit,' Kwaku suggested.

'Who?'

'Sidonie, the buck woman. She know everything. Everything, I tell you.'

'Like what?' Suarez asked, his interest aroused.

'One day when he was going out she say, "Don' go there." "Where?" And she tell him where he was going. He couldn' believe his ears.'

'You asked her how she thinks Correia died?'

'No,' Kwaku answered. 'I should have, but I didn'.'

It seemed to Kwaku that Suarez was trying to solve a puzzle.

'Let's go round and see her,' he suggested with that note of authority Miss Gwendoline detested in her son-in-law, but admired in him.

Kwaku led the way into the yard in which Correia's polygamous wife lived and Suarez, following close behind, could not avoid crushing underfoot fruit that had fallen from the overhanging trees.

'Don' ask her to put on the light,' Kwaku said.

'Why?'

'Since Correia dead she won't have any light.'

Kwaku went up the stairs first and rapped three times in quick succession.

'Sidonie, is me. Kwaku.'

Precipitate steps were followed by the drawing of bolts before the door opened no more than a finger's breadth.

'Is me,' Kwaku said.

She allowed the two men to enter the dark room.

'I bring a visitor with me,' Kwaku reassured her. 'He was Correia good friend. . . . Is where the child?'

'Inside. You wan' see him?'

'Yes. Jus' for so.'

It was during the short space of time when she opened, and light entered from the nearby house that Kwaku noticed she had been drinking. On reaching the bedroom door she had to support herself against the partition before going inside.

'You don't have to get him out,' Suarez said.

'Leave her,' Kwaku corrected him. 'She want to.'

Kwaku knew how much the child meant to her and never failed to make much of it when he came visiting.

She brought out her baby, who was not awakened by the disturbance.

Kwaku took the boy from her and fondled him for a few seconds before giving him back to his mother, while Suarez stood aside, unsure what he was expected to do.

'Put him back to bed then,' Kwaku told her and she complied, walking back to the bedroom with the same drunken gait.

'Sidonie,' Kwaku said, when she came out again, 'turn on the light, ne?'

'No!' she answered with unusual firmness. 'The light dead!'

Kwaku did not insist.

'Why you been drinking?' he asked, as much to temper her agitation about the light as to express his concern for her drunken state.

'I in' know,' she answered.

'Correia did always say you talk a lot in your own language. Why you don' talk more in English?'

'I in' know,' came the ritual answer.

Kwaku was as far as ever from asking her the pertinent question, but when she sat down, and they followed suit he made his resolution at the risk of upsetting her.

'We want to find out who kill Correia. We think we know who, but don' have proof. Did he say why he was goin' to see the Minister, or if they were goin' out together?'

'He been to see a minister?' she asked.

'He tell me so himself,' Kwaku pursued, eager to get something out of her before she went back into her shell.

'I don' know 'bout a minister. All he keep saying was, "All or nothing." I ask him what he mean, but he didn' explain. But I see in my eye that he was going to *Mara*.'

'Where?' Kwaku asked.

'To Mara.'

'What's that?'

'Mara,' she could only repeat.

The word meant 'Dark Pool' in the Macusi language but Sidonie, unable to find a suitable English equivalent, repeated it with a distressed expression of frustration.

'You saw anything else in your eye?' Suarez asked, speaking for the first time.

'I see many things. I don' want to talk, though.'

'You see a man in your eye?' Suarez asked, afraid they would get nothing more out of her.

'I in' see no man,' she answered. 'I see a woman.'

'What!' Kwaku exclaimed.

Suarez did not believe a word she said and reckoned it a waste of time to continue questioning her.

'This woman,' Kwaku said, 'what she look like?'

'I can't talk no more. He shouldn' have come back to town. No more.'

Suarez thought he caught sight of a rum bottle on the floor behind her chair.

'How the child?' Kwaku asked.

'He dey good.'

'And you?'

'I dey good too.'

'You want to go back to the bush?'

'Yes.'

'Where you would go to?'

'Family.'

Suarez and Kwaku exchanged glances. Suarez felt it was time to go, but Kwaku could not leave her alone after such a brief visit. Correia had told him often enough that the Indians feared loneliness more than anything else.

'I goin' arrange to send you money to Lethem,' Kwaku told her. 'But you must stay in town till the end of the year.'

He had the idea of setting a specific time in case she had to testify at a trial. It was probably best for her to return among her people, he thought, yet saw no reason to withdraw his request.

He had spent many happy evenings in that house, where Correia exposed another side of himself, speaking of his fire-raising days, when the sight of a conflagration gave him a peculiar thrill, especially when a large crowd gathered to witness its progress. Even after the flames subsided, and the blackened skeleton of the house resembled a building in its early stage of construction, and the crowds had gone away, he would remain to watch the firemen directing their hoses onto its forlorn remains. The way he felt was a secret he had shared with no one since then. So often had he stayed on after the excitement died down that people became suspicious, and rumour went the rounds that he was the bringer of ill fortune. In the end, following the unfounded accusation that he had started a warehouse fire, the police apprehended him, but released him when he claimed to be attracted by fires but had never committed arson. From that day onwards the compulsion to witness a conflagration became the need to start one himself.

He spoke of his time in prison, the years in Lethem, his trips into Brazil across the Takutu river that swelled in the wet season and took boats down to the great Black River, then to the Amazon, mother of inland waters, which struggled with the ocean until it expired one hundred miles beyond its mouth. He had seen the territory where Indians hang up their dead to rot and devoured their crushed bones after scavenging birds had picked them dry. He was reborn into a world where humans knew their place, he became fond of saying. Yet there remained a longing in him that grew with time: the need to settle a matter of honour. Like the Indians he was unable to forget an injury and for that reason he came back to town not for good, but to stay as long as it took him to right his private wrong.

For the first time Kwaku saw Suarez at a loss for words, in the presence of a woman whom he was unable to fathom. Yet he, Kwaku, felt at ease in her company, a fact that made him proud and provided a measure of the progress that had put the clown in him to sleep.

Suarez wanted to let Kwaku know that he was ready to leave but could not find a way of doing so in the dark without attracting the woman's attention. Everything about the unusual circumstances of the gathering unsettled him; the lady's laconic answers, the unlit room and the fact that it was his first meeting with an aboriginal Indian. Besides, their visit had proved fruitless. Correia's lady wanted to go back to the bush and clearly had no intention of helping them, while Kwaku's demonstration of tolerance increased his impatience with the pointless visit. He was about to declare that he was going when the infant began to bawl.

'Is alright,' Kwaku said, anticipating an excuse Sidonie did not make.

She returned with the infant, and once seated gave it the breast. Thereupon the sound of the child attempting to suckle mingled with the hum of mosquitoes attracted by warm flesh.

'Is the mosquitoes,' she said, explaining why the infant had woken up.

The bedroom window, the only one open in the house, had served as an entrance for the insects, which had followed the infant and his mother into the drawing-room.

Suarez, seeking a reason for his lack of compassion towards the woman and his growing irritation at the prolonged visit, found none; rather, he could not help blaming her for Correia's death which, in spite of Kwaku's assertion to the contrary, seemed to have left her unmoved. He would never have admitted to feelings of contempt for her *just* because she was an aboriginal, since she had welcomed them barefoot and lacked the basic manners of any townswoman who let him into her room. What is more, he would have protested violently at any accusation of bias against her as a member of the opposite sex and pointed to the respect he showed his aunt and Miss Gwendoline, and the fact that no woman had ever accused him of discourtesy.

'It's time we made a move,' he told Kwaku, who was sitting motionless in the dark, like a stranger on his best behaviour.

'Right!'

'You goin'?' the woman asked.

'Yes,' Kwaku answered, and stood up. 'I goin' come the day after tomorrow.'

Suarez still found it difficult to believe that Correia had been murdered. He was one of those people who criticized the administration harshly, backing up assertions of corruption with facts and figures, but in the last resort remain unconvinced by their own logic unless they witness with their own eyes the vice of which they complain. And though he came to grasp the reality of that corruption, he still could not credit that those responsible were capable of murder.

Among the fraternity of watchmen and messengers, a secret society in its own right, he was regarded as aloof, and colleagues were careful to avoid discussing their conspiracies in his presence. Many were involved in some racket or other, either under the aegis of a superior or on their own account and, knowing applicants who did not fancy waiting months for a certified copy of a birth certificate or a passport, first approached them, rather than an official of the department concerned, with a sum of money corresponding to the current unofficial tariff. The fraternity had their agents, and even sub-agents, who could break down the global sum into its component parts: so many hundreds for the messenger's or watchman's cut, this proportion for the first clerk, and so on; and in the end the applicant would be in for a figure several times the official cost.

Suarez's high probity was not unique in the Civil Service. There were Christians who could not reconcile this kind of dishonesty with their Bible reading; there were men and women who, intimidated by the weight of a strict upbringing, felt unable to confront a watchful conscience should they soil their hands. Some, like Suarez, never married, while others married women who earned well and put off for as long as necessary the burden of conception.

But if Suarez belonged to those who managed to maintain their standards he attributed to others the desire to behave in like manner and reacted with a child-like surprise on discovering that this was not the case. For that reason his aloofness was, in the view of certain colleagues, the eccentric form of an inveterate naïveté.

In spite of his demand for incontrovertible proof that the Right Hand Man was a murderer, Suarez could not help but look at him askance whenever their paths crossed at the ministry; and his utter conviction that a creole government was the only one he could ever contemplate could no longer be maintained in the light of the suspicions that tormented him.

Suarez, Kwaku, the Teacher, Heliga, Eunice and Bertie attended Correia's funeral, which attracted little attention outside their circle because his relations had all emigrated to the United States and Canada, following the exodus of Portuguese which began in earnest soon after independence from Britain. At the sight of the dead man being lowered into the earth Eunice nearly fainted and had to be led away by Bertie to a point where they looked on at the ceremony from a distance. And afterwards, while the friends drove away in the large car hired by Kwaku, Eunice started recounting a joke about the last funeral she attended. A Trinidadian who came to Guyana and had no idea where the Le Repentir cemetery was, got separated from the procession of cars at changing traffic lights. He asked a number of passers-by to show him the way, only to be frustrated in his search by a deaf couple, a drunk and finally a smiling old man who confused him with contradictory directions. And when at last he arrived, after a vain trip up the East Coast road, the cemetery gates were already closed. Eunice's nervousness became even more acute when her story was received with a frigid silence and a series of cut-eyes from her husband.

The friends drove to one of the many Chinese restaurants on the edge of town, where they were ushered into a dingy back room with a large open doorway leading into a concrete-covered yard. High up on one partition were a series of red-tasselled lanterns, while on the wall near which their table stood were faded pictures illustrating scenes from the Sino-Japanese war with ancient aeroplanes bombarding a port on fire.

The proprietor himself brought them the menu and, on his way out, switched on a turntable which began playing a reggae song entirely unsuited to the occasion. Suarez, who invariably performed the function of spokesman on such occasions, left the group to request that the machine be turned off. But the silence that followed, a long, lugubrious interlude, was worse than the intrusive beat of the music it replaced, and the company sat consulting their menus with strained expressions.

Nothing would have pleased the Teacher more than the opportunity to take the stage and entertain his friends from his storehouse of anecdotes, for he had never met the dead man and could only affect a sadness he did not feel. As for Eunice, now mother of a boy and two months pregnant, she was only too pleased to have a break from her domestic responsibilities and be out with her husband, as in the old days when they were courting. Motherhood had not tempered her ebullience, and she was at her wit's end to give a suitable performance of the staid housewife the men expected of her. Much as she had admired Correia, he was now dead, and the ceremony for committing him to the other world was over. It was now time for merriment and the celebration of life.

The proprietor, back to take orders from his well-dressed clients, made notes of their requests: chow mein, lau mein, sweet and sour pork, fried rice, bean sprouts and soya cakes. And even Suarez and Kwaku, genuinely grief-stricken, ordered sumptuously, as though yielding to a need to assuage an unconscious longing.

The Teacher, sensing that the atmosphere became less tense with the arrival of the victuals, began to expose his theories on the connection between food and death and declared that they ought not to feel ashamed of eating well at a time like this because it was the most natural thing in the world. The subject was not to the others' taste, however, and soon they were talking of other matters, while avoiding any mention of the deceased.

Bertie maintained that things were not as bad in the country as people claimed, a view the Teacher shared, pointing to the new industries that had sprung up on the East Bank. But Kwaku disagreed and spoke of the general deterioration in the standard of living among his clients, who dressed more shabbily than when he set up his business.

'Lots o' people does come 'bout money matters now. That does tell me more than industries on the East Bank.'

And soon they were exchanging words in a discussion as animated as any they used to have at Surinam's flat. Night had fallen, and the electric bulb that lit up the concrete yard swayed in the evening breeze, creating shifting shadows on the corrugated fence. Occasionally conversation from the front shop filled the gaps in the friends' discussion, and, distracted for a moment, they would listen, cocking their ears involuntarily. But it was their laughter that filled the shop, and their loud arguments, which made the proprietor wonder at the behaviour of a company all dressed in black.

'Alyou eat as much as you want and drink as much as you want,' urged Kwaku. 'Don' bother 'bout me. My wife say I musn' come home drunk, so I not drinking no more. "Don' drink a lot," she say. " You did lose your character one time already. Nex' time people not goin' forget." So she say. She don' like funerals, so I din' bring her. Tobesides, she din' know Correia.'

There was no reason why Kwaku should have explained his wife's absence, since everyone knew that Miss Gwendoline was blind and could not attend a funeral. But an inexplicable urge had obliged him to make the statement.

'I use to know a man who was only happy when he had all his relations round him,' he continued. 'Some people does complain 'bout their relations, but he did love them all, down to his in-laws. Me, I only love some people. Ah, these books! When you come to think of it, there's so much experience in books. An' yet, so many things they don' say! So much cut out, like the writers was frighten to talk 'bout them. Is where the old people in our books, for instance? Suarez does make me read things I din' know exist in this world. But where are the old people? . . . I know I'm a lil' drunk, but I got to confess something before I stop talking: I terrified of dying. I was shiverin' on the edge of the grave. And look who faint! Eunice! But none of you suspect how I did faint long before her, and only keep upright through will power. Youal think I talkin' nonsense. But everything I say is true. I don' lie no more, like in the old days when I was free. One more thing: You know anybody who ever satisfied? The man who did like his in-laws, I wonder if he was really satisfied? I got everything I want an' I not satisfied. What do people want, after all? I thought I was longing to be rich, so as to know where the nex' meal coming from, 'cause waking up in the mornin' and not knowing where you is is like living in Hell. But apart from the security, there's only one thing I would miss if I was poor again. Since I been rich people does listen to me when I talk. Anyway, let's drink a toast to Sidonie.'

'Who's Sidonie?' Bertie asked.

'The buck woman Correia leave behind,' Kwaku answered.

'That's enough!' Suarez snapped.

'To Sidonie!' Kwaku exlaimed.

Everyone raised a glass of beer except Suarez, whose disgust with Kwaku's monologue was manifest.

'Sidonie!' Kwaku said in a loud voice. 'Sidonie don' appreciate wealth. She don' like our town or our fine houses. She like the bush! After all she born there. Don't you like the town? Well I can't understand how people can talk 'bout freedom. If you born in the desert how can you like the forest? All this I get from books, you know. From him!'

And Kwaku pointed half accusingly to Suarez who, by now tight-lipped, was daring him to stop with his eyes.

'A compendium of fantasies,' Kwaku continued. 'So one book called itself. A compendium of fantasies. I had to look up the two words, and from what the dictionary say it could've be a description of my life.'

Kwaku took a long draught from his glass and Bertie, seizing the chance, raised his own and said, 'Let's drink to old times.'

'To old times!' they all said enthusiastically.

On the way home in the hired car Kwaku fell silent, regretting that he had made a fool of himself. Until then everything had been going well. He was especially ashamed that the monologue had been witnessed by Suarez, from whom he had learned so much. The reading sessions, when the younger man had deployed an extraordinary patience in explaining what to him was obvious, came back to him. Had not the very books of which he complained raised him in his own estimation? If he had been certain of anything it was that he had once and for all put his inability to control himself behind him. But with his friend's burial and the thought of Sidonie and her baby in the dark house the old feeling had surprised him again, like an unwanted companion who refused to go away.

One by one the friends were dropped off home until Kwaku was the only passenger left in the hired car and, for the first time since Miss Gwendoline came to join him in town, he felt alone.

Chapter XXXII

A burly man of about thirty was waiting for Kwaku. But no sooner had he been shown into the consulting-room than the door opened, and the Right Hand Man came in after them.

'Don't be alarmed,' the Minister said. 'This is an employee at the ministry. My bodyguard.'

'I din' expect you. . . . You come 'bout the flat?' Kwaku asked, his anger giving way to unease about the burly man's presence.

'No,' the Right Hand Man said.

'I'm sorry,' Kwaku went on. 'I can't have more than one person in here. Which one is the patient?'

'This isn't a professional call,' the Minister said. 'In any case he can wait outside.'

Immediately the ministry employee left the two men alone.

'May I sit down?' the Right Hand Man asked.

'Of course.'

Kwaku's heart was thumping, for he knew full well the purpose of the Minister's visit and, although he had anticipated the call and rehearsed a hundred times how he would face his former employer, he was thrown into a confusion made worse by the bodyguard's presence on the other side of the door.

'Well, Mr Cholmondeley, are you surprised by my visit? Of course you are not. A poet like you must have seen it coming weeks ago.'

'Why should I expect you to come an' see me?' Kwaku asked, feigning surprise.

'Aren't poets visionaries? . . . I saw you at the funeral yesterday. Oh yes, I was there. I take an interest in my employees, even after they leave my employ.'

The Right Hand Man got up and drew the window-blind.

'You never can be sure,' he said, returning to his seat.

'What can I do for you then?' Kwaku asked.

'Nothing. . . . I came to say, "Nothing".'

'So why you come?'

'To say, "Nothing". I don't want the extra rent I should have charged for the long occupation of my expensive flat. I don't want you to thank me for giving you a start in Georgetown, when you would have died like a dog in the street. I want . . . nothing.'

'But you must've come for a reason.'

'You're rich, but you're not bright. I want nothing. I want you to do nothing. That's all. I was very fond of Correia and I'm very fond of you. . . . Death is so mysterious. You see a person walking round one day and the next you're throwing earth on him and relegating him to a corner of your memory with beautiful words: "Man born of woman hath a short while to live", something like that. But how noble! I don't know what you thought when I used to give you my "In Memoriam" poems to publish. Maybe you had no idea how much they meant to me. I used to say to myself, "If you can't become a great poet you must have power." Poetry or power. Yes, people have no idea how things are connected.'

In his agitation the Right Hand Man kept emphasizing his words with jerky movements of his head and arms.

'I'm too stupid to understand why you come to see me, Minister,' Kwaku said. 'I'm a peaceful man who only want to feed his wife and family and not get mixed up in anything that don' concern me.'

'That's what I came to hear, Mr Cholmondeley. Did I say you were a fool? You're no fool. . . . But there's something else. A woman. A buck woman. I hear Correia's buck lady's got a child. You know them?'

'Me? I don' know no buck woman.'

The Right Hand Man's expression changed to one of anger.

'I thought we were being straight with one another, Mr Cholmondeley. You used to visit Correia and his little family. Don't bother how I know. I know everything.'

Kwaku stood his ground. He had conceived a plan to meet any threat with a threat of his own.

'You got to take my word for it,' Kwaku insisted. 'I don' know any buck woman.'

'Do me a favour and see if you have any patients waiting.'

'No,' Kwaku said. 'There's a bell and I hear when they arrive. In any case, nowadays I don' start before ten o'clock.'

The Right Hand Man consulted his watch.

'I want to find this buck lady to help her,' he said. 'And you will find her for me.'

'You know, Minister, your mother. . . .'

'Don't you mention my mother!' shouted the Minister at the top of his voice, in an outburst that recalled a similar incident years ago.

The burly man, attracted by the noise, opened the door, but at a gesture from the Minister closed it once more.

'Whatever you do,' the Minister continued quietly, 'you don't ever speak to me of Miss Rose. A louse like you . . . well, you know what I mean. To come back to the subject. You will bring her to my office tomorrow, this buck woman. . . .'

'I repeat what I tell you some time ago,' Kwaku interrupted. 'You touch me an' you're finished. . . . What you waiting for? I invite you to touch me. You can always kill me like you kill Correia, an' God know who else.'

Kwaku went to the window, opened it and shouted, 'Murder! Murder!' only to be seized from behind and knocked to the floor. He heard the window being closed but remained staring at the floorboards, ready, almost willing, to be brutalized. He saw the feet approaching, the enclosed feet that announced authority with their very posture and impeccably polished leather. To look upwards would be to acknowledge the terror behind his courage, and so he held his gaze on the strangely shaped appendages; and for the first time in his life he found himself examining closely a pair. of shod feet and brown socks that performed no other function than a concession to taste. Beyond the feet he saw the door, and only then realized that it must have opened when he shouted 'Murder'. Then it closed slowly and with a gentle click, as though the bodyguard had come upon an intimate scene and decided to retire.

'Get up!' came the Right Hand Man's order.

'I staying right here! Is my house.'

He only saw the right foot in its backward flight, then felt the pain in his side, just above the hip.

'Tell me where the buck woman lives!'

But before Kwaku could react there was a knock on the door.

'Mr Cholmondeley! I been waiting long!'

Kwaku jumped up and rushed to the door.

'Come in, mistress!' he blurted out, even before he managed to open the door and face the impatient client. 'The man just going.'

And the Minister took himself off without a word, raging at the intrusion.

The Minister had decided to make the visit, not least because he knew that with so much to lose Kwaku would be unlikely to spread rumours about him. Nevertheless, he had a great deal to lose and could not leave matters as they were for, with the elections in the offing, the ruling party could not take the risk of backing a candidate tainted by rumour. Although the money and land he had acquired during the tenure of office guaranteed his future and a modest standard of living, the thought of giving up the power he wielded as a government minister and the privileges attached to the post was unendurable. The armed guard at the entrance to his home, the chauffeur-driven car, the trips abroad in a first class berth, the obsequiousness of underlings, all went to create an aura of superiority which could not fail to distort anyone's vision. But if, before his elevation to the post, he believed he was immune to such influences, he saw himself yielding to them with little attempt at resistance soon after his appointment as Minister of Hope.

His worst fears centred on the aboriginal wife of Correia. Had he known that, like Kwaku, she only wanted to be left in peace and lived in terror of Correia's enemies, he would have done nothing, just as he intended to do in Kwaku's case. But, unable to lay the nagging anxiety about the mysterious woman, he thought it best to approach Kwaku, only to discover that in doing so he had opened yet another can of worms. Correia, Kwaku, the aboriginal Indian woman . . . who else might be standing behind them in a line of indeterminate length? That night, when the noise of a body falling into the Conservancy roused the birds from their roost, was it not a symbol of something with much wider implications?

He had stood in the presence of this underling, completely at a loss. From the start of their acquaintanceship in Georgetown there was something strange about him, something shadowy. He resembled in no way the successful healer of his childhood whom he directed to the rich East Indian's house in Canje and who came round to his mother's hovel afterwards. Then Kwaku had struck him as a man of the world, who condescended to visit them and who resembled, in his self-assured deportment, his own absent father. If, years later, he accepted his mother's assurance that it was indeed Kwaku the healer who applied to him for help, he could not do otherwise, in spite of the metamorphosis in his appearance and the palpable decline in his fortunes. The past counted for nothing. Beside his desk had stood a man in an advanced stage of deprivation, whose poverty provoked not only his sympathy, but also a deep-seated need to exploit him. However rich Kwaku became, he could see in him no more than an uneducated petitioner who, having taken advantage of his generosity, had proceeded to blackmail him into living in his property at little cost. The unspoken blackmail, the unerring choice of the right formula for success could only be evidence of unsavoury, obeah connections. Had he thought of the matter deeply beforehand he would have left Kwaku in peace. Now, however, his defiance made him see his position in a different light. But what could he do?

Kwaku rushed round to Sidonie's house after dark and made her collect her personal belongings. Then, after scrutinizing the yard and street in the immediate vicinity, he moved her and the child to a guesthouse with a view to sending them back to Lethem by plane the following Tuesday.

'The child sick?' Kwaku asked when, having installed them in the spacious guest-house room, he was about to go.

'No, he jus' sleepy.'

A flood of tenderness for Sidonie and her child overcame Kwaku, who wondered at the unwritten rule that obliged him to keep his generosity a secret from Miss Gwendoline. He would have liked to take them home with him, feed them and put them to bed as a tribute to his dead friend, whose ghost must surely be grieving for his manner of departing this life — furtively, Sidonie might think. He recalled the night in Lethem when on an impulse he opened the door and stepped out into the darkness under the cashew trees, terrified in his display of courage. It was the very first time that he had displayed a degree of bravery that attracted the admiration and respect of acquaintances; yet he had no idea what had caused him to act as he did. Perhaps his affection for Correia and his polygamous wife grew out of that one impulsive act.

Kwaku's respect for Miss Rose was tainted by suspicions he harboured regarding her son, especially as he was certain she would never believe any ill report about him, however well-founded it appeared. He was a good son and had stuck by her. Widely admired by powerful colleagues, his ministry was famous for its efficiency. But above all she *knew* him! He was incapable of evil. Kwaku's imagination presented her vividly before him and he could almost hear her protesting the Minister's innocence.

Miss Rose, like him, had known the poverty of the gutter; like him she became familiar with the interior of notorious New Amsterdam rum shops and knocked about from pillar to post until she came to rest in a place the Right Hand Man had bought for her. She had brought him into the world and boasted of his prowess while he was still a child; and it was he who had led Kwaku to her all those years ago, clutching a fistful of notes. How then could he dissociate the one from the other? The mother was identified with the son and in branding him a murderer she, too, fell in his esteem.

Kwaku had no doubt that, once he had contrived to get Sidonie and her infant back to Lethem, he would wash his hands of all concerns that did not directly affect his family. His work had proved so absorbing that he discovered in it his true vocation and, with Suarez's help, was preparing a casebook to serve as a guide in future consultations.

Ambling along the thoroughfares, he would recall how once the open spaces, the balustraded entrances to avenue walks and the grand houses of Main Street had intimidated him. Now they held no terrors for him whatsoever. And this flux was so extraordinary he found it difficult to call to mind its principal events: his betrothal and marriage, his apprenticeship, the vengeance he practised on his master, his wanderings and sojourn in Winkel, his rise and fall as a healer and his descent into the urban gutter accompanied by Miss Gwendoline. Everything about the past seemed shrouded in shadows, as though recollection was a cross he had grown too old to bear. Now, at least, he stood at the helm of events, armed with resources he never dreamt would one day be at his disposal.

Back home Kwaku told his wife of the Minister's visit and, for the first time, of Sidonie's existence. She in turn reminded him of his long association with Blossom, his old school friend and wondered whether he did not belong to that body of men who longed to be associated with more than one woman.

'What you got to take care of this Sidonie for? At least Blossom independent.'

'I not takin' care of her,' he lied. 'I jus' helpin' her to go back to Lethem in case Miss Rose son want to do her harm.'

'You sleep with her?' Miss Gwendoline asked.

'No! Is not like that at all. I wouldn' want to send her away if we had relations.'

Satisfied with his answer, she let him tell her what she had heard a hundred times before, namely his account of the trip to Lethem, where men rode horses bareback, and no one passed you without a greeting. He was certain that its great attraction for Correia lay in the many fires that dotted the landscape.

'Let's go out tonight,' he said, not certain whether she accepted the account of his relations with Sidonie at face value.

'Where?'

'Somewhere we can buy liquor.'

'But I don' like you driving when you drink. I don' like you driving when you sober even.'

'We goin' walk, like in the old days.'

They decided to dine out for once in an expensive restaurant, an indulgence that did not usually find favour with Miss Gwendoline, who disliked wasting their money and found, in any case, that public cooking was inferior to the mouth-watering meals she used to prepare before she went blind.

'Jus' this one time,' she said.

She put on the dress with a braided neck made by her seamstress from a pattern recommended by Philomena. And the neighbour, his wife and children all looked out of the window to watch them leave.

The moon was up and the stagnant water in the nearby trench gave back its wan reflection; and the footfalls Kwaku did not hear reverberated for Miss Gwendoline as eloquently as his words or the conversation of a welcome visitor. She liked and judged people by their voices and looked forward to taking her seat in the eating-place and building a picture of the waitress according to her speech.

In her circumscribed world she was content to harvest muted pleasures, attended by a housekeeper who also demanded less than those around her.

The couple went by the guest-house where Sidonie was staying, entirely by chance it seemed, so that Kwaku looked up in surprise at the brightly lit windows, each decorated with an earthenware jardiniere.

'We pass the cathedral yet?' she asked.

'Not yet,' he answered, while looking back involuntarily.

'A lot of people about tonight,' she said.

Then, realizing how sparing with words he had been since setting out, Kwaku made an effort to entertain her, describing a passer-by or a building he had never spoken about before. They walked on, she with her arm thrust under his, and he scanning the pavement for obstructions.

On the way back home she complained of having eaten too much, and, glancing at her, Kwaku realized how portly she had become on rich food and an inactivity that contrasted markedly with her younger days. But when she declared that she was happy he pressed her arm in gratitude.

On their return only the night-light in the neighbours' house was burning, while in theirs the housekeeper had turned on all the bulbs in every room out of an exaggerated fear of burglars.

'She probably been praying all the while we been out,' Kwaku said, knowing the housekeeper's propensity to sink to her knees and pray aloud as an antidote to every manner of danger.

The old woman drew the bolts and unlocked the front door even before they were halfway up the stairs; and, unable to contain her relief at seeing Miss Gwendoline again, she threw her arms round her in a lengthy, effusive welcome.

'Miss Gwen it had noises at the back an' when I go to investigate it start creaking at the front. I nearly jump out of m' skin!'

'Why you didn' start praying?' Kwaku suggested mischievously.

'Don' bother with him,' Miss Gwendoline consoled her, 'you safe now. Go to bed.'

She retired, cooing with delight.

'She right you know,' Kwaku said. 'They say things getting worse now the elections coming up.'

When Miss Gwendoline complained that her digestion would keep her up till the early hours of the morning Kwaku suggested that they should go out on the porch and talk.

'You 'member Winkel?' she asked.

And they recalled incidents from long ago: the boy with the falsetto voice who sang in places of ill repute; her first visit to his uncle's house before they married; the infestation of coconut trees that ruined whole plantations; and her first labour pains, when village women filled the house and banished all the men except Kwaku, who took refuge on the back stairs, wondering whether she was about to die.

They reminisced like two people who had not seen each other for years and took refuge from their loss of contact in a delusive evocation of the past.

In the end only the occasional vehicle went by, breaking into the deathly quiet of the night. It was the middle of the dry season and constellations that glimmered against an ashen sky stretched like portions of a fisherman's net to the long horizons beyond the trees.

Kwaku spoke of things he and Suarez read, matters beyond his comprehension, but which sank deep and remained to trouble him, like a Hindu web of illusions through which everyone glimpsed the surrounding world.

'What you mean?' Miss Gwendoline asked.

'I don' know 'cause I don' understand. But I feel it's right.'

'You should never read what you don' understand,' she chided him. 'It can only lead to bad things.'

She no longer spoke disparagingly of Heliga and Philomena, which Kwaku attributed to the greater security she enjoyed. She, however, was certain that the housekeeper had made all the difference.

'I did need companionship. Is not the money. I keep tellin' you, is not the money.'

'But is the money that buy companionship,' Kwaku insisted, to which Miss Gwendoline could find no answer.

Kwaku fell asleep and, as always when he slept in company, he wore a smile, no doubt to parry accusations that he had not been listening.

'Kwaku, wake up!'

'I tell you not to come late!' he exclaimed.

'You talkin' nonsense. You dreaming!'

'Me? I been listening to you all the time.'

He retired, leaving Miss Gwendoline at her post above the street, and her short wave transistor with its miraculous ability to wander around the universe.

Chapter XXXIII

The Minister's car was waiting in the drive. The chauffeur, on hearing the front door close, started up the engine, got out and held the door open for him.

'Where's the guard?' he asked.

'I don't know, sir.'

'Didn't you see him when you came?'

'No sir.'

The Minister hesitated, reflected for a moment, then took his seat.

On approaching the Ministry of Hope building he was seized by a vague feeling of unease, and as the car came to a halt a clammy hand seemed to seize the back of his neck.

'Morning, comrade,' came the greeting from all sides as he walked through the office. Nothing had changed. The sweat coursing down his face got into his eyes and he was obliged to use the handkerchief which peeped out of his shirt-jac pocket for show.

'Tell Mrs Correia to come and see me,' he said to a young woman whose desk was near his secretary's.

'She hasn't arrived yet, comrade.'

'What? That's not possible.'

She had said goodbye to him before she left and kissed him with unnecessary fervour, as he recalled.

'Very well. As soon as she comes I want to see her in any case. It's urgent.'

But no sooner had he settled at his desk than an acquaintance from the Ministry of Foreign Affairs appeared in the doorway.

'Can I come in?'

'Come on in! What's wrong with you, standing on ceremony like a stranger?'

Once more the unnerving chill on his neck; and the smiling face of his visitor was incongruous, grotesque, even though he knew him as an uncommonly pleasant man.

'Want something to drink?'

The visitor only raised his hand as a sign that he wanted nothing.

'You know why I've come,' he said.

The Right Hand Man, the image of self-possession, could only wipe his face once more. And curiously, the more he perspired the less efficiently he salivated.

'You know?' the visitor asked.

'A minute, please.'

The Minister went to the door and asked the young woman typing at the table next to Mrs Correia's to fetch him a glass of water.

'What's wrong?' the Minister asked, now standing ceremoniously by his chair.

'This is very unpleasant for me. You must understand I was sent. . . . A warrant for your arrest has been issued.'

'On what charge?'

The visitor bowed his head, apparently ashamed to answer.

'Murder. I thought you knew Mrs Correia made certain allegations. . . . I don't believe that a warrant has actually been issued yet, but that's what I was told. They're giving you forty-eight hours to leave the country. After that you'll be taken in for questioning if you haven't left. It's the elections. The party can't afford a scandal.'

'Do you know whom I'm supposed to have killed?'

'Correia and an aboriginal Indian lady he was living with.'

'Good God! I. . . .'

He held back in time, and the two men sat staring at each other.

'But I thought. . . .' the visitor said. And the Minister understood very well the meaning of the hiatus.

'She's not at work,' the Minister said. 'She said goodbye this morning. . . . When did she make the allegations?'

'I've told you too much,' the visitor declared with great dignity, thinking that the moment for firmness had come.

His bearing, the tone of his voice, almost hallucinatory in its effect, had marked him out as a diplomat with a promising future, and he was entrusted with the mission of persuading a man many feared. In spite of his conciliatory manner, however, he actually relished the task, seeing it as another test along the road to rapid promotion. Fully aware of his effect on people, he deliberately cultivated the qualities which produced that effect, and he watched the Right Hand Man succumb, apparently with no resentment toward him.

'Can you tell me. . . ?' the Right Hand Man began.

'If you ask me any compromising question now,' he said, 'it would be an invitation to prevarication.'

'Yes, of course. . . . What about my work here?'

'That'll be taken care of. Arrangements have been made for the bank to close your account today. And as for the loan you took out with them, well, you can pay it off from abroad.'

'What about transport . . . abroad?'

'You'll receive a plane ticket within the next few hours for Barbados.'

'Barbados?'

Typists, clerks, computer operators and other workers saw their minister leave in the company of the personable young man, who smiled as he engaged him in an apparently agreeable exchange. Downstairs, where the palms rose over white-painted fences, two chauffeurs were in conversation, and the guard presiding over his bayonetted rifle like a redundant butcher looked neither right nor left at the actors in the scene.

The dry season was coming to an end, and the clouds, almost immobile, gathered to form a thick, oppressive lid above the earth.

'Couldn't it be changed to Trinidad?'

'I'm afraid not. They've settled on Barbados.'

'What do you think my chances are if I stayed?'

'That's a question I can't answer,' the young man said. 'In any case I've said too much.'

They parted, the visitor in his car and the Minister on foot.

Amy Correia had sought an audience with the Attorney-General a week before. She had sat on a bench in the Promenade Gardens for hours before taking the decisive step. At lunch-time she watched the employees of the office leave and, an hour later, return on foot or on their cycles, thinking that they dressed more neatly than their opposite numbers at the Ministry of Hope.

At precisely half past two she crossed the road and went up the stairs of the elegant building — once a private house like so many ministries — clutching the note she hoped the Attorney-General would consider reason enough to see her. But in the event she was shown into the office of a man she recognized as a legal draughtsman from Sri Lanka, who had come to the country a few years back to fill a vacant post.

'What does this mean?' he asked her. 'The Attorney-General will be very disturbed at a serious allegation like this against a minister.'

He placed an exaggerated accent on the word 'minister', accompanying it with a frown of disapproval.

'Would you rather I said nothing? Suppose someone else knows.'

'If you tell me exactly what you know . . . I can't have a shorthand writer take down these allegations. . . .'

'*This* allegation!'

'Are you a barrister?'

'No,' Amy answered.

'Can you write an account of what you know and bring it to me? Then we'll make our investigations. Meanwhile please say nothing about what you know, nor about this visit.'

The following day she handed him her account of the incident that led up to the Minister's night journey in Correia's company, their conversation when he came back, and her visit to the dark empty house where Correia used to live. And the day after that he asked her to come and see him at his house in the evening, lest her visits to the office aroused suspicions. Then he questioned her thoroughly, so as to tempt her into making remarks inconsistent with her deposition — a long, carefully worded document flawlessly typed on Ministry of Hope paper. He pointed out how unusual it was for someone in her position — as the Minister's mistress and secretary — to make an accusation like that. A defence barrister would destroy her in the witness-box.

'Are you prepared to face that kind of hostile examination? And he can pay for the best.'

'I've already done what I had to do,' she said calmly. 'It's for you to decide now.'

'So you don't mind if we let the matter drop,' he remarked.

'I don't mind. I've done my duty.'

'Very well. We'll get in touch with you, Miss Correia.'

'Mrs.'

'Mrs?'

'Yes.'

He looked at her as if her status name had thrown an entirely different light on the matter.

'I see.'

'Does it make a difference?' she asked.

'No, of course not.'

When she left the legal draughtsman lost no time in making a photostat copy of her statement and arranging a conference with the Minister of Home Affairs. The wheels were set in motion and, within seven days, the decision to issue the Right Hand Man with an ultimatum had been made after consultations with the highest authorities, who were unanimous in their view that the affair, if made public, was capable of tilting the elections in favour of the East Indian opposition party.

Amy Correia was informed by messenger that it would be unwise to go to work on the day of the ultimatum, and when she got up that morning, awakened by the muezzin's voice in the mosque next door, she went and stood on the verandah at the back of the house.

Numb, confused and frightened, as in a dream when she woke up to find herself in the company of venomous snakes, she thought how purposeful her life had been at the time of striving, when she made those cramped journeys by plane. Yet, looking back, was she not like an insect flying towards a distant light? Her first act of adultery was in this house with its countless rooms, a tentative act of independence fraught with guilt. Even now, in denouncing a murderer, she wanted to beg him for forgiveness, unable to escape from the debt of an unendurable dependence. 'Thou shalt not kill!' Yet I am ashamed for pointing a finger at him. Ah yes! I had my husband killed and I'm sending my lover to his death.

' "Women long for peace," they say. But no man's had such murderous thoughts like mine.'

She called to mind her childhood, untroubled by the painful experiences that were Correia's as a boy which, she had always assumed, provided the explanation for his pyromania. She believed now that deeper motives impelled them to act as they did, connected with their impotence as individuals. How else could one explain the absence of guilt in those who achieve power, than by their *capacity* to exercise power? She remembered the Right Hand Man when, as a powerless assistant, he could not influence events; and she, like all his underlings, wondered at his expressions of concern for all who depended on him. But the night when he returned from his trip along the coast with Correia she detected no sign of remorse, only an arrogant indifference to her anxiety.

Her reflections led her into by-ways in which she became lost, unable to separate myth from truth, and even now indulging in an exaggerated admiration of the man she had trapped into taking her husband's life.

The full awareness of the change in her situation only came on receiving instructions not to go to the ministry that morning. Until then she had not worked out the consequences that would follow the Minister's arrest, a curious lapse in her powers of organization. What would she tell her parents and relations, with whom she was already in disgrace since she began living with a man who was not her husband? And her work? It might not be desirable or even practical to continue working in the Civil Service, knowing from experience the fate of those responsible for bringing powerful men into disrepute. She weighed up the possibility of taking up the teaching profession once more, but rejected the idea, not because of the wretched pay, but because disciplinary problems had compromised her dignity to the point where she used to look forward to the holidays with an expectation bordering on indecency.

She prepared for work as usual, made certain that the Minister's breakfast was made and kept warm and went into his bedroom to bid him goodbye. And although she planned to behave as if everything was normal, she involuntarily avoided his gaze.

'You look stylish this morning,' he remarked, sitting up on one elbow to examine her from head to foot.

'I just felt like dressing up. There's no special occasion. Your breakfast's ready.'

She bent down and kissed him, first on his forehead, then full on the lips in a manner that took him by surprise.

On passing his wardrobe it occurred to her that she had not discovered his characteristic scent, unlike Correia, with whom she had become so familiar that, in anticipation of intimacy, her nostrils were filled with the musty odour of his body.

Amy Correia, on leaving the Minister's residence, walked a short distance to the main road, where she boarded a taxi-van to her parents' home, a Costello House on Vlissingen Road.

Chapter XXXIV

Kwaku saw his protégée and her son off at Timehri airport and even stayed to watch the box-like plane taxiing on the runway. He had brought them to the airport himself, unwilling to make the journey in the company of his chauffeur, whose inquisitiveness, fuelled by hours of enforced idleness, had assumed the character of a compulsive itch.

Sidonie, without uttering a word, held onto his arm when they were about to separate at the barrier, and he was moved to wonder whether anyone had ever seen an aboriginal Indian shed tears. People said their children did not cry, that their women gave birth while displaying the same monumental indifference to pain as the spirits and heroes of their lore. Time and again he had attempted to characterize the relationship between himself and Miss Gwendoline, or even himself and Blossom, but it was no more comprehensible than those excrescences that oozed out of certain trees. His relationship to Sidonie left him in no doubt as to its character, however. He was her patron, and his reward was a gratitude that swelled his heart. Philomena, the only one of his children he loved unreservedly, could never conceal a certain contempt for him which, like scum, surfaced to offend him with its murky character. Sidonie reminded him of the daughter he fondly imagined Philomena would turn out to be.

On the way back he wondered if time would ever erase her from his memory, as it had after his first visit to Lethem. Time, the true culprit behind the woes of his patients, whom he often sent away with no more than the hope that it would heal as mysteriously as it had ravaged them.

And indeed, the fascination Sidonie had unwittingly spun round him, provoked in the beginning by envy and fed subsequently by his own vanity, waned with the passing months; and although he continued to send her money in lined envelopes, he did so as an obligation, in testimony to his old friendship with the drowned man.

On the Attorney-General's advice it was decided to charge the Right Hand Man rather than run the risk of his deed being made public by Amy Correia or some other person privy to it, a decision vehemently opposed by certain highly-placed members of the party executive. On learning of the Minister's arraignment for the murder of both Correia and an unidentified aboriginal woman, Kwaku went and informed the police that the lady he believed to be the subject of the indictment was alive and resident in Lethem with her son by Correia. And the Attorney-General, relieved at the news, arranged for the prosecution service for the indictment to confine itself to Correia's murder.

Kwaku attended the brief proceedings before the magistrate, who decided that there was a case to answer and at the same time took the unusual step of freeing the defendant on bail. Kwaku hoped that Miss Rose's son would look his way, but he kept his gaze fixed on the magistrate, no doubt out of embarrassment that he was exposed to the public gaze.

The same night Suarez, during one of his regular visits to Kwaku's flat, expressed the opinion that the authorities hoped that the Minister would attempt to escape. And the accuracy of this speculative statement, made without a shred of evidence, was to be borne out in the rumour that a man who had been given special permission to visit him in his cell offered to help him flee, claiming that he had the means and the permission to guarantee the plan's success.

It was believed that the Right Hand Man's refusal of the first suggestion to flee was due to his ignorance of the mass of evidence against him. But when he rejected the second offer — his visitor having explained in detail about the tyre marks and Amy's willingness to tell the Court of the conversations that led up to his trip on the fateful night — his highly-placed colleagues panicked, fearing not only for the effect the case would have on the planned elections, but also the dirt the Minister of Hope could stir up out of vengeance that his fancied inviolability had not been respected.

Various individuals and delegations to the Church Street mansion followed one another, offering unheard-of wealth to the Minister of Hope if only he would show Guyana a clean pair of heels. Did he want to be a martyr like Walter Rodney? What *did* he want, dammit? Had he forgotten that hanging had not been abolished as a punishment for murder? Did he relish the feel of a cord round his neck and the slow death afterwards? Had he not seen pictures of hanged men with their tongues hanging out? He was not even fighting for a cause! Jesus! Did he wish the East Indians to win the elections and force them all to become good Hindus and worship a multiplicity of Gods? Be reasonable! If he was not interested in his own skin what about his *mattee* creoles? Did he want the Indians to do to us what we have been doing to them for the last twenty-eight years? Where was his civic sense? The last delegation raised the stakes, promising that if the Indians lost the elections he would be allowed back into the country immediately afterwards *and* given an honour into the bargain. The Golden Arrow award? He only had to name the honour he desired, and it would be his! What was he? Some kind of pervert? Or was he impotent and did he care little for this life? Take care! We know all about your illegal currency dealings. And wasn't his adultery common knowledge? Which jury would not believe that he wanted his lover's husband out of the way to have her all to himself? They would pack the jury with Christian feminists who cannot abide adulterous men. Had he ever had dealings with the products of Methodist austerity, who went one better than the Catholics and abolished purgatory? His naïveté in this day and age was extraordinary! If only he would say what he wanted, a way could be found to accommodate him! Everything was possible with the resources of the state at their disposal.

The same young man who first urged the Minister to flee suggested that since neither incentives nor threats were working another approach to the problem was needed. Why doesn't someone pay a visit to his mother? People said he worshipped the ground she walked on and kept her in style in a New Amsterdam cottage. He himself was given the task of looking up Miss Rose and deploying his charm and tact in the interests of a matter that had got dangerously out of hand.

The same young man knocked on Miss Rose's door and waited. The woman who opened up was well-dressed but wore the jaded expression of the chronic insomniac. Her uncompromising frown took him aback, but he smiled warmly and explained that he had come on official business.

Seated opposite his unsmiling hostess the suave young man found it difficult to begin. Usually his good looks and sociability inspired confidence and made it easy for him to seduce women into a co-operative frame of mind. But Miss Rose, tight-lipped and apparently hostile, sized him up as she would have done when faced with any intrusive salesman.

'The drive from Georgetown took less time than I imagined,' he began, 'but I had to wait two hours on the Berbice ferry stelling. Two hours!'

He received no encouragement from her and so, his first tactic having failed, he decided to change his approach.

'This is more difficult than I imagined,' he said.

'I know why you come, so stop beating 'bout the bush.'

'You know. . . ?'

'Why else you would come all the way to New Amsterdam?'

'It's about your son, the Minister.'

'I say come to the point! What you want?'

Confronted by someone who would not observe the niceties of polite conversation, the suave young man could only flounder.

'As you know he's been charged with a serious crime. . . .'

'How old you are?' Miss Rose asked.

'I'm twenty-seven.'

'I'm forty-five. I been down here eighteen years longer than you an' I know more than you. But I don' know more than my son. When you talk 'bout him you mus' talk respectful.'

'But I am respectful,' said the young man. 'I was asked to come because I admire your son.'

The profession of admiration and the sincere tone of voice had the desired effect, and Miss Rose, as tight-lipped as ever, offered to make her guest a drink.

She brought back a tray with iced lemonade in a jug and two glasses.

'I prefer cups, but you people like glass.'

Soon they were chatting about the cemetery whose white grave-stones could be seen from her back stairs. She said that no one stole from graves in the country, like the *barbarians* did in Georgetown, apparently with little concern that her visitor might be offended.

'Can you help us?' he asked, certain that the time was opportune.

'Who is "us"?' Miss Rose demanded.

'The administration. They've made an offer to your son to leave the country and come back immediately after the elections.'

'He tell me. But if he run away people would say he guilty. And if there's one thing 'bout my son I'm sure of, is that he can't stand violence. He's like his father. He was respected in the islands as one of the best pan-boilers. Six foot tall an' wouldn' raise his hand to my son or me. You ever notice how big men does keep calm? My son is even more tall than his father. What he goin' go round drowning people for? Anybody only got to take one look at him an' *know* he's innocent. An' you want me to get him to leave the country?'

'Suppose he's convicted?' the young man asked.

'While there's a God up there he won't get put down, you take it from me. How old you say you is?'

'Twenty-seven.'

'You can't be wise at twenty-seven. . . . Nobody did stand by him when he was arrested. I always use to tell him, "What you want to fly high for? The higher you fly the less friends you got. They does drop off at different heights." But alyou don' listen to your mothers. Look how men make this country go to the dogs, eh? Is not the mothers drag the country down. . . . Is when the trial for?'

The young man did not know.

'I believe he's not guilty as well,' he declared.

'I tell you!' she exclaimed. 'One look at him an' you know he couldn' kill nobody. You ever hear of a man who love books resorting to violence? You would think that people at the top would see all this . . . . I believe is that woman he been living with. You see, men don' understand certain things. I meet her a couple of times at the house an' right away I say, "I don' trust that woman. She too efficient, jus' like a machine." And her hands! You ever look good at her hands?'

'What's wrong with her hands?' the suave young man asked, unable to get the better of Miss Rose. If her naïveté should make her fair game this was not borne out by her behaviour. Besides, she was so convinced of her son's invulnerability she was unlikely to see things as they were.

'What's wrong with her hands?' Miss Rose asked, echoing the young man's question. 'They're bony!'

'Miss Rose, I'm all at sea,' the suave young man declared, a touch of exasperation in his voice. This, the most difficult diplomatic mission of his career, had gone badly wrong. 'I'm at sea Miss Rose, because I can't make you see the danger your son's running. . . .'

'Drink up your lemonade, the ice melting.'

He drank up to please her.

'God may be too busy to help the Minister,' he said when he finished. 'I mean it. There *have* been miscarriages of justice, against men as good as your son.'

This statement was greeted with a long, eloquent suck-teeth that conveyed unmistakably her contempt for the suave young man's flawed view of God's omnipotence.

He, in turn, despaired of penetrating Miss Rose's defences against persuasion and resolved to listen rather than try to bring her round to his way of thinking.

She excused herself, disappeared for a minute and came back with a Bible held high above her head.

'God never busy!' she declared. 'You open the good book at any page. Go on! Yes, anywhere!'

Thinking it best to humour her he opened the Bible, then looked up at her.

'Close your eyes an' put your finger down 'pon the page.'

He complied, then waited for further instructions.

'Open your eyes.'

He did so.

'Now read where your finger pointing to.'

'The upright man is laughed to scorn. . . ,' the suave young man began, but she interrupted him, continuing where he left off.

'. . . He that is ready to slip with his feet. . . .'

And after quoting several verses she said:

'Job, chapter twelve. The good book is God's word, an' the word don' got time or place. It does never sleep. Alyou persecuting my son 'cause he's a upright man. Job was persecuted by God 'cause he was upright too, but in a good cause. Why alyou persecuting my son? Is it because the malefactor not comfortable in the company of decent people? My son don' got no money stack away in a Swiss bank account. He don' got more than one car. He don' seize public property an' give it to his lady friend. Alyou t'ief so much. . . .'

'You'd better be careful with your words, lady,' said the suave young man, his affable mask slipping to disclose for a brief moment the suggestion of a sinister bent.

'Ah,' said Miss Rose, 'but now you understand. If you convict him you goin' have to silence me, 'cause I goin' go to that newspaper alyou try to suppress an' tell them all I know. And when I start talking I goin' quote chapter and verse. . . . Now you want some more ice? . . . I'm a proper virago! Not one o' your well-bred convent-educated city women who does sit still while they husbands drink rum an' argue with their friends.'

'I think you've made your position clear,' said the young man.
'May I remind you of what I said at the beginning. I told you I admired
your son. What's more he's widely admired in official circles for the
efficiency of his department.'

'Truly?'

'Yes. . . .'

And he went on to give examples of the work done by the Right
Hand Man and his staff.

'Now I can see who he inherited his talents from,' he concluded.

'No, it's from his father,' she corrected him. 'He was the sort of
man who couldn' stand the second rate. You know when he was home
he use to sweep the yard hisself. Alyou men would drop dead before
you pick up a broom. But the thing is, he use to boast that no one in the
country could sweep a yard like him. Truly! And he was a respected
pan-boiler. Some of his pan-boiler friends was so great they wouldn'
look left or right when they walk on the road. But he, he was too proud
to look down on anybody. An' my son take after him, not me. I mean,
I would quarrel all day, then wake up in the mornin' an' start over
again. Not my husband or my son. How can a man like that take
somebody life?'

The suave young man, aware that he was trying to breach an
impenetrable wall, acknowledged to himself that he had been given
a lesson in advocacy. Miss Rose, surrounded by her bric-à-brac, the
mother of a once highly-regarded minister, would almost certainly
carry out her threat to damage an increasingly nervous administration, whose representatives no longer believed that their future was
assured. A recent unofficial census, using a new technique perfected
in the United States, put the East Indian population as high as fifty-
seven per cent. And though experts in demography claimed that
only a census carried out on traditional lines could lay claim to
accuracy, publication of the result was considered a significant
success in the psychological warfare being waged between East
Indians and creoles.

'Miss Rose, I have to go now.'

'Why?' she asked. 'Stay, man. Not 'cause we don' see eye to eye
you have to go. Let me get you another drink.'

She filled up his glass and put a lump of ice in it.

'When I was a girl my aunt did keep a cake shop in Canje. An' I use
to help her on a Saturday afternoon. The first thing she teach me is

how to put a big lump of ice in the glass so that you only did need a little bit of drink to fill it. The poor customers didn' even notice what was happening in front of they eyes.'

Miss Rose laughed, slapping her thighs and lifting her legs immodestly.

'I not frightened for my son,' she said. 'When they acquit him he will be strong as a lion, mark my words.'

'I can't understand,' said the young man, 'how you can take his impending trial so lightly.'

'But you wrong! I not taking it lightly. The planning is over. Now the waiting begin. I tell you *my son will not be convicted*! You're one of these people who got to hear something ten times before you believe it. *I* don' have to worry. *You* do.'

Not one of the ministers, the managers or the senior civil servants in the diplomatic service had ever had the effect on him that Miss Rose, with her defective logic and defective grammar, produced in the short time they had been together.

How extraordinary that it was a woman — Mrs Correia — who had obliged the administration to prosecute the Minister! Now an apparently more dangerous opponent in the form of another woman was threatening action if the prosecution succeeded.

The suave young man got up to go.

'Come again, in better times,' she said.

And he looked hard at her to see if he could detect any resemblance with the deposed Minister of Hope.

'He probably looks like his father,' he thought.

She saw him to the gate, watched him get into his car, waved goodbye in return and reckoned that she and her son could, between them, make a better job of running the country than the young man's superiors.

He had not underestimated her. She believed implicitly that her son's rise to power had been ordained by God and that his arrest and forthcoming trial were a test on a par with Job's, whose torments she knew by heart. Imbued with an exhilaration that often accompanies the onset of some great danger, she saw the suave young man's visit as a sign of weakness on the part of her son's enemies. And while they schemed and plotted she had little fear, knowing that the Almighty was on her side. She idolized her son with the same fervour with which she once deified her husband while still a young woman. Since his death, presumed from his long absence, his misdeeds, eroded by the weathering effect of time, laid bare once more that youthful admiration. And with every promotion her son received, she endowed him with something borrowed from the memory of those early years.

She imagined his trial: the crowded courtroom, his enemies' sneers and a hostile judge presiding over the machinations of his tormentors. But just as the Lord 'blessed the latter end of Job better than the beginning' so her son would be relieved of his torment in the fullness of time.

Chapter XXXV

Kwaku's reputation was such that he was obliged to put up his fees in order to reduce the number of people seeking treatment and advice. At first, reluctant to exclude poor folk from his clientele, he met the problem by enlisting his son-in-law's assistance. But Heliga, more interested in rehabilitating himself as an acupuncturist, began running down his father-in-law's work. And even after his ingratitude reached Kwaku's ears and he was warned to confine himself to counselling and prescribing herbs, he could not resist the temptation to display his needles in their velvet-lined boxes on the table in his consulting-room. Kwaku, on learning of this from a patient who came downstairs for a second consultation, brought the arrangement to an end.

He raised his fees and inevitably his waiting-room took on the appearance of a repair for well-heeled clients from the wealthy residential districts of Greater Georgetown. Some sought solace in an arid marriage; others, unable to obtain permission to live in Canada or the United States, believed that they were the objects of persecution; yet others were treated with herbs for pains in various parts of the body, or for diabetes, cramp and a number of different afflictions. One woman living in Republic Park, who complained of swelling in her stomach, *knew* that an envious neighbour had interfered with her, and Kwaku, despite his recently acquired book-learning, agreed with this diagnosis and prescribed a protective phial of aromatic vinegar to be hung over both her front and back doors. A few months later her husband, on a surveyor's advice, raised the floor of their house and installed air-bricks in the walls as a means of ventilating the space under the boards. This done, the woman's swelling went down soon afterwards, and Kwaku, already well-known in Republic Park, acquired the status of a modern-day saint.

A psychologist, who wrote about the case in a newspaper, pointed out the benefits of superstition and ended his article with the following words: 'Your religion is my superstition. If I believe in the beneficial properties of aromatic vinegar, that belief can only be good for me. It is a mistake to exaggerate the advantages of rationalism. In our great forest between the Orinoco and Amazon rivers there are men who will abandon a planned hunt because they discover that there is a menstruating woman in the clan. The conviction that the hunt will be successful only if certain taboos are observed is of immeasurable assistance in preparing them for their enterprise.'

Kwaku, on arriving at his surgery early one morning — he had extended his hours of business, so that he now began at half past seven instead of half past eight — on arriving at seven o'clock he saw a well-dressed lady standing in the doorway.

'So early?' he asked involuntarily as the car turned into the drive.

'Is Mrs Correia,' his chauffeur said.

Kwaku hesitated before opening the door and, had he followed his instincts, would have ordered that the car be driven off.

'What could she want?' he thought, recalling the circumstances of her previous series of visits.

She was the last person he wanted to see, imagining that associating with her could be construed as taking her side in the controversy the Minister's trial was bound to provoke.

Her hair was dishevelled and her usually immaculate attire gave the impression of being unironed.

'Good morning, Mrs Correia,' he said, greeting her in the hearty manner that was now an indispensable part of his technique.

'Good morning, Mr Cholmondeley. I hope you don't mind me waiting like this.'

'No, no. You're not just a client, but a old friend. Come right in.'

As he fumbled with his bunch of keys the car drove off, and the guard dog he kept inside overnight began barking furiously.

'I see you've got a dog now,' she ventured, unable to suppress her nervousness.

'Thieves break in las' year. You know what is like.'

She leaned against the partition as the hound leapt up at Kwaku in an effusive greeting.

'He won't even notice you when I'm here,' he reassured her.

Kwaku expected Amy Correia to remark on the improvements that had cost him a small fortune: the enlarged window through which the early morning sun was streaming, the recently painted interior and the new balustraded staircase to the upper storey. But she appeared to notice nothing and followed Kwaku silently through the waiting-room and into his enlarged practitioner's chamber.

'Things change up a bit since you come here last, as you can see,' he said, fishing for a compliment.

Without any warning Amy Correia burst into tears and hid her face behind her raised hands. Long ago, the fact that he had slept with her would have been enough to make him put his arm round her in a gesture of sympathy. But now he held back, more concerned about his deportment since he had been treating women whose refinement did not permit liberties or any physical demonstration of sympathy.

'Sit down an' let it out,' he advised, genuinely touched by the contrast with the Amy Correia who once was the embodiment of Georgetown women's aloofness.

How could she bear to come and see him after having made such a fool of herself? Her kind simply did not behave like that. For the first time he noticed that she was not wearing make-up. Her unpainted nails were strewn with white spots he diagnosed as indicating a diet poor in zinc, and strands of her hair seemed broken at the ends.

Kwaku discovered, with years of practice, that his vulnerability to suffering was capable of surprising him when he professed to be inured to its manifestations. And though he had every reason to dislike his dead friend's wife, her crumpled figure, sunk in his most opulent easy chair, aroused in him a compassion he was unable to resist. She was Sidonie, his protégée, Miss Gwendoline, his blind wife, Miss Rose whom he had once abused, the village teacher with her illegitimate boy he had come to know through Blossom and all the vulnerable women to whom he had been drawn in the past, succumbing to the pull of an inward magnet he had never been inclined to define. Perhaps they were images of the mother he used to boast about as a child, but of whom he had no recollection whatsoever.

'I'm sorry,' she half whispered. 'Just give me a minute.'

Kwaku went and stood at the window, which was covered with a film of moisture that had persisted since the refurbishment.

'All these people who does come here believing I can help them,' he reflected. 'Yet I'm the same fraud I was when I use to practise in New Amsterdam an' did treat people with nothing but garlic. One thing I learn in this very room is that people don' change. If only they did know how I still long to play the fool an' how frighten I be that people goin' find me out!'

He called to mind the woman who confessed to him how she threw a party for all her old men-friends the day before she became engaged, and came to see Kwaku because she longed to confess what she had done. She dared not say it to her best friend, who would not have hesitated to judge her. Nor did she dare tell the priest, to whom she had always presented the face of a uniquely virtuous woman.

'I needed to see them all at one table,' she had told Kwaku. 'I had the urge to get them to know one another. The priest would never have understood because he's a man. And my best friend, as a woman, would have judged me more harshly than most men.'

This nagging desire to confess fascinated Kwaku all the more because it was contrary to his nature; and he, who harboured many secrets, swelled with a feeling of power at the time of each confession, like a miser who adds a wad of notes to an already impressive pile.

'Why has Mrs Correia come?' he asked himself again.

He drew his hand across the window pane, making a horizontal mark in the film of vapour. Outside, the uncut grass grew unevenly in contrast to the adjoining yard, where bora beans were cultivated on frames along shallow furrows in the black earth. Kwaku reflected on the startling contrasts between people's characters, their lives and destinies. Yet, judging from his patients' problems, everyone was alike; so much so that he was often able to advise, 'Do such and such a thing, and such and such will happen.'

'I'm wasting your time,' Amy Correia said, wresting him from his reflections.

'No, no. I was thinking. Of course I want to know what bothering you.'

'I don't know. That's it. I don't know what's bothering me. I read about the woman you cured in the papers and I thought . . . well, we've been underestimating him. . . .'

'Some people . . . but not all,' Kwaku told her.

'Well, I underestimated you,' she confessed.

'You've got a problem?'

'Yes. . . .'

'Nobody does come here to see me socially,' said Kwaku. 'Even my daughter upstairs. When she want to see me she does come to the house.'

'Oh . . . your daughter lives upstairs?'

Amy Correia was so surprised at the news, Kwaku drew the

inference that nothing much could be wrong with her. What did it matter if all his children, their wives and husbands and their children lived upstairs or underground, or floated in the air above his house?

He looked at his watch.

The hint was not lost on her.

'I'm sorry,' she said. 'I came because I'm frightened.'

'Of what?'

'I don't know. . . . A few nights ago I undressed for bed and went into the bedroom. I'm staying with my parents. I put on the light and in one corner about six, I don't know, seven, eight or more buck women were standing around, and all of them were holding a baby. And every baby had the face of a monkey. I . . . I. . . . You. . . .'

She was staring straight ahead as though unable to avert her gaze from some object on the wall.

'You din' call someone. . . ?'

'I called my father. I went and got my father, but when we opened the room they had gone. I didn't dare tell him exactly what I saw, because he would have said I was being punished for my sins. He's like that.'

'Aren't you like that too?' Kwaku asked.

'Me? I'm not like that. I'm the opposite.'

'Where you slept the next night?'

'In the room with my parents.'

'You see anything in that room?'

'No.'

'An' the next night?'

'I told them I was frightened and wanted to continue sleeping with them.'

'That's not what you come to tell me, Mrs Correia.'

'You don't believe me that it happened?' she asked.

'Yes, I believe you. . . . One lady used to see people coming to scratch her eyes out,' Kwaku said, 'but the reason why she did come to see me was to tell me *why* she had her visions. We know everything 'bout ourselves, Mrs Correia.'

'You think I'm pretending not to know.'

At no point in the conversation had she lost her composure.

'Yes. I think you pretend not to know. I not saying you lying. I say you know.'

She reflected for a moment.

'I think I'd better go.'

'Suit you'self,' Kwaku told her. 'But the visions goin' get worse. And when you start seeing them in daytime it might be too late.'

She sat down once more, and her agitation was only betrayed by the way she kept pressing her hands together.

'Those books on the shelves,' she said at length, nodding towards a line of thick tomes disposed on a shelf running the length of the partition. 'You've read all of them?'

'Read an' studied. I won't say understand. That's another story. They got a lot of nonsense in them, though. People saying the opposite an' swearing it's true. Suarez know far more 'bout them than me. He was a good friend of your husband.'

She turned to face him.

'Why did you bring up my husband's name?'

'Nothing. I think of Suarez, so I mention Correia. They were friends.'

'I didn't come here to talk about my husband, Mr Cholmondeley.'

Her defensive attitude made Kwaku think that he had opened a door into a forbidden room.

The clock above the door chimed half past seven and Kwaku excused himself, saying that he had to put out magazines for clients who might be waiting.

She heard bolts being drawn and an exchange of greetings, followed by a short conversation between Kwaku and another man, presumably a client. The sudden realization that Kwaku was there for others as well provoked a feeling of betrayal.

He came back, but instead of taking his seat remained standing.

'It's I who killed Mr Correia,' Amy said, pronouncing the words with the official voice she used for answering the telephone and intimidating the clerks and typists at the Ministry of Hope. Kwaku's heart sank. He feared becoming somehow embroiled in her troubles, and here she was confessing to a matter that could bring him directly into conflict with certain elements of the ruling party.

'I lied to the Minister of Hope about Correia threatening him and suggested he should get him out of the way.'

Kwaku waited until he was certain she had finished.

'You need a lawyer, Mrs Correia.'

'No, Mr Cholmondeley. I don't need a lawyer. I know what to do about my position. . . . I can't bed down with my parents forever, so last night I went back to sleep in my bedroom. In the day I put cloth and paper in the chinks between the window and the frame and kept the window closed. I went to bed about ten o'clock and fell asleep quickly, after I'd drunk a shot of my father's rum. About . . . I don't know . . . about two in the morning I sat up and put on the light, but nothing was wrong. I turned off the light and was about to get into bed when I felt I. . . . Anyway I went and turned on the light again and I saw. . . . It doesn't matter. All I want is sleep.'

She looked at him with such an expression of despair he was tempted to put out a hand and stroke her head.

'What you saw?' Kwaku asked her.

'The whole bed was covered with women suckling their children. The first time . . . the last time I saw them they were all staring at me. This time they behaved as if I wasn't there . . . as if I didn't exist.'

'What you do then?' asked Kwaku, who had forgotten that he wanted to get rid of her as quickly as possible.

'I didn't do anything. I couldn't move or speak. And the women kept on squeezing and adjusting their breasts. But there was an extraordinary thing: the children's heads were normal. I didn't want to run like the last time. It was as if I was interested in the feeding. What. . . ?'

Kwaku did not wish to tell her what he thought. After hearing the first dream he jumped to the conclusion that she was consumed with guilt about something in her past; and her subsequent confession of being an accessory to murder appeared to confirm the tentative diagnosis. But her interest in the feeding and the children's loss of their simian features threw a completely different light on the unfolding drama.

'Can you do anything, Mr Cholmondeley? People say. . . .'

'People say!' Kwaku burst out. 'People don' know. . . . Don' worry about what people say. Give them a rumour an' they'll do God knows what with it. They don' know what does go on in this room an' you should hear the stories they tell. The fact is I can't do anything for you.'

'But a man like you must have an opinion!' she exclaimed. 'I can't sleep in my parents' house any more.'

'You say you wasn't disturbed by the second vision,' Kwaku reminded her.

'I didn't say that. I said I was interested in the children feeding; but I was frightened.'

'If I was to tell you what I think, Mrs Correia, you'd be offended.'

'I prefer that than you being silent.'

Kwaku felt that his judgement would be clouded by his dislike of Amy Correia.

'Do you suffer from . . . about what you make the Minister do to your husband?' Kwaku asked.

'Oh yes! Terribly! I spend all my spare time praying in church, and I've burnt scores of candles for him. Yes, I suffer.'

She had spoken precipitously, with clasped hands, as though she was praying, and for the first time since she stopped crying she dropped her pretence at composure.

'I can't help thinking, Mrs Correia, that you not capable of feeling guilt.'

'What?'

'Please,' Kwaku enjoined, 'the clients outside goin' hear you if you cry out like that.'

'You think. . . . But that's what is making me sick. Guilt!'

'You see,' Kwaku said, 'you say just now you din' know what's wrong with you, but now you're sure is guilt. I think one thing bothering you. You need a man.'

Mrs Correia's contempt for Kwaku was mirrored in her face so clearly that a stranger entering the room at that moment would have come to the conclusion that she was of a hysterical temperament.

'I'm sorry, Mrs Correia. The trouble with what I do is that I make a lot of mistakes. But I *did* say was my opinion. If I ask you what in that jar you'd probably say "water". Then when I pour the contents out and you see is rum you'd be surprised, 'cause people don' put rum in a jar. Is the same thing with my work. I din' mean to offend you.'

She seemed to be crying again, but her head was turned away from him. He now felt he should have followed his first diagnosis of guilt feelings that were tormenting her. All the evidence appeared to point that way. Yet he believed that her pretence was a salient feature in her make-up and that when everything else was stripped away she would be revealed as hard and ruthless. The confession of being an accessory to murder was the only evidence he need take seriously.

On the other hand her visions contradicted flatly this view, and

Kwaku came to the conclusion that his prejudice against Amy Correia had affected his judgment.

'I goin' have to see my next patient now,' he told her.

The clock was pointing to a minute before eight, and the session would never come to an end if they carried on as they had done.

'I came to ask you if you could give me a herb, *something*. I heard you've got a herb for every complaint.'

'I can give you a herb to make you sleep through the night.'

He went upstairs and came back with a packet of dried leaves.

'No, no payment,' he told her when she opened her purse. 'Where're you going to sleep?'

'Where else? With my parents.'

Kwaku asked the next client to wait a few minutes, unable to cope with another request for help right away. The session with Amy Correia had increased his growing unease about the work he was doing, which he compared to encounters in the dark. A patient had once asked him whether he would take the risk of befriending someone whose face he could not see, to which he could give no answer. Was he not taking a similar risk with every consultation? Was not the inner person perpetually hidden? And worse still, was there not an elaborate, impenetrable curtain drawn across the face of the most innocent among those who visited him?

But gradually Kwaku's preoccupation with his last client was overcome by his fear of encroachment upon ground about which the ruling party was sensitive, and, as he invited the next client to join him, he was wondering whether Amy had not been followed by one of the army of faceless government informers.

Chapter XXXVI

The very night of her consultation Amy Correia sought out a distant cousin who lived alone and stayed with her until the morning of her visit to the police station, where she intended to make a full confession. But the vision of the aboriginal Indian women pursued her there. As she was about to get up from a kneeling position after her nightly prayers, she saw them climbing through the bedroom window one by one while balancing their children miraculously on their hips. And though she no longer experienced the paralyzing fear of the first two occasions she, none the less, saw herself at one and the same time the victim of an assassination by degrees and a bystander with no power to intervene. She closed her eyes, not daring to look at them, and lay down on the floor by the door, where she eventually fell asleep. The following afternoon she had no hesitation about going to the police and confessing her part in Correia's murder, having made up her mind to accept the cup that had been prepared for her by her own conscience or by some external force, some regulator, not apprehended because it had yet to be given a name.

After much to-ing and fro-ing and innumerable telephone calls, the sergeant asked her to make a statement, which was committed to shorthand by a surprisingly young secretary with rings on all her fingers. Then followed a long wait in a room cleared of constables who had been sitting around chatting noisily and playing cards. Regretting that she had not accepted several offers of a meal, her hunger began to gnaw at her inside like an assiduous, malevolent worm until, ashamed at her weakness, she asked a passing constable to fetch the sergeant.

'I'd like something to eat if you don't mind,' she pleaded.

'I'll send for something right away.'

She did not care what, as long as it was not fish.

'The inspector's coming down to see you within the hour,' the sergeant told her, more kindly than she thought she deserved.

She had not gone to work for several days now and imagined that the office must be in chaos without her firm guiding hand. As for the Minister's absence, the consequences of that would be disastrous. The ministry would never recover, she felt certain, for she was familiar with the critical influence a minister exercised on his or her staff, which affected everyone, including the messengers. They were known as the 'tavern boys' in one ministry, on account of the time they spent in the nearby liquor restaurant consuming local beer and gossiping about their superiors. Not at the Ministry of Hope!

Her heart was filled with sadness at these recollections and the enormity of her treachery. What had contributed to her deep satisfaction over the last few years was not her circumscribed life at the mansion in Church Street, but the indescribable warmth that overcame her on entering the ministry building where she knew the place of everything and the details of the work required by everyone.

While she was eating her meal a constable came in and immediately apologized. He had mistakenly opened the door of the room he and his colleagues usually used. Amy was touched by his courtesy, for she had imagined a brutal reception and the badgering tactics she knew of from hearsay.

Finally the inspector came, long after the promised time had passed, when the night air made her button her blouse to the top and fatigue had replaced the torpor of the first hours.

'Mrs Correia, I'm sorry it took so long, but there are developments. Now please listen to me very carefully.'

He informed her that *she* was not to be prosecuted, since a successful prosecution of the Minister depended entirely upon her own testimony. Furthermore, she was to speak to no one about the matter and was expected to accept an appointment in the North West.

'You're hardly in a position to refuse,' he added.

'I'm not refusing,' she said as in a daze. 'I . . . I want to be sent where I'll be alone.'

'That would suit everyone,' the inspector added. 'Arrangements will be made for your transport. You'll have a house at your disposal and everything. If you leave your address with the sergeant we'll get in touch with you.'

'I can go?'

'Yes. Do you want someone to drive you home?'

'No thanks.'

'It's advisable, in the dark.'

'No, I'll manage.'

Later she was to learn that the charge against the Minister was dropped, since the Administration had managed to get her out of the way.

And so Amy Correia left Georgetown to live in a remote settlement at the confluence of two rivers in the Pomeroon district, as an administrator whose duties were so vaguely defined that they left her with a great deal of time to ponder on her past and future life. Her only certain responsibility was for stores — mainly medical — to be dispensed as she saw fit to visiting Medical Officers, who held a clinic for the Warrau Indians, and a peripatetic teacher who came and went like the wind and laid claim to all her stocks of aspirin on the grounds that he doubled as teacher and sick-nurse, maintaining a tradition that began as far back as the eighteenth century when the Caribs of the region were endowed with twice-yearly gifts in recognition of their services as hunters of runaway slaves. Incapable of idleness, Amy Correia took upon herself the task of championing the Warraus' cause. Dismissed as the most degenerate Indian tribe in the country, they were held in contempt by officials responsible for their welfare and neglected so blatantly that she foresaw little difficulty in alerting Georgetown officials to their plight. But she soon learned that just as the Ministry of Hope had acquired its reputation for efficiency, there were Government departments with a notoriety for ineptitude and sloth. Indian affairs attracted — so it seemed — the least able officials, most of whom had come by a knowledge of Indians from American Western films, according to their detractors.

The year after her arrival Amy set up her own school, unique in its conception of reciprocal learning. In exchange for being taught the Indians' handicrafts she gave them lessons in reading and mathematics, and within months their cooperation led to the manufacture of casreep on a large scale and its sale to a Georgetown merchant who undertook to supply them with cork stoppers and old bottles for the black cassava sauce.

Her delusions ceased once she left the capital, and she came to understand that what had been for her visitations of terror were the currency of Indian piai-men, who readily fell into a trance in order to make long visionary journeys to treat with spirits during healing ceremonies. Here was a world far removed from coastal certainties and Christian austerity, in which a solitary flute possessed mesmeric resonances, and fires burned throughout the night.

If at first Amy Correia regarded her stay in this Pomeroon backwater as a penance, she soon came to realize that the black nights and rainy days of her new home, the cluttered huts, the intrusive domestic animals living cheek by jowl with the Indians, the belief in a world of three levels, the ité palms they cultivated as the tree of life, the monkeys wailing at sunrise like tormented souls, presented to her the possibility of rebirth; and that here, as a woman, her self-esteem was capable of remaining intact.

In spite of adapting to her new environment with a rapidity that belied her background she still clung to her Christian beliefs, reading the wafer-thin pages of her Bible which crumpled progressively with the humidity and the wear and tear of three generations. And for the first time she did not shun the Songs of Solomon and their sensual evocations, but rather dwelt on the liberating images of a woman's poetry. And once when Teacher-Nurse came on his rounds she seduced him in the medicine shed, then offered him as recompense an extra ration of aspirins. From then on he came more often, fell under her spell and would have married her but for the plague of mosquitoes that descended on the Pomeroon River banks during the rainy season, and were for him reason enough to avoid settling in the area.

On reading that Miss Rose's son's trial had been abandoned and that he had left the country, she felt a pang of regret; but her sedentary life as a secretary at the beck and call of her superior seemed in such contrast to her adventurous huckster days and her present experience in the forest that she wondered at the depth of her past corruption.

Chapter XXXVII

Now that the Minister's trial was averted, the ruling party could get down to the business of preparing wholeheartedly for the forthcoming elections which, however, were postponed once again in response to objections that the electoral roll was incomplete, a factor that would have been of great advantage to creoles, it was said. They had had things their own way for more than two decades, with their falsified registers and mysterious resurrections of the dead, who appeared at polling stations, voted and promptly returned to their resting-places in cemeteries all over the country; not to mention the transmigration of would-be citizens domiciled overseas, whose ocean-skipping antics would have done justice to the comic strip plastic man. They had voted in impressive numbers during previous elections alongside Jamaicans and small islanders masquerading as Guyanese, but with no knowledge of Guyana's whereabouts.

During the breathing-space of a few months while the electoral register was being revised, the ruling party tried desperately to persuade the people that the general economic, financial and moral collapse was the result of a conspiracy conceived abroad and owed nothing to the incompetence and fraud of which their enemies accused them. Meanwhile foreign banks were busy processing applications for special accounts from Guyanese who had battened on the people's misery, accumulating fortunes in American dollars in the process, which they now decided to off-load in anticipation of the anarchy they feared would follow an East Indian victory.

The ruling party pinned their hopes on the Working People's Alliance, whose leader it had been accused of blowing to bits years ago by means of a bomb placed in his car. If only it could attract enough votes away from Dr Jagan's opposition party with its vast East Indian support there was more than a chance of winning, in spite of the threatened international supervision by people who would not be persuaded to mind their own business and let the Guyanese get on with living in the way they alone knew how. Were we not all one, when all was said and done? Was not inter-marriage between East Indians and creoles on the increase? Give us a few hundred years and we will be a nation of *douglas,* mixed Indians and Creoles, with dim memories of our ancestral homes in Africa and India, the alpha and omega of man's destiny. At the end, with the marriage of Shango and Durga, will not our mutual resentments be washed away in the torrential rains of history?

When men cease to think they can only hope.

Chapter XXXVIII

Miss Gwendoline believed that the time had come to broach a subject calculated to make Kwaku lose his temper.

'The twins getting married,' she told him one morning just before he was about to leave for his surgery.

'Eh, heh,' he answered.

'I been thinking,' she went on, reflecting that had she been able to see she would pretend to adjust the tablecloth or set about some task, so that he would not detect her nervousness.

'How you know?' Kwaku asked.

'What?'

'They getting married.'

'Philomena say so. She know everything. . . . I been thinking, we can hold the reception here.'

'Why?'

'To please me, that's why,' Miss Gwendoline declared testily.

Kwaku sat down, recalling how he had gone to great lengths to help Sidonie, a stranger, and how he had discovered a pool of compassion in himself since his future was assured. Yet the mere mention of his twin sons was enough to make him forget the ties of blood that bound them.

'To please you, yes,' Kwaku said.

How much he had done to please her! How ashamed he had been at any evidence of her displeasure! Was she similarly afflicted by any show of displeasure on his part? This new passion for reflection was becoming increasingly burdensome. Logic was the least effective means of persuasion, he had read recently. It was also little use in instructing him on his own relations with those around him.

Kwaku, while acutely sensitive to the calm success had brought him, longed, nevertheless, for his old status as buffoon; like the gilded butterfly of a fantastical tale that hankered after the pristine home of its tomb-like cocoon.

'Right,' he said, 'let them come . . . to please you.'

Kwaku and his family lined up for a photograph in the small studio.

The occasion was the double marriage of his twin sons, who were invited by their father to forget their past resentments. Travelling down from New Amsterdam with their fiancées, they stayed the night at Kwaku's expense in the same guest-house where he had installed Sidonie on the eve of her departure for Lethem.

They arranged themselves in two rows: his strapping sons, their wives attired in bridal gowns and holding modest bouquets of white artificial flowers standing at the back; Miss Gwendoline and Kwaku seated in easy chairs in the front row. Philomena, Heliga and their daughter squatted beside them on the floor, since the camera did not have a wide-angle lens to accommodate them with those standing.

After the photographic session they went home with Kwaku and Miss Gwendoline, where Suarez, his aunt, Surinam's wife, the house-keeper, the Teacher and his wife were waiting for them, standing on the porch and on the stairs. And as the brides and grooms stepped out of the car the neighbours, assembled in groups on the grass verge, began clapping vigorously.

Surinam's wife, who had only just arrived, was still standing with two presents under her arm which she had hardly had time to unwrap. She gave one each to the brides, two simple country girls who could not make head or tail of the framed canvases with splashes of colour on them — pictures by her husband who, on hearing about the marriages, had painted them both in one night as a tribute to his defunct friendship with Kwaku. They were intended as a summary of the images in his adjoining rooms.

Kwaku, still deeply suspicious of his twin sons, soon forgot his concern when Miss Gwendoline began kissing him on his cheek and dragging up memories of the bright days of early married life.

'I look forward to the day when all my children goin' sit with me in the same room. All seven. Or is it eight?'

She laughed out loud at her lapse of memory.

'Imagine not knowing how many children you have!' Suarez joked.

And they all laughed. And Philomena's daughter laughed with them although she could not see the joke.

The two little girls from next door had climbed the stairs and were looking through the open window at the family, some at the small table and others scattered about the room.

'Quiet!' exclaimed Miss Gwendoline suddenly. 'Somebody watching us.'

'Come in,' called Philomena. 'Is the girls from next door.'

'Come darlings,' Miss Gwendoline called out in turn. 'Come inside.'

The two girls went in eagerly and took the slices of cake offered them by the housekeeper. And Philomena could not help noticing the contrast between the affectionate way her mother had addressed them and the detached manner she used in speaking to her own daughter.

'I propose a toast to Suarez getting married,' Miss Gwendoline blurted out, as though she had sensed her daughter's discomfiture.

'Me? I leave that to the young people,' Suarez said, a remark that once more provoked laughter, for he was himself a young man.

He did his best to avoid Philomena's eyes and make a fool of himself.

'Make a speech then,' Kwaku suggested. 'You does talk long an' loud with me, but as soon as you in company you shut up as if Ol' Higue holding your tongue.'

Everyone clamoured for a speech from Suarez, except Philomena and the two girls from next door.

And Suarez was suddenly overcome with emotion, overwhelmed by his acceptance in this household where he was once an outsider like any other stranger. With a deep distaste for any kind of display, he could only hang his head and wait for his weakness to pass.

Kwaku, partly to cover his friend's embarrassment and partly to impress his violent sons with his improved status as a true patriarch, got up and made a speech peppered with big words for the occasion. He spoke of the country's promising future, comparing it with the erstwhile decline in his own fortunes and the eventual regeneration of his powers as a healer and father.

The twins sat staring at him with their baleful eyes, their hunched frames embodying a kind of secret power. One had never worked and the other had filled many temporary posts since his first job at the post office, but no one had ever managed to discover how they managed to survive. On noticing the way they were staring at him, Kwaku faltered and quickly brought his speech to an end.

'Teacher, you make a speech!' Kwaku shouted, feigning a hilarity impossible to achieve in the twins' presence.

The Teacher, whose inhibitions about public speaking had long vanished before captive audiences of admiring school children, accepted the challenge and launched into a panegyric of Kwaku's family, whom he knew only from hearsay. His devoted, heroic sons would make excellent husbands, just as his daughter Philomena was an irreproachable wife. Scattered about the country, Kwaku's numerous offspring were the flower of Guyana's youth, who, attached to their homeland by an umbilical cord, had not been seduced into emigrating to Babylon.

And as the Teacher spoke Miss Gwendoline came to the conclusion that he was no less fraudulent than Heliga, her son-in-law. But her soft suck-teeth was drowned in the welter of words that would have done justice to a funeral oration pronounced by a white-robed Mason.

For Kwaku, however, the Teacher's speech was a vindication of his own view of himself. He had survived where others had foundered and now, in his forties, had arrived like the legendary boatman at the longed-for haven from turbulent waters.

The street bulbs flared soon after the housekeeper switched on the gallery light and, when Kwaku's borrowed record-player began to emit back-ball music, neighbours gathered on the parapet under the almond trees to listen and watch the dancers as they passed by the casement windows. Miss Gwendoline appeared with her tentative steps, her head swaying to the music and looking upwards with her sightless eyes; and the children from next door, dancing together with the aplomb of adults; and the Teacher and Surinam's wife; and the two brides like identical puppets in chiffon gowns back-balling with their husbands. Only Philomena and her husband were not dancing, emphasizing as it were their status as Kwaku's dependants. And while Philomena rocked the little one who lay asleep athwart her lap, Heliga stared absently at the others, contemplating in his tight-lipped manner the celebration that seemed no less than a metaphor for his own despair.

The girls from next door paid no heed to the time until their mother came to fetch them. And one by one the others were taken home by Kwaku in his car, until only the twins and their wives were left dancing with indefatigable fervour, having resisted Kwaku's pleas to drive them back to their guest-house on Republic Avenue.

In the end they consented, long after their mother had retired. And Kwaku, watching his two sons in the rear-view mirror, with their wives affectionately installed on their laps, recalled that wedding-night almost out of time when he and Miss Gwendoline engaged in their first act of intimacy. He smiled at the thought of how things had changed. Nowadays they did not wait that long.

The national elections, finally held towards the end of 1992 before the rainy season broke, ended in victory for the East Indian political party, which gained fifty-six per cent of the votes, a figure that represented exactly the mean between their population as assessed by the outgoing government and their own calculation. Stunned at the apprehension that an era had come to an end, the latter ceded the trappings of power to the chagrin of many supporters. And while most East Indians, mindful of the terrible events of 1963, fêted their triumph in muted fashion, some, unable to contain their delight, spoke openly of the vaunted Co-operative Republic as a gigantic fraud.

In the aftermath of the elections so many gratuitous prescriptions for rehabilitating the country's finances were bruited about, it was tempting to conclude that twenty-six years of misrule had ended in an orgy of collective folly. One man even suggested the reintroduction of the paddle-steamer as a cure for all financial ills, while a community of ascetics made exorbitant claims for the power of yoga to unite the multiplicity of races and creeds.

But none of these things prevented Kwaku from carrying on with his work for, as far as he was concerned, nothing had changed. Heliga, his son-in-law, was urged to come downstairs from time to time to help him sort and dust the green-tinted ammonia bottles, the neatly labelled boxes of sapodilla leaves, the petroleum jelly in grease-proof paper and all his other containers with their 'cures', which did not require a licence for their sale. Mindful of appearances, Kwaku decorated his waiting-room with lattice-work and trailing shrubs, and subscribed to several copies of each daily newspaper so that his patients should not be bored.

He put up a sign which read, 'Suffer the little children to come unto me', a commentary not on his fondness for the young, but rather a vague recollection of deprivation during his infant years.

One afternoon, on coming down from lunch with his daughter and son-in-law, he found Miss Rose reading a newspaper in the waiting - room.

'You?'

'Why you ask?' she said, with mock surprise. 'We quarrel?'

She accompanied him into the consulting-room and stood in silence to admire the maidenhair ferns and lattice-work that divided the space into equal parts.

'Some people!' she exclaimed. 'I suppose this is why you never get in touch with me.'

'I thought. . . ,' he began, but left his observation unfinished, knowing that she understood.

'Yes, well. My son business is his business. My business is my business. Tobesides, I got to keep in good with you, 'cause you're a important man. We women can't afford much pride.'

Apart from his family she was his only connection with the early time — his country days — when it was the general belief that the creole party would never relinquish power.

'What I goin' worry for?' she said, replying to his question about the new government, 'I got my new home in New Amsterdam an' I live near the burial ground. When I dead they won't got far to carry me.'

They spoke like sparring partners in a boxing ring, unwilling to disturb the equilibrium of uncertainty. Her son stood between them, the Right Hand Man. And although he never used to mention Kwaku's name in conversations with his mother, she none the less apprehended his resentment in the silences that followed her evocations of times past.

'I gettin' married you know,' she said.

'You!' Kwaku exclaimed, unable to hide his surprise.

'Yes, me.'

'What 'bout your husband?'

'He gone missing all these years the court had to presume he dead. I *know* he dead. . . . I need companionship.'

'I did know a man who had two wives,' Kwaku said, smiling at the thought of Correia's misdeed.

'They din' lock him up?'

'They din' know.'

'They should lock up men like that.'

Kwaku did not bother to explain. What was there to explain? And to what purpose? Presiding at his daily table of complaining, he came to accept his patients' fractured lives as a kind of norm, refusing to sit in judgement on them. Every impulse, every feeling was a manifestation of life, and what surprised him more than anything else was the oft discovered shame behind the meanest acts. Perhaps his own wrong-headed conduct when a young man was informed by that same sense of shame. Yet he had been unaware of it, while those around him never took that view.

The two friends talked until they were interrupted by a knock on the door. Three clients were waiting for a consultation.

She held him in a long embrace, then went without a word, leaving in her wake the hardly audible sound of a closing door.